MW01108000

UNKNOWN REALMS

A FICTION-ATLAS PRESS ANTHOLOGY

C.L. CANNON   KATE REEDWOOD   CHRIS HEINICKE

K.A. WIGGINS   TRISH BENINATO   ERIN CASEY

K. MATT   C.A. KING   DEVORAH FOX

MACKENZIE FLOHR   MELISSA E. BECKWITH

FICTION-ATLAS PRESS LLC

UNKNOWN REALMS

A FICTION-ATLAS PRESS ANTHOLOGY

FICTION-ATLAS
PRESS LLC

Unknown Realms: A Fiction-Atlas Press Anthology
Copyright © 2019 Fiction-Atlas Press
http://fiction-atlas.com

ISBN-13: 978-1-7323406-6-4

First Edition: October 2019

10 9 8 7 6 5 4 3 2 1

CONTENTS

THE MIDNIGHT CITY

BY C.L. CANNON

You ever get that feeling that you don't belong—well anywhere? I mean, you can travel the world in search of a place that calls to you or a person who understands you completely, and still, you may never find either one.

Sometimes you can sense those lost people, the ones who don't belong. The ones who don't conform, who stumble through life as if they are standing at the edge of a precipice, balancing their pain, fear, sadness, and grief against the call of sweet silence on the other side of it all.

And then there are the ones who mask their otherness with the trappings of life—work, family, even humor. These persons are not so easily called out, chameleons upon the ordinary.

I guess what I'm trying to say is, I was one of those people, the ones in hiding. And my brother, Eric, he was one of the balancers at the top of that precipice, until one day he jumped and changed both our lives forever.

When we were young, it was easy to believe that our lives didn't belong to us. There had been some mistake. Our true father couldn't possibly be the drunken shell of a man we often found passed out on the kitchen floor after school. Our real mother would never leave us without so much as a goodbye.

No, we'd been whisked away from loving parents, who were desperate to find us, or perhaps we were long lost fae royalty, and one day, we'd find our way back to our people. We dreamed up a thousand different scenarios to explain away our situation, but the place we always came back to was called The Midnight City. Everyone knew us and loved us there. We were the secret keepers, the beloved travelers from far away who'd adopted the city and its inhabitants as our family.

As its name implies, The Midnight City only appears at midnight and only to those lost souls who need it. I'm not sure if it was me or Eric who came up with this magical escape, but I'm almost certain it was Eric. He always had a vivid imagination and took me along for the ride to help transform his vision into order. Together we dreamed up people to live in the city. A baker who only ever made sweets, a street musician who sang just like Tom Petty, Mr. and Mrs. Mortimer, who owned the grocery and fed us when we'd had nothing for supper. We transformed all the troubles of our day into delights within The Midnight City. It was the one place that was truly ours. No adult could tell us no, and the possibilities were only limited by our imaginations.

We'd been inseparable our entire childhood, but somewhere along the way, we started losing each other. It was gradual at first. We started hanging out with friends, and then we developed relationships, got jobs, and suddenly birthdays and holidays marked our time together. And then, one day, time ran out.

I ran my hands lovingly over the old oak door. It felt like a lifetime ago since I'd last seen it. I dug for my keys when my phone suddenly began to ring. It was eleven-thirty, and I'd just left most of the people I knew in my life back at the church. It had to be my boyfriend, Nathaniel. I located my key and unlocked the door, discarding my purse and jacket onto the ancient barker lounger before taking the call.

"Where are you?" I asked without waiting for the voice on the other line to say hello.

Nathaniel's exasperated sigh greeted me. "I'm sorry, my flight was delayed, but I'm on the next one, I promise."

"You missed the wake," I pointed out, jiggling my keys out of the brass lock.

"I know, I'm so sorry, Kat. I wanted to be there for you." His tone was sincere. I was sure he meant it too, but being alone and yet bombarded by relatives and acquaintances for the past few hours had made me snappy.

"It's all right. I know you're busy, and I know you can't control the weather."

"How was it?"

"Exhausting," I answered truthfully.

"Well, get some rest. I'll be there in the morning. Love you."

"Love you too."

I set the phone on the entry table then sank down into one of the overstuffed chairs in the living room.

Being back in this house brung a flood of memories to the surface. It was the only place in the real world that I'd felt safe as a child. My grandmother would sit by the hearth with a basket of yarn at her side, telling stories as Eric and I listened intently. Here our bellies were never empty, and we had clean clothes and a huge down-feathered bed to share. The ornately carved grandfather clock that we used to pretend was a door to Narnia ticked its melodic rhythm just across from me. I couldn't help but smile at the thought. It was fitting that Eric chose to be buried in Branton rather than Seattle. This was our home.

The wake had been almost unbearable. Family members I hadn't seen in decades, ex-girlfriends who treated Eric like shit while he was alive suddenly crying their eyes out over his tragic passing, and work colleagues who didn't know Eric from Adam, but who had come to offer moral support. I knew they meant well, or at least most of them did, but it was all too much. I needed time to myself to relax, to grieve? To move on? To forget him?

I grabbed a bottle of wine from the fridge, kicked off my heels, and made my way up the steps to the bathroom. I shut the door, relaxing for a moment against it. I was just me now. I could let the mask fall away. I breathed out a long, slow sigh, but the heaviness in my chest felt stronger than ever, and no well wishes, condolences, or flowers could quell the utter sense of loneliness. He was gone, and he wasn't coming back.

I slipped my black blouse and shirt off, then turned the ancient taps on, letting the tub fill to the brim. I eased my body into the water, watching as my skin flushed crimson. The heat loosened my knotted spine and tired muscles. The house was silent save for the distant ticking of the grandfather clock.

My mind began to wander back to last week when I had been on a massive deadline for a new client. I had to have been sitting at the computer for sixteen hours straight at that point when suddenly my messenger dinged. I pushed my glasses back up my nose and grabbed my phone. A bubble with Eric's smiling face stared back at me. I blew out a breath and swiped open the message.

Want to see a movie? They're playing a Kevin Costner marathon at Twin City.

Sorry, too much work. Next time? I shot back, throwing my phone to the side.

I jumped back into my work, ignoring the three other dings. I didn't have time to debate Costner with him. If I didn't finish my report on time, I would be losing out on a considerable opportunity. Instead, I worked into the early morning hours and submitted the report with twelve minutes to spare.

If only I'd know what else I'd have to sacrifice for that decision.

I awoke the next evening to a phone call from one of Eric's students. He'd missed their morning guitar lessons, so the boy had shown up at the apartment. When no one answered the door and Eric couldn't be reached by phone, the super unlocked the door. They found him suspended from the beam that ran across his studio.

There must have been some misunderstanding, though. Eric would never kill himself. Eric had so much to live for. He had a job he loved, cool friends, a nice apartment, an enviable Blu-ray collection, and, most of all, he had me... or did he?

I hung up on the poor student and frantically pulled up messenger.

It's okay. I understand.

I love you, Kitty-Kat.

Never forget how much I love you. Meet you in the MC.

He'd done it. He'd stood on the precipice for too long, and instead of pulling him back, I let him take the leap. And now I was standing on the edge, looking down into the chasm, and all I could see was Eric's face and the twinkling lights of The Midnight City. He was waiting for me. The only thing separating us was the fall. How much could that hurt compared to the constant aching in my chest or the knowledge that I'd never hear his voice again? The choice was the easiest one I'd ever made. The clock began to chime, and I slid the blade up one wrist and then the other. The water tinged pink as my life source emptied into it. This was't so bad, like falling asleep.

"Katherine?" The darkness was hard to navigate, and I felt myself stumbling through thick, sticky clods of mush. My vision returned slowly, and I could see that it was mud, bright red clay covering my whole body. I looked as if I had crawled through one side of the earth and came out the other.

"Katherine? Is that you, my girl?"

My eyes adjusted, and I could see an old woman standing over me, a look of concern plastered across her features. "Mrs. Mortimer?"

"Of course? Who else would I be?" she asked incredulously.

"I don't-"

"And how did you get in such a state," she continued, pulling a handkerchief from her purse.

She dabbed at me for a moment with the handkerchief, and miraculously I was once again clean from head to toe—the magic of The Midnight City.

"I'm back," I said more to myself than anyone else.

"Well, of course you are. We always knew we'd see you again."

"Mrs. Mortimer, have you seen my brother?" I clutched the woman's arms, looking directly into her wise eyes, hoping against hope that she could help me.

My desperation seemed to puzzle her. "Eric? Oh, I'm sure he's around here somewhere, dear."

"I have to find him. I have to tell him I'm sorry."

I sped past Mrs. Mortimer and out into the city square, twisting my head this way and that, searching in vain. There was Bruno the street performer strumming a song that vaguely resembled "Won't Back Down" and across the street sat Mr. Hemlock's sweet shop with glistening chocolate lava cakes in the window.

Citizens began to recognize me.

"Miss, Katherine," Latimer, the city's librarian, greeted me, tipping his hat as he hurried along. How many hours had I spent whiling away the hours between the stacks of books there?

Next, Rosa, the doll-maker bustled through the square carrying a box of fabric. "Good evening, Miss Katherine, wonderful to see you."

More and more familiar faces rushed forward to greet me and then disappeared back to their lives. The city was different. It was as if it had grown without us.

It should have felt euphoric to be here. To confirm that it was real, not just the imagining of two scared children, but instead, all I could feel was dread. This was not my home anymore. I wasn't seven, and though I did feel lost, I knew this wasn't where I was supposed to be, not yet. I had so many things to accomplish, so many dreams unachieved. This was wrong. It was all wrong.

I took off in a race across the square and down the alley by the sweet shop. The walls seemed so much taller and dirtier than they had in my childhood, like a real city, not a child's dream. Steam rose from the pavement as I rushed even farther into the darkness, and then I connected with something…or someone.

I heard the other person groan and then felt a large hand wrap around my elbow to keep me from falling.

Suddenly, a lamp in the alley sprung to life. The fluorescents hummed as they warmed up, spilling yellow light upon both of us.

"Kat? Is that you?"

I couldn't contain myself. I knew those eyes. I knew that voice better than my own. I wrapped my arms around Eric, pulling him so close that my ribs ached.

"What are you doing here?" he asked, pulling back out of my arms. He seemed to be looking me over for any sign of injury, and then his eyes narrowed to my wrists and has gasped.

I hadn't noticed them before. I hadn't really even thought much about how I had gotten here, but the two red welts up each arm told the story well enough.

"I'm sorry, Eric. I'm so sorry. I should have been there for you."

"I'm the one who's sorry," he said, not meeting my eyes.

"No, I know it was my fault," I insisted as hot tears leaked down my cheeks. "I should have answered your messages. I should have known something was wrong. I was too caught up in work to notice."

His arms wrapped around me once more, his tallness enveloping my petite stature. I couldn't keep the dam from breaking any longer, so I sobbed into his chest, clutching his long-sleeve shirt in my fists. He let me calm down for a moment, rubbing my arm and whispering comforts until my breathing evened out, and my tears slowed.

"It's different than we imagined," he began. "Everyone here is such a damn hurry."

So, he'd noticed the change too. "I know. I don't understand what happened."

"I think I do." He nodded toward the square, and we began to walk arm and arm.

"What do you mean?" I asked, curious how he'd managed to figure anything out so quickly.

We took a seat on the bench in front of Mr. Hemlock's sweet shop.

He removed his jacket and placed it over the back of the bench, and in the street light I could see a thin line of red circling his neck. I tried not the stare. I tried not to even think of why it was there, but I'm not sure I succeeded.

"So, what's your theory?" I asked, trying to ease the tension.

"I think it's the architect. I mean, she's here way before her time. She's rushing to finish everything. Rushing to make it perfect. But it's not time yet. Not for a long while."

He thought he was being clever. He thought he was being vague, but I knew *I* was the architect. I always had been.

"You left, what was she supposed to do without you?" I asked.

"Live. She has so much to live for. She's so smart and so talented."

"We can drop the *she*. I know who you're talking about," I informed him.

He smiled for a second, just a second. Just long enough to let me know that my Eric was still in there, not this somber regretful person who looked like him, and then his worried frown appeared again.

"This is not what I wanted for you. And none of this is your fault. It was a decision that I made, and I'm not even sure if it was the right one."

His mahogany eyes bore into mine, pleading for me to accept his words.

"But if I just answered the phone-"

"Then I probably still would have ended up here at some point. It was moment of weakness, Kat. It was everything pressing down at me at once until I couldn't breathe. Even you couldn't shoulder that burden for me."

"But, I wanted to," I whispered, trying to quell the aching in my heart. I would have done anything for him, been anything for him if he'd let me. I was the big sister, that was my job. He was my responsibility.

"I know you did, and I love you," he confessed, gently tilting my chin up to look at him. " I love you so much, Kitty-Kat, but this is a place you can't follow."

"It's too late," I said, my voice quivering. I started to run my fingers over the puckered flesh of my wrists to emphasize my point, but there was nothing there. They were unmarred with pale blue veins, still ribboning across them, no longer rent open for all to see.

"Eric? What's going on?" I asked, frightened.

"It's not time, Kat. But I'll see you when it is, and we'll build the city to right way. Until then, take care of yourself, please."

Eric's words began to echo, and a sudden dizziness came over me until, at last, my whole world went black.

I awoke practically freezing. Most of the water had drained from the bathtub, and what little remained was frigid, but clear.

"Kat? Kat? Are you in there?" Nathaniel's worried voice called through the thick wooden door.

"I'll be right out," I managed to croak.

"Are you sure you're all right? Do you want me to make you some tea?" Nathanial asked.

"Yes, I'll be fine. Tea sounds lovely."

It was a dream. It was all a dream. I'd fallen asleep in the bath. I hadn't taken the leap, and Eric didn't want me to. More importantly, I didn't want to. He was right. I had things to live for, places to explore, and stories to tell about my little brother. The boy who made me laugh like no one else in the world. Who made me feel safe in the darkest times of my life, and who would be waiting for me in The Midnight City... someday, but not just yet. Until then, the architect would plan, but she'd also do the most important thing of all... she would live.

C.L. Cannon is a USA Today Bestselling Author, publisher, publicist, editor, designer, and lots of other occupations with the -er sound at the end! She is a woman of many talents who never gives up or stops improving. She enjoys writing about love and friendship. She loves it even more when she can add fantasy and science fiction aspects to those themes! She's a self-proclaimed Harry Potter freak (Slytherin Pride people), lover of anything Joss Whedon (Spuffy forever), Tolkien fiend (who enjoys second breakfast), and addict of classic literature (Social class struggles turn me on... literally ;) yah see what I did there?) She spends her days trying to #bookstagram (and probably failing), helping other authors grow and succeed (I love my job), and loving on her two babes (velociraptors), Seth and Petey. She's also sort of a social media enthusiast! You can find her basically everywhere on the net (man I just aged myself). Or, you can visit her website or join her street team for more content!

https://clcannon.net
https://facebook.com/groups/clcannon

facebook.com/clcannonauthor

twitter.com/clcannonauthor

instagram.com/cl_cannon

THE DEMON OF CORPUS CHRISTI

BY DEBORAH FOX

If I failed to submit my story on time, I'd never get a chance like this again. The deadline loomed, but I couldn't be more firmly stymied if I were in cast in quick-drying cement. I couldn't squeeze out another syllable if my life depended on it. My life didn't, but the opportunity sure did. I'd accepted an invitation to contribute to an anthology. My first publication credit! My writing career would only go up from here. I was nearly done but needed a killer ending, something to resonate with readers. The closing date for submissions hanging over my shoulder cast a shadow on my keyboard. I felt the deadline's hot breath on the back of my neck.

I fired up my work playlist, jazz instrumentals that I find relaxing and freeing, but I did more chair-dancing than writing. I left my living room writing niche and fixed my favorite coffee. The legend on the mug mocked me—*Writer's Block: When Your Imaginary Friends Won't Talk To You.* I tried all my trusty block-breaking tricks to no avail.

Ernest Hemingway once said, "In order to write about life, first you must live it."

He might be right. I should step away from this desk, go experience something.

A drive. I'd take a short excursion away from the city. A long blank stretch of blacktop without traffic to contend with would allow my thoughts to wander. I'd stop trying to force the words to come and would instead open my mind, take inspiration from my surroundings.

Making sure that I had a pen in my purse, I grabbed a bottle of water. I got into my little Kia Soul crossover. When I leaned over to stash my water in the cup holder, the edge of my bag hit a button, which activated the navigation system.

"Enter your destination," prompted a disembodied woman's voice.

Yikes, the car was talking to me! I had, at times, talked to the car and in admittedly harsh terms, but this was creepy.

I didn't have a ready answer. Where to go? I glanced at the electronic display for the navigation option, a feature I never use. I rarely go anywhere unfamiliar.

"Enter your destination," the voice repeated.

I felt on the spot, like being called on by the teacher when I hadn't done my homework. Frantic, I scoured the display prompts for help. *Home?* No, I was already home. *Street Address?* No, I had none to supply. *Points of Interest?*

Okay, now we were talking, no pun intended. I selected that and received *Nearby Restaurants, Nearby Gas Stations, Nearby ATMs.* None of those were what I had in mind. The *Search By Category* option looked promising. I chose it and scrolled through the selections until I found *Tourist Attractions.* I had been to most of them, but one was new to me: *the Selena Museum.* I had seen her memorial statue on Corpus Christi's bayfront but a museum? What could be in it? How big could it be? It might be the ticket for a quick jaunt. Then revitalized, recharged, back to work.

Another choice caught my eye: *the Demon of Corpus Christi.*

Say what? I chuckled. I guess I had heard something about that: a huge fiberglass construction, once part of an amusement park ride that was salvaged by a scrap-metal business.

Oh, why not? I said to myself, but not to the GPS lady because who knew where that would send me? I selected *the Demon of Corpus Christi* and backed down the driveway.

"Head southeast for 358 feet," the lady said.

Before I figured out how far that was, the lady told me to take a "slight right toward Ennis Joslin Road, for one-tenth of a mile," followed by "slight right onto Ennis Joslin Road, eight-tenths of a mile. Turn right onto Nile Drive. Get on Texas 358 West, eight minutes, two-point three miles."

Why didn't you just say, "Get on SPID?" I wanted to ask but didn't for fear of what response that would provoke. I headed for the familiar freeway.

"Turn right onto South Padre Island Drive," my electronic copilot said.

See? Why didn't you say that in the first place? I retorted silently.

Further instructions directed me toward the Leopard Street exit. An industrial area, it houses recycling centers, spare car-parts lots, an asphalt plant, a metal fabricator.

I jounced over a stretch of road where the expansion joints sounded like horses clomping. "Sorry," I said to the GPS lady. The audio for the navigation system crackled, and for a moment was a flurry of static. "Recalculating," came a garbled voice.

Was there a problem with the system? Had I jarred something loose, annoyed my navigator? What if she deserted me? I didn't know the exact location of the Demon of Corpus Christi. I supposed that if I couldn't find it, I could simply turn around and go home. After all, I did get a little drive. Maybe I would be ready to get back to work.

The navigation system crackled again. "Recalculating. Exit onto Mckinzie Road," said a new voice, this time a male. I knew the system offered a variety of narrator personalities. Perhaps the interruption to the signal had made a new selection. I could restore the female voice if I dared to fiddle with the controls. But this voice was intriguing: clear, authoritative, with a hint of seductive charm, like a voice-over artist for a TV commercial.

I followed the instructions, although the further I drove, the less populated the area became. I passed a concrete plant, a distribution warehouse, and a nursery. Then structures of any kind became fewer and farther between. I drove past a lot of open country, the scrubby foliage crisping in the summer sun. It made me thirsty and glad I had brought water.

I drove for miles, keeping to the route to which I had been directed. Finally, I decided that not only was I not nearing *the Demon of Corpus Christi*, but also I was lost. How did that happen? If I took a wrong turn somewhere, why hadn't the piloting system put me back on course?

Sun streaming through the window created a wearying glare. The heat in the car rose enough that I glanced at the air conditioner settings. I had it cranked up to "Max." Had that system malfunctioned too?

I pulled onto the shoulder and stopped, idling. Where the heck was I? I studied the display. The graphic showed exactly what surrounded me as far as I could see: one road, the one I was on, with no side road, not even some obscure graded farm-to-market road.

I pulled my cell phone from my purse, thinking I would get directions from a search engine which I should have done in the first place. To text or talk while driving within the city limits was prohibited, but I wasn't driving, I was stationary. It didn't matter; the signal was down to one bar. Besides, I was sure I was no longer in the city, but in the Outer Limits. Was I even still in Nueces County? I might have strayed as far as Kleberg County, featuring desolate ranchlands traversed by illegal immigrants who sometimes made it no further north. I glanced with misgivings at my empty water bottle.

The phone's battery was low, too. I fished out the car charger and plugged the phone into the power supply socket.

"Home?" I said to the car's navigation system in a voice that sounded a little piteous.

The reply was a distorted "Recalculating."

So much for the funky electronic guidance. Looked like the interference in the signal did scramble something. And so much for my outing. Not only had I drunk all the water, now I was hungry and needed to pee. Time to head back to civilization, find a gas station. Hit the restroom, grab a drink and a snack and get directions from a live human.

I pulled a U-ey and started back the way I came, hoping that before long, I'd spot something familiar.

"Recalculating," said the GPS guy. The static had resolved, and the narrator's voice was clear and confident. I could swear he also sounded peeved. "Turn right onto County Road 13. Continue on County Road 13 for five miles."

I didn't recall traveling a County Road 13 on my outbound trip. This might be an alternate road or even a shortcut. I made the turn. If in five miles I hadn't arrived at something promising, I'd change direction and retrace my path, regardless of what the electronic mapping said about it.

"Your destination is in one-half mile."

Really? Half a mile? That would be some shortcut.

The system was still glitchy because what I found 2640 feet down County Road 13 was not my house. It wasn't a gas station either, but a motel.

Out here in the middle of nowhere? I guessed it had been built during the oilfield industry's heyday when housing for workers popped up like toadstools in the morning dew. The industry cratered, and many of the newly opened accommodations stood empty, having never seen a single guest.

This could be one of them. It looked like many of the other hastily erected facilities. Of slump-block construction, its glossy white paint gleamed in the bright afternoon sun. Wings of single-story guest rooms flanked a taller main building housing the lobby and offices.

The sign read Nomed Motor Lodge. Shouldn't that be "Nomad," I wondered, and figured Nomed must be a family name.

It wasn't a gas station, but it would have a restroom and a water fountain. Their marquee touted high-speed internet. At the very least, there'd be someone at the front desk who might be able to point me in the right direction.

I grabbed my cell phone, which now had half a charge but no signal at all and strode to the front door. The big sliding glass panel opened automatically, a welcoming gesture. The front desk area washed in late afternoon sunlight boasted a Saltillo tile floor. In a nod to the area's south-of-the-border heritage, the decor featured bright primary colors, serape-draped windows, and Talavera-style pottery with silk Mexican-bird-of-paradise plants and cacti. I thought all those reds, oranges, and yellows created warmth unnecessary for the summer months, but it all looked clean and fresh, almost unused. Either the facility had gone up recently, or it didn't see much traffic.

At the end of the hallway branching off to the left, I glimpsed a small dining room. I figured restrooms must be nearby and made a beeline for where I hoped to find the ladies' room.

My most pressing need taken care of, I rehydrated at the water fountain. Either I was super-thirsty, or the establishment had one hell of a filtration system because the water was crisp, almost effervescent. Refreshed, I checked my phone. Still no bars. I swiped my way to Settings to connect with the motel's Wi-Fi. Sure enough, I found a connection, but it was secured. I needed a password.

I headed back in time to catch a man stepping out from behind the front desk. Tall and lean with groomed black hair and a goatee, outfitted in a tailored suit, and possessed of eyes of the most intriguing redwood-brown, he was good-looking enough to be well worth the detour. A small gold name tag pinned to his breast pocket read "L. Siffer. Manager."

"Excuse me, but may I please have the password for the Wi-Fi?" I asked.

He gave me a polite smile. "You're not a guest here, are you?"

"No."

His smile warmed a degree. "I didn't think so. You don't look famil-iar. I'm sorry, Wi-Fi is a benefit for our patrons. You understand, don't you?"

My searching for a way home wasn't going to inflate his internet bill, but I did get his point. If his Wi-Fi were free to everyone, people from town would fill his lobby to use it. Assuming there was a town. "I do. Well, could you tell me how to get back to Corpus Christi? I'm afraid I took the wrong exit somewhere."

He continued to stride down the corridor to the dining room. "You did go out of your way, didn't you? I'll help map it out for you, but we're about to start the Guest Mixer hour, and I'm the host. My name's Lou." He held out his hand for me to shake. "May I ask you to wait?"

"Well, sure." I tried to rein in my impatience. It would do no good to pressure him. He might tell me to get lost, which I already was.

He waved at me to accompany him. "Let me offer you some of our hospitality in the meantime."

"That's very kind," I murmured. Might as well rather than mark time in the lobby. I followed along in the wake of his pleasantly-scented sandalwood-and-cognac aftershave.

He stepped behind a bamboo-paneled counter, put out cocktail plates, napkins, and small clear-plastic cups, and held out a tray. I would have expected cheese cubes cut from a brick and crackers from an "economy-size" box, but he offered me pigs-in-blankets, my favorite snack. I've gone to many a party for those munchies alone. "Help yourself."

"Don't mind if I do." My stomach growled, and I had no idea how close was the nearest source of food. Trying not to make a dinner out of his free hors d'oeuvres, I put two on my plate. He set the tray at the edge of the bar.

"May I offer you a glass of wine to go with them?"

"I shouldn't--"

"I know. You're driving." His polite smile broadened to a grin, and he winked. "It's a small glass."

"Well, maybe a sip." I was lining my stomach with food after all, and by the time I got back on the road ...

"Red or white?"

"Red, please."

I expected him to serve from a huge jug of No Name Burgundy, but from behind the bar, he brought out a bottle of Entice Zinfandel, definitely not the cheapest vintage around. I know because it happens to be my special-occasion indulgence.

I climbed onto a barstool and took a sparing sip from the dainty glass.

Manager Lou set out more snacks that ran the gamut from plebeian to patrician. To huge bowls of chips and dips, he added sushi bites,

Brie, crostinis with smoked salmon, mini meatballs, pate de foie gras, and was that caviar? Along with the bottle of Entice, Lou served other top-shelf wines and liquors as well as cans of convenience-store beer. Guests drifted in and helped themselves to refreshments.

Lou served generous pours in conventionally-sized glasses. People settled in at the divans and took seats on counter-height stools. They gave each other nods in greeting and seemed to be well acquainted. I wondered if this was an extended-stay facility. On the other hand, they weren't the least bit conversational or for that matter, hungry or thirsty. No one spoke. Their snacks and drinks sat untouched on the tables.

Reluctantly, I polished off the last of my Zinfandel. "Thank you for your generosity," I said to Lou, "but I should hit the road."

"You wanted the password for the Wi-Fi." He reached for a cocktail napkin and pulled a pen from an inside jacket pocket.

"I thought you said I couldn't have it."

Lou beamed and handed me the slip of paper. "Well, now that you're our guest ..."

I took the paper, which had four numbers written on it: 1134. "Oh, I'm sorry. You don't understand. I don't mean to check-in." I frowned at my empty wine glass. "I guess I misunderstood. I thought this was on the house." I reached for my bag and pulled out my wallet. "What do I owe you?"

Lou's smile was still broad but tinged with forbearance. "I'm afraid you're the one who doesn't understand. You have partaken of our hospitality, and so you are now our guest."

I shook my head. "I don't think so." I turned on my phone and punched in the password to log onto the motel's Wi-Fi, but the password was invalid. "Hey, what gives?"

With a tilt of his head, Lou replied," I suspect that you entered it wrong. Most people make that mistake." He took the paper, turned it upside down, and handed it back.

The numbers 1134 now read h E l l. "Is this some kind of joke?"

With his smile still in place, Lou shook his head.

Okay. I guess once you knew the trick, it would be an easy password to remember. With a shrug, I gave it a try. It did indeed log me in, but it didn't do me any good. When I attempted to access a search engine, I received an error message reading "Not connected to the internet."

Possibly it was unreasonable to expect that Manager Lou would help me use a network to which I wasn't entitled, but I looked up, about to ask for assistance. A trick of the light from the setting sun streaming through the window made Lou's face look crimson-tinted. His redwood eyes had the color of a pinot noir and glowed as though backlit by a candle.

"I ... I can't seem to connect to the internet."

Lou's lips split into a wide grin. Against his scarlet-hued complexion, his teeth gleamed very white. "You won't need to," he said. "You don't need the internet. Everything you want is here." He took my phone from my hand and laid it screen-side down on the bar. "Another glass of wine?"

I heard myself saying, "Sure," with my brain chortling "in for a penny, in for a pound," "might as well be hung for a sheep as a lamb," and other ridiculous justifications.

Lou took my tiny glass and exchanged it for a goblet, which he filled almost to the top. "Will you want a key?"

"A key?" I sounded like a tipsy parrot, but I couldn't seem to shift my brain into gear.

"To your room. You may have one, although, after a while, you won't need it. No one here uses them after the first night or two."

Oh? What kept unscrupulous lodgers from stealing someone else's stuff, I wondered, but my lips moved of their own accord. "A key. Sure." Apparently, I would be staying the night, although I wasn't aware of having made that decision.

He reached into his jacket pocket. He handed me not an electronic card, but an old-fashioned bronze key, the inch-long shank topped by an ornate filigreed bow. "Room One. In the Tower."

I couldn't recall having ever stayed in a motel's Room One. My incredulity must have shown on my face because Lou grinned and said, "It's our Presidential Suite."

Like presidents actually stayed here? Whatever. I didn't intend to stay the night, but a nap before I hit the road seemed like a good idea. Who knew how long it would take me to find my way home?

Room One was a penthouse arrangement, so the elevator opened to a vestibule leading to the room's door. I turned the key.

Ahead of me loomed a sitting area so spacious it could span the width of the Tower. Room One seemed larger than my apartment. I minced across the thick, pale Berber carpeting and stroked the ultra-plush velvet sofa facing an ebony coffee table. A gleaming crystal pitcher of ice water sat waiting to be poured into the matching faceted goblet. At my right stood a dining table set with linens, glasses, silver-ware, and golden chargers. The flat-screen television atop the enter-tainment center could be viewed from both the dining and sitting area. Ahead, an archway outlined the bedroom. The mound of fluffy spank-ing-white pillows and a plump comforter whispered my name, but the marble-clad bathroom invited me to wash off the road dust.

A crystal tray held full-sized supplies of premium shampoo, condi-tioner, and shower gel. A thick Turkish terrycloth robe hung on a padded hanger, and an etagere held stacks of lush towels.

I considered a therapy bath but felt so fatigued that I feared falling asleep in it. I stripped off my clothes and stepped into the spa shower bristling with spray nozzles. Wrapped in the robe, enveloped in the scent of lily and bergamot, I peeled back the comforter, laid my head on a satin-smooth pillow, and stretched out.

I fell asleep immediately only to be awakened by a noise. I turned my head toward the bedside table to find it absent of a clock, but it was late enough that the open curtains revealed a night-dark sky. I fumbled for my wristwatch. It read a few minutes past three. Either I had slept through to the middle of the night, or my watch stopped earlier this afternoon, about the time that I walked into the motel.

Subdued lights from the sitting area dark silhouetted a figure framed by the bedroom archway. I bolted upright.

"I'm sorry. I didn't mean to disturb your rest." The voice belonged to Lou, the manager. "I wanted to check on you, make sure that you found everything to your satisfaction."

I was about to ask him how he got in when I realized that as the manager, he could, of course, gain access to everything. It was unsettling, though, that he had let himself in. "A phone call would have been fine."

"That would have woken you for sure."

"I'm awake now." Pulling the robe a little closer, I swung my legs over the side of the bed. I crossed to the burled wood dresser where I had set my handbag and fished out my cell phone. I clicked it on to check the time, but the screen was dark. The battery had run down again.

"I thought you might be hungry, and I brought you something to eat." He stretched out his arm and pointed to the dining table, which now held a covered tray.

"Thanks, but I've already taken way too much advantage of your generosity. I'll pick up something on my way home." I wasn't eager to leave, but I was certain I had overstayed my welcome.

"No need to hurry." Lou strode to the coffee table and plucked a champagne bottle from a silver ice bucket. Music wafted from the sound system as though triggered by the popping of the champagne cork. The notes of a soft trumpet evoked images of long lazy nights spent lounging on a red velvet banquette in an intimate jazz club. Tension melted from my face and shoulders.

Lou filled two flutes with bubbly. He drew close enough that his sandalwood fragrance infused my nostrils, and I submerged in the Merlot-colored depths of his eyes. Soothing warmth enveloped me like a silk shawl.

He put his arms around me. Swaying with the music, he led me in a dance that was more embrace than movement. No effort was required of me. Supported by his arms, his torso, I melted into his warmth. His firm, smooth lips caressed mine, then aroused a craving for more intimacy. As if of their own accord, my clothes fell away. His capable hands pressed all the buttons, including some I hadn't been aware of.

Hours later, I opened my eyes to a window framing a night sky with twinkling stars. I lay in bed for a moment, marveling at my unprecedented abandon. Were I not still tingling, I would think I dreamed it. Whatever the price tag would be for my stay at the Nomed Motor Lodge, I could hardly complain. I wanted an experience, and I got it.

I eased off the bed and collected my clothes. Headed for the bathroom, I stopped short at the sight of someone seated on the couch.

Manager Lou turned and smiled at me.

"About this evening. It was ..." I fumbled for words that didn't sound hyperbolic.

He stood. "It was. We know what you like." He winked.

I wondered how many other sojourners had received such *service* and decided I didn't want to know. "I'll, uh, dress and be on my way. Will there be someone at the front desk so I can settle up?" I stepped toward the bathroom.

"No need. You won't be leaving." Lou's fixed expression matched his firm tone. "I thought you understood earlier. You are our guest."

While part of me was willing to linger, another part of me was annoyed. "What do you mean, I can't leave? You can't stop me."

"But I can." Lou stepped closer. "You are in Hell."

In Hell? He had to be kidding. He wasn't. His unblinking rapacious gaze left no doubt. The smell of something smoldering seeped into my nose. Terror flooded my veins.

Wasn't dying a prerequisite for eternal damnation? If I was dead, why did I have sensations? Despite the abrupt rise in the room's temperature, I felt chilled through and through, and my skin shrunk tight against my bones. When did I die? If I had a traffic accident, wouldn't I remember it? I opened my mouth to protest, but nothing came out.

Lou shook his head and flashed a predatory smile. "You got what you were looking for. You sought out the Devil. I am he."

I sank to the velvet couch. "I wasn't," I stammered.

"Oh, but you were. You selected it as your destination. You have arrived. Admit it. You were enervated. You lost your spark. Don't worry," he said. He stepped close to me and rested a hand on my shoulder. "You have come to the right place. Your struggle is over." His voice was as persuasive as the GPS navigator's. "Goodnight," he said with a smirk and exited the room.

I slumped against the cushions.

The next thing I knew, it was morning. My normal practice was to start the day with a shower, but I didn't feel the need. Nor was I hungry, although I couldn't recall when I last ate. My choices for dress of the day were the robe supplied with the room or the clothes in which I traveled yesterday. I put those on, expecting to find them less than fresh. Instead, though they hadn't been laundered, they didn't smell sour. They had no aroma at all, not even the residue of the perfume I had applied on my last morning at home.

I drifted from the room. Lou had said something about room keys. I recalled being given one but didn't bother to lock the door, there being nothing to secure. I understood that now.

I took the elevator to the main entrance. I found it bright with sunlight streaming in through the glass doors and windows, but empty of people. Even the reception desk was unmanned. I walked up to the door. Yesterday, it opened by itself at my approach, but today it remained closed. Had I sought to open it manually, I would have been thwarted; there was no knob to turn or handle to pull. I lacked the will even to try.

I drifted to the dining room. The breakfast buffet included not only the expected beverages, pastries, and cereals but also smoked salmon, eggs Benedict, cream cheese spreads, croissants. Guests wandered in, filled their plates and mugs, and took seats at the tables, but no one talked. No one ate. I had neither an appetite nor anything to say so I returned to the lobby. I spent the day on one of the couches staring out the window, watching wispy clouds cross the sky.

That afternoon, happy hour was a repeat of the previous day's gathering. Lou manned the bar, which offered an impressive assortment of food and drink. People helped themselves to hors d'oeuvres and beverages they didn't consume. I took a plate of pigs-in-blankets, but one bite proved them to be flavorless. I accepted a glass of Entice. It, too, was tasteless.

With an avaricious leer, Lou offered to join me for the evening.

Though I recalled our coupling as the best sex I'd ever experienced, I could muster no enthusiasm. After a while, I went to my room. I left the big-screen TV dark, the media player silent, and ended up on the couch, watching the light in the sky fade. The sun set. The moon rose, a crescent sliver. Stars came out and formed constellations, the names of which I used to know but couldn't bother to remember.

Time passed like that. I slept. I woke. There was no difference between one hour and the next except that some were lit by the sun, others by the moon. Some were marked by breakfast and others by cocktails, which didn't matter since no one ate or drank, including me. Lou noticed that the luxury appointments in my room went unused. He assigned me to smaller, simpler accommodations; he needed Room One for a new guest. The bed, a simple cot, was a narrow board compared to the downy king bed in Room One. I could as well have slept on the floor. The room offered no shower, toilet, or sink, which wasn't a problem as I had no need for them.

Pigs-in-blankets and upscale wine didn't tempt me, nor did a limitless supply of consummate sex. Maybe I was dead. But how could I explain a nagging edginess? By day, an odd disquiet plagued me, as though I forgot something, something vital. The feeling wouldn't subside. I lay awake at night and wracked my benumbed brain.

Unease worsened to distress. Distress became torment. Had I missed a dental appointment or someone's birthday or a bill payment? I gave a mental shrug. None of that was important enough to cause my torture.

One night as I sat staring out the window, the sky seemed brighter. It occurred to me that there had been a new moon in the sky when I first arrived, and now the moon was much brighter, a waxing gibbous. I had spent almost a month here, I observed and quickly dismissed. There was no point in marking the days. After all, I was in Hell. Time and its passing had no meaning.

Then I remembered. My deadline! The deadline for my submission to the anthology. A lifetime ago, I had had a month. Now I had a day, two at the most. Not that there was a thing that I could do about it, even if I wanted to.

Except I did want to. I had an idea for how to finish the story.

The concept was brilliant, perfect. It would mirror the story's opening and echo its motifs, tie up loose ends, and provide a stunning indelible conclusion. Sentences formed in my head and grew into paragraphs. Scenes presented themselves to me. I scoured my mental catalog of synonyms for the most accurate and descriptive words.

In any other roadside lodge, the nightstand would have held a lamp, a phone, plus a notepad and a pen for jotting down messages. My cell had no such accessories; it didn't even have a bedside table. I had a pen in my purse but no paper. I couldn't jot down my thoughts in my phone's Notepad or even leave them as a voice memo since the phone had no power.

It was of no consequence, I despaired. Even if I finished the story, I couldn't submit it. Here I had what amounted to the best writing I had ever done, and I was powerless to do anything about it. I was indeed in Hell. I didn't know what sin I had committed, but this was the worst penance I could pay for it.

I sighed and lay down on the unyielding cot, but physical discomfort didn't keep me from falling asleep. My brain would not turn off. Words assailed me. They pounded their little fists against my cranium clamoring for release. I had to write them down to let them out, or they would drive me mad. Maybe that was to be my eternal punishment.

I stared up at the ceiling. Lacking even an overhead light fixture, it was as featureless as a blank sheet of paper. I slid my eyes to the bare walls. With a smile, I rose from the cot. I fished out my pen and in the meager light of the moon, scribbled on the wall, unleashing the flood of words with the urgency of a graffiti artist.

The moon set, and sunlight peeked over the horizon. With a sigh of relief, I wrote "The End" and stepped back to regard my scribbles. To my dismay, as daylight crept up the wall, one letter, then the next faded. Flecks of black ink lifted from the wall and burst in a puff of smoke.

Frantic, I ransacked my brain for a way to preserve my writing. If only I could reach my car, I could charge my phone. I could photograph the walls.

I grabbed my phone and my handbag and bolted from the room. With not a moment to spare to wait for the elevator, I raced down the stairs towards the lobby. Ahead, the unyielding glass doors gleamed like gold in the light of a new day. At a run, I charged the exit, determined to crash through the glass if that was what it took.

Instead, I almost fell on my face as the doors slid open and I stumbled onto the driveway. Certain the hounds of Hell, or at least Lou, the Manager, would be at my heels I didn't risk even a backward glance but made a beeline for my car. Behind me, a swelling vortex peppered my back with hot grit. I clicked the door open with my key fob and threw myself into the driver's seat. I roared out of the driveway.

Sunshine lit the road before me, but behind me was darkness. The lodge's neon sign glared red in my rearview mirror, the reversed letters gibberish except for the motel's name.

With a shriek, I swerved onto the road, headed in the direction from which I had come. One hand clutching the wheel, I got my phone plugged into the car charger and babbled a voice memo, the highlights of my story's ending.

The navigation sputtered to life. "You have passed your destination," the navigator bellowed. "Turn around." Though sunlight suffused the sky ahead, darkness overtook me from the rear. I jounced over rumble strips high as hillocks. Lighting flashed, and thunder rattled the windows.

"Not on your life," I yelled back. I punched off the navigation and jammed the accelerator to the floor. I didn't know where I was going, but away from the Nomed Lodge had to be the right direction.

In much less time than it took to arrive at the motel, I turned onto my street. Without questioning how I made my way home, I pulled into my driveway, screeched to a stop, and slammed the transmission into park. I sprinted into the house and raced to my desk. With a click of the mouse, the screen came to life and displayed my work-in-progress. The cursor blinked at the spot where I had left my story hanging. I typed as fast as my fingers would fly. Praying that the keyboard wouldn't jam, I saved the document every few seconds.

Breathless and dizzy, I again inscribed "The End." I signed into my email account. With mere minutes to spare, I submitted the story. I took a deep breath, leaned back in my chair, and exhaled. The document was riddled with typos, but I didn't care; it was done.

With smug satisfaction, I realized that I had written my way out of Hell.

—END—

"What if?" Those two words all too easily send Devorah Fox spinning into flights of fancy.

A multi-genre author, she has written a best-selling epic fantasy series, an acclaimed mystery, a popular thriller, and co-authored a contemporary thriller with Jed Donellie. She contributed short stories to a variety of anthologies and has several Mystery and Fantasy Short Reads to her name.

Born in Brooklyn, New York, she now lives on the Texas Gulf Coast with rescued tabby cats ... and a dragon named Inky.

Visit the "Dee-Scoveries" blog at http://devorahfox.com.
Sign up for the free e-mail newsletter and get a link to
a free gift, http://eepurl.com/LrZGX

facebook.com/DevorahFoxAuthor

twitter.com/devorah_fox

pinterest.com/devorahfox

A SONG OF DARK THINGS

BY K.A. WIGGINS

I sing of dark things.

Not that it's actually my voice, but I know the feeling of it: shards caught in my throat, shrieks only the sea hears in the twilight.

There are dark, glittering things listening in the shadows and dark skittering things in the bracken where the speaker is hidden. Dark creeping things scrape the inside of my skull and dark, biting things swarm, scouring my ears and face and the inside of my mouth as I take that powerful voice for my own.

And dark places open for me because of it.

———

There are tales of those who've walked this path before me. Lost children, wayward girls and lazy boys, drunkards, and fools, and others besides. Musicians and artists, the mad and the holy, and those without border or limit most of all.

Some have stumbled unawares onto the dark paths—and I've mapped those to be sure. But if I want to take anything of worth back with me, it's the other type of story I'll need to find my way into.

Themselves have a special liking for the strong, the beautiful, the gifted. It's said they cannot create beautiful things for themselves—or create at all. I wonder, though, if it's not that they cannot create, but that they can find no delight in their works?

And if they should find me delightful, who am I to deny myself their favor?

Or so I think as I stare down another summer of scrubbing and hauling and chopping and scrubbing some more. The worst of it is, at the end of the summer, there'll be no escaping to the classroom. All there is for me now is breaking my back on two shifts a day in the high season and one in the shoulder, drinking the pain down at nights until it hurts more to go out than it does to stay in, then shivering through the dreich days on what's left only to do it all again come the thaw.

The city folk and foreigners who swarm through on holiday call it beautiful. But they see only the fantasy of blue and green and gold; birdsong, and pipers in the hills, and a dry bed and a dram at the end of a day of tramping, all cozy and clean by a peat fire (or coal, more like) before the midges come out to play of an evening.

But I've no interest in the waves and the heather, and I'm already banned from two of the three pubs in town on my da's account if not fairly my own. None'll book me for a session anyway, not with me dragging his fists and his bruises and all the rest behind me. They see it clear as I; his helplessness and rage and senseless violence reflected in every mirror I polish and every pot I scour.

I'll make them regret it one day, turning me away. They'll all be telling stories, real and remembered or imagined and embellished, putting up pictures to draw the fans, turning their shops to shrines to extract another few pence, and I'll begrudge them every penny they can scrounge from the fringes of my fame.

That thought keeps me warm when I trudge into the hills late in the season, just as the sun paints the islands red.

I've spackled over my spots and darkened my lips and eyes for the occasion, aware Themselves prefer the pretty ones and hopeful they'll not see past the layers of artifice until it's too late.

Mud seeps through the cracks in my boots and bracken tugs at my skirt. The case slung over my shoulder is just as battered as my boots;

dents and scrapes colored over with marker that might misdirect the casual eye but will never keep out the damp.

I'm stronger than I look, if softer looking than I feel.

Here. I shove the wireless speaker into the bracken at the edge of the ring and plant my feet nearly on top of it. The islands are black in the distance, color leaching from the sky as the light drowns.

It's time.

The vocals are powerful, the lyrics achingly fierce: inventive, intimate, eternal. I feel them in my soul, channel them with my body, but nothing but midges passes my lips as I move to the music, claiming it.

My eyes are pinched against the biting swarm. When the last note fades, there's nothing left but darkness and the breeze rustling in the bracken. I choke on the taste of failure along with the grainy bitterness of the flying pests.

"Human children used to know better."

A voice like the creak of branches in a gale. The good neighbor is so near it blots out the emerging stars. Its green-brown skin has a swirling grain to it, under loose-knit, trailing, dappled greenish-gray homespun. Its irises swim with the same shades, like a breeze rippling the surface of a peat pool. Its locks are long and black and quite possibly not hair at all and its breath is the still air of a glen in the gloaming as the haar comes in and—

"You will play for us," it says, and it is not a question.

It smiles, and its lips are the rich shade of Hawthorne berries, and its teeth are the hue and sharpness of shattered shell, and I smile back because I called Themselves, and they came.

"I will play for a price," I say, because the good neighbors are fair when they will or their ways demand, and I am not as innocent as they believe. But, after having called them, this bit is the trickiest, because they may hear the deception in my voice.

The good neighbor's expression does not change, but it is no longer a breath away, but an arm's length. "A good tune shared among friends is its own reward."

"And yet, a player is paid for her work."

"Our Lady will provide handsomely for your needs."

"I place a high value on my skills."

I kneel and lift the battered case at my feet. The good neighbor's eyes gleam. I have won this round.

"But perhaps you are in no need of a fiddler as well?" I sling the case over my shoulder and pivot on my heel. Damp grasses squelch underfoot, tearing as they're driven into the muck.

A sharp jangling of bells, the suggestions of horns, strings, a distant, broken snatch of music—the good neighbor speaks over the sudden noise: "What do you seek?"

This I have given great thought to, knowing full well deals with Themselves have a pronounced tendency to go awry. I toss the words over my shoulder with artful casualness, but the details of my request are precise, unambiguous, and comprehensive.

The terms are rejected immediately. One song will not be sufficient, nor one night's worth, nor even one moon's, for a prize such as I demand.

This is no surprise, but it's always better to offer low and never let on just how high you'd be willing to go. For my heart's desire, there is no price too dear, though I'd rather buy at a bargain than a loss. But what I didn't count on was negotiations being cut short.

The good neighbor's attention drifts, its glimmering eyes distant, then sharp. "Your price is granted," it says, hauling me back. "Your terms, however, are subject to the Lady's discretion."

Its grip chafes my wrist, rough as tree bark. I draw blood struggling.

"I do not agree to this deal."

"It is done."

It drags me out of the low ring of grassy mud and into the surrounding bracken. I dig in my heels and trip almost immediately on the hidden speaker. It lets out a squawk of protest, and I yell and dive into the good neighbor headfirst to cover the noise.

It whips around between one heartbeat and the next, its limbs over-long under those shifting layers a bare shade darker than its skin. It curls them around me, and I'm a fish in a net, my struggles only serving to draw the trap tighter.

"Let me go." I pretend the rising tones are imperious instead of panicked.

It bends over me, luminescent in the scant light of rising moon and stars. My heartbeat spikes, and my breath grows ragged. Themselves come in many types, and not all those they have dealings with return in one piece.

I will.

I clamp my lips together and surge in instead of away, pressing for an instant against the good neighbor's. His wide eyes widen further, and his knotted grip uncoils all at once.

I collide with the ground, teeth clacking, head ringing, tailbone stinging with the impact. I clutch the battered fiddle case as damp earth soaks through my skirt and tattered leggings, and the not-so-good neighbor rustles with laughter. But its voice is dry when it speaks.

"Sealed with a kiss. How . . . traditional."

My face flames. "Negotiations are not concluded."

It picks me up, case and all, and tucks me under one arm. Blood rushes to my head, and I kick and flail, shrieking my protest. This is not how I planned this.

But I can work with it.

I might be able to capture it in a song. Perhaps. Words alone are not enough to understand what happened next.

One moment I was fending off scratches from the heather and gorse and bracken rushing by as I dangled from the good neighbor's spindly arm. The next, we walked right into the earth.

That makes it sound like we came up to a cave in the side of a hill or a hole dug in the ground or something, but it wasn't like that at all.

There was/wasn't a moment of transition, a threshold. You could/couldn't see it, feel it, taste it. It was/wasn't a separate thing again from the brisk night air we left behind and the fragrant gloaming we stepped into.

It's always twilight. Always on the cusp of day and night, summer and autumn, autumn and winter, winter and spring and summer again. It's a place of becoming and ending, like the breath before you sing the first note.

No, more like the half-conscious ripple of muscle and flesh and air and fluid that prepares the way for song but can subside into silence with half a thought.

And by fragrant, I do not mean perfumed or spiced or anything near as nice. Though there certainly is perfume and spice and a lot else besides in the mix. It tends to change based on who you're standing by —or running from.

But I'm not here to run. I'm here to sing.

Which is why I never open my mouth.

It turns out to be a he, and he turns out to be important. I call him Twigs because he's spindly and treelike and Themselves aren't over-fond of giving out names and also because I think he hates it.

I don't know if feudalism caught their fancy one fine century, or if the Middle Ages were modeled after their nonsense in the first place, but the good neighbors do love their court intrigues.

Twigs is a knight and not just any knight. The Queen's Knight. I've never been too into all that pseudo-historical high fantasy nonsense, but his position seems to be a big deal, which turns out to work in my favor.

Their queen didn't seem too pleased when I showed up and failed to demonstrate my supposedly mad pipes. I mean, it's not like I can't sing. I can. Just . . . not like that. Not yet.

Which is why I grabbed a killer track off the web and blasted it instead: bait.

Themselves haven't yet figured out the trick. And if I can keep my mouth shut long enough, they never will. Their moods are said to be as mercurial as the endlessly shifting seasons here. They'll tire of waiting. They'll forget what I was here for in the first place. The singer will become the player and, being a better-than-adequate but less-than-prodigy fiddler, they'll eventually tire of that too and grant my price in order to get rid of me. Essentially, I'll just wait them out, adjust the terms in my favor, and then remind them of a reality to my liking.

It seemed like a good plan when I was making it. Turns out, I misjudged the good neighbors' level of interest in my supposed talents and living up to their reputations alike. Badly. The only thing keeping me alive is kissing Twigs. Somehow, he got woven into my deal, bound to ensure my safety until its completion.

I pluck the strings of the fiddle they brought me when my last collapsed, teasing out a half-remembered radio jingle, the theme from a film, a nursery rhyme, the bass line from a rock song . . ..

Things wear out fast here. My clothes were falling off me within an hour of arrival. Human-made things don't last. Apparently, humans don't either—unless one of Themselves takes an interest.

I strum a discordant chord, repeatedly, until a string snaps. I lift the instrument by its neck and wave it at Twigs. He looks away.

I poke him with the bow. He swats it. It snaps.

"I just brought you that," he complains.

I smirk and poke him with the scroll of the fiddle instead. Its neck cracks, and the remaining three strings whip loose and lash my bare arm. Blood springs from long welts, and a dozen heads swivel in my direction, inhuman eyes glittering.

Twigs hisses and twists my arm behind me, pressing the stinging cuts against the back of my shirt.

"You're more trouble than you're worth."

I grin wider in response and nudge the splintered heap of polished wood at my feet meaningfully. He shakes his head.

"I don't have time to get you another one. You can always sing for your supper."

I twist my shoulders, yanking against his grip. It doesn't loosen, and the movement grinds the cuts against my shirt, widening them. I wince, but Twigs has no sympathy.

I'm not certain if that's because Themselves don't feel, or if he just doesn't like me. Though the answer could always be both.

Blood is warm and sticky on my shirt, and the others are still staring. My eyelids drift lower without permission. I sag in his grip, too drained to keep the game going. He grumbles but scoops me up and hauls me out of sight before it turns into another fight.

It's not for my sake he saves me. I'm not yet clear on whether the good neighbors would eat me, or just thoroughly enjoy my death—odds are the answer would be both—but they certainly wouldn't fight me. They'd have the pleasure of fighting the Queen's Knight to get the chance to decide my fate, which is a win-win on their part. Their own human to enjoy, plus one of the highest ranks in this twisted kingdom into the bargain. If they win.

The fact that Twigs shreds his opponents into so much mince doesn't stop a new one from trying its luck every few days. Or what pass for days in this eternal twilight. If it seems to have gotten a shade darker since I arrived, I'm fairly certain that's only because my energy's running low.

I'm starving. Slowly. It's an ongoing, unending process. Between my bargain with Twigs and the interestingly unpredictable physics of this place, death by starvation doesn't seem to be on the table, so to speak.

Which I don't. Speak, or sing, or even eat, that is. For once in my life, I keep my mouth closed.

It's the only way to make it back intact. Don't eat anything in the good neighbor's realm. Don't take anything away with you, but the prize you win from them. And, in my case, definitely do not let on you tricked them into taking you in the first place.

So here I am, considerably less soft-looking than when I arrived and also much weaker, but no less determined.

Twigs hauls me through the castle. It changes like the seasons, its massive halls and spiraling stairs and endless corridors crumbling one moment, pristine the next, and shifting into a sort of elaborate tree fort in the breath after that.

I fell right through the floor when I tried to go exploring on my own, but it stays firm underfoot for Twigs, and his room is always the same. Among the many forms the castle of the realm takes, this one place remains mainly of the tree-fort persuasion, woven of branches and cozy, like a rather posh nest in the crown of some impossibly enormous tree.

Twigs dumps me on what passes for a bed and leaves without a word. I blink sleepily and smirk. He'll be off to find me another fiddle. A half-decent fiddler is worth more than a silent singer to the queen, though I'm sure she'd rather turn me into a coat or a rug or something for refusing her.

I tip myself out of bed and crawl across the floor, placing one hand across the threshold to test the wide trunk beyond. It shifts to marble under my fingers, and then through them as they slip below its surface.

I crawl back to bed. The cuts on my arm burn.

Whatever force keeps me from starving also slows my healing. The scrapes and bruises I got on the way in have barely faded. The gouges of the queen's talons at my throat before Twigs reluctantly intervened are still deep and painful. I can barely clamp the fiddle under my chin without starting the bleeding afresh.

I think that's why she orders me to play. Not because she finds my music lovely, but because she likes to see me squirm.

I'd rather not find out just how much damage I can sustain without dying. Starvation is quite enough, thanks. But on the plus side, I can see how my newly sharp bones and hollow eyes will set me up for success when I'm done here. Rockstar chic. Burned up by talent and fame and the kind of life everyone else can only dream of.

Time passes. I might have slept. Then Twigs hauls me out of bed and into a hall that shifts from gilt and mirrors to bowers of flowers and thorns as fantastic figures weave elaborate patterns around one another. The dances always start formal and spin out from there.

There is music, but I never see other musicians. I like it that way. I'm free to join in, to surf the beat and slip inside the melody, filling in countermelody, pushing and changing until it becomes something new. I seize control, pushing, pushing, taking it darker, higher, sharper, and then mellowing out for an aching breath before driving the pace faster once more.

The hairs of my bow spring free, snagging at the strings, and Twigs is at my elbow with a fresh one. A string snaps and I shift up. Another, and I'm balancing a melody at the tips of my fingers with a droning pulse of a bass line on the lower string—until the higher is lost entirely.

I hold that pulse as Twigs pulls the instrument away, following his arm down and away with my own while fresh blood surges at the gouges in my neck. I swallow convulsively. He shoves another fiddle in place, setting the wounds on fire as I bend to the new instrument and pick up the drone without a moment's lapse. My heart flutters, and my fingers slip from the neck with a screech that drags my focus back to the dance. I repeat the eye-watering sound, turning it into a rhythmic wail, deliberate discordance becoming the eerie centerpiece of a fresh tune.

And the dance continues.

I never choose to stop playing, nor do I catch the moment the dance ends. There is the music, and little else. And then there is nothing, and I'm waking up in Twigs' nest of a room, or in his arms, or on the floor at his feet with the splinters of yet another spent instrument beneath me.

Time passes. My fingers, already calloused, grow harder. The callouses flake and split and peel, and new ones slowly take their place, and eventually these too crack until the strings are never not slippery with blood.

I don't mind. My fingers sing of dark things for me, and the shards once caught in my throat have spread to my chest, and my feet and my hands and I am a knife bent to the will of no master but myself. I make them feel it, the sharpness, the hardness, the burn of rage, the void of rejection, the ache of frustration.

And then it's over.

The queen holds up a hand, and Twigs pulls the instrument from my bleeding hands with a screech. I shriek my rage, and my voice echoes with power and bottomless darkness, and the dancers sway with it, caught between hunger and the bare edge of obedience they're bound to.

The queen smiles, and her lips are redder than Twigs', and her teeth are sharper, and her eyes are much, much darker.

"You have served us well," she says in a voice of earthquakes and tsunamis and galaxies engulfed by darkness, and yet I do not tremble before her. "Will you not sing for us before you go?"

And I have forgotten why I should not open my mouth.

No, it is not the knowing that I have lost, but the caring. I stare down the Queen of Air and Darkness and howl my song across the grove-ballroom-lagoon-ruin, and the walls shatter, and the dancers leap to its twisted rhythms, and the queen bares those sharp teeth in delight.

Twigs stands at my side, not dancing, nor smiling, nor even trembling as I wish him to. As I wish them all to.

My breath goes before the song is done, and I slump to the floor, glaring into the queen's mirthful eyes to the last. She starts the applause. The darkness swallows the rest of it.

Twigs lays me down on the damp grass under an oorlich sky. Icy mud seeps through the thin layers I wear, and for the first time in longer than I can count, I shiver. I don't have the energy to lift my head, so the world is little more than bracken and gorse and heather looming against the stars. And Twigs.

"You may go now, human child," he says.

I blink slowly, meaning to glare. But my face feels thick and heavy and it's taking too long to assemble it into the correct positions. My words slur, thick as the mud beneath me. "Not a child."

Twigs looks at me with those enormous, liquid eyes and nods, slowly. "Nonetheless, your bargain is complete. You are free to go. As am I."

I close my eyes. Every part of me aches. My stomach is a hard knot, clenched with emptiness. My mouth is filled with sand, and the inside of my throat, and quite possibly my veins as well. Every scratch and gouge and split callous burns, and all I can think is that Twigs is going to go back to the dance and I—I am not.

"How . . . how long," I croak.

"A year and a day."

It's more than fair, and better than expected. Time had not passed as I was used to on the other side, but my impression had been of years, decades, even centuries.

I return to a world I recognize. One that will recognize me. I don't know if it's a gift or a curse. Knowing the good neighbors, undoubtedly, it's both.

"You haven't delivered on your end of the deal," I say very deliberately.

It takes a long time. Twigs waits until I'm finished forming each slow syllable. Then he stoops and snakes one of those long arms into the bracken, rustling about. He stands and tosses a slimy lump of something at me.

"Haven't we?" he says.

Night is lifting behind him, the stars fading. Then he's gone, and there is only the sky, washed out and dull with the first light of dawn.

The bracken rustles, and I am no longer afraid of the things hiding in it. I've seen worse.

The world wasn't prepared for my music. My power. Not that I cared.

I lay in the mud and the grass that morning, soaked and bleeding and starved and exhausted. Then the sun warmed me, and I rose with it. I didn't walk back to town. I didn't go back to my da's place or to my work. I didn't even stop for the small packet I'd so carefully hidden away, currency I'd hoped would survive the centuries I might be forced to serve.

I staggered down to the roadside and got into the first car that would stop for me. I didn't look back.

I staggered out of the hospital and into a pub with live karaoke the next night. It didn't matter that I didn't know the songs. I dragged the band with me. At the end of the set, they begged me not to leave. The ones who could still talk, at least.

My manager takes credit for discovering me there.

Hardly. I just used the first willing fool to come along. He had the contacts and the expense account. I had the darkness.

I never opened for anyone. Never played another pub, unless I felt like it. And there was nothing better than wandering into a late-night club after a stadium show and shredding a roomful of strangers into awestruck shambles.

I thirsted for live shows, but I did all the rest too. Albums and films and talk shows where I glared at the inane hosts until they let me get up and sing. Preferably to the kind of in-studio audience I could feed off of, seize the energy of and spin it into something more. And so, I sang of dark things until the world overflowed with it.

It was everything I'd hungered for and more. I was everything. Sharp and hard and fierce and untouchable. Everyone wanted me and wanted to be me, and I cared for none of them.

And then they moved on.

They said they were tired of the darkness. Heroin-chic was vintage cool until it wasn't. Soft and bright and happy and light were the new trend.

And though I choked on the unbearable twee-ness of it all, I discovered I didn't care for the fame or the money. The fans dwindled, and the stadium shows turned into clubs, and the hotels got smaller and dingier, and that manager I'd put up with for his connections had only been putting up with me as long as he could skim money off the top. And the bottom and all the damn way through.

The crowds get sparser, and the fans crazier. Some come for the music. More come wanting attention I can't be bothered to give. Bands shrink into the odd player here and there, and then it's just me, in the corner of a too-bright pub, and the owner's telling me he was a big fan back in the day, loves what I'm putting out—if I can just maybe dial it back a couple notches? Or several? People are just out for a good time, after all, a quick catch up with their mates, that kind of thing. It's all a bit heavy for their crowd; maybe I could try something lighter?

My knuckles whiten around the mic, old scars stark and jagged, white on black, and the owner's eyeing me nervously and crooking a finger at the bouncer and I'm reaching for the battered case I still lug around everywhere and pull out for the odd bridge or intro and wondering if I can even do it, if it's even worth trying to change, if I even want to.

And then the mic is bouncing against beer-steeped planks and feedback is squealing in the monitors and I'm scooping up that case and stalking out of there, because there's just one thing left I want and it sure as hell isn't to play a light background set to add a little flavor to these sots' night.

I'm set to walk all the way back to that clearing outside that town on the edge of the world that I swore I'd never return to until the hot burst of blisters drains the heat from my head and I can think clearly enough to remember the real way home.

I can't wait until the next dusk, and midnight is already a fading memory. Dawn will have to do.

There's no bracken here. No circle to step into, no heather to break my fall, but the sharp sea air should still carry me home.

I kick off my boots and let the sand and salt scour the blisters. My jeans are too skinny to roll up, so I let the waves soak them to the knees. I cast my empty case up onto dry sand behind me and raise the fiddle.

I play of dark things and hidden things. I play of leaving home and finding it, of losing myself and becoming and losing it all again. I play of forgetting and remembering and wanting and hunger and gaining your heart's desire and discovering it was not enough, it will never be enough, and there's nothing more ahead but disappointment and diminishing.

I play of dark things, and then I sing of the other things. The glittering in the darkness, the secret light, the grace unasked for, the love unspoken. I sing of being young and foolish and older and foolish and older still but perhaps a little wiser. I sing of life and death and the goodness in both, and of loving the darkness too much and not enough to see through it.

And then the salt is burning in my throat, and my eyes as well as my feet and I choke on my song of the sea and let it die in the rising light.

But my hope does not die.

I made a simple mistake. The doorway does not open here; that is all.

I know my worth. It may be a long journey, but I will be able to open the door at the end of it. I turn to the shore.

He's there, just as I remembered him, and not at all.

And when he opens the door, I follow him through on my own two feet. And on the other side, all is just as I remembered and not at all. Including me.

I sing for them.

And I play for them. And I eat with them, and I dance with them. And I am them, and they are me. Fierce and forbidden. Unending. Enduring. Stronger than they look but softer than they seem.

The good neighbors love the dark as I do, because they are made for it, as I am, and see through it, as I have learned to. As I have an eternity to do.

And so I play and I sing and the one I call Twigs and other things beside stands at my side and brings me new instruments when they cannot keep up with me and a day comes when he sings with me, and a day comes when I dance with him, and a hunger I did not know I had is satisfied. And we continue.

And one day, a ragged girl stands in-between places and sings to us of the darkness. And we invite her in.

END

K.A. Wiggins is a Canadian writer of fantasy with a speculative edge for young readers. Her work explores social movements, environmental crisis, and identity issues through intricate, dreamlike tales of monsters and magic. She's currently hard at work on book two in the Threads of Dreams series.

Website: https://kaie.space/

facebook.com/kaiespace

twitter.com/kaiespace

instagram.com/kaie.space

MESSING WITH THE MULTIVERSE

BY K. MATT

REALITY #671

'So far, not so good,' the young man thought to himself, punching the wall in response to his umpteenth failure. For the past three years, he had been trying, trying, and trying yet more to open up a portal to another universe and pull someone through. He had a very specific variety of targets in mind. But the one time he thought he'd succeeded, it turned out to be nothing more than a dream.

The walls of his bunker were littered with cracks, aged blood, and dents. His knuckles broke each time he punched those walls. Were he a normal human being, his hand would have been rendered entirely useless several times over by now. But that was the thing: he wasn't a normal human. Not anymore. Not after *He* had experimented on him, leaving him with one off-colored eye, freakishly long prehensile hair, those damnable monkey traits, and that downright unnatural healing ability. But the thing that had unnerved him most was that part of him that never actually had healed. His left eye may have had a black sclera by now, with a red iris, but his right was gone entirely. His face below that eye wasn't scarred so much as *cracked*. He could have sworn he was a being of flesh…so when did that cheek become like porcelain?

All of this had been done on purpose by someone he'd thought was his friend. And who knew how many more of this bastard had to be out there? How many universes had a Dr. Spencer Abbot?

He had to find out. And he had every intention of rounding up as many of them as possible. He might not receive much (if any) recognition for his valiant efforts, but if he could keep the good people of other universes safe, he didn't *need* that adulation.

Shaking his head, the green-haired monkey-man pulled himself out of his own thoughts, nursing his cracked knuckles and looking over the portal generation spell once more. He would figure this out. He had to.

He muttered the spell under his breath, focusing all of his energy into it. As had happened the last twelve times he'd attempted the spell, he could feel the electricity spark its way through his veins, causing him to convulse. But unlike those last twelve times, he could actually *see* some sparks this time.

The sparks began to form into swirls of purple, pink, and blue. He opened his eye, his jaw-dropping. Holy crap...he'd done it! He had actually created a portal to another world! At least, he was pretty sure that was the case. But now it was time to see if he'd be able to carry out his plan. A long green tendril of his hair shot through the portal. The monkey-man gave an excited yelp as it wrapped around something warm and solid. He had a bite!

He yanked whoever it was through the portal, dropping them on the concrete floor of his bunker. But as he looked at the figure, his smile gave way to a frown. Lightly, he kicked the aqua-skinned woman in the side. Her fish-like tail twitched, and she pushed herself upright. Waves of dark and light blue hair fell down her back, her blue eyes studying the guy that had dragged her...wherever she was. Not taking her eyes off of him for a second, she moved to pull the skirt of her black-and-turquoise uniform down a bit.

"Well. This is a setback," the monkey-man grumbled.

"Pff. You're tellin' me," the semi-aquatic woman replied, pushing herself to her feet. "Where in the hell am I, and why?"

A tendril of hair wrapped around her waist, and she was lifted off of the ground, letting off a few colorful curses as this happened.

"Your name. Now," the monkey-man demanded, staring her down with his one red and black eye.

She scoffed. "I've been trained not to give in to people like you. Answer my questions."

The hair gave her a painful squeeze. "No. You tell me who you are. Is your name Spencer Abbot?"

The woman shook her head. "Nope. Ivy."

With a grumble, he tossed her to the floor, giving a wall another punch with his less-injured hand. She pulled herself to her feet once more, the young man not even noticing how she stared at him, clearly wondering what his problem was.

REALITY #6

Just another normal day in Hell Bent, PA, the Lab Capital of the US. Of course, *normal*, in this case, varied depending on the individual. For the Baker family, it meant two overwhelmed parents preparing their brood of six for school. For local snake/human hybrid Sherman Pataki, *normal* was just another word for *petty theft*.

And for Dr. Spencer Abbot, that meant spending his day off from the hospital doing some combat training with his brother-in-law. The slim mage pushed up his glasses, sweat drenching his light brown hair. His monkey-tailed opponent pulled a shard of ice from his arm, the puncture wound healing in seconds. Said opponent, Travis, tossed the shard over his shoulder.

"Best you got, Spence?" he teased, flipping his ridiculously long red braid over his shoulder.

The doctor chuckled. "Travis…you know I'm only holding back because I don't like hurting you, right?"

Travis was about to respond when another voice chimed in.

"If that were a real fight, you might not do well to hold back."

The guys turned to see a dark-haired, part-feline woman with cybernetic limbs. Travis' aunt Beast. With her was a close friend of hers, a mostly-human woman with huge waves of black and brown-streaked hair.

"Yeah, Beast is right. Like, for both of you," the latter of the two stated, opening her flask and taking a healthy swig.

"So, Ivy, any advice?" Spencer asked.

"Yeah. Don't hold back. Try not to die," she replied. "And don't worry about hurting Trav...he can take a *lot* of punishment."

Travis blushed as she smirked at him. The two had been together for a year or so by now after she'd shown up to help with a particularly rough time in his life. He was dealing with some immense trauma, and she had the ability to read (or even enter) others' minds. One thing had led to another, and they eventually became a couple.

Spencer opened his mouth to reply when the sparks began to form and swirl nearby. Beast was the first to notice, her ears folding back as she hissed and brandished the huge metal claws of her right hand. Ivy and Travis turned to see what the matter was, as did Spencer.

There, hovering inches above the lawn was a swirling vortex of purple and orange. A dark green tendril shot out of the vortex, aimed right for Spencer. Without a second thought, he conjured a sword of ice, swinging it at this new offender. The sword broke, and the tendril grabbed a hold of the doctor. Beast, Ivy, and Travis all ran forward to attack, Ivy focusing her energy on willing the tendril off of the doctor. Travis was trying to pull Spencer away, and Beast slashed at the tendril itself. But it refused to move, and Beast's claws were dented a bit from her attempts.

And with that, Spencer was pulled through, Travis being pushed back by some invisible force. The portal closed and faded into nothingness. Beast stared at her claws. Those things could cut through human bone like butter, so what the hell had just happened? Ivy cursed, kicking a nearby rock. Travis, a man who didn't normally like to put his fear out for others to see, was shaking. It was either fear, rage, or some combination of the two that had caused him to shake.

But one thing was certain: they needed to get to the bottom of what had just happened, and soon.

REALITY #5124

It was annoying enough for an actual cat to disrupt his paperwork, Spencer realized. But the presence of steel feet, attached to a feline-human hybrid was even worse.

"Beast," he sighed, pushing up his glasses. "Unless you intend to file some of this, please get your feet off of my desk."

Beast, having been trying to take a nap, cracked open her good eye. One of her fuzzy black cat ears twitched, and she grinned at her fellow mercenary. "Am I bothering you, Doc?"

"Not at all," he snarked. "You're just disrupting my paperwork, is all. It's not like I need to get it done or anything."

Rolling her eye, she moved her feet from the desk and stood. Both of them were part of an up-and-coming squad of mercenaries known as The Hammer. Beast was their leader, being the most physical fighter of the quartet. Her second-in-command was Ivy, who was off in the corner and nursing a bottle of whiskey. The two weren't what one might call *tall*, but they were the more intimidating of the group. With her steel arms and legs and her razor-sharp claws, Beast could do a fair bit of damage to a man twice her size. Aside from that, she was the very picture of femininity in a short red dress, albeit with a scar over her right eye. Ivy's long black and brown waves and large blue eyes, combined with her slim frame, made her look delicate, to some. But she lived on that whiskey, and those that underestimated her were bound to get one of her thigh-high leather boots to the face. Spencer was the group's medic, also working as part of the area's local law enforcement. He was the one that got their group jobs, and he was just as underestimated as the women. However, he genuinely *was* as delicate as his slender frame suggested and therefore needed magic (and the occasional firearms) to defend himself. Rounding out their quartet was Travis, currently settled next to Ivy and reading some new thing called a *comic book* or whatever. The half-monkey had an eyepatch, and most assumed him to be the leader. But really, he was more a hugger than a fighter. He could fight, yes, but it wasn't his first choice.

"So, anything lined up for today?" Ivy asked, going to take another swig of her booze.

Spencer shuffled through his papers, even less orderly than they had been thanks to Beast. "Let's see…there are a few listings I nicked from the tavern yesterday. Could see if any of those appeal to us."

"Just so long as I'm not bait this time," Travis said. "I know, I'll recover from pretty much everything, but way too many assholes have taken us up on the offer."

Spencer nodded. "I'll keep that under consideration. Beast, how about you?"

The cat-lady scratched behind one of her ears. "I guess that's fair…"

As they continued to debate the merits of their habit of using the regenerator as bait, they failed to notice the portal beginning to swirl into existence nearby. Travis was the first to see the dark green tendril start to snake its way out of the portal, setting down his reading.

"Hey, anyone else seeing that?"

Spencer was the next to turn toward it, followed soon by Beast and Ivy. Beast's head tilted a bit.

"Is it odd that I find it sort of adorable?" she asked, her ears twitching.

When it lunged for Spencer, however, Travis pounced at it with a screech. He might not have been much for fighting, most of the time, but when it came to Spencer, everything else got pushed aside. Spencer had started launching ice spells at it, Ivy and Beast both attacking the tendril as well.

But unbroken, it picked Travis up and flung him right into the two women, before grabbing Spencer and dragging him through the portal. The others rushed forward to attempt a retrieval, but it closed just as Travis reached through it. He screeched and stumbled backward, a rush of electricity coursing through his arm.

Ivy leapt to his side, inspecting his now-burnt wrist. Beast watched the area that used to contain the portal, her ears folded back. They'd just lost one of their own to a power they'd never encountered before. Scratching the back of her ear, Beast had to wonder one thing…

"Are…are we supposed to file this?"

REALITY #671

Ivy played a bit with a lock of light blue hair as she watched the green-haired monkey-man (whose name, she'd found, was Travis) dance around happily with some kind of tablet in his hands. She hadn't bothered to ask much about his plan. She just knew he was after some guy named "Spencer Abbot" or whatever. And his plan clearly involved portals. Without those, she wouldn't have been there. She might have just been on the Red Joker with her crew, getting somehow even less respect than this guy had shown her thus far. Also, for the past three hours, she had been watching portal after portal being created. Nothing ever exited those portals, save for the tendrils of hair he'd been sending out.

Leaning against one of the dented walls, she finally let her curiosity get the better of her. Her blue eyes ticked over to her unintended host, an eyebrow raised.

"So, um…Travis, right?" she asked.

"Yes, YES!" he cheered, before turning his red-and-black eye toward her. "Hm? Oh, right, you're still here…" His smile didn't leave his face; his mood was too elevated for that. "What the hell do you want?"

Ivy shivered at the effect of his cracked face combined with that shit-eating grin. "What's your plan, anyway?"

The monkey-man skipped over to her, holding the tablet out proudly for her to see. She narrowed her eyes, studying the display before her. There were portals of various colors depicted, practically identical to those that'd been generated in front of her over the past few hours. The difference between these portals and the ones she'd seen so far was the output. Specifically, each portal she saw through the screen spat out a figure. Each of these figures was tall, with short light brown hair. Each of them had glasses and a lanky frame. Though she couldn't help but notice that one of the figures there was a little shorter, with long red hair, a red coat, and a monkey tail.

"Okay…and just what am I looking at, here?" she asked.

"Those are all of the Spencer Abbots I've gathered so far," he said, beaming.

"Uh-huh...so, a couple more questions: 1) is that redhead in the long red coat also a Spencer, or one of you, and 2) what are you planning to do with them all?"

Travis blinked, before looking at the screen once more. "Huh... yeah, that *does* look kinda like one of me...weird... Anyhow, to answer your second question, I...haven't actually thought that far ahead just yet. I'm thinking I'll just, like, toss 'em all in a maze or something until I figure out a better plan?"

Ivy rubbed her temples. "I see...and you're not gonna kill them, are you?"

His grin widened. "Well, of *course* I'm gonna kill 'em! It's just a matter of how I wanna do that after I get all of them rounded up, is all!"

He cast a few more portal spells, tendrils of hair launching through each one. Ivy watched, unsure what to do next. She could stand by and just let Travis do this, but that would lead to countless casualties. After all, she had no idea how many of these Spencers there were out there. But she had this need to help people, and who would she be helping by letting him get away with this? But she knew that attempting to fight him one-on-one would yield worse results than seeking out help.

So with that, she charged ahead, to the next open portal. It was red and swirling like any of the others. Travis hadn't plunged one of his tendrils through it yet, and she could feel it calling to her. She had no idea what would await her on the other side, but she had to try.

Travis didn't notice her rushing through, as one of his tendrils snaked after her and toward the portal—and her. She leapt through the vortex, focusing all of her telekinetic energy into closing it. To be honest, Ivy wasn't entirely certain it would work, but again: she had to try.

The last thing she saw before the darkness overtook her was a diminishing red light.

REALITY #723

Blackness greeted the semi-aquatic woman as her eyes opened again. The last thing she recalled was slamming a portal shut with her powers and then...nothing. Shakily, Ivy rose to her feet, taking a few hesitant steps around her new location. As she roamed about, she could hear a different set of footsteps beginning to approach. If she could see anything around that she could throw, she'd be attacking right now.

But the only thing visible in the darkness was a red glow. It was faint at first but began to illuminate more and more. And before long, she could see that the glow began to a staff. No, not exactly a staff... more like a scythe. It was unlike any scythe she'd ever seen before, with four blades, all in different colors. Its wielder? Another monkey-man. He looked a lot like this "Travis" fellow she'd managed to escape, but with a few key differences. For one thing, his hair was pure white. Secondly, his eyes were a solid glowing red. He dressed in black and had an almost alarming number of piercings; she was sure he had fifteen of them in only his tail.

"Huh...well, this is a rare sight," he remarked, scratching the back of his head with the silver scythe blade. "You're from...Reality #4408, right?"

She shrugged. "Well, you'd probably know more about that than I would. I'm not as versed in different realities. I know one, and that's mine. Or at least I *did*... Could you tell me where I am? And is your name Travis, by any chance, and would you know a Spencer Abbot?"

The scythe-wielder shook his head. "I'm afraid I don't know who you're talking about, 4408. My name is Death PA-6, and there are plenty of Spencer Abbots in this world. But I've never met anyone by that name. Why do you ask?"

With that, she went over what she'd experienced with the green-haired monkey-man, about his plans. She brought up the part where he looked a lot like PA-6, but with different hair and one eye. PA-6 listened, his expression growing more and more concerned by the second.

"You say he's been using a spell for this?" he asked, his thick white eyebrows knitted.

She nodded. "Yes, he has. A portal spell, and he's been ripping Spencers out of them and dropping them into a maze. Um…are you okay? You look worried."

PA-6 scoffed. "Well, *yeah*, I'm worried! Do you know what happens when too many universes are compromised at one time?!"

Ivy shook her head, shrugging. "No, I can't say that I do…"

There was a long pause, and she gestured for him to get on with the explanation.

"I…I don't entirely know," he admitted. "Could be nothing, or it could bring the fabric of reality crashing down. Either one, really."

Was there nothing in between? Ivy had to wonder that, as she rubbed her temples and kicked at what she hoped was a wall. She knew she hit something solid, at least, though it was obscured by darkness. The pained hiss told her that she had either hit Death himself or that the walls were alive. Somehow, neither of those seemed a comforting thought.

"Hey, I know you're frustrated," said PA-6. "But is there any need to take it out on my shins?"

"Sorry," she muttered as Death began to pace. "So, how do we wanna resolve this?"

He scratched the back of his neck again, this time with the purple blade. "That's the thing. I don't know. The simplest solution would be for me to fight this Travis and then find the Spencers and send them all to their respective realities. But here's the thing…" He looked back and forth as if someone were watching him from the darkness. Then he leaned in and whispered to her. "I *suck* at fighting. I mean, I had to be saved from a human once."

"Well, I can't take 'im on!" Ivy snapped. "And it's not like we can let him get away with it…"

And that was when PA-6 had an idea. It may have been mildly insane. Or it could have been a good one. But either way, the wheels were beginning to turn.

"What if we assembled a small army of some kind?" he asked.

Ivy put a hand on one hip, rubbing the bridge of her slim nose. "And where do you propose we find one of those?"

In response, PA-6 conjured a screen of some sort before them. He asked Ivy to describe these Spencers she had seen. It took a few minutes, but he had gotten a visual. What they saw was a scene of a young woman who, aside from her slight curves and longer hair, matched Ivy's description of Spencer exactly. With her was another monkey-man, with no shirt and long red hair. The pair seemed to be embroiled in a fight with some sort of demon. The scene shifted to a city, where they could see another male Spencer relaxing with a red-haired monkey man that Ivy could only assume to be another Travis. With them was a scantily-clad cybernetic cat-woman with huge leathery bat wings. Other scenes came up, depicting various Spencers. Some were with their Travises, but some of those Travises were left without their Spencers and mildly panicked.

"Welp," said PA-6. "Those taken have friends left behind. We can portal to those ones and recruit them. We'll have an army in no time."

Ivy nodded, though she did see one teensy hole in the plan. "I thought we weren't supposed to toy with that," she said. "Y'know, the whole 'compromising universes' thing?"

"I also said I didn't know," PA-6 reminded her. "There's a chance that not doing this will *also* screw the fabric of reality.

With that, PA-6 drew a circle in the air with his scythe, creating a deep red portal for the two of them to step through. Ivy didn't know quite where she'd end up, but the fact that she wouldn't be going through the portal alone was certainly a plus.

REALITY #1780

The first stop on PA-6 and Ivy's recruitment drive had brought them to an alley. Tall chrome-plated buildings sat on either side of them. Outside of the alley, they could see apes of all sorts roaming about like this was their city. Of course, given the infinite possibilities of a multiverse, this was quite likely the case.

But what ultimately drew their attention was the young woman standing before them, her bright green eyes narrowed. Her almost-absurdly long hair was held in a pair of pigtails, and her equally red monkey tail was flicking with what could only be annoyance.

"Are you this universe's Travis?" Ivy asked, head tilted with curiosity.

The woman scoffed. "Yeah, that's my name. What'd you do with him?"

Ivy and PA-6 exchanged glances. This Travis had already lost her Spencer, hadn't she? PA-6 simply shrugged.

"Miss," he said. "You'll have to tell me what you mean."

Truth be told, he knew perfectly well what had to have happened. But something told him that if he let on that he knew, she'd suspect him of being responsible for her Spencer's disappearance. And from that look in her eyes, she was itching for a fight.

"I'm looking for a gorilla," she spat.

Ivy scratched the back of one of her fin-like ears. "Uh, we've seen a few gorillas around here."

The redhead shook her head. "He'd have glasses. Goes by the name of Spencer. Was pulled through some kind of glowy swirling thingy like the one you two stepped out of. Now, I don't know of too many people around here that can do that, so...where is he?"

PA-6 tossed his scythe from one hand to the other a few times. "Well, I don't really know that..." he said. "Because I still have no idea who you're talking ab—HEY!"

The redhead had snatched the scythe away from him, growling. "Tell. Me. Where. He. Is! You want me to break this little stick of yours? Because I totally will!"

Ivy glanced at the currently dumbfounded PA-6. She could hear him muttering something about how nobody had ever stolen his scythe from him before. She turned her attention back toward the redhead, offering a smile.

"So...you said a portal was involved, hm?"

Travis nodded. "Yeah, if that's what it's called, I guess. Kind of an orange and purple thing, and this green hair-tentacle or whatever dragged him through."

"Yeah, that sounds about right," Ivy sighed. "There's been a lot of that going around. So tell me, just what makes you think it was us? I mean, you saw that this dude's portal was red and that any hair tendrils he'd send out would be white, right?"

Travis thought on that for a moment, her lips moving a bit as she pieced this whole thing together to herself. And then she slapped her forehead, letting out a long groan.

"Oh my God, I'm such an *idiot...*"

She handed the scythe back to PA-6, backing up sheepishly with her tail hanging low to the ground. "Sorry...it's just that with the situation, I can't help being a little paranoid, y' know?"

The reaper put a hand on her shoulder. "Hey, that's entirely understandable. Though we do have an inkling of what's going on. So, y' know, sorry about not being up-front about that part..."

And so, the pair explained to Travis just what they knew of the whole situation, about this other green-haired Travis collecting the various Spencers of the multiverse and dumping them off in some maze. She seemed a little confused but nodded as she listened to the whole thing.

"I see..." she said, tapping her chin. "If you need reinforcements, I'm in. I want my Spence back..."

PA-6 smiled. "That, my friend, is exactly why we came: a recruitment drive."

With the pair's first new recruit gathered, the reaper opened up a new portal and prepared to take them to their next destination. In the back of her mind, Ivy wondered if they were, in fact, going to screw the fabric of reality. But she shook her head, trying not to think too hard on it right now. Thinking too hard about the whole situation would give her a headache.

REALITY #1059

The Spencer Abbot of this reality pushed up her aqua-framed cat eyeglasses, having been pushed back by the demonic entity she and her Travis had been fighting. Well, *she* was fighting it. He was trying to get out of its smoky grip, as it held him by the waistband of his baggy black jeans.

"Hey, did I *not* just tell you to let him go?" Spencer called.

The smoke demon roared (or perhaps more of a snarl; it was hard to tell, really) at her. But her bright brown eyes took on a solid aqua glow, as she summoned a small living tornado to her side, directing it toward their assailant. The force of the twister nearly knocked her off-balance, ripping the nearest fire hydrant straight off of the sidewalk. The witch cringed, already not liking how much that was probably going to cost in property damage. She'd have to summon something else to fix it when this was done before anyone at city hall got on her back about it.

But even with the property damage, her plan worked. The twister slammed into the smoke demon, causing it to drop Trav. The redhead charged back to Spencer, getting in front of her.

She chuckled. "I'm still more powerful than you, Trav. You don't need to defend me."

He looked back at her with a smile. "I know. But I still don't want you to get hurt, and know how I'm kinda hard to kill?"

She chuckled, playfully slapping his shoulder as the fight continued. Between the witch, her familiar, and the twister she'd summoned, they made short work of the smoke demon. It dissipated within moments, leaving the pair with the damage.

"All right..." Spencer said, taking a moment to adjust the star-shaped brooch on her short purple cape. "I'm going to see about getting everything fixed. Can you cover for me if anyone asks?"

The half-monkey nodded. "Got it."

As the witch began to summon more creatures to help repair the damage, she failed to notice the orange and violet portal beginning to swirl into existence. She hadn't actually noticed it until she heard the screech of her half-monkey familiar as he leapt to intercept the dark green tendril snaking its way toward her. Spencer looked to see it just inches from her ankle, unable to fully reach because of Travis. He had a hard grip on it, biting the tendril and growling.

Spencer summoned a spectral chimp, sending it after the tendril, but it wasn't enough. Travis was pulled through the portal, which pulled itself closed as soon as it'd been fed. With a scream, she charged forward, trying to summon the portal back to her.

Portals were not really a part of her skillset, but dammit, she had to try! She needed her familiar back. Things didn't feel right without him.

In her attempts to summon it back, she saw another portal appear. It glowed deep red, and through it stepped three figures: two half-monkeys and a short blue woman. Both of the half-monkeys looked quite a bit like her Travis, though one had obscenely long white hair and solid red eyes, and the redhead was quite noticeably curvy, her hair in twin-tails.

"You're not my Travis," she breathed, confused. "Where is he?"

The white-haired one stepped forward. "Spencer Abbot?" he asked.

Her eyes began to glow, and she prepared to summon forth more fighters for her side. "How do you know my name?"

The short woman rubbed the back of a fin-like ear. "Well, it's kind of a weird story…"

And that was when the newcomers began to tell her the tale of an evil Travis and the disappearance of multiple Spencers. much to her consternation. She appreciated her Travis's willingness to take the attack for her, of course, but she still wanted him back.

"Whatever it takes to retrieve him," she said. "I want in."

And thus, the trio became a quartet, as their universe-hopping adventure continued.

REALITY #671

The walls were tall and concrete, seeming to stretch past the sky. That was the first thing that occurred to the Spencer of Reality #6 as he regained consciousness. The second thing to occur to him was to check his leg for any damage, as he rolled up the left pant leg and pulled down the argyle sock. No damage to the cybernetic limb. Okay, that was a relief.

The third, and most drastic, thing that he noticed, however, was the collection of people that appeared to have his face and hair. One of them wore suspenders. Another looked especially indistinguishable from himself. One of them, through what Spencer felt had to be a miracle of some sort, actually had a full beard. Though he also had a bit of gray in his hair and his clothing was a bit tattered. His boots didn't even match at all. There was also a gorilla that had glasses, with a bit of fur that tufted up in a similar manner to his own. There were also two red-haired monkey men that reminded him of Travis. One wore no shirt, just a pair of baggy black bondage pants and a snakebite piercing in his lower lip. The other was clad in a sleeveless red jacket, tattered red pants, and wore thick leather cuffs on his wrists and ankles, with a matching collar.

"The hell is going on?" he muttered to himself, watching as a few of the others began to come around.

The gorilla was the first to wake, hefting himself up onto his knuckles and adjusting his glasses. His brown eyes widened before he leaned in to analyze him further.

"Are...are you what I'd look like if I were human?"

Taken aback, the doctor shrugged. "I...guess? I don't really know. Are you what I'd look like if I were a silverback?"

"Huh...well, I'm not sure if this is time travel or what it is, exactly," stated the one with the beard as he stood up, squinting at the pair.

The three Spencers stared at each other in confusion. None of them had ever considered this turn of events.

"Oh, dear, I've had nightmares about this..." grumbled the one with suspenders. "Am I in some whacky funhouse or what?"

He strode toward Reality #6's Spencer, gently poking his cheek and recoiling as he realized that he was touching actual skin rather than the smooth reflective surface of a mirror. Shaking, he backed away.

And right into the fifth Spencer, who was pulling himself upright once more. The shriek the one with the suspenders let out split the air and roused both of the Travises from their own unconsciousness.

"You're not my Spencer," the snakebite-pierced one began. "Like, none of you. Unless one of you became a dude after landing here."

The Spencers gaped at both of them, the Travis in red adjusting the cuff on his right wrist a bit. The Spence of Reality #6, who shall be referred to from this point on as *Spence Prime*, pinched the bridge of his nose.

"All right...so, what's the last thing any of you recall?" he asked.

They began to launch into their stories. One of the Travises (the one with the cuffs) had been yanked through a portal by a tendril of hair, and he wasn't sure why. All of the Spencers had similar stories: portals, hair tendrils, and then finding themselves wherever this place was. The other Travis mentioned seeing something just like that coming for his Spencer, but he wasn't about to let it take her. At the same time, he wasn't entirely enthused to have taken her place.

But now that they had pieced together how they had gotten there, they had three more questions: where was here, why were they here, and how were they supposed to get the hell out of here?

The only solution that came to this small logic of Spencers was to walk straight forward. Just keep on going ahead, until they found a door. Or even just some sign of a way out.

The men (and ape) began their trek, having to make a few turns here and there. It took about ten minutes (give or take) of walking for them to realize something. They seemed to be in a huge maze. And the realization of that fact did not seem to sit well with Spence Prime, who began to shake a bit.

"Oh, God...not another maze..." he muttered.

There were murmurings of concern amongst the Logic and the two Travises before the one with the leather cuffs spoke up.

"What's wrong with mazes?" he asked. "Do you get lost easily too?"

Spence Prime shook his head. "It's not that," he said as they kept walking. "It's just that my Travis and I were once trapped in a maze. It was a studio that created snuff films, and my Travis was cut by these blades that came out of the walls. I haven't been able to look at a maze without thinking of that incident..."

The others cringed at the thought, not noticing that a number of razor-sharp blades were beginning to manifest, protruding from the walls.

"I'm sure it's perfectly safe," stated the leather-cuffed Travis, putting a hand on Spence Prime's shoulder.

Cold iron sliced through his extended arm, lopping it off just below the shoulder. He screeched in pain, and the whole group then finally noticed the blades reaching toward them. The one Travis continued to screech at the burning sensation of the blade. It wasn't bleeding, but the pain was blinding. The gorilla had hoisted the injured member of their party onto his back as the group bolted through the maze.

They hit a few dead ends, pursued by the blades at every turn. There were a few shouts of regrets they all had in life, but they all kept running. But eventually, the blades stopped. It had taken twenty turns, some of which they thought they'd repeated, but they were finally able to take a break.

But a break wasn't going to get them out of this maze any quicker. They would have to keep going.

They needed to find an exit as soon as possible, or the only survivors might have been the Travises.

REALITY #6

Dr. Serena Taylor looked over her notes once more. Travis, Beast, and Ivy had told her all about the portal that'd taken Spencer from them, and she had consulted her boyfriend, Silas, about the whole thing. She could deal with science with ease, but magic was more his thing. Even with that slight discrepancy, she got something useful from the line of questioning: there existed a spell that could create portals to anywhere, ranging from a room over, to another country, or even to entirely different realities. And since Ivy had been unable to trace him at all, Serena had begun to pursue the "alternate reality" theory.

The good news was that it was theoretically possible to find him using that information. The downside was that there were infinite alternate realities out there to explore. They could search those other universes for decades, leaving their descendants and even their descendants' descendants to search and never learn where he ended up.

Of course, what didn't help her train of thought was the pacing. Beast's hulking metal feet were the worst of it, the light thudding of her footfalls disrupting Serena anytime she began to think. Travis wasn't much better, as he muttered his concerns. The most tolerable of the three right now was Ivy, and *she* could feel the psychic probing her mind, reading her thoughts before she could so much as commit them to paper.

"If you three would like to contribute anything of *use*, I'm open," she deadpanned. "Really, anything would help if it'd get you to stop pacing."

Travis cleared his throat. "Mom…we're just worried, all right? Like, what if we never get Spence back?"

The scientist sighed, her feline ears flattening as she got up to give Travis a reassuring hug. She was literally a step away from him when the red vortex swirled into existence. It started first as a few sparks, before expanding enough to cover the entire wall of her lab.

Serena stepped back to her desk, prepared to call in the security droids, as Travis, Beast, and Spencer approached the portal and prepared to fight. Of course, they would soon come to find themselves vastly outnumbered, as the procession entered the lab.

Leading the pack was a white-haired monkey man with a four-bladed scythe, three women with him: a short aqua-skinned lady with a tail, a redhead that looked just like Travis with an hourglass figure (come to think of it, the white-haired one also looked quite a bit like him), and a lady with shoulder-length light brown hair that reminded him so much of Spencer. Following them were a few more Travises: one with an eyepatch and tattered clothing, another with an eyepatch, wearing just a pair of baggy jeans and an olive duster with the sleeves torn off, and one with a red shirt and enough facial piercings to make him wonder if maybe he'd lost a fight with a nail gun. And with the Travises was one more Spencer, this one in long blue wizard robes, the trim depicting stylized waves. Three Beasts and two other Ivys followed. One of the Beasts had more streamlined red metal limbs, with paws rather than slabs for hands and huge leathery wings. Another had what looked like steel armor on her arms and legs, and—most noticeably—a dress that actually covered her midriff, a baggy trench coat on over that. The last of the Beasts was the most bizarre, her arms and legs looking to be made entirely of flesh. Her hair was pulled into a long ponytail, and she wore some furs here and there. She looked for all the world like a barbarian warrior of some kind. As for the two Ivys, one wore a short trench coat and thigh-high flat-soled boots, the other clad in fine purple and gray silk, a gold and amethyst crown upon her head.

The Travis, Beast, and Ivy of Reality #6 stared for a good long while, trying to wrap their heads around the small crowd around them. Silence cut through the lab like a chainsaw, before one of them had the nerve to speak up.

"All right, since nobody else is saying it, I guess I will..." Reality #6 Travis (or *Travis Prime*, as we'll call him) began. "Just what in the holy blue *fuck* is going on here?!"

The scythe-wielder smiled, gesturing them to sit down. He had quite the tale to tell them all about the multiverse. He told them everything the aqua-hued woman had told him, as well as how he went about recruiting the Travises of the Spencers that had been taken. In a couple of universes, it had been the Travises that were taken instead (one without intention, the other in an instance of self-sacrifice). In another one, that universe's Beast had viewed Spencer as almost like a second son to her and wanted to help Travis retrieve him. In a different one, that realm's Beast and Ivy had witnessed the disappearance, and their team of mercenaries had no intention of leaving one of their own behind. As for the queen and the barbarian, they were good friends with the robed mage and didn't exactly relish the idea of someone coming for him. The queen especially didn't like the thought, as he was *her* royal mage, and that was his half-fae familiar that was taken.

As the whole group began to strategize, Serena let out a sigh. It was clear that this was going to be a massive headache for her. Name tags and nicknames were definitely going to be a priority, she realized, as she left the room to raid her supply closet.

REALITY #671

None of the Spencers (nor either of the Travises, for that matter) knew how long they'd all been wandering the maze. Sometimes, they had hit dead ends. On at least one occasion, they passed by a wall they could have collectively sworn they'd passed already. But there were no more blades chasing them, so that was the biggest takeaway for the group.

"So…a gorilla, hm?" Spence Prime asked, just hoping to keep things from being too quiet and awkward.

The gorilla (who will be known henceforth as *Spence Kong*) nodded. "That's right. Pretty normal, where I'm from…though my own Travis is kind of odd…she's half-human. You know, like these two." He gestured toward the two Travises. "I try not to eat bananas around her, though…deathly allergic."

"Mine is the same way," the bearded one—Grizzled Spence—stated. "But I suppose that since the world came to an end, we haven't been able to be particularly choosy with our meals. Thankfully, we haven't found very many bananas in our travels over the years."

The one with suspenders (*Iceman*) cleared his throat. "I'm sorry… did you say the world ended where you're from?" he asked.

"Sure did. 'Bout thirty-odd years ago. Well, what's your home like?"

Iceman shrugged. "My friends and I work as mercenaries. I'm also an officer of the law. Of course, this may sound like a slight conflict of interest, but it saves on paperwork. Somewhat."

"I learned magic from a shop owner somewhere in town," the last Spencer (*Normal-Leg*) said. "Just found him in this little hole-in-the-wall establishment, begged him to teach me, and now…"

The Spencers chatted away about their respective magical experiences, the two Travises talking amongst themselves.

"So, half-fae, huh?" the one with the snakebite piercing (Snakebite) asked.

The other one scoffed. "Half-fae and cursed, thank you very much. Horrible stuff always seems to happen to me."

To emphasize his point, he gestured to the maze, and then the stump where his arm used to be. "Hell, that's why I wear the cuffs and collar in the first place. Too many humans have come after me, and they seem to favor cold iron restraints. Since that burns in the worst possible way..."

Snakebite nodded. "Makes sense. My luck was kinda the same way before I became soul-bonded to my Spencer. I'm her familiar and her roommate, and we'd do anything for each other."

"Hey, I'm my Spencer's familiar, too!" said the other one, who shall be called Jinx.

"So, like, is yours afraid of spiders, too?" Snakebite asked.

Up ahead, the pair could see the entire mini-logic cringe as a group at the mere mention of spiders. It seemed that arachnophobia was a universal constant amongst the various Spencer Abbots of the multiverse.

And that arachnophobia was not helped at all by the horrible skittering that echoed through the halls. The entire group froze, looking around for the source of the noise. But the only thing they could see was each other.

Which was a shame, because if they *did* get a better look, they would have seen what grabbed Jinx from the rest of the group, causing him to elicit an ear-splitting screech.

Normal-Leg was the first of the Spencers to cast a light spell, illuminating the entire hallway to reveal what the entire logic viewed as their nightmare come to life: a giant spider. It stood at seven feet in height, taller than anyone in the group. And it was in the process of creating a cocoon around Jinx. The half-monkey didn't seem particularly disturbed...more resigned to his fate than anything else.

Somehow, Snakebite had found himself the one monkey-man shield to five arachnophobic mages. Rolling his eyes, he unleashed a screech of his own, rushing forward to attack their assailant. As he leapt at one of its legs, it slapped him away with one of the other seven. He managed to dodge the stream of silk it had shot at him, if just barely.

"Hey, a little *help* here would be nice!" he shouted to the Spencers. "I know y'all are scared of them and shit, but I can't do this al—"

He was cut off when another huge spider jumped down from above, landing on his back and going to inject him with its venom.

The realization that they would be next was enough to snap the Spencers out of their frozen far, as Iceman stepped forward and cast a downright merciless ice shard spell, raining the frozen blades down upon the spiders. Spence Kong joined him in the attack, letting out a roar before he pounded on the ground with his huge fists. Ice jutted up from the ground, hitting one of the spiders square in the middle. It dropped Jinx, who was hurriedly yanked to safety by Grizzled Spence's magic. Finally, Normal-Leg and Spence Prime finished the spiders off with a spell that would encase each of them in 3-foot thick ice.

"Okay, anyone *else* notice that anytime one of our fears is brought up, this kind of thing happens?" Spence Prime demanded.

Grizzled Spence stroked his beard. "Yeah, you're right...okay, nobody mention any kind of fears from here on out, got it?"

The whole group nodded in agreement, save for the still-paralyzed Snakebite. It was also decided that it was probably for the best that they didn't free Jinx from the cocoon for now, as a means of possibly keeping him (and the rest of them through association) out of trouble.

Spence Kong slung both of the half-monkeys over his back, as the party continued along their quest for an exit.

REALITY #6

Serena rubbed her temples, wondering if it was too late for her to take up drinking. Things like *debates* and *strategizing* were supposed to be at least halfway dignified affairs, weren't they?

Not with this twisted little menagerie in her lab. All of them stood in a circle, screaming over one another to assert their dominance. She saw one of the Beasts produce a whip from her metal paw, flapping her wings in one of the Ivy's faces.

"I'm telling you, our best bet is sheer aggression!" she roared.

Serena wondered if maybe she should have given this one a name tag reading something other than *Mom-Beast*, but the cat-woman had mentioned having a bunch of kids back home.

"It's better to be direct, ya cheap floozy version of Beast!" the Ivy retorted, taking a swig from a large bottle of whiskey. "We find that evil version of Travis that's been messing with things and beat him into submission."

Ah, yes, the mercenary, or as her name tag read, *Barfly*. From what Serena had gathered, this one came from a realm that was much like the 30s or 40s, but with much more magic than she ever recalled hearing about in history.

"Well, the blue chick there said something about a maze, right?" the female Travis asked, twisting the end of one of her pigtails around a finger. "So why don't we, like, find that maze, storm it ourselves, and pull our guys out?"

Serena had dubbed this one *Twin-Tails*. Though she did realize that "Fridge-raider" would have been equally valid, as this one had done just that shortly after their arrival. She dreaded her next grocery shopping trip.

"We could always use one of the Spencers as bait and hop through the portal," said the Travis with the tattered clothing and eye patch (who Serena had called *Ponytail*).

"I refuse to be used as bait!" declared the Spencer in the blue robe (or, *The Mage*, as Serena labeled him).

Ponytail jumped up from his seat, nearly knocking the aqua-skinned Ivy (or *Aqua-vy*, to Serena and those who read the name tag) over.

"That's just the thing! You two would be magic and could probably use that to kick this guy's ass!"

"Except that they never made any contact with Evil-You," Aqua-vy told him, resting her chin on her hand. "He's just been dumping them off in the maze with no idea what to do about them."

"Surely he has to have people guarding this maze..." murmured the fur-clad Beast (*The Warrior*). "So it only stands to reason that we kill all those who get in our way. Preferably quickly. They'd only be doing their jobs, after all."

"Yeah, I agree with Beast!" called Beast Prime.

The fourth Beast, who Serena was calling *Modest Beast*, arched an eyebrow. "Which one? There are five of us here, for God's sake!"

Beast Prime blinked. "Okay, for the last time, Beast, that fifth one's name is *Serena*."

It was times like this that Serena regretted being an identical twin. She was fairly sure that in whatever universe Modest Beast hailed from, she didn't exist. That was the only reasonable explanation outside of too much catnip.

Damn, did catnip sound like an amazing idea right now...

The female Spencer, whom Serena had called *Witch Spence* smoothed out the corner of her name tag, which was already starting to rise off of her shirt. "It might actually be worth it to distract any such guards. I'd be more than willing to summon all sorts of creatures for that, and I'm sure my D&D counterpart here would be able to do the same...sorry, I'm not sure on your areas of expertise, Other Me. Are you more proficient with combat magic, summoning, healing...?"

The Mage smiled. "I excel mostly at combat magic, but I'm certainly capable of summoning."

"Great!"

"Well," said Travis Prime. "If you're so great at this *summoning* thing, why not just summon our Spencers and your Travises back to us?"

Travis Prime and both Spencers began to argue amongst themselves, as the two remaining Travises (*Redshirt* and *Patch*, as Serena called them) and the fourth Ivy (*Her Freaking Highness* Serena had been getting frustrated in making out the tags) looked on. PA-6 sat near them, nearly falling asleep.

The only one to notice the ripple in the space before them was Patch. This particular Travis, the one hailing from the same reality as Barfly and Modest Beast, squinted his one good eye. Through the ripple, he could see an off-white wall as opposed to the shiny blue steel of the lab. Near that wall, he could see some heavy-set long-haired figure hunched over a laptop, writing and chuckling to themselves. And then, just as quickly as he had seen that the ripple disappeared, the lab's wall back to its full glory.

"Okay, so, nobody else saw that?" he asked, clutching at the bottom hem of his sleeveless olive duster.

"Saw what?" Redshirt asked, raising a pierced eyebrow.

"I thought I could see into a different reality entirely. I saw it, then it disappeared..."

PA-6 started from his nap, his eyes shooting wide open. "Oh...oh, hell, it's started..."

Her Freaking Highness stood, adjusting her crown. "What's started?" she asked.

Aqua-vy leapt to her feet, staring. "Is...is it that thing you mentioned about the fabric of reality?"

PA-6 nodded. "We have no more time to debate this. We've already wasted enough time as it is. So what we'll do is head to this other Travis's home reality, go with the distraction idea, fight all that oppose us, locate the maze and try to extract your friends, battle him if possible..."

He was interrupted by a slight vibration. The two silver skulls he wore in his long white hair were the source of the vibrations, their eye sockets glowing red. He muttered under his breath.

"Hell of a time for a soul escort...Look, I won't be able to join your battle. Sorry to disappoint."

The entire group stared at him expectantly, wondering what the plan was if he had to simply bugger off like this. PA-6 raised his scythe.

"So, what I'm gonna do here is open up a portal to Reality #671 for you all. You may have to wander for a while to find them. I'll regroup with you all as soon as possible, and wish you the best of luck."

He drew a circle in the air with the scythe, a huge red portal forming once again. Off to the side, he generated a much smaller one for himself, striding through it. It closed behind him, leaving the horde to go through their own vortex.

"We ready to do this?" Travis Prime asked.

Ivy Prime took a good long swig from her flask. "Let's do this."

There were murmurings of agreement amongst the others, as Trav Prime led the way through the portal and into whatever this "Reality #671" had in store for all of them.

"Come back safe!" Serena called to the Primes.

Of course, she also hoped for the others to return safely to their own homes. Not her lab, though. That was a place for science. Science and the copious amounts of catnip she required to deal with this whole thing.

REALITY #671

The mega-portal opened to...nothing. At least, it looked like nothing but flat ground as far as the eye could see. Every so often, there would be a mound of dirt or some random bones. A gentle breeze would blow in here and there, carrying with it the slightest smell of death. All of them looked around, trying to decide where to go first.

"Any ideas, folks?" Patch asked, his hands shoved into the pockets of his duster.

They all thought for a moment, The Mage and Witch Spence discussing tracking methods. The Travises all seemed a bit lost. Beast Prime, however, had a thought.

"Hey, Ivy...and I do mean all four of you. How many of you are telepathic?" she asked.

Ivy Prime, Barfly, and Her Freaking Highness all raised their hands. Aqua-vy rubbed her arm awkwardly, mentioning that she was only telekinetic. But either way, the other three caught onto Beast's idea right away.

Ivy Prime took a swig from her flask, as Barfly did the same with her whiskey. Her Freaking Highness looked to The Mage, who conjured her favorite goblet, filled to the brim with wine. She took the goblet and drank from it, and soon the trio had powered up entirely.

The three stood in something of a triangle formation, facing away from each other, as they all began to scan the region for Spencers. The two with them already pinged their collective radar. But soon, in the distance, they could sense a third Spencer. Barfly was the first to start tearing in his general direction, Ivy Prime running right after her. Her Freaking Highness tried to run, but given the heels on her boots, that was easier said than done. Shrugging, she ultimately used the tele-kinetic part of her skillset to levitate and propel herself along.

Mom Beast also took to the air, flying after them. The other three Beasts, both Spencers and all of the remaining Travises followed. The half-monkeys all ran on their knuckles, keeping to all fours.

What they found was a dead tree, and seated beneath this tree was the Spencer that most of the hangover of Ivys had detected. He wore a white lab coat, long black gloves, and knee-high black boots. His eyes were entirely obscured by a pair of goggles. He picked his head up to see the crowd gathering by him, a smile crossing his face. This Spencer closed his book and stood.

"Well, *hello* there!" he greeted, enthusiasm dripping from each syllable.

Travis Prime stepped forward, waving. "Hey...so, we're looking for a bunch of dudes that look kinda like you. All go by the name Spencer Abbot?"

The tall goggle-wearing man stroked his chin. "Hm...now this is fascinating..." he said.

He looked from Travis Prime, to Redshirt, then Patch, Ponytail, and Twin-Tails. They might not have been able to see his eyes clearly, but he did seem particularly focused on the small plague of Travises that stood before him. He approached them slowly, gripping Twin-Tails' arm gently.

"Hm, yes, quite fascinating...I could probably help you all five of you out if you follow me..."

Aqua-vy reached out with her powers, yanking this other Spencer away from the Travises. The rest of the hangover, along with the full destruction of Beasts, glared at him.

"And why, might I ask, are you so interested in them?" Ivy Prime asked.

The shadier Spencer, who will be known as "Recneps" smirked, shrugging. "Well, look at them. Those feet and tails, and I assume that ever-so-tantalizing regenerative factor..."

The plague backed away, as Aqua-vy glared. "Did you happen to have a Travis with dark green hair?" she asked. "Black and red eye, cracked face…?"

The smirk became a grin. "Sure do! Oh, he was my best work by far… If you would all give me a chance, I could happily do the same for all of you!"

The aqua-skinned woman dropped him, clearly disgusted. She looked to the others.

"This bastard is the reason your Spencers have been targeted in the first place. He wants revenge for this prick's actions."

Much hissing came from the entire group, as The Mage hurled an ice shard at him, and Witch Spence summoned a small demon to chew on his ankle until it could inject the venom. But then Her Freaking Highness stepped up, gripping him by the front of the lab coat. She shielded them both with her powers before her attention turned entirely toward him.

"You have orders. You will tell us where to find your Travis. And then? Then we're doing an exchange. You hear me? We'll trade you for them."

He tried to get out of her grip, but the queen wasn't about to let go. "W-why would I go and do a thing like that?" Recneps demanded.

Mom Beast took to the air again, pointing her knees at him. The kneecaps slid back to reveal a small missile in one thigh and a flamethrower in the other. The mad scientist gasped, as all of the others (save for Redshirt) gaped at the sight.

"How long have you been hiding *those*, and why in the hell hasn't Serena given me any weapons like that?!" Beast Prime asked.

She got no answer, as Recneps eventually relented. "Yes, yes, fine, I'll take you to his compound! Just please, don't shoot either of those off!"

Mom Beast smirked, putting the weapons back and returning to the ground. Taking Redshirt's belt, they bound Recneps' hands in front of him. In return for Mom Beast not reducing him to a pile of viscera and ash, he began to lead the way to his Travis's compound.

They *would* be reunited with their friends, or this entire wasteland was going to burn.

Speaking of the Travis they were targeting (Sivart, for the sake of sanity), he had his tablet out once more. He had a live feed of the maze and could see the logic of Spencers as they traversed through the maze. That one Travis with the snakebite piercing was mobile once more (as was Jinx; the spider webbing had just sort of dissipated somewhere along the line), and he saw them face many more challenges. They faced off with living vines (which tried to eat Jinx), flooding (which again, nearly took Jinx from them), and even evil versions of themselves that tried to kill and replace all of them. That one had successfully killed Jinx...but the half-monkey had a habit of not staying dead. Sivart had to cringe as he saw that last one. And there he was, thinking his own life was horrible.

"I'd kinda forgotten about that part of the maze," he chuckled to himself as he saw it manifest threat after threat.

The monkey man patted himself on the back for the accidental brilliance on his part. Maybe his Spencer was wrong, after all. Maybe he *did* have two brain cells to rub together! He watched it all with glee, rubbing his hands together. Ooh, if he only had that rat bastard at his feet right then and there, he could really make him pay. But he supposed that this was the next best thing.

He barely even noticed the sound of his bunker's door being blown clear off its hinges by a small missile. But Sivart *did* notice a sudden draft.

"Who left a window open in here...and for that matter, *since when did I have a window in here?*"

He looked at the wall, seeing a window glitch in and out of existence. Shaking his head, he noticed eight figures: four were half-feline, three had wide hips and big black and brown-streaked hair, and one was that rat bastard he had been hoping to see again. Grinning, Sivart stepped toward them, tossing the tablet aside like it wasn't a semi-delicate piece of technology. He didn't even care that it broke upon landing on the concrete.

"Well, well...been a while, Spence, hasn't it?" he taunted.

Recneps spat at him, and Ivy Prime stepped between the two. "We'll let you get your revenge," she said. "But only if you let all of those other Spencers and both Travises go free. Understood?"

Sivart tapped his chin, before chuckling and shaking his head. "No, I don't think I will. You're cute and all? But I'm on a mission to wipe them all out. Just because they're not like that one now, who's to say they wouldn't be in the future?"

"Oh…" scoffed Barfly. "So we're reading the future now, are we?"

And then Ivy Prime kneed him square in the groin, as Her Freaking Highness stepped forward and kicked him in the face with one of her stiletto-heeled boots. There was a bit of levitation required on her part, but she got the point across.

"See *that* coming?" Barfly asked.

Sivart bled for a moment, but the wound on his face healed. And then the fight broke out. Seven against one may have sounded like unfair odds, particularly when three combatants were partly made of metal, one was a warrior by trade, and the other three could kill without so much as laying a finger upon their opponent. But when their collective opponent was an entity that could not stay dead no matter what and was driven by stubborn vengeance, it became a bit more complicated.

Beast Prime had begun to slice into him with her razor-sharp blades. She sliced right through to the rib, but he grabbed her neck with his hair and flung her backward into Her Freaking Highness, who had been using her powers to keep the wound open for a bit. Barfly leapt on him from behind, wrapping both arms around his neck as he slammed his back into a wall to knock her off. Ivy Prime had opted more for a telepathic attack, focusing on trying to make him forget everything, up to and including his own name, while Modesty Beast and The Warrior both charged him, the latter unleashing a downright terrifying war cry. His legs received immense gashes, his pants becoming more and more shredded and bloodied by the second. With his hair, he tore the two of them away from his legs, slammed them into each other, and threw them across the room. Mom Beast dodged, before taking a knee and aiming the flamethrower at him. The fire hit, but it was soon doused by the bunker's sprinkler system.

· · ·

Meanwhile, Aqua-vy led the five Travises and both Spencers on their search for the maze. Or rather, the exit to the maze. From the immense size of the black building to the spray paint scrawl of "GET LOST" on the side, they were sure that that had to be the right place.

"So, how do we wanna go about this?" Travis Prime asked.

Ponytail shrugged. "Well...I know my Spencer has this tracking spell he likes to use sometimes. Involves using the hair and/or blood of whoever you want to find. He has a bracelet of my hair for just such purposes."

"Mine too!" said Patch. "Not that it helps with the reverse..."

The Mage pushed up his sleeve, revealing a small orange-red bracelet around his left wrist. "Is it anything like this?" he asked. "I crafted it shortly after my Travis became my familiar."

Redshirt flipped some hair over a shoulder. "Okay, great! So, using that to find yours and that'd help us find the others, right?"

"Ideally," stated The Mage. "I just need a moment to concentrate.

He closed his eyes and held the wrist with the bracelet forward. As he began to focus, the others stood around him, keeping a close eye on the area. If anything attacked, they would be ready.

The fray continued, with the destruction of Beasts and most of the hangover of Ivys trading blows with Sivart. The Warrior came close to losing her non-scarred left eye at one point but managed to avert that fate when she used her own claws to slice through Sivart's hair. Or rather, when she attempted to do so. It didn't cut at all, but it did withdraw upon her attack. Mom Beast had brought out the whip and her claws, using them both to attack this depraved double of her son.

Ivy Prime and Her Freaking Highness both focused on ripping some concrete from the walls, pelting him with it. Whenever he tried to focus on one of them, the other would increase her barrage. Beast Prime had taken to slamming him in the back with one of her hulking arms, as Modest Beast sliced his back anytime the other pulled her arm away.

As all this was going on, Recneps was left unattended. The mad doctor slipped free of the makeshift restraints, soon rummaging through his lab coat pockets. There was a small, but powerful, grenade in there that he had every intention of using.

There was only one person allowed to defeat this green-haired monster. And if there were random casualties in the process, that was okay by him. He was even fine with not surviving it himself if it came down to it. All that mattered to him was making sure that he finished what he started with that damn monkey man.

His eyes lit up behind his goggles as his hand brushed against the explosive, as he pulled it from his coat…

The good news was that The Mage had a bead on his Travis's location. The less good news was that in the plague's search for a threat, they had found one. A small army of large spiders scrambled toward the group. Five of them in all.

Twin-Tails and Ponytail both rushed one of them, with her ramming into its legs as hard as she could. He pulled a knife and leapt for the eyes, both screeching the whole time. Travis Prime took on another one, opting to bite its leg, kicking said leg at the same time. Patch rushed for its thorax with his own knifes, intent on slicing it open. Aqua-vy had set to work on it with her telekinesis, intent on tearing it apart. The Witch, though severely afraid of the arachnid before her and wishing she were very much at home with a nice cup of coffee, her familiar, and a trashy sci-fi romance, saw fit to summon a huge spectral gorilla with a war hammer, directing it to kill the giant spider. She then went to help the Travises with theirs.

Within minutes, the threat had been neutralized, and The Mage had exited his trance. A glowing blue arrow hovered ahead of him, pointing ahead and turning the corner. They had their lead.

The group began to follow the arrow, preparing for the next stage of their plan: breaking into the maze and following the arrow that way. As they moved, a few more things glitched into and out of existence. Aqua-vy sighed, remembering again about the "screwing with the fabric of reality" thing. At this point, nobody thought to question it.

However, they wouldn't have to worry about that next stage, as by the time they reached the arrow's stopping point…

BOOM!

The black wall exploded outward, with Travis Prime and Twin-Tails both receiving a face-full of shrapnel.

"Holy crap…Trav? Are you okay?!" two identical voices called.

Spence Prime and Spence Kong charged out first, each rushing to their respective Travises. Twin-Tails had lost a tooth, spitting that out, but she didn't care as she wrapped her arms around her gorilla friend with a delighted squeal. Travis Prime pulled his Spencer close, the embrace threatening to crush the slimmer man's ribs. Normal-Leg and Redshirt charged at one another, with the latter ultimately instigating the embrace. Iceman and Patch greeted each other with a handshake, which turned into one pulling the other into the tightest hug of his life. Snakebite tackled Witch Spence upon seeing her again, and she laughed, ruffling his hair a bit.

"Missed you too, buddy," she said.

Patch lifted Grizzled Spence in his arms, the two pressing their foreheads together. The Mage ran to Jinx's side, shaking his head at the missing arm. But ultimately, he held his familiar close, the half-monkey wrapping his remaining arm, and tail around him.

Aqua-vy watched the reunions, smiling a bit. Her smile faded when a huge hole appeared in the sky, before it swallowed a good chunk of the maze and disappeared in a flash.

"Okay, it's great you're all back together, but we should really look into getting you all home. I mean, anyone else notice the glitchiness of stuff lately? That's probably reality deciding 'Yeah, to hell with everything!'"

Of course, that would be much easier if PA-6 had returned. Ugh, where was that reaper, anyway? And there was still the matter of the other three Ivys and the four Beasts. Aqua-vy wished they would hurry up and regroup with the others, already.

All froze when an explosion sounded from not too far off, shaking the ground. The plague and the logic both charged ahead, hoping to find the source of that explosion. Some of them had loved ones around the area, and while they realized they would outlive them eventually, they were not ready for that to be today.

The bunker lay in ruins. Recneps had taken the brunt of the explosion, and Sivart was underneath a pile of rubble. A shield of telekinetic energy, held up by all three Ivys, was all that stood between the hangover, the destruction, and a live burial under hundreds of pounds of debris.

"E-everyone, okay?" Ivy Prime asked, not breaking her focus for a moment.

"Yeah," Modest Beast replied. "Are you three sure you can keep this up?"

Barfly hesitated before answering. "Not sure how long..."

"But we've got this! Don't worry," said Her Freaking Highness.

She was probably trying to reassure herself as much as anyone else. She was straining to keep up her third of the shield. Her nose was starting to bleed from the pressure.

The trio's focus was so strong that they had not paid attention to who was approaching the ruins of the bunker, as the plague of Travises, the logic of Spencers, and Aqua-vy charged to their aid.

The Spencers focused on the area around the shield, the area that threatened to crush the others if they didn't have that shield up. All they needed was to hold that up long enough for them to get out.

"Okay, so, Ivy, Ivy, and Ivy, you can all drop that shield now, all right?" Witch Spence called. "We got them all back!"

The shield came down within seconds, all three Ivys collapsing soon after. Beast Prime lifted Ivy Prime, as Modest Beast grabbed Barfly, and The Warrior slung Her Freaking Highness over her shoulder in a manner that might have been undignified for a queen. But this wasn't a time to bring that up, and it wasn't like the queen was currently conscious to complain about it anyway. Mom Beast made sure the others made it out as quickly as possible before flying out of the ruins, herself.

The Spencers let the rest of it collapse once all were present and accounted for. The Ivys and Beasts regrouped with their respective Travises and Spencers, as a small red portal appeared to everyone's left.

"Hey! Sorry I'm late, and I know I really should've gotten here sooner, but I had to report to the Grim about the escort, and then I had to do three more, and...oh, damn, I'm rambling...but I see the mission was a success?" PA-6 panted, finally taking a moment to breathe.

The group nodded, and the reaper took a moment to count the groups. Once he had his number, he created the first portal. A golden-hued vortex, it waited for its occupants.

"Reality #402, here you go," PA-6 stated, looking to Mom-Beast, Normal-Leg, and Redshirt.

The three of them walked to their portal. They could see their hometown on the other side and turned back to wave their goodbyes to the larger group. They stepped through the portal, and it closed behind them.

The next to be created was a rich green color. On the other side was the messy office that Iceman and his ilk knew all too well: Reality #5124. Iceman was hesitant to enter, knowing the chaos that awaited them on the other side. But Barfly needed to rest, and thanks to these multiverse shenanigans, reality was falling apart. He'd even had to dodge a piece of what he assumed to be reality as they stood by the portal. He let Patch and Modest Beast through first, turning toward the other Spencers with a nod before ultimately joining his team.

A soft teal and violet vortex was created now. On its other side lay a lush forest with a large palace nestled in a clearing. Good old Reality #1407. The Warrior sauntered through it first, the queen still in her arms. The Mage and Jinx entered next, giving a quick farewell to the diminishing group. As the portal closed, it nearly cut off the tip of Jinx's tail. Thankfully for him, The Mage stopped it.

PA-6 created a tan and green swirled portal next, leading to some apocalypse-ravaged wasteland. "Okay, Reality #2929? You guys are up."

Ponytail and Grizzled Spence stepped up, the half-monkey throwing up a peace sign as they entered back into their ever-familiar nomadic lifestyle.

A blue portal was next, leading to Reality #1780 and an ape-filled city. Spence Kong had Twin-Tails on his back, the monkey-woman not planning to let go at any point in time. He didn't mind that, either, smiling as she dozed off on him.

"Thanks for your help," he said to the group, keeping his voice down so as not to wake her before stepping back into their home reality.

The blue and purple portal leading to Reality #1059 was next, and it waited for Witch Spence and Snakebite. There was another demon attack happening on the other side, and both rushed forward to fight it without another word. PA-6 waved them off, anyway.

A pink portal swirled open to Reality #6, making Beast Prime cringe. She'd always hated that color, and she looked at PA-6. "So...you can't choose the color, then?" she asked.

He shook his head. "Afraid not. That's the color of your reality. Now please go through, so the multiverse doesn't fall apart."

With a groan, the cat-woman stepped through it with the Ivy in her arms and into her sister's lab. Her Travis and Spencer followed, the portal closing behind them.

And that just left Aqua-vy and PA-6.

"So, you're sure it's time for me to go home?" she asked, rubbing the back of her head. "The other members of my crew don't really respect me..."

The reaper smiled at her. "You'll turn it around. I believe in you," he said, before drawing a circle in the air with his scythe.

A swirl of purple, pink, blue, and aqua appeared in the air.

"There you go. Reality #4408," PA-6 told her. "And no matter what that crew of yours tells you, you're more than capable of great things."

She hugged him for a moment before turning away and entering the portal. This time it led to a bar. Good thing, because she needed a drink after all that insanity.

Once she was situated, PA-6 breathed a sigh of relief. Reality could balance itself once more. And as he opened a red portal to Reality #723, he began to have a thought.

He looked so much like all of those Travises. Each and every one of them had their own Spencer. He had to wonder...

Did he have one of his own at some point? And if so, why couldn't he remember? Muttering to himself about a headache, PA-6 strode through the portal. If he could avoid thinking too much about this line of questioning, he could probably avoid a headache...

Right?

END

K.Matt is both an author and an illustrator living in upstate NY. When she's not writing or drawing, she's planning to write and draw and getting neither done. No matter what, she feels incomplete without a hilariously long project list. The multiverse story she's done for this anthology is particularly special to her, being one of the more ambitious things she's ever written.

f facebook.com/HellBentBookSeries

🐦 twitter.com/MarieTwixie

g goodreads.com/kmatt_hellbent

FAE PROTECTION SERVICES

BY ERIN CASEY

Cadenza Wilde flicked her fingers, sending a spark of magic sizzling towards a nearby candle. Night had descended on the fae realm, Apsaras, but Cade's work had just begun.

She lit a few more candles, illuminating the wooden walls of her cabin. Ivy curled around supporting posts, bearing brilliant blue flowers that couldn't be found on earth. Their sweet fragrance reminded Cade of a nearly over-ripe fruit mixed with caramel. Too bad the flowers weren't for eating; she'd end up a bloated corpse with a single bite.

The cabin wasn't her every-day home. No, she spent most of her time on earth with her wife Naomi in a lovely little ranch house in the suburbs of New York City. That didn't mean that Cade didn't sometimes want to come back *home* to check on her ferocious little garden.

The midnight plants that lined her walls awoke to the glow of her magic. A bulbous black plant with gnashing teeth and golden stripes snapped at her hand as she reached for its evening dinner.

Cade snickered and poked its pot. "Too slow," she teased and tossed a slug into its mouth. She tried to drown out the unpleasant squelching noises by checking on her other vicious foliage.

Suddenly, one of the oblong glass jars lining her desk started to glow crimson. Cade rushed to it and pulled out the cork. A cloud of red smoke flowed into the room, taking the shape of a circle. A moment later, a face appeared in the center of the mirror message.

The other person looked human to the untrained eye with slightly wrinkled dark skin and white hair pulled back in a severe bun. But Cade saw the flicker of magic in the woman's green eyes. She was dressed in a business suit commonly found on earth with a billowy white blazer and a crimson jacket that echoed her hidden fire magic. "Good evening, Cade."

"Riley," she greeted and bowed her head. "I await your command."

Riley snorted. "Wilde, how many times do I have to tell you not to be so formal?"

Cade set her jaw. What was Riley expecting? She wasn't talking to just any fae. She was talking to the head of the Fae Protection Services on earth! And Cade knew how important decorum was in that realm. "I apologize. What mission do you have for me?"

Riley sighed and waved her hand. "My, my, such a change in disposition." She curled her finger, and writing began to appear in place of her face. "You brought to my attention an Elena Maverick of New York City, New York, Earth, yes?"

Cade's heart skipped a beat. Finally! She'd made that request months ago. "Yes, ma'am. It's under my professional opinion that the child should be extracted and sent to Ezekiel's lair." She stared at the child's name along with the numerous complaints Cade herself had made about Elena's living conditions.

"I'm in agreement," Riley said. "However, you need to be mindful, Cade. Other children that we've pegged for relocation have gone missing."

"Missing?"

"The Piper."

Cade growled under her breath. The Pied Piper. Of course he'd be behind that. Humans told fairytales about the mysterious Pied Piper, but none of them knew his true intentions. Too many children had gone missing, sucked away to his realm, never to be seen or heard from again. Some said he drank in the innocent music they sang to help him fuel his magic. Other fae murmured that he actually swallowed their life force because it *tasted the best*. Cade wasn't interested in finding out which was the truth. "I'll be careful," she said.

"Good. I recharged your crystal so you can shift to Earth without going through the Gatekeeper."

The crimson smoke flashed brightly, nearly blinding Cade before ebbing. A glistening ruby dangled from a cord in the center of the cloud. Cade took it and looked it over, sensing the Gateway magic inside that allowed her to shift.

"He's not still cross with you for giving it to me, is he?"

Riley grunted in reply. "I promised him extra payment for his agreement to let you shift so easily between Apsaras and Earth."

Cade arched an eyebrow as she put the necklace on. "It's peanut brittle from Clair's Candies, isn't it?"

Riley quickly cleared her throat. "Our transactions are private, Cadenza, you should know…um, Cade, is your plant-eating a bucket?"

Cade whirled around and found her carnivorous plant upending the snail bucket over its head. "Why you little," she growled and threw herself at the bucket. She yanked it out of its leafy hands and set it up on a higher shelf. "You're impossible."

The plant whined and shrank back into its hole on the shelf.

Riley sighed. "Be on your way, Cadenza. I expect a full report in the morning."

"You'll have it." Cade lifted the jar and held it in the air until the crimson cloud turned white and rushed back into the bottle. She corked it and breathed out slowly. The Pied Piper. She wasn't looking forward to crossing paths with him again. Hopefully, tonight would not be one of those nights.

Cade gripped her crystal necklace and held out her hand. Magic rushed along her arm and to her fingers, sparkling like starlight. With a grunt, she threw her hand forward and created a rift between Asparas and Earth.

The moon hung like a crystal ball in the smog-filled city sky. Sirens blared through the streets as ambulances raced the wounded to hospitals or cops pulled people over for speeding. Teenagers laughed in the alleys, shattering beer bottles against brick walls, their glass shards tinkling as they struck the ground. And from within a tiny apartment, a man bellowed in a drunken rage.

Cade listened to it all as she perched on the fire escape of a run-down building. She watched a police car speed by, the officer completely oblivious to the crimes being committed in the apartment building across from her. It didn't affect anyone else, so why should they care? She wrinkled her nose, her mood souring and glared at the open window.

The shouting resumed. The words didn't matter to her, but the actions did. A tall, hefty man towered over an eight-year-old girl. He pointed at a dirty table overflowing with his beer bottles and cans and shoved her towards them. She stumbled over something unseen, a white trash bag clasped in trembling hands against her chest.

Cade narrowed her eyes and leaned forward, planting her booted feet on the railing. The man's tirade sounded all too familiar to her. How many homes had she visited where parents abused their children or foster children? She and other child protective service workers tried valiantly to free the kids, but not all parents would relinquish their rights. That's where Cade came in; when things had to get messy.

The girl dropped a bottle on the ground with a clatter. She reached for it at the same time the man raised a meaty hand.

Cade tensed, muscles poised to leap—

A dark figure flew vertically in front of her. A whoosh of wind knocked her off balance and onto the fire escape. Cade grabbed the wall to steady herself and glowered as her assailant fluttered down and landed on the railing in front of her.

"Now, now, Cadenza, what did Riley tell you about rushing into an assignment?" the woman said with a Cheshire smile. Her average-height body bore faint muscles around her biceps and thighs, exaggerated by black leather on her arms and legs. Her shoulder-length ebony hair waved lightly in the wind. She wouldn't have looked special, except for the pair of iridescent wings on her back. They glittered in the moon, soaking in the lunar light and spreading it through the green veins. Monarchs would have envied the intricate pattern. She raised her deep emerald lips into a smile, everything about her a perfect copy of Cade except for the mischievous smoky purple eyes.

"*Reg,*" Cade growled. She leapt forward and swung two thick, leafy vines from her hands. They wrapped around the mirror image of herself and sliced the body into three sections. No blood spurted, of course. The pieces vanished into smoke and reappeared into a black shadow floating in midair.

Ugh, changelings, Cade thought.

Reg looked down at the three glowing marks on their ghostly frame and scoffed. "It's only a flesh wound," they said, betraying their insatiable love for *Monty Python and the Holy Grail.* Reg blurred and reformed at her side. This time, they took on the body of a young man with a boyish complexion, a nose covered in freckles, and copper hair. A blue and beige scarf fluttered around their neck as they leaned forward and inspected the apartment. "I thought this was a no-kill mission."

"It is." Cade settled her wings down her back and leaned against the railing beside Reg. The man and girl were gone for the moment, but the tv blared in the living room. "I *hate* it when you turn into me."

"It made you stop, didn't it?" Reg flashed a false smile at her. As a changeling, they didn't really have a true form. What she saw before her was a culmination of their favorite parts of humans, the one that they chose most often when they didn't have a target. Whether Reg went by Regina or Reginald depended on the day, time, and position of the moon, or so they said.

Cade settled for Reg to avoid headaches.

"I didn't ask you to interfere."

"Oh come on, don't look so sour. We're going to get her out of there."

Cade huffed. "It's taken too long as it is. We gave CPS a chance. I told Riley we should have gone in sooner." She'd also included in her report *not* to send Reg of all changelings, the very one who couldn't take a single mission seriously. What had the woman been thinking? "Why are you here?"

"Oh, that." He sighed dramatically. "It seems poor Derek has suddenly come down with food poisoning. He sends his best."

Cade groaned. "What did you feed him this time?"

"Moi? I'm hurt you would think such a thing!"

Cade gave them a deadpan look. "Do Vail, Malachi, and Laina ring a bell?" All victims of Reg's exploits when they wanted to *help* Cade.

They lifted a chin. "I simply have no idea what you're talking about. Anyway, want to fill me in on what we have?"

"You didn't even read the report?"

Reg flashed their auburn eyelashes at her. "Why read when I have you to parrot it?"

"Oh for...*fine*." It wasn't like Cade hadn't read the report back to front ten times over. "Elena Maverick, daughter to Julian and Sora Maverick. Mother deceased; died from cancer about two years ago. Julian Maverick is Elena's sole caregiver and only family. Reports indicate child abuse. CPS has fought to get her out, but Julian has a damn good lawyer. I've been watching them."

"Of course you have, you creeper."

Cade shot them a look. "I've seen the dad go after her more than once. She's definitely a candidate for Ezekiel's hoard."

Reg hummed under their breath. "School? Clubs? Activities?"

"School, yes. Cubs, no. And it doesn't sound like she has any friends, or if she does, no one checks in." Her wings trembled with rage. It wasn't the first kid she'd have to take from a home, and she doubted it would be the last. She didn't get it. She and her wife had spent years trying to adopt a kid but had been rejected due to their gender. Yet this scum-of-the-earth kept a little girl walking on jagged glass, waiting to see if her father would hit the bottle, or her.

"Um, you want to calm down, Poison Ivy? You're kind of turning the fire escape into a garden."

Cade looked down. Sure enough, moss, grass, and flowers grew beneath her fingers. Vines coiled around the black bars and dipped over the edge of the platform. She shook her hands, and the plants vanished in a cloud of emerald dust. "Sorry. All right, you know the routine. I'll get the girl."

"I'll eat the dad, got it."

"*Reg...*"

"Kidding, kidding. Sorta." Reg climbed onto the railing and crouched down, their fingers curling around the bar. "Hey, just to warn you, I heard P. Piper has taken some interest in this one. His portals have been popping up all over town lately."

"Riley mentioned. Why has he taken particular interest in *this* one, though?"

In an instant, the mirth fled from Reg's face. They looked somberly at the building and shook their heads. "Easier to call away a kid who doesn't feel loved."

"Yeah, well, that's going to change," Cade said. She hopped over the railing, spread her wings, and fluttered towards the ground. The cool night air washed over her, carrying her towards the brick-paved alleyway below.

Reg jumped and floated in the sky after her. "Cade, quit it with the scary face. You're trying to comfort the girl, not chase her away."

"*Reg!*"

"I'm going. I'm going."

She looked up in time to watch them burst into a cloud of smoke. Reg raced for the door, unseen by anyone except for fae and changelings. It was a good thing too, because just as Cade landed, the back door to the alley swung open. Cade fought back a snort as the door smacked Reg in their smoky face.

Elena emerged carrying a white bag full of bottles and cans. Freckles dotted the little girl's nose, her face angelic, save for the stress lines that shouldn't have appeared on someone so young. Her mahogany hair swept across her cheeks, one white, the other blossoming red.

Cade clenched her teeth, then took a calming breath. Right, no scary face. She used her magic to hide her wings and approached the girl slowly.

Elena tossed the bag into the dumpster. She looked up when Cade got close and jumped back a step.

"Hey, hey, I'm not going to hurt you," Cade said. "You remember me? From your school? My wife, Naomi, is the guidance counselor there."

Elena fidgeted with the tips of her hair, but her shoulders eased up a little at Naomi's name. "Y-yeah." She glanced behind her. "I need to get back inside."

"Don't worry, I won't keep you long," Cade assured her. She crouched down and held out her hand. "My name is Cadenza, but you can just call me Cade." Elena kept her hands to herself, ignoring the greeting. Cade quickly lowered her arm. The kid looked petrified, but Cade didn't think she was the source. A shout up above and Elena's sudden tense shoulders confirmed it. "Hey, is everything okay at home? I hear a lot of shouting from your dad."

Elena tugged at her hair harder, causing a few loose strands to fall out. "I'm fine."

"No you're not, sweetheart," Cade whispered. "I can see the mark on your cheek." Elena tried to hide it with her hair; Cade didn't stop her. This was a delicate moment, and she didn't want to send the kid running back upstairs. "I know you're scared, but I'm not going to hurt you. I just want to help."

"You can't help," Elena whimpered. "No one can."

Cade's eyes softened. "I have a couple tricks up my sleeve, some that Naomi taught me." She knelt down on the ground to get more at Elena's eye level. She knew not to beat around the bush; this kid had seen things that some adults never would. "Naomi told me that you're scared of your dad. That he's hurt you. I'm here to make sure that doesn't happen again."

Elena looked at her in confusion, but the truth slipped through the practiced fog. "I don't know what I'm supposed to do," she said with a soft sob. "I know I deserve it. I...I don't know why I'm not good enough. I try to be good. I try—" She broke down crying, hiding her face in her bruised hands.

"Oh, honey." Cade scooted closer and held out her hand. "Do you want to be held? I won't touch you if you don't want me to." Naomi always told her consent and choice were of the utmost importance in a situation like this.

But the little girl must have been through too much. She threw herself into Cade's arms, almost knocking her onto her butt. Cade hugged her close and glared at the open window above.

"How come I'm not good enough?" Elena cried.

Cade stroked her hair and buried her face against the girl's uninjured cheek. Oh, how she wanted to slam her fist into the guy's face and make sure he never saw the light of day again. "You *are* enough. He's the one who isn't good enough for you. What he does to you is wrong. He shouldn't hurt you like that." She pulled back and lifted Elena's damp chin. "You're worthy, Elena. You're important, and I'm going to make sure someone helps you believe that."

"How?" Elena asked.

Cade chuckled and used her sleeve to help brush the tears out of Elena's eyes. "Your mama used to read you stories about magic and fairies, right?" When Elena nodded, Cade leaned forward as if to keep a special secret between them. "That's how. I'm going to use a little magic to get you someplace safe." And just so the girl couldn't argue that magic didn't exist, Cade unfurled her wings.

Elena gasped but didn't pull away. She stared in wonder at the glittering appendages, the moon causing them to glow in the dark alleyway. "You-you're a fairy?"

"A fae, actually, but yes." Cade stretched out a wing so Elena could touch it. Her little fingers danced along her dark markings, her touch as light as a hummingbird's foot. "I'm going to take you somewhere safe."

"But how? My dad will know I'm gone," Elena said.

Cade snapped her finger at the door. "I have a friend who's going to help with that."

By the time Elena turned, Reg had transformed into a replica of the little girl. They stepped out of the doorway and waved their right hand. Elena gaped then raised her left arm. They stood across from each other, mirror copies. Whenever Elena moved, Reg followed, going so far as to dance in a circle.

Elena giggled. "What are you?" she asked.

Reg grinned. "I'm Elena!"

"No, I'm Elena!"

Reg smiled. "Okay, okay, *you're* Elena. I'm just going to pretend to be you. I'm a changeling."

Elena spun towards Cade. "They're *real*, too?"

Reg scoffed. "Oh, of course, you believe in fae, but you don't believe in changelings. I think I should be offended!"

Elena blushed crimson, and she shied away from Reg's mock anger. "I-I-I'm sorry."

Cade pulled the child to her, shooting Reg a look. "Leave the jokes for later, Reg."

Reg's mirth vanished. "He sure did a number on her, didn't he?" With a quiet growl only Cade recognized, Reg rounded on their foot. "Whelp, let me go take care of daddy dearest. Get the girl out of here, Cade."

"Be careful," Cade said. Honestly, the guy had more to worry about than Reg, but she still fretted. Even if Reg could be a pain in the ass. She held out her hand to Elena. "If there are any toys or clothing you want, you tell me, and I'll let Reg, my friend, know. They'll get what you need."

Elena looked at Cade's outstretched hand. This time, she took it in her tiny fingers. "Is this really happening? Or am I dreaming?"

Cade chuckled. "It's really real. Now I need you to trust me. I'm going to fly us up; I promise I won't drop you." She swept the girl up. Elena wrapped her small arms around her neck and tucked her face beneath Cade's cheek. Cade's heart melted, and the ache to have a child of her own struck her all over again. A faint smell of lavender shampoo with a ghostly scent of beer-filled Cade's nose. It made her want to get the kid away even faster.

She spread her powerful wings and flapped into the sky.

They were airborne for but a moment when a hauntingly beautiful song filled the area. Cade knew the melody in an instant and she swore. *"Piper."*

Cade tried to fly out of the music's range, but it was too late. Golden magic-filled Elena's eyes until they closed with a butterfly flutter. Her body sank heavily in Cade's arms.

Cade turned around with a growl and flapped a few feet above the ground.

A young man stepped out from beside another dumpster, a golden portal open behind him that led to his lair. All she could see of it was a stone wall and chains, but that was enough to put her on edge. He walked towards her, his body swathed in jeans, a white shirt, and a scaly black trench coat with golden buttons. A multi-colored beret sat upon a bed of perfectly smoothed brown hair held back in a single braid. He smiled up at her as he wiggled his fingers in the air. Gold magic danced along the keys of a flute, capturing Elena in his spell.

"Well, seems you beat me to it," Piper called out, and yet the music continued to play.

"Let her go, P, this one's mine," Cade snarled. She held Elena close, but the girl's dead weight started to pull her down, too, or maybe it was the magic yanking on the child.

"Hm, how many times are we going to do this, Cadenza? She's not yours until she's free of the spell." He tipped his beret up, revealing gold eyes. "You couldn't save the last one. What makes this little morsel any different?"

Cade narrowed her eyes, his words slicing her like a knife. She didn't need to be reminded of the children he'd stolen from her before she could save them. None of the Fae Protection Services liked to be reminded. "I'm not letting you feed off of her."

Piper sighed and waved his hand. The flute floated to the right and continued to play with his magic. "Are we going to do this tired dance again? Cadenza, I really don't think—"

She lashed out with an ivy vine before he finished speaking. Her magic whipped at the flute, wrapping it up to try to plug the sound. She succeeded for a moment before a snap of Piper's fingers caused her vine to turn to gold. Magic raced up her vine, and she tossed it to the side. It clanked to the ground, solid, dead.

Piper glowered. "Rude. But fine. We'll play it your way." He took off his beret and tossed it onto the downstairs doorknob. His hands filled with golden magic that he hurled up at her.

Cade dodged the first two blasts and flew towards the ground so she could put Elena down. She didn't want the little girl to get hurt. She tucked the child against the wall then flew back up and sent her magic into the earth. Bricks split beneath Piper's feet as vines shot up to twist around him.

He curled his lip, a single tooth shining gold, as he hopped through the green tendrils and slashed at them with his magic. One by one, the vines fell, but Cade didn't care. She grabbed onto the dumpster behind him with two more vines and swung it at his back.

This time Piper didn't dodge. He yelped as the hard metal slammed into him, sending him sprawling across the ground.

Cade circled and brought more vines down on him, trying to wrap him up in earth and brick.

But Piper only laughed. "Oh, you're cute." He pounded his fist into the ground.

Vibrations ran through the dirt, which Cade felt in her bones, but nothing flew at her. She frowned in confusion, circling him, binding him with more dirt and brick until only his head was exposed.

She hovered in front of him.

The ground exploded.

Water shot up from burst pipes, striking her and sending her flying backward with wet wings. Cade gasped and dried them with magic, but not fast enough. Bricks rushed to meet her and cracked into her arm and shoulder. She rolled several feet away, ending up in a heap. Cade shook herself, dazed, and struggled to rise.

Piper started to hum and twitched his nose since his hands were hidden beneath the earth.

The water pipes broke free and shot towards Cade. She lashed out with vines, knocking them away as fast as she could. Suddenly they broke apart into pieces. Two cut across her arm, another along her leg.

Cade cried out in pain, not from the cut, but from the feel of iron on her skin. Many cities had worked to eliminate iron particles from construction, at least in fae territories, but there were still old pipes lurking about. Her body burned where the shards slashed her.

She dodged another piece, causing her to miss seeing the thick pipe swinging at her stomach. It struck, winding her and sending her back to the ground. Cade rolled to her hands and knees. At the same time, more pipes broke through the earth. They twisted around her arms and legs, effectively pinning her in place. They would have burnt her too, if not for her clothing. Cade struggled and swore, but the restraints held her tight.

Piper broke through his prison with a combination of magic and pipes. He picked up one and spun it in his hands, whistling all the while. "Nice try, Cadenza. I do so enjoy our dance, but I'll be on my way." He draped the pipe over his shoulder and winked. "Just in case you try to follow, eh?" A flick of magic brought his beret back to his head.

"Piper, don't!" Cade shouted as he scooped the sleeping Elena into his arms. "She's just a kid. Give her a chance!"

Piper looked down at Cade, his eyes devoid of pity. "You fuel your magic your way, and I'll fuel mine my way. Thanks to your changeling, she won't be missed. Try, try again, little Cadenza." He laughed as he stepped past her, his flute floating and playing merrily behind him.

Cade shouted in outrage. Not again! She refused to lose another child to that monster! She struggled against the iron, ignoring any burns that blistered her flesh as her hands brushed her bonds. There had to be something she could do! She looked around frantically then stared at the flute.

Cade clenched her teeth and grabbed hold of a brick with another vine protruding from the ground. She glanced over her shoulder, aimed, and hurled the brick as hard as she could.

The flute gave a tortured squawk as the brick connected, knocking it from the sky.

Piper yowled as if he'd been the one hit.

Cade blinked. Wait; was the flute more than just the source of his power? She opened up the earth beneath the flute and dropped it down before Piper could grab it.

"Where is it?" he bellowed.

Cade dragged the flute through concrete, brick, and dirt, bashing it side to side.

Piper yelped with each new blow. He dropped Elena to the ground and scrambled after the flute, his nails clawing at the earth in desperation. "Where is it? Where is it!" He raced along the alley, sent on a wild goose chase.

Cade concentrated and brought the flute towards her.

Piper spun on his foot. He pulled the pipe off of his back and raised it above her, his eyes glinting red instead of gold. "Where is it!" He swung.

Cade jerked the flute up through the ground and put it in front of the pipe. The moment Piper struck it, the flute cracked in half. He unleashed an inhuman cry as he collapsed backward, writhing, clawing at the air. Before he hit the ground, he vanished in a cloud of golden smoke. At the same time, the portal behind him sizzled out of existence.

Cade knew he couldn't be dispatched so easily. He'd be one pissed Piper once he reformed.

She slumped in her prison, exhausted, and looked at Elena.

The girl jerked awake, gasping. She touched her head, and her face then looked around at the demolished alleyway. The moment she saw Cade, she sprang to her feet. "Cade!"

"Hey, kid," Cade said with a half-smile. Elena dropped to her knees next to her and tugged on the pipes, but they were stuck.

"I can't get you out!"

"It's okay. It's okay," Cade said. "Reach into my pocket for my Cell. Yeah, the right one." She waited until Elena turned the screen on. "You see the name, Ezekiel? Call that and put the phone to my ear."

Elena did as she was asked and pressed the phone close. Cade closed her eyes wearily. She'd used a bit more magic than usual against Piper, not that she regretted it. She would do it again for the kid.

Ezekiel answered after the third ring. "Cade." His deep voice rumbled through the phone. "Are you almost here?"

"Ah, about that. Ran into Piper. I'm a bit tied up."

"Hm, figuratively or literally this time?"

Cade made a face. Why did he always have to make it sound like she ended up in trouble? "Literally. Iron pipes."

"He got creative, I see. And the girl?"

"Safe with me. How do you think I called you? Can you make a pick-up?"

"Very well. Stay where you are."

Cade glared at the phone. "Funny, Ezekiel."

The call ended.

No sooner had Elena put the phone away did Reg lean out through the window. "What the hell happened down there?" they asked in Elena's voice.

"Piper," Cade said. "The dad?"

"Passed out on the couch."

Elena rocked back on her heels. "Can you help her?"

Cade gave a sad smile. "It's iron, sweetheart. It would hurt them too. Besides, Ezekiel will be here shortly."

"Who—"

Elena didn't get to finish.

A rift appeared in the air in front of them in a glowing silver line. It unzipped from the other side, parting the alleyway to reveal a library just beyond the split. Children played on the floor, rolling balls, stacking blocks, reading, all of them smiling and laughing, exactly what Elena should be doing instead of hiding from her father.

Ezekiel stepped out, his great-horned head rising high above the rift. He loomed ten feet tall, though he measured even longer from snout to tail. He stood in his biped form, his taloned feet the size of serving platters. Gold and brown scales covered the dragon's body, matching the wizened beard flowing down his chin. Spectacles rested in front of his violet eyes, his irises matching his tweed jacket, which he wore over a white shirt and black pants modified for his gigantic frame. He folded his leather wings along his back and looked down at Cade with a wrinkled nose.

"You always make a mess," the dragon scoffed, kicking a brick away.

Elena's mouth dropped open, her eyes growing wide. "Y-y-you're a. You're a...a...."

"Dragon is the word you're looking for," Ezekiel said kindly. He crouched down but the child still barely reached his chest. "Elena, I presume? My name is Ezekiel. I'll be taking care of you from now on." He held out a mighty, clawed hand.

Elena looked at Cade for guidance, her eyes a mix of wonder and absolute bafflement.

"Go ahead. He's a friend."

Elena eyed his hand once more, then slowly took it. Magic wrapped around her, chasing away her bruises and pain. She sighed, and the biggest smile Cade had ever seen stretched across her face from ear to ear. "Nice to meet you."

Ezekiel chuckled. "Likewise, little Elena. Now, let's help your friend." He pulled Elena to his side and swung out his tail. Two vicious blades sliced through the iron, keeping Cade pinned. She flopped to her stomach with a grunt of pain and rubbed her sore limbs.

"Couldn't have been gentler?" she complained.

Ezekiel snorted and sent another wave of magic across her to heal her hurts. "I don't question your methods. Don't question mine. Now, I'm going to get this little one home. Be sure the father is dealt with."

Reg perked their head out the window. "Does this mean I get to eat him?"

"No!" Cade and Ezekiel shouted back.

Ezekiel started to scoop Elena in his arms, but she stopped him. "Wait," she said. He set her down, and she rushed to Cade, wrapping her small arms around her throat. Cade rocked back, surprised, but she returned the hug. "Thank you," Elena whispered.

Cade smiled. "You're going to be okay, kid."

"You'll come and visit?"

Cade glanced up at Ezekiel and received a nod. "Yeah. Of course."

She took a breath and nudged the girl towards the dragon. "Go on. You don't want to keep your new friends waiting."

Ezekiel held out a clawed hand for Elena. When she took it, he guided her into the new realm. Elena looked back once with a smile, then vanished from sight.

An eerie silence fell over the area. Cade settled back on her butt with an exhausted sigh and looked up at Reg. "How many 911 calls do you think there's going to be with this mess?"

"Eh, I wouldn't worry about it. I put a cloaking spell on the alley before I went inside so no one would see or hear you."

Cade arched a defined eyebrow. "Cloaking spell? Since when did you learn cloaking spells?"

"Since Ezekiel complained, I made too much noise and gave me an amulet to create the spell." They pulled the necklace out from beneath their shirt.

Cade grunted. "Thanks for the warning." She leaned back and drank in the light of the moon, letting it fill her. Moon flowers grew through the damaged earth around her, their buds opening up to the silver light. There would be questions in the morning, but she didn't care. Her mission was complete.

Another kid would wake up to a better tomorrow.

Erin Casey is an urban fantasy and YA fantasy writer. She published her first book, The Purple Door District, in December 2018, and the sequel, Wolf Pit, is coming out December 2019. A lover of all things magic, she enjoys dabbling in stories about fae and other worlds. "Fae Protection Services" won a silver honorary mention in Writers of the Future. And there are more stories to come from this world.

Learn more about her at www.erincasey.org.

facebook.com/rerincaseyauthor

twitter.com/erincasey09

instagram.com/erincaseyauthor

MICROSCOPIC MAYHEM

BY KATE REEDWOOD AND CHRIS HEINICKE

CHAPTER 1

Shiznit woke up, a realization that made him most happy.

For one thing, his beautiful Plovanian girlfriend was lying next to him in bed. For another, waking meant he hadn't died, a circumstance he considered to be a completely, frelling awesome start to the day.

Not that the young Gho'bar expected to die in his sleep. His kind were *long-lived and sturdy* as his starship captain, Blake Bronson, had explained. Gho'bars were, apparently, *built like mountain goats...with feelings*. But as Bronson was without a doubt the craziest human Shiznit had ever traveled with, he doubted such a comparison was a good thing. And, thanks to Bronson's constant run-ins with beings who wanted to see him and his friends dead (a circumstance one would think easily avoidable on a ship capable of time travel, but which seemed to have the opposite effect) the possibility of a bounty hunter killing them as they slept was higher than Shiznit liked.

He climbed out of bed and walked to the hotel room window. With a wave of his hand, he activated the motion sensor that increased the window's transparency from *opaque night* to *morning light*. Blazing sunlight immediately filtered into the room, causing Shiznit to blink and glance away. Not that he minded the view of his bed anyway. Marsais. What a sight she was, her slightly feline features relaxed, and her soft skin glowing in the warm light. He'd never known a species like hers before leaving his home planet of Gho'barchreig and venturing out into the galaxy. He'd never known a lot of things, except mountain passes and the constant disapproval of his tribal elders. His life had changed so much in the last three solar cycles that his past seemed more like a dream than reality.

Did he miss the craggy landscape and routine familiarity of his home world? At times. But the chance to travel on the Queen Bohemia with Bronson and his crew was one he'd never regret, despite the constant danger the captain seemed to attract. He'd met Marsais, and that was maybe the best thing to ever happen to him. She was different with her tail and tufted ears, soft curves, and sweet laugh. Not at all like the females of his own species with their curled horns and trim, muscled bodies. But differences were a very good thing, he'd found, and exploring them over and over again could be quite enjoyable. He grinned, remembering the night before. It was a bit hazy, which was odd as he didn't think he'd had more than one or two drinks before retreating to his room with Marsais, but he was certain that once in the room things had been…well, frelling awesome.

So far, Bronson's plan for the six-member crew of the Queen Bohemia to spend a few days at the Celestia Six Paradise Hotel and Resort for some much-needed relaxation had turned out to be a good one. Rare, considering the captain's track record to attract danger. But no one had died, at least not yet, and Shiznit felt the tension leaving his body, despite himself.

He looked through the window. With his room on the one hundred and eighth floor of the space station, he was treated to an awe-inspiring panoramic view of the vast pool and beach area that made up the inner sanctum of the resort. The artificial sun, which brightened the dome of holographic sky above, highlighted the blue water with tranquil glints of sunshine. He stretched, easing the stiffness from his muscles and let out a relieved sigh. He wasn't much of a swimmer, but yeah, he could get used to this place. That moonlight dip in the pool they'd done last night had been epic. Perhaps they would go for another before meeting with the rest of the crew from the Bohemia for snacks and drinks today. Although, maybe not like the ones they'd had last night. He couldn't quite remember what he'd done while at the bar, but the impression of it left a bad taste in his mouth.

An ear-piercing shriek from behind him made him jump and nearly fall into a dead faint, despite his recent improvement with controlling the goat-like startle response.

"What the frell?" Marsais yelled. "Who the frell are you?"

He turned to face her. "What?"

She stared at him, her expression full of confusion as if he'd grown another pair of horns on his head. "What are you doing in my room?"

"Marsais?" He took a few steps toward her, and then stopped when her gaze traveled over his naked body. Rather than showing her usual appreciation over his fully exposed appearance, she seemed shocked. Which didn't make sense at all. "Are you okay?"

"No, I'm not. You...you...pervert!" She peeked beneath the sheet and yanked it all the way up to her chin, her violet eyes frantic. "I'm naked."

"Yes." He smiled, hoping she'd ask him to join her on the bed again.

"You think this is funny? How about you wipe that stupid grin off your face, goat-boy, and get the frell out of my room before I shoot you?"

He raised his hands outward and spread his palms wide. "I don't understand. What did I do wrong?"

"Oh, my frell, get out. Get out!" She grabbed her laser blaster from the nightstand where she'd left it close by the night before, in case a bounty hunter showed up unexpectedly. It was a precaution he'd always thought a good idea in helping to extend their life expectancy, except now the gun was pointed at him. Yes, he was willing to admit he may have been mistaken with that belief.

"But, Marsais..."

He dived to the floor as a laser bolt missed his head by a matter of centimeters. *Frell.* "Okay, I'm leaving." He raised his hands over his head and raced for the door. Whatever was wrong, he'd have to talk to her about it later. Right now, he was in danger of being her next kill. Not that he'd ever seen her kill someone, but he didn't doubt she knew how to use that blaster.

In a fluid motion, he activated the door release and tumbled outside into the passageway, just as a second laser bolt sizzled past him and hit the wall in front of him.

He turned as the auto-close function on the door activated, providing a barrier between him and Marsais. At least a temporary one until she came after him.

The holographic figure of a humanoid male dressed in a well-pressed black hotel uniform flickered to life next to him. "May I be of assistance, sir?"

Shiznit eyed the hotel's auto-attendant. "Not unless you can figure out women." He hurried down the hall and around the corner away from the line of fire, completely naked and more confused than he'd ever been in his life, which was saying something.

The auto-attendant kept pace, floating beside him as he walked. "Girl troubles? Shit, that's not good, mate."

Shiznit did a double-take. The auto-attendant had changed from *Prim and Proper Concierge* to *Poolside Tiki hut Bartender* complete with tan, bleached hair, and the script of an informal life coach.

The hologram shook his head at the Gho'bar. "Mate, come with me, and I'll get you something to hide your tackle with."

"Tackle?" Shiznit tapped his comm device. Was he hearing this right? "Why would I want to tackle anyone?"

"You know, your old fella." The auto-attendant gestured at Shiznit's naked midsection.

The Gho'bar shook his head as understanding dawned. "Why couldn't you just say penis?" Universal communication devices weren't always as universal as they should be.

"Tackle is a bit less trouble, mate. But you can't be letting it hang out like this. Some of the guests might complain."

"And do what? Shoot me? Already been there, done that today."

What in the flaming fires of Gho'barchreig was going on? Marsais had seemed fine when they'd fallen asleep last night. Had he woken up in an alternate reality? Considering the Bohemia traveled between realities on a regular basis, anything was possible. Maybe Bronson would know what had happened because he sure as frell didn't.

He stopped in front of a door on the left side of the hallway and raised his hand to knock, but the door hissed open before him.

"Ah, good timing," Bronson said. He glanced between Shiznit and the auto-attendant. "Perhaps one of you gentlemen would be good enough to tell me where I am?"

Gentlemen? Shiznit studied the dark-skinned, bald-headed captain of the Queen Bohemia and muttered an expletive. "Has everyone lost their mind today?"

"You are currently a guest at the Celestia Six Paradise Hotel and Resort, mate."

"Oh, right, right." Bronson's gaze flicked over Shiznit, then back at the auto-attendant. "Is this one of those clothing-optional places?"

"Naw, not on these levels. Best to keep your tackle locked up, mate, if you know what I mean."

"*What does it matter?*" Shiznit shouted. "There's more important problems happening."

"Oh?" Bronson glanced at the attendant.

"Girl problems," the hologram said with a solemn nod.

"Ah," Bronson said as if that explained everything.

Shiznit snapped his fingers in front of the captain's face. "Hey, Bronson. It's me, Shiznit. One of your crew?"

The captain of the Queen Bohemia's brows drew together as he studied him. "A naked Gho'bar is part of my crew? I don't think so."

He pushed passed Shiznit and set off down the hallway, chuckling. Then he abruptly stopped and turned back. "Wait. What crew? I don't have a crew. The resort handles everything when I need it and sets up and clears the stage for me. Speaking of which," He focused on the auto-attendant. "I need you to secure my flight to Hell spaceport for later today."

The attendant changed back to *Prim and Proper Concierge* with a nod. "Very good, sir. As you wish." The hologram flickered and disappeared.

Shiznit stared at the captain. "Bronson. You own a frelling starship, the Queen Bohemia. Not a band."

"Of course, it's not a *band*," Bronson scoffed. "It's a musical extravaganza experience on a starship tour of the galaxy."

Shiznit twitched. He rubbed his chin, hoping it would help him think, but wasn't surprised when it didn't.

"Little goat man, you need to check out the show. We're performing today. I think." He frowned. "Wait, you said I'm a captain?"

Shiznit frowned. First, Marsais seemed to not recognize him, and now Bronson didn't either. What's more, Bronson thought of himself as some kind of performer. "Yes, a starship captain."

Bronson scratched his head. "Shit, I need to talk to my manager. See you later, and damn, put some clothes on. Waving your tackle about. That's not cool. You'll scare the fans."

Shiznit stood with his jaw agape as Bronson retreated into the room he'd emerged from, leaving the Gho'bar alone in the hallway just as naked as before, but more confused than ever.

CHAPTER 2

Shiznit had seen a lot of strange things since he'd departed his sheltered life on Gho'barchreig and traveled through tesseract portals to alternate realities and dimensions with the crew of the Bohemia. The weirdest had probably been the reality where inanimate objects were sentient, including the chair he'd tried to sit in and almost been eaten by because he'd not asked it for permission. Frell, he'd freaking died once, sort of, but that had been in another reality, which, of course, wasn't this one.

But this situation…this was one he'd never encountered before, and he was having a hard time making sense of it. Marsais and Bronson appeared to have no memory of him. But the hotel auto-attendant still recognized them all as guests, so, whatever was going on…well, he had no idea what was going on. It was just really frelling confusing.

He stared at Bronson's closed door, trying to decide what to do next. But all that rose to the surface of his thoughts was that he'd not yet eaten breakfast and that he missed being in bed with Marsais, even if she now wanted to kill him. Maybe it was okay to go back to his room? She couldn't stay angry with him forever, could she?

When Marsais appeared around the hallway corner a second later, paused mid-stride upon seeing him and screamed, "You!" at the top of her lungs, he realized, however, that she could.

Her quick glance took in his proximity to Bronson's door and narrowed when it landed back on his bare midsection, making him wish, once again, that he'd remembered to at least bring a towel when he'd run out into the hall.

"Harassing other guests now? Disgusting." She raised her blaster at him and spoke into her comm. "Security—"

He took a step backward and raised his hands. "Wait. No!"

"Save it," a familiar female voice said from behind Shiznit at the same time a low-pulse energy discharge passed above his shoulder and hit Marsais square in the chest. "She isn't listening right now."

Marsais froze mid-step, the surprised expression on her face mirroring the one on Shiznit's.

Oh, frell!

Caught off balance and unable to move, she started to tip forward, freeing him from his momentary shock paralysis.

"Marsais!" Shiznit leaped toward her, catching her before she hit the floor. "What the frell?" There was no visible damage to her, but she was stiff in his arms, eyes open and staring. He glanced up as the shooter approached them. T-183, the Queen Bohemia's third-in-command. She stood with one hand on her hip and the other holding her blaster. Was the cyborg suffering memory loss too and had gotten trigger happy? "Why the frell did you do that?"

"She has not been permanently harmed," T-183 said. She lifted the weapon so Shiznit could see it. "Stasis blaster. Lowest setting. Our bigger problem is what she will do when it wears off in a few seconds."

"I'll tell you what she'll do. She'll really frelling kill me!" Being hit by a stasis blast felt like you were buried in a dark tunnel, unable to move or breathe.

The auto-attendant flickered to life beside them, this time dressed

as a Monsatan security officer. The orange-faced, three-legged creature held a laser weapon in each of its four hands and pointed them at
the three people in the corridor. "Celestia Six security reporting as
requested. Do you require assistance?"

"No," T-183 said in her emotionless tone. She moved her stasis gun
behind her back and assumed a casual stance. "False alarm."

"Your companion is unconscious," the auto-attendant observed.
"And may require medical treatment."

"She fainted," Shiznit said. "When she saw me." He pulled Marsais
closer to him and smiled at the holographic projection, hoping the
hotel's Artificial Intelligence would believe him. It was the kind of
place that catered to the needs and beliefs of many different species,
hence the non-confiscation of personal weapons upon check-in, and
the lack of interference in a guest's business unless requested. But
general rules of conduct did apply, such as don't kill anyone or
break things, unless you really wanted to be detained and handed
over to the Core galactic authorities. Which he didn't. He'd had
enough run-ins with the Core during his recent travels to last him a
lifetime.

The auto-attendant focused on him for a long second and, with a
nod, changed back into the Tiki hut bartender persona. "Not surprising, mate. I told you to lock up your tackle. You're scaring the sheilas
into a dead faint."

Marsais began to moan slightly and move. Which was good, but
frell, they needed to get rid of the auto-attendant before she
completely revived and had them arrested. "No, no. It's not that. She's
my girlfriend. She just found me so...so..." He glanced around, struggling to find a word to describe himself.

"Awkwardly compatible?" T-183 supplied.

"Exciting," Shiznit said as he glared at the cyborg, "that she passed
out. She's fine. See?"

As he kissed Marsais on the cheek, she moaned and lifted her hand
to bat at him weakly.

The auto-attendant studied them, then nodded. "Okay, mate. I'll
leave you to it then. But no more trouble from you lot, you hear?" He

pointed at the three of them. "Or I'll report you to the management." The attendant disappeared with a flicker.

Marsais blinked. Then blinked again, her eyes flashing bright with anger as her gaze focused on Shiznit. *"You!"*

T-183 quickly placed a transdermal applicator to the Plovanian's neck and pressed the injector with a click. Marsais's eyes rolled back in her head, and she went limp without uttering another sound.

"Frell!" Shiznit stared at the cyborg. "Will you stop doing that?" Breath still passed between Marsais slackened lips, so at least she wasn't dead. But this day was beyond frelled up. Even T-183 seemed intent on shooting people and jabbing them with shit. "What the frell is your problem with Marsais?"

"She is unstable."

Shiznit frowned. "Well, she isn't the only one."

"You are correct. Help me lift her onto the luggage cart." The cyborg indicated the anti-gravity platform that hovered behind her in the corridor. She took one of Marsais arms and shouldered the weight, leaving Shiznit to support the other. "We need to get her and the others back to the ship as quickly as possible. She would not cooperate if awake. Sedation was the only viable option for us to move her with expediency."

"Well, you could have warned me."

"I could not. There was no time."

"Really? Well, what the frell is going on that you couldn't even contact me using the comm?" Shiznit grimaced as they struggled to place his unconscious girlfriend onto the rectangular platform. T-183 didn't appear to have the memory problem that was affecting Marsais and Bronson. She recognized him at least, and she was handling things with her usual hyper-efficiency, even if he didn't really like it.

"I am uncertain." T-183 scanned Marsais with a device strapped to her wrist. "The medical scanner on the Queen Bohemia will be more precise, but it appears that members of the crew are suffering a hallucinogenic episode."

"A what? Like they are seeing things that aren't really there?"

"No. More precisely, a disruption to their memory processes."

"How? Is it a temporal anomaly?" He was familiar with how frelled those things could be with unsticking people in time.

T shook her head. "If so, it is extremely localized as it appears to be affecting only the crew of the Bohemia."

"Just us? No one else?"

"Currently."

"You think it might spread?" He wasn't affected, yet. But what if it happened to him as well?

"Unknown."

"What caused it?"

"Unknown."

"Frell. Is it serious?" He stared at Marsais. Maybe he'd become jaded by all the seemingly impossible possibilities he'd encountered while traveling on the Bohemia, but his shock over her trying to kill him was fading into the realization that whatever had gone wrong could be potentially lethal. What if it killed her? And the others? And everyone?

"Uncertain. But I feel it prudent for all of the crew to retreat back to the Bohemia as soon as possible." She placed a sheet over Marsais, hiding her from view. "She will stay safely sedated for the next several hourly cycles." The cyborg glanced at her wrist unit and activated a sequence of holographic buttons. "However, three members of our crew remain at large." She glanced at the door across from them and reset the transdermal applicator with a click. "I will retrieve Captain Bronson. You collect the Rhinernan. He may have been affected as well. If so, I will sedate him if needed. We will retrieve the Travanian together. She is not in her room and is on a passageway two levels down. I will meet you back here in five."

"Five?"

"Chrono units." T-183 turned away and knocked on Bronson's door.

Shiznit smacked his forehead. "Why can't people just say what they mean?"

T-183 glanced at him and knocked on Bronson's door a second time. "Time is of importance in this instance."

"Okay. Yes. I get it." The Gho'bar hurried past the lump of floating luggage that was Marsais and down the hallway toward Remler's room. "Frelling cyborg," he muttered. For someone who lacked the capacity for sarcasm, T-183 sarcasmed very well.

He paused before knocking on Remler's door. He hadn't seen the Rhinernan since he and Marsais had left the bar to retreat to their room alone. Remler had seemed fine, from what Shiznit could remember. He'd been enjoying the party going on, celebrating his new temporal-dampening implant by having a few drinks with the others. Or more than a few, maybe. It was all a bit fuzzy, but Shiznit remembered Remler giving a thank you speech about how happy he was to be able to leave the Bohemia for a change without feeling like he was going insane.

Shiznit had always thought it weird how Rhinernans were born being able to see multiple realities simultaneously. He had enough trouble keeping track of the one he was in, let alone how chaotic it must be to see numerous possibilities forming every instant. Remler normally stayed on the Bohemia, where the ship's temporal shielding acted like a dampening field, giving him some peace from the multiple reality chaos. But thanks to the new implant that Bronson had acquired for the Rhinernan, Remler had been able to join the rest of the crew off-ship for the first time without a problem.

Unless...there was a problem. Was it possible that a malfunction in his implant was affecting the reality around him? Would that cause the memory hallucinations the others were having?

There was only one way to find out. Shiznit knocked on the door.

"Go away. I told you before, unless you have more Plovanian ale, you aren't welcome." Remler's voice boomed through the room's comm as the remote viewscreen activated.

"It's me, Shiznit. I need to speak with you." He pointed at himself in front of the viewscreen, indicating that he was who he said, remembering belatedly that he was also completely naked.

After a moment, the door opened, and the large, gray-skinned, single-horned, completely butt naked Rhinernan appeared. He looked the Gho'bar up and down with a stern gaze.

"What the hell's a Shiznit?"

The Gho'bar groaned inwardly. Not Remler, too. Maybe it *was* his implant that had frelled everything up. T-183 was right. They needed to get everyone back to the ship as soon as possible and figure out what was going on before they all lost their connection to each other.

"A Shiznit is a person who has access to copious amounts of Plovanian ale."

"Oh, yeah? In sales, are you?"

"Let's just say I know how to hook up the right buyer." Shiznit tried not to outwardly cringe at the story he was spinning. But if it got Remler's cooperation while avoiding the need for sedation, it was all good. Wasn't it?

"Hey, now we're talking. Come on in for a moment. I need to take a piss."

"A mental image I don't need," Shiznit muttered. He followed the Rhinernan into the room and waited by the exit while Remler disappeared into a small chamber adjacent to the closed-off sleeping quarters.

"Geez, I've never seen one of you before," Remler called out through the cracked open bathroom door. "You sure are strange looking. You've got weird-shaped eyes, and your horns are all twisted. Did that happen in a fight?"

"No."

The sound of the toilet flushing and then water running in the sink preceded Remler's reappearance through the doorway. He looked at Shiznit and smiled. "So, where's the Plovanian ale?"

"Well, I couldn't bring it here with me." Shiznit felt his fur bristle as he attempted to ad-lib the situation and get Remler to accompany him to the ship. The Rhinernan's obsession with alcohol wasn't a good sign. Getting drunk was how Remler had coped with the multiple reality chaos before joining the crew of the Bohemia. "We need to go to it. But first, can I borrow some pants?" At the Rhinernan's unspoken question, he added, "Girlfriend kicked me out."

Remler nodded. "Ah man, sorry. That's harsh. Where are my manners? I need pants too." He opened the frosted doors to the sleeping area and gestured for the Gho'bar to follow him.

A large bed dominated the room where two sleeping figures rested. Remler picked up his clothes off the floor. "I had company last night, if you know what I mean." He grabbed an extra flight suit from a bag by the door and tossed it at Shiznit. "Might be a bit big on you, but you can have this."

"Thanks." Shiznit turned to the wall and put the flight suit on, self-conscious of the four pairs of eyes that had blinked open at the sound of voices and were studying him from the bed. The green-skinned, multiple-limbed, tentacled beings from the outer rim planet, Gerome, were not to his taste, but then, he wasn't a Rhinernan.

"Don't worry about them," Remler called out. "I'm pretty sure they've seen it all. I met them at the bar last night. Frelling incredible time, might I add."

Shiznit finished fastening his flight suit, which hung on him like a deflated bag. But at least he was now clothed. So, there was that. He turned to see Remler sitting on the bed, pulling on his boots. "Wait. You remember what happened last night?"

"Sure, I do. I finished an author event in the convention room, went to the bar, and hooked up with these two exquisite creatures." The nearest one to him blew him a kiss, which he trapped in his hand and caught to his lips.

Author event? Shiznit squeezed his eyes shut and lowered his chin to his chest. "Frell it to frell."

"Hey buddy, language, please. There's ladies present, albeit, sleepy and deliciously exhausted." Remler put a finger up. "You said Plovanian ale, right?"

"Yeah, come on. I'll show you where the shipment is."

Shiznit headed for the door. Behind him, he heard Remler tell the two Geromians to rest up, and they could stroke his horn some more when he got back. The Gho'bar frowned and stepped out into the passageway, allowing Remler to say his goodbyes in private. He met T-183 with the baggage cart, coming around the corner in the hall toward him. Two large lumps covered in white hotel sheets now occupied the cart.

"I have Marsais and Bronson," the cyborg said. "How is Remler?"

"We've got a problem."

T-183 grabbed her stasis pistol from her holster.

"No, not that sort of problem. Wait a second—"

The door to Remler's room opened, and the Rhinernan stepped out into the passageway. "So, where's this...Oh, hello, who have we here?" He eyed the cyborg.

"She's with me," Shiznit said. "Imports and Acquisitions."

"Sounds great, let's get going then." Remler pointed to the luggage trolley. "Is that the Plovanian ale shipment?"

"No, no. It's just...ah—" Shiznit quickly moved to step between Remler and the cart, but the Rhinernan had already peered past him and had his hand on the nearest covered lump.

"Are there people under there?" He lifted the sheet, revealing the two unconscious bodies beneath.

T-183 and Shiznit glanced at each other. *Well, this is awkward,* Shiznit thought. T raised her stasis blaster and pointed it at the Rhinernan's back.

"Well, you haven't put them on right," Remler said. "They'll fall off if you leave them like that. You need to secure them with luggage straps. I'll show you."

"Um...thanks," Shiznit said. He exchanged another glance with T-183 and gave her a small shrug. This day had been so frelled-up, nothing could surprise him anymore. *I hope,* he added as an afterthought.

The cyborg lowered her blaster but kept it at the ready.

The large-framed Rhinernan threw off the sheets covering Marsais and Bronson. "Wow, that's a pretty one," he said as he repositioned Marsais so that she was seated upright, her back to the rear frame of the trolley. He put Bronson next to her, packed them tightly together, and covered them over again, securing them both with the luggage straps. "There, that should hold your friends." He turned to Shiznit and the cyborg. "How about that shipment of ale, then?"

The cyborg pressed a device on a metal band around her wrist. "The ship is in Bay 183. We need to retrieve Bubbles on the way."

"Bubbles?" Remler asked. "You have sparkling Plovanian wine as well? Impressive cargo, I must say."

"Bubbles is one of our traveling companions. She's a Travanian," Shiznit said.

"Really? I'm not sure I like that. The size of the heads on those creatures is enormous. She better not acquire all the cargo for herself."

T-183 checked her wrist scanner. "She's headed this way."

A familiar gruff voice spoke from down the hallway behind them, "Okay...but I don't understand why you'd deliver it to a different room."

Shiznit twisted around and saw the Travanian's familiar face. She walked in their direction without noticing them. Her attention focused on whoever she was speaking to through her comm.

"Bubbles," he called out. He had no idea what her real name was. Something unpronounceable that Bronson had replaced with the teasing nickname, which had stuck because Bubbles was anything but bubbly. Her personality was as cheerful as a constipated Borbian guard with a hemorrhoid problem.

As she looked up and saw them, she pulled her blaster from her holster and aimed it at his head. "Who the frell are you?"

Shit. Not her too. He opened his mouth to reply but nearly jumped out of his skin as a blast from T-183's stasis gun hit Bubbles with a shot that caused her to fall face-first to the floor. The thud as her head collided with the ground caused an uneasy feeling in Shiznit's stomach.

"Damn," Remler said. "I know I was worried she'd take the whole shipment, but that was a bit harsh."

"She was going to shoot the Gho'bar," T-183 said as she holstered her stasis gun. "Her finger was on the trigger."

The holographic attendant appeared in the passageway with a flash. It glanced at the immobilized Travanian and then at Shiznit. "Another fainter, mate?"

"Um...yeah," Shiznit said and grinned at the hologram, hoping it looked like a smile rather than the insane grimace he really felt. This day was getting more out of hand by the second.

"Crickey. You've got some skills, mate."

"Well, if you'd like to excuse us, my new friends and I have an important rendezvous with a supply of Plovanian ale," Remler said to the attendant. He picked Bubbles up from the floor as if she weighed nothing and placed her on the luggage trolley opposite the other two. "I assume you'd like your friend to go on here too?" he asked Shiznit.

"Correct," T-183 said.

"That is an improper use of a luggage cart," the auto-attendant said, changing into the concierge persona.

"It is an efficient mode of transportation."

"Well, yes, but..." The auto-attendant peered at Bronson as if he could see him through the covering of sheets. "Now, what has happened to this gentleman? Why is he unconscious as well?"

"I'm just that exciting, I guess," Shiznit said, unable to suppress the hysterical laughter that was building inside him.

"I think you three are hindering the enjoyment of these other guests. I will report this to the management." The auto-attendant disappeared with a flicker of static.

"Shit. Time to leave." Shiznit said, not wanting to hang around in case the report did get placed, and the hotel security arrived. He quickly rearranged the sheets over the three unconscious bodies on the cart, covering Bubbles as well in case they encountered any other guests. Less questions the better. Always.

"Agreed," said T-183. She waved at Remler to follow, who grabbed the controls and propelled the cart down the hall toward the elevator at a fast trot.

Shiznit sighed as the happy visions he'd woken up with of spending time at the hotel with Marsais vanished completely. He should be used to it by now, the hasty exits. It always ended the same wherever they went. Running from places had become a habit, usually because they were being chased out by someone Bronson had offended, though he always claimed to be innocent. Well, this time, Bronson was not the problem, but maybe the giant Rhinernan lumbering down the hall, whistling a happy tune about Plovanian ale was. Either way they needed to get to the Bohemia, and fast, because they had clearly outstayed their welcome.

T-183 put a hand up and came to an abrupt halt a few steps from the elevator. She turned to Remler, who had to bring the luggage trolley to a sudden stop.

"Oy!" Remler frowned at her. "You nearly made me tip the whole cart."

"This one is waking." She indicated Bubbles, who was trying to throw off the sheets covering her. The cyborg injected the Travanian in the neck with the transdermal applicator. Bubbles stopped struggling and fell back unconscious with the others. "I'm going to need a stronger sedative to keep her down. Her species is more resilient."

"Wow, you're really serious when it comes to protecting your interests," Remler said with an appreciative nod. "I think I like you, new robo-lady-friend."

"You can admire me from a distance, thanks."

Shiznit grinned, if only Remler remembered what happened when anyone mistook her for a pleasure-bot, he'd be more cautious about giving the cyborg flirty compliments. He swiped his hand across the wall panel, calling for a lift to head downward.

"We need docking level B52."

"That's like, nearly one hundred levels down," Remler said, his eyes widening as he studied the station's layout on the wall display. "Did it have to be near the bottom?"

Whatever had gone wrong to cause his memory difficulties, the tall, stocky, armor-skinned Rhinernan was apparently still uncomfortable with the velocity shift of gravity-well lift systems.

The door slid open in front of them, presenting an empty elevator car, big enough to fit the luggage trolley as well as the three of them who were on foot.

Remler studied the others as they boarded, seeming reluctant to follow.

"Speed is of importance. We must hurry," T-183 said.

"Speed is the problem," Remler said. He boarded the lift and grabbed onto the railing, shutting his eyes. One wouldn't think it possible for a gray-skinned creature to turn pale, but the Rhinernan had found a way to make it happen. "It's for the ale," he whispered.

Shiznit smiled. "I once flew with someone who had this rule, if you vomit on it, you clean it up." Which had proven to be sound advice on many occasions, including this one, he noted, as the lift lurched into action, and Remler turned from pale to a faint shade of vomit green.

CHAPTER 3

Onboard the Queen Bohemia, inside docking bay 183, Shiznit decided that what had started out as a bad day, had in fact, gone straight past bad and into indescribable.

Remler looked at him apologetically. "I tried to stop it. I'll help you clean it up."

Shiznit pushed the Rhinernan's hands aside as the single-horned being began trying to wipe vomit from the Gho'bar's baggy flight suit.

"No, no, I'm good."

"But you said if you vomit on it you—"

"It's fine. Really. Just go sit over there." He indicated the scanner bed that was in the ship's medical bay and pushed at the sticky goo on the front of his chest with a cloth. He frowned and then quickly gave up. Rhinernan vomit appeared to be particularly hard to remove from clothing. As soon as he had the chance, he'd just get changed.

Remler sat on the scanning bed and looked around the small room. "This is a curious ship. Lots of gadgets and interesting pokey things. This isn't where you store your cargo, is it?"

"No," T-183 said from the open doorway of the room. She fired her stasis blaster at the bulky Rhinernan, hitting him square in the chest and freezing the confused expression on his face in place. She turned to Shiznit and re-holstered the blaster.

"Pre-flight is complete. You secure the rest of them for take-off, while I get us out of here before the hotel A.I. decides to not let us leave."

She was gone again and heading back to the bridge before Shiznit could blink. "Okay, then." He shrugged and fastened Remler to the scanning bed, then looked at the other unconscious bodies in the room who they'd removed from the luggage trolley as soon as they'd boarded.

Marsais sat in a chair against the wall. She was easy enough to secure with the seating restraints so that she didn't fall during any sudden acceleration, but Bronson and Bubbles were a different problem. Bronson was on the floor, propped against a wall, Bubbles lying next to him. Shiznit felt a rumble move through the ship as T activated the engines.

"Hey! Can we slow it down for a minute?" He called through the comm. "This isn't as easy as it looks." Dead weight was dead weight and hard to lift into a seat.

"We cannot."

"Frell." He glanced around the small room. No time for seats then. He'd have to improvise.

He dragged Bubbles as fast as he could to the small recessed compartment near the back of the room, which Bronson had named *The Impenetrable Cage of No One Gets Out*. It had only been used once since Shiznit had been made a member of the crew, and that was to stop a damaged cyborg from harming everyone. If it could secure a cyborg safely, he was pretty sure it would do the same for Bubbles and Bronson, even if the Travanian woke up and tried to use her head as a battering ram to escape.

The engine rumbling increased as he dragged the captain to the recessed area and placed him next to Bubbles.

"Are all bodies secured?" T called out over the comm.

"Wait!" Shiz shouted. "Almost got it!"

"We must leave now. Prepare for disembarkment."

"Okay! Okay!" Shiznit slapped the button that activated the restraints and rolled to the side as the shielding flickered into place, partitioning the small recessed area from the rest of the medical bay.

Bronson's eyes popped open. "Great Scott!" The captain stared at the ceiling. "Has anyone seen Great Scott, our lead singer?" Then his eyes shut again, and he was unconscious as if he'd never spoken.

The ship lurched as it accelerated under T's control, causing Shiznit to slide across the smooth flooring. He grasped at the bottom of the scanning bed and clung on tight. *"This day is just frelling crazy!"* Whatever the cyborg was doing to leave the docking bay in a hurry was stressing the inertial dampeners. It was also making his stomach insist it wanted to escape out through his nose. He closed his eyes and focused on breathing before he added to the mess on the front of his flight suit. At least the Rhinernan was still in stasis.

The ship lurched sideways, and he almost lost his hold on the scanner bed as well as the contents of his stomach. *Frell.* He should have switched places and piloted the ship while the cyborg took care of the restraints. T-183 was efficient in her actions, but there was an art to flying she didn't possess.

Abruptly, the movement stopped, and the feeling of being tossed about and squeezed like a nutcracker eased. He lay flat on his back, arms outstretched, and stared at the ceiling as he tried to catch his breath. Maybe he would just stay like that for a while. The cool flooring felt good on his back. Maybe he would just not move ever again.

The door to the medical bay opened, and T's face appeared looking down at him, obscuring his view of the ceiling. "Gho'bar. It is an inappropriate moment for rest. We must utilize the medical scanner to investigate the cause of our crewmates' aberrant behavior." She moved from his line of sight and toward the scanning bed.

Shiznit groaned and rolled onto his side. No rest for the weary, as Bronson often said. "What happened out there." He gestured with his hand indicating beyond the ship as he slowly got to his feet.

T kept her focus trained on the Rhinernan on the scanning bed. She reinforced the stasis field holding him in place as she activated the complex machine. "We encountered a Borbian bounty hunter as we attempted to exit the station. Evasive maneuvers were required."

Bands of light crossed Remler's body as the scanner followed the cyborg's instructions. Shiznit turned to her more concerned at the moment by what she'd just said. "Frell. A bounty hunter? Was it lying in wait, or did the station report us?"

"Uncertain. I activated the slip drive, which put us safely out of phase with this dimension and allowed us to leave the docking bay without further altercation."

"The slip drive?" *Fracking frell.* Well, that explained why he'd felt like his insides were trying to escape. While the ship's multi-phasic, temporal shielding protected the crew from the harmful effects of traveling between dimensions and realities, he'd never gotten used to the physical feeling that using the slip drive caused. He shook his head. "Okay, but where are we now?"

"We are currently orbiting the station, but out of phase and unobservable until we have an exit destination. It was the most efficient course of action to provide safe cover while we investigate the situation."

"Fair enough." Going out of phase with a dimension was a tactic they'd used many times before to hide in plain sight. During his travels through the galaxy, he'd never encountered another ship quite like the Queen Bohemia. Did another even exist? He really wasn't sure how Bronson had gotten his hands on it in the first place. Of all the stories the captain liked to tell, that was one he'd kept to himself. "The bounty hunter must have found it confusing when we just disappeared."

T shrugged slightly. "The Borb species is not intellectually significant."

Shiznit nodded agreement. Borbs were angry green blobs full of acid, dangerous to get into a fight with but not particularly bright. He frowned as he studied Remler. "I think his new temporal implant is the cause of all this mess. Yesterday was the first real test of it. I don't think it's working right."

"A valid hypothesis." The cyborg initiated a secondary set of scans as the first concluded, this one involving a lozenge-shaped tool that pressed against the Rhinernan's neck and took whatever samples it required through contact with his skin. "However, if a fault existed in his implant, causing it to affect the reality around him, you and I would be affected as well." She input another sequence of instructions into the scanner that the machine acknowledged with a beep. "And we are not."

Shiznit frowned. "So, what is it then?"

T-183 studied the readouts from the scanner. "The Rhinernan's implant is functioning within correct parameters. However, his physiological readings indicate the presence of a toxic substance in his blood that is creating a hallucinogenic effect. Most likely route of introduction into his system was through ingestion."

"So, something he ate or drank?"

"Correct. Time frame is uncertain, but his usual rate of digestion would predict twelve chrono-hours prior to now as a likely moment."

"So last night at the bar?"

"It is a logical assumption."

"You said toxic. Do you mean poison?" He glanced at Marsais. Had someone slipped something into their drinks and deliberately tried to kill them?

"The substance is not listed in our current database. It is possible it is the result of a chemical reaction during digestion. But unless we can isolate the specific cause and determine a method to counteract it, the affected parties will continue to lose mental cohesion as the toxicity increases and destroys their brain cells. Unchecked, the result will be fatal." She touched her wrist unit to the medical scanner. "I am cross-checking now with samples I took from the others earlier to see if the same substance exists within them."

Shiznit didn't need to wait for the beep from the scanner and the cyborg's affirmative nod to tell him that it was. Bubbles, Marsais, Bronson, and Remler had all come down with the same symptoms at the same time. Marsais. He looked at her slack, beautiful face. She appeared as if she was simply asleep, rather than seriously ill. He couldn't lose her. Not now. Not ever.

"How long?" It was hard to speak with his heart in his mouth. He wet his lips and spoke louder. "How long do they have?"

"Uncertain. Hours. Perhaps days. It would be prudent to find a remedy as quickly as possible." T-183 poked at him with her wrist scanner. "Do you recall what you consumed last night? Was it the same as the others?"

"I'm not sure." He tried to think past the gray cloud in his brain. There were faint images, impressions. The thumping music in the bar.

The sound of laughter. The taste of sweet heat on his tongue. "Plovanian ale." He snapped his fingers and looked at Remler. "He had quite a bit. So did Marsais and the others, I think."

"And you?" T-183 asked.

"Yes. I had some too."

She shook her head. "You are not affected by the substance. There is no trace of it in your system."

"So not the Plovanian ale then. Something they had eaten or encountered, but I didn't." He shook his head and gritted his teeth, trying to remember if anything unusual had happened. They'd arrived at the bar, where they'd had a selection of snacks, and maybe more drinks than he'd first thought. T-183 had left early on. He remembered that. "Frell. There's just too many things it could be."

"Were any of the foods offered of foreign origin?"

"If you are meaning: 'Did we eat alien space food?' Then the answer is yes, of course. It's a freaking galactic resort. But we often do that wherever we go, and no one has gotten sick before, other than when Bubbles' head nearly exploded from an allergic reaction to cotton candy." That had been unpleasant. But they'd gotten her med help in time.

"If I had a sample of what they ingested, I could isolate the precipitating substance in its pre-digested form, and potentially synthesize a cure."

He stared at her. "We need to go back to the station to do that."

"Correct."

"And we're not exactly welcome there at the moment."

"Correct. There is also the possibility that whatever food was ingested is no longer available. It may have been disposed of. It is best to return to the most likely point in time that contamination occurred and collect samples directly."

"You mean, go back in time to last night and figure out what went wrong and bring whatever it is back to the ship now so you can turn it into a fix?"

She smiled. "Correct."

Shiznit grinned. "Have time travel ship, will, er...travel in time."

There were no guarantees with any of it, of finding the cause, of being at the right moment that things had gone wrong, or if they did find the problem substance that T could use it to create a cure. But it felt good to be doing something other than sitting around wondering what had gone wrong and watching the others die. No frelling way was that going to happen. Not on his watch.

"I will stay aboard the Bohemia and do a more thorough examination of the others." The cyborg glanced at Remler as she put on a pair of protective gloves. "I may find more information in their excremental substances."

Shiznit nodded. He wasn't entirely certain what excremental meant, but the nearest translation his comm could come up with was *shit*, which didn't sound like something he wanted to be involved with at all.

"I'll head to the bridge and set course for the nearest tesseract that intersects the timeline we need." He was a good pilot. He knew how to fly a ship better than she did. He could do this. As he exited the room and hurried down the short corridor, he glanced down at his baggy flight suit, still covered in Rhinernan vomit. "But, I think I'll quickly get changed first."

CHAPTER 4

"Remember, your primary purpose is to observe and collect samples," T-183 said over the coded comm channel that they had chosen to use while Shiznit went off-ship to the Celestia Six's Tiki-lounge bar. "The more you directly interact with this timeline, the greater the risk of creating a paradox."

"Understood." Shiznit marched out of the elevator on the Lido deck and headed toward the bar. It was a little-understood fact (or so Shiznit had found in discussions with others, though it made perfect sense to him) that time was an ever-expanding dimension of space, measured by infinite moments and possibilities. And that traveling back in time was not really traveling back in time at all, so much as traveling to an alternate reality to re-visit a particular moment.

The trick, of course, was choosing the exact reality that a person wanted out of the infinite possibilities that existed, some of which were so similar they were virtually indistinguishable, which is where Remler's unique ability to see simultaneous realities had always proven useful. But he was lying in the medical bay, currently undergoing an examination of his excremental secretions. Shiznit had relied on the ship to choose the correct tesseract they needed. Was it the best choice? He shrugged mentally. The best he could do was to try and avoid any unwanted paradox problems while in a reality where another version of himself already existed. Meeting himself face to face wouldn't cause the universe to implode or anything dramatic, but it would create a very confusing conversation, which he'd rather avoid at the moment.

Time, as Bronson often liked to say, was of the essence. Which in Gho'bar, roughly translated to *delay, is death.*

Up ahead, the lounge bar was a welcoming oasis within the network of the many levels of the space station. It was one of many such common spaces, and, exactly like the previous night that Shiznit had observed, many different lifeforms drank and ate at the tables and seating areas. Others lounged near the main bar itself, talking and laughing as music pumped throughout the area mingled with the curses and cheers of gamesters playing their credits on a roll of holo-dice.

It felt weird walking through a place that he'd recently been to, and even more recently been chased out of. He half-expected the hotel auto-attendant to pop up any second and toss him into a detainment room. But he was revisiting a time before any troubles had started, and he passed through the room without incident as he headed for the main bar.

As he took a seat at the long counter, he kept his eye on a group of beings seated at a nearby table, his alternate-self one of them. *Frell. Is that how I really look when I'm talking?* As Marsais said something funny, his alter-self, who was seated next to her, grinned like an unseasoned Gho'barling about to get his horns stroked for the first time. *What the frell does she see in me? I need to work on that.*

A droid arrived at the table with an order of amber liquid that Bronson called *Faster's Larger*, a drink he claimed to be an Earth delicacy, but which Shiznit had decided was nothing more than watered-down beer. The captain took several tall glasses of it from the tray and passed them around the table to Bubbles, Remler, and the alter-Shiz. Marsais declined it with a downward turn of her plump lips and reached for her glass of Plovanian ale. The contaminant couldn't be the beer then, as Marsais had never drunk it. At least that was one thing he could rule out.

"G' day, mate. What can I get you to wet your whistle with then?"

Shiznit turned to the droid bartender who resembled the auto-attendant persona in both appearance and voice. "Plovanian ale." Best to keep to what he'd had the previous night. Well, as much as he could remember. A good portion of this experience was still lost to him, but being back in the bar and observing himself and the others was helping him remember.

The bartender handed him a drink.

"Thanks." Shiznit offered his wrist unit for the bartender to scan. One extra charge from himself to himself wouldn't look suspicious. His alter-self was going to be leaving in a hurry the next morning anyway if the current reality kept to the same path.

"Going it alone tonight, mate?" The bartender picked up an empty glass from a tray of them and began polishing it.

Shiznit made a non-committal sound and took a sip of his drink. He turned sideways in his seat so he could observe the others at the table without it being obvious.

"We don't see many of your kind here, but this evening, there's two of you." The bartender placed the polished glass on the counter. He nodded past Shiznit toward the nearby table. "Is that a friend of yours? He looks like he could be related to you, mate."

Shiznit turned his back on the bartender. "I don't see the resemblance." Frell. So much for being inconspicuous. The other Shiznit sat close to Marsais, so close, in fact, they constantly made physical contact. Laughing, smiling. Marsais whispered something in his alter-self's ear that made him blush beneath his fur. Not that anyone else could see it, but Shiznit knew the heat she caused with the soft sound of her voice. He clutched his drink. Was it possible to be jealous of oneself?

"Oy, she looks a friendly sort. Plovanian sheilas are sweet as, yeah? Why not go over and introduce yourself? Could be just the thing for you, mate. That other guy looks a bit of a wanker, if you know what I mean."

"Thanks. I'll, uh, think about it." Shiznit shuffled away and found a secluded place behind a large, leafy pillar-plant that wasn't currently occupied by anyone, and more importantly, no nosey, frelling bartenders. He didn't know what wanker meant, but it didn't sound a good thing. He peered through the leaves, keeping his eye on the table where the others continued drinking and chatting. He activated his comm.

"Got anything for me, T? I feel like I'm wasting my time looking for something that may or may not be the problem."

"I have concluded my examination of the excremental secretions." The snapping sound of protective gloves being removed filled the comm. "And I have determined that you are in the correct time frame for this investigation. The substance was in an item consumed during the evening."

Well, that's something. "Any clue as to what the culprit might be?"

"Due to the longer period required for absorption into the system, I believe it to have been in an item that was eaten rather than a liquid."

"So, a food then."

"Correct."

"Well, what did they eat that I didn't?" Or anyone else in the bar for that matter. "Have there been any reports of any other guests getting sick with these symptoms?" He knew how thorough T was and that she would have been monitoring the station comm channels for signs of unusual activity.

"Negative."

"So, it must be something very specific."

"Correct."

"I will keep searching." He closed the comm channel. They'd all ordered several rounds of snacks throughout the evening, shared along with their drinks. What could they have ordered that no one else had? He shook his head. He'd just have to keep watching until he figured it out.

He moved out from behind the pillar-plant and chose a seat at an empty gaming console close to the others where he could observe them at their table without being overtly conspicuous.

The brightly lit gambling console flashed its holographic game of chance before him. Some kind of numbers play with dice, requiring him to guess the outcome in order to win, which didn't make any sense to him. Other beings were playing the same game on nearby consoles, some in jubilation, others staring at the cause of their loss with rage. Shiznit had never understood the point of gambling when one could earn credits and save them.

The holographic screen before him flashed with a series of numbers, which appeared in large blocks before dropping to the bottom to join a series of other numbers. *What the frell is the point of this game?* Shiznit thought. *How could one predict a string of numbers between one and one hundred?*

"To Remler," Bronson said loudly, drawing Shiznit's attention. The captain had stood and was addressing the others at the table with a drink in his hand. "May time always be on your side, my friend." He raised the drink in a salute Shiznit knew was customary on Earth to honor a friend, and, as was expected, the others at the tabled followed the action and joined in, each taking a sip from their drinks.

Remler grinned and thanked the captain, then launched into the same 'thank you' speech that Shiznit remembered him doing, at the end of which T-183 politely excused herself to head to her room for the rest of the evening. As she didn't eat or drink in the same manner as the rest of them, bars really weren't her scene.

"Better luck next time," the holo game announced. Shiznit glanced at the display as the sequence of numbers floating there spiraled downward and disappeared, accompanied by a musical reminder that he'd just lost the turn. It would probably help if he was playing. He cued up the next turn, and the game reset. Not that he'd do much better with it now. He still didn't understand how to play it.

He turned back to watching the table. His alter-self was gone, his seat next to Marsais empty.

Wait. What the frell? Shiznit glanced around and caught a glimpse of himself disappearing around the corner, heading to the restroom area. His heartbeat steadied as the memory of doing so surfaced. Yeah, that's right, he'd gone to 'drain a snake' as Bronson liked to call it.

"Oh, my frell!" he heard Marsais shout.

Shiznit turned to her, his heart leaping into his mouth.

But Marsais was smiling, her eyes wide with excitement as she peered into a small, plain white box that Bronson had placed onto the table.

"Yeah, I thought you might like those," the captain said.

"Aren't they for Bubbles?" Marsais asked, glancing at the Travanian.

Bronson nodded. "Yeah. But he sent them for everyone. Well, everyone except for Shiznit, because he's weird and doesn't like them."

Shiznit's fur bristled as he watched the group at the table. What the frell had he missed when he'd left to go to the bathroom?

"His loss," Remler said, looking into the box. "Our gain."

Marsais whispered in Bronson's ear, which caused him to laugh and smack the table with his hand as Remler removed a small serving container from the box. It was filled with round, frosted baked treats that Shiznit knew Marsais loved almost more than she loved him.

"Oh, my frell," Shiznit said. Do-nuts! Mid-evilian do-nuts. When the frell had Bronson gotten his hands on those?

He'd tried the do-nuts once, when Bronson offered them to him during the trip to Mid-evil but hadn't liked them. He wasn't sure if it was the taste so much as the fact Marsais practically worshipped Arfustor, the so-called Master Baker that made them.

T-183, being a cyborg, never ate that type of food either. But the others did, Bronson, Bubbles, Remler, and Marsais, and those frelling do-nuts were disappearing out of that container as if the four of them hadn't eaten in a week. And his alter-self was still not back from the bathroom, so hadn't seen a damn thing.

Shiznit ignored the holo game as it sounded its displeasure through mournful music that he was about to lose again. He opened the comm channel to T-183. "I'm pretty sure I know what happened last night."

"Explain."

"Do-nuts. Bronson got do-nuts from Arfustor. It's the only thing that the others ate, but I didn't. And it wasn't ordered at the station. He must have saved some from the last time we were in Arfustor's dimension." It had been several weeks since they'd visited Mid-evil, but these do-nuts appeared fresh rather than stale.

"You are certain they are from Arfustor and not a similar item?"

He watched Marsais eyes close in near orgasmic bliss as she took a bite of the do-nut in her hand. "Yeah, I'm sure."

"You must retain a sample and bring it to the ship for analysis. There may be more to this than we first expected. Arfustor would not deliberately harm another with his livelihood."

"I agree." The cyborg had a good point. Arfustor was annoyingly good at what he did and took great pride in his ability as a baker. He was odd with his four eyes that moved independently and the fact he lived in a different dimension. But Bronson had considered him a trusted friend for as long as Shiznit had known him, and he'd never seen Arfustor do anything to suggest otherwise. "There has to be more to it."

"Procure a sample and bring it back to the ship as quickly as possible. It is the only way to be certain." She disconnected the comm before he could answer.

Shiznit looked at the game flashing before him, the numbers once again spiraling downward. He frowned as he focused his mind on the new problem he had. How was he going to get a sample of the do-nuts without being seen by the others?

He turned back to watch his friends at the table. His alter-self had not yet returned, and Marsais was licking pink icing from the top of a do-nut. The way her tongue moved made his jaw drop, and he couldn't take his eyes off her, until hers locked onto his.

"Oh, shit," he whispered, seeing the Plovanian pause mid lick, and her eyes widen, then narrow. She placed the half-eaten do-nut on a napkin and stood, her gaze firmly fixed on him.

"Game over," the game announced as the words flashed on the console.

"Frell," Shiznit said. "I think you're right." Then he turned and bolted for the exit, heart pounding like he was running a race. Which maybe he was. Talking to Marsais right now could really frell things up. He did *not* have time to explain why there were two of him hanging around.

As he hurried through the bar, he called the cyborg through the comm. "Got a problem. Marsais made me out at the bar and is pursuing me. I'm trying to lose her and double back to get the sample, but I'm not sure if I can."

"She cannot know what is to happen the next morning. Events need to occur the same, or else both timelines will form a paradox loop."

"I think one already has." Shiznit could feel his blood pressure rising as he tried to move quickly without seeming suspicious. He didn't dare glance behind him to see where Marsais was. How close was she? Had she given up? He couldn't get to the elevator shaft soon enough.

"Shiznit, I'm coming to you. I will attempt to draw her and the others away while you get the sample." T-183 said through the comm. "Remain on your present course."

"Okay." He didn't want to feel nervous about what was to occur, as the cyborg was more than efficient at making the right call. After all, it came down to her programming, and if there was a fault in her logic, then they were all really frelled.

Meters ahead of him, the elevator door opened. He slowed down and stopped, allowing passengers to disembark, none of whom were T-183.

"Shiz?"

Shiznit froze at the sound of Marsais sweet voice behind him. *Frell.* What was he supposed to do now? He attempted to disguise his voice. "I'm not Shiz."

A pair of fingers pinched the fabric on the arm of his flight suit and forced him to turn slightly. Marsais stared at him. "What are you doing?" She glanced at his clothing, her brow furrowing. "Are you going somewhere? Why did you get changed into your flight suit?" Her eyes narrowed. "And why did you run when you saw me?"

Shiznit's heart pumped so hard he thought it was going to burst out of his chest and launch itself at his lover. Of course, she'd think he was his alter-self even if he was dressed differently. "I...was going to surprise you."

Marsais put her hands on her hips. "Mission accomplished, sir."

Shiznit waved his hands in a crisscross manner. "No, no, no. I mean, I was going to take you on a walk through the nature reserve."

"In a flight suit?"

"Well, I'm guessing the atmosphere..."

Marsais smiled and stepped closer, hugging him tight. "Oh my, you are so romantic, but you're also silly. The nature reserve is in a dome, so you don't need a flight suit. I hear there's a waterfall. Maybe we could take a late-night dip."

"I don't have any swimming clothes on me."

Marsais winked. "Neither do I."

Shiznit took a few seconds, then his eyes widened at what she was insinuating. He stared at her as the image of her swimming naked with him burned in his brain. He never tired of her, so much so he wondered if he had an addiction to her. But he'd never met another being who was so, so... beautifully smart in all his life.

Her smile slipped a little as she studied him. "Are you sure you weren't running off because you were mad?"

"Mad? Why?"

She looked at her sticky fingers and shrugged lightly. "I know it bothers you how much I like Arfustor's do-nuts. I wasn't trying to sneak them behind your back. I promise."

"Oh, babe." He wrapped his arms around her waist and drew her close to him. "You can like whatever you want. Just because I don't enjoy them, doesn't mean you can't." He traced his fingers over the of bit of frosting and tiny crumbs that had fallen onto the soft skin of her chest above her low-cut top. "I think it's sexy when you get excited about stuff."

She giggled. "You do?"

"Frell, yeah."

She leaned in close and locked her lips with his.

He tightened his grip around her waist as Marsais sagged against him. After almost half a minute, she pulled away.

"Wow...Shiz..." She put a hand on her chest. "It's like you haven't seen me for a week."

"Just trying to prepare you for our upcoming romantic interlude." He winked. "I'll go and get changed again and meet you back in the bar in a few minutes. Enjoy the rest of the do-nuts."

"Okay," she said, seeming breathless. Her sweet smile and the soft look in her eyes made him melt inside as it simultaneously filled him with panic. She gave him a little wave as he stepped onto the next lift. *Frell.* Could he feel more like a deceptive piece of shit right now? Maybe she had more reason than he'd thought for screaming at him and trying to kill him when she'd woken up.

Frelling do-nuts.

Little round pastries with stupid holes through the middle. They were not cute. They were not tasty. But they were the toast of all Mid-evil. And knowing they were more than likely contaminated, telling her to go back and eat more of them had nearly killed him just now. The last thing he ever wanted was her eating something that would make her sick, but he couldn't have her following him either right now. And he had no frelling idea how what had just happened would play out for his alter-self in this timeline now.

But on second thought, it would explain why Marsais had been so cuddly when he'd gotten back from the restroom and had been big on seeing the nature reserve to go for a dip before they'd headed to their room. So maybe he'd not changed anything at all just now, and his presence at the station had been a paradox all along.

He really didn't want to think about it anymore. His head was hurting with the idea of multiple realities blooming into existence, ones in which he and the others possibly didn't survive.

The elevator reached its destination. As he stepped through the doors and into the landing bay, he came face-to-face with T-183.

"Where is the Plovanian?" She raised her stasis blaster at the lift, causing its occupants to look at her warily as they exited and went about their business.

"Don't worry about it." Shiznit gestured for her to put the gun away. "I got what you wanted." He showed her the icing and crumbs smeared on his fingertips. "You don't need to shoot everyone all the time."

The cyborg nodded and holstered her weapon. As they headed for the Queen Bohemia at a fast pace, T-183 pressed something on her wrist device, which powered up the ship in its docking bay. Another series of presses opened the side door of their vessel, ready for their imminent arrival.

"I will analyze the sample of the do-nuts you have provided," the cyborg said as they entered the ship. "Assuming it is the cause of the toxic reaction in the others, I will attempt to synthesize a cure. But if it originated in Arfustor's dimension, it would be prudent to investigate why."

Shiznit let out a sigh. To do that, they'd have to use the slip drive again while they passed through a micro black hole that connected with the right dimension. A tricky feat for even a ship like the Bohemia, which was designed to navigate both time and space. As T headed for the medical bay with the sample she'd taken from his fingertips, he headed for the bridge and began to mentally prepare for the trip ahead. But he knew that no amount of preparation would ever make the sensation of having his nostrils shoved inside his ass as he was squeezed to the size of tardigrade remotely pleasant.

He sat in the pilot's chair and began making calculations but didn't have to wait long for T-183's confirmation over the ship's onboard comm.

"The do-nut sample is positive for the toxic compound."

Frell. Not that Shiznit was at all surprised. *I knew there was a reason I don't eat the frelling things that guy bakes.* "Setting course for the Mid-evil system and Arfustor's place."

CHAPTER 5

The realm of Mid-evil was perhaps one of the more unexceptional looking places that Shiznit had traveled to during his time on the Bohemia. Often shrouded in gray mist, the landscape reminded him of Gho'barchreig with its craggy hills and grassy plains and the scent of woodfires burning inside the stone huts, which made up the small village of Shiresteadham.

But today, as he and T-183 walked down the cobblestone lane that led from where they'd docked the ship in an open field, to the round thatched hut Shiznit knew only as "Arfustor's place", the mist had lifted, and a castle could be seen on the distant green hillside, it's colorful pennants blowing in the breeze. Not that the idyllic vista put him at ease or improved his mood any.

"Squint," he said.

"The correct word, I believe, is quaint," T-183 corrected. "Mid-evil is within acceptable parameters for such a description."

Shiznit stared at her. "No, I mean, *squint*." He pointed at the horizon and shadowed his eyes from the sun. "What is that above the castle?" A black dot floated in the sky in line with the pennants.

The cyborg focused her vision on the direction he indicated. "It appears to be a banner of some kind, as is befitting the royal household. This society is feudal in its origins, and symbolism is the common currency of power recognition within the populous."

"Uh… whatever that means." Shiznit wrinkled his brow as his comm struggled to translate. "But I hope it's not a Nombard. I frelling hate those things." The flying, clawed, bird-like creatures reminded him of Braptors, which lurked in caves on Gho'barchreig. But unlike Braptors, which were easily startled away, Nombards pursued their prey relentlessly. They also had a particular taste for goats, apparently. The last time he'd been here, he'd had to run for his life while one chased him back to the ship.

"We must focus on our purpose here, which is to save our crewmates."

"Yeah." Shiznit hurried his step as they neared the door of the hut they wanted. T-183 had been unable to isolate the compound from the small sample he'd given her and create an anti-toxin. But the do-nuts had definitely been contaminated. Which meant Arfustor had a lot to answer for. Shiznit pounded on the wooden door with his fist so forcefully the booming sound echoed off the nearby buildings.

He waited a moment then repeated the action when the door didn't open.

"If he isn't home, I swear I'll—"

"What in the blooming hills of Bottomhole is all this racket about?" Arfustor said as he opened the door and peered out through the gap, all four eyes moving independently on their short stalks.

Shiznit pushed the door open wide and faced the Master Baker of Shiresteadham as if the Hagarrian wasn't a horn's length taller and twice as wide and couldn't mash the Gho'bar with one of his meaty fists. *"What the frell did you put in those do-nuts?"*

Arfustor took a step back. "Blimey, little goat-man. All right, hey?"

"Greetings, Master Baker." T-183 moved between Shiznit and the Hagarrian and inside the bakery. Sunlight streamed through the windows, catching the floor in bright square patches. The place smelled of lemon polish and the few end-of-day leftovers from the morning's bake that were arranged in baskets on the sales counter.

The cyborg bowed as was the customary greeting in this realm. "Our business is both grave and urgent. Four members of the Queen Bohemia's crew have fallen ill due to a toxin, which I have traced to baked goods they consumed, that came from your establishment."

"They what? From me?" Arfustor glanced rapidly between Shiznit and the cyborg, his eyestalks bobbing. He tossed an envelope he'd been holding onto a nearby wooden table and dusted his hands on his flour-covered apron. The sunlight streaming through the open windows was the only source of lighting, but the frown on Arfustor's face was clear to see. "Ill, you say? My Bubbles is ill? And Bronson?"

"And Remler. And Marsais," Shiznit said. "They're on the ship right now in medically-induced stasis. They will die if we can't find a way to save them. *What did you put in the do-nuts you gave Bronson last time we were here?"*

Arfustor sagged against the workbench at his back and wiped his face with his broad palm. "I...well, now." He shook his head. "That would have been a couple of weeks back, yeah?"

"Correct."

He shook his head. "I don't understand." Arfustor glanced between Shiznit and the cyborg, his expression changing from confused to stricken. "You're saying something I did made my Bubbles sick?"

"Correct."

The anger pumping through Shiznit cooled. He'd never understood what Arfustor found attractive in the Travanian, but he did understand the feeling of devastation that the baker was experiencing at the thought of being responsible for her illness. He'd rather tear off his horns than hurt Marsais.

The bulky man puffed up his chest and folded his arms across it. He stared down at the Gho'bar and cyborg. "Now you listen here. I would never, on my life, ever do something like that. There must be a mistake."

"Have any of your customers here become sick recently? Maybe forgotten where they are or who the people are around them?" Shiznit asked.

"Not that I have heard." Arfustor's bushy brows furrowed. "Shiresteadham is a pretty close place, ya follow? Princess Fussy-Bits knows if anyone's got a secret before they've even got one. What is this all about?"

Arfustor's memories appeared to be intact, which meant it was doubtful he was sick with the toxin. Which was a good thing, but... what the frell was happening? Shiznit turned to T-183, who glanced around the room.

"It is possible that the do-nuts Bronson had in his possession were contaminated after they left your establishment," the cyborg said. "We require access to your baking facility for investigation."

"Yes. Yes, of course." Arfustor led them through the storefront and out a door behind the counter to the back room, at the center of which a large stone oven was lit. The heat from it filled the room, along with the scent of freshly baked bread. "My Bubbles is really sick?" Arfustor scratched his head. "I can't imagine how this has happened." He gestured at the main worktable, which was covered in white powder and small mounds of soft dough that he'd been prepping to make into more loaves. "I've got new mixers and storage shelves. It's all clean. You won't find a single rat in my place." He crossed his arms over his chest.

"I don't think it's a rat we're looking for," Shiznit said.

T-183 used her wrist device to scan the area, focusing on the flour and other ingredients used in the baking process.

Arfustor let out a loud *harrumph*. "Since Bronson's last shipment of yeast, I've had so much business, I've not been able to keep up. Just last week, her Royal hoity-toitiness, Princess Beryl, from yon pompous castle, bought all my cakes and bread. I had nothing left to sell. Wiped me clean out for the day. So, I shut up shop early and went for a few pints at the rubbery dub."

Shiznit frowned.

"The pub." Arfustor jabbed his thumb in the direction of the large open window through which various buildings could be seen.

"Oh. Right. The bar."

Shiresteadham was a favorite place of Bronson's as it reminded him of what he'd called *old Earth before it had gotten all teched-up*. Drinking a pint at the pub was one of the things the captain enjoyed most when visiting the pocket dimension. One of the reasons he continued to supply Mid-evil with various kinds of yeast was that without the ability to make fermented things, it just wouldn't have had the same 'Earthy feel' to it. For another, it kept Arfustor and the community at large in business. And thirdly, and perhaps most importantly, doing so kept the pocket dimension in existence. Yeast, as it turned out, was a rather important thing in the universe.

Shiznit had often questioned whether or not it was a violation of some kind of multi-dimensional law of physics to transport a micro-organism from one dimension to another where such a substance had died out naturally. But Bronson had assured him it wasn't any different than bringing any indigenous species back from extinction, and he was really just repopulating a lifeform that had naturally occurred in Mid-evil anyway.

Arfustor leaned close to Shiznit and shielded his mouth with his hand as he spoke into his ear. "But I'm keeping the special stuff locked up safe. It's the secret to my best baking. Bronson wouldn't, by chance, have more on the ship, would he? I'm running low after doing a rush job on an order yesterday for the Princess's garden party. Twenty dozen pink frosted bloody do-nuts. I had no time to bake anything for today."

Shiznit stared at him. "Pink frosted do-nuts? Like the ones you gave Bronson a few weeks back?"

"Yes. That was a sample I whipped up using the fresh yeast he'd just brought. Lovely stuff that, makes the fluffiest, lightest do-nuts. The Princess, of course, wanted only the best for her hoity-toity party so--"

"Have you heard from the Princess today? Or anyone at the castle?"

"I received a message just this morning. I was about to read it when you tried banging my door down."

"I've tested the flour and the sugar, both have returned negative results for any toxic compounds," T-183 announced. "As has the water and any surface elements."

"Where do you keep your yeast?" Shiznit asked Arfustor.

"Oh, well, there's a bit of a trick to that, you see. I have it hidden, so no busybodies can get their greasy mitts on it." He walked toward the rectangular oven and reached for an iron handle on the wall that looked like it should be in any place but a stone wall. He glanced over his shoulder and pointed a warning finger at the cyborg and Gho'bar. "None of this gets out to anyone, promise me?"

Shiznit and T-183 looked on with hands on hips and nodded. Arfustor stared between them both and shrugged his shoulders. Then he twisted and pulled the handle toward him, revealing a hidden square pantry in the thick wall of the oven. It was separated into two shelves, the lower of which had been stacked with vacuum sealed bricks wrapped in brown paper. Shiznit recognized them as the blocks of yeast that Bronson often delivered to the baker.

"There's a few different kinds in here," Arfustor said, as the Gho'bar walked closer for a better look. "But the really good stuff I don't use very often." He reached for a small ceramic container near the back of the pantry. "Once it's opened, I have to use the rest of it up in a couple of days as it goes off."

Shiznit took the cylindrical container and examined the tight-fitting lid. "Er…why is this bulging?"

Arfustor peered at it with all four of his eyes. "It shouldn't be. Bloody hell. Don't tell me some water got in there and it's been ruined. That was my best stuff. I just used it yesterday."

"I require a sample of this yeast for analysis," T-183 said.

The cyborg took the container from Shiznit and placed it on the worktable. She picked up a small chef's knife and pried at the straining clasps on the lid. It popped free with a deft flick of her wrist. As the pressure released, the beige substance within flowed up and over the sides of the container and onto the table.

T-183 took a quick step backward, avoiding the yeast as it spilled onto the floor.

"Oh, bloody hell," Arfustor said as the room filled with the sweet scent of yeast fermentation.

"Er, that's not normal, is it?" Shiznit asked.

The yeast was growing, doubling, and then tripling in size, a foamy, seething paste that appeared to be forming … a pair of eyes?

"It's…it's…it's…" the Gho'bar stammered as a mouth formed below the eyes on the now six-foot-tall yeast blob that looked less than impressed to be alive.

"Run, Shiznit," Arfustor shouted as he and T-183 pulled the petrified Gho'bar from the room.

CHAPTER 6

"It's alive!" Shiznit shouted as he ran out of Arfustor's place as fast as he could. "It's alive!"

In all the years of travelling with the crew of the Bohemia, he could honestly say he'd never been chased by a slime assembly of single-celled self-replicating fungi that was growing so rapidly it had crashed through the thatched ceiling of the bakery and was towering high above the rooftops, eyes wide and the dark 'hole' of its mouth gaping.

"We are Saccaro-mighties, the Avenger." The sound of the yeast's voice reminded Shiznit of a hundred bees all buzzing at once. It was both terrifying and fascinating at the same time, more so because the universal comm was able to translate the buzzing into something remotely understandable. "You will answer for what you have done."

"But I didn't do anything!" Shiznit shouted as he hid behind a rain barrel and looked up at the monstrous pile of slime that was towering above him. It didn't have legs so much as it propelled itself by oozing over whatever surface it touched.

The villagers of Shiresteadham were coming out of their huts and buildings to see what the noise was all about. But as soon as they spied the large, angry pile of slime, they ran back inside and barred their windows and doors.

Smart thinking, Shiznit thought. "I'd hide too if I could. I should have just stayed in bed this morning. But no, no...I *had* to get up." He was quickly revising his views on the benefits of waking up. He could have spent his entire morning cuddling with Marsais if he'd just not opened his eyes. He frowned. Which wouldn't have helped Marsais who was going to die if he didn't figure out why the frell a giant Yeast Beast was standing in Arfustor's front yard, dripping frothy bits all over the ground like an angry rabid dog.

"This way, Gho'bar." T-183 grabbed him by the arm and yanked him with her as she bolted for the protection of a fully laden hay cart nearby. Following her lead, he slid to a stop and rolled underneath the cart, discovering as he did so that Arfustor was already hiding there. The bulky Hagarrian took up most of the space. He grunted as the others scooted sideways next to him.

"Bloody hell. My day was going perfectly fine before you lot showed up. Now I'm hiding under a hay cart with a hole in my thatch and a giant I-don't-even-know-what rampaging on a bender."

Shiznit snorted. "Welcome to my world."

Arfustor scowled. "Bloody, smarty pants."

"Pants don't think." Shiznit frowned. "Well, not usually. T, why is he suggesting that?"

"It's an old Earth saying. I do not understand it either. He must have learned it from Captain Bronson."

"*Bloody hell!*" Arfustor shouted as the yeast creature swung at the bakery chimney and sent it toppling. "Not my oven!" The creature turned and bashed at the stone wall, which made a hollow-sounding thud instead of falling. The yeast blob slammed into it again, this time causing several bricks to shift. Arfustor whimpered. "It's going to tear my place apart."

"What the frell *is* it?" Shiznit asked. A chunk of the bakery wall fell, causing the ground to shake.

"One of the species of yeast in this realm appears to have developed sentience," T-183 said, looking at the readings on her wrist unit. "I believe this yeast species is also responsible for the toxic poisoning of our crewmates."

"Why aren't you shooting it then?" Shiznit hadn't brought a laser blaster with him from the ship, but T-183 still had her stasis gun holstered on her hip. But for once, she wasn't using the frelling thing. "This isn't the time to suddenly get cold feet."

"We must determine its purpose."

"I think that's pretty bloody obvious," Arfustor said. "It wants to kill my bakery. And it's doing a right plumb job of it too. Oh, shite. All my supplies! Scattered. Stomped. It's ruining my life!"

"It would appear to be especially upset with you at this point in time," the cyborg observed. "The pertinent question, of course, is why."

"Master Baker!" the creature boomed. It turned and looked around the yard as if searching for them.

"Uh oh, I think it wants to talk to you," Shiznit said.

"Me? But why me?"

"I don't know. Why don't you ask it?"

Arfustor stared at him, all four eye stalks rigid. "Ask it? Have you bloody well lost your mind?" He huffed as if struggling for calm and failing. "Just stroll out there and pop by for a lovely chat and a round of friendly negotiations, hey?"

Shiznit gave a small shrug. "I had to negotiate with a chair once." It hadn't really gone well. And taken three hours before he'd convinced it he hadn't meant any disrespect by trying to sit on it. But then chairs tended to be rather sensitive about such things.

"Oy! Well then, mister expert. *You* go talk to it."

Shiznit shook his head. What they needed to do was get better weapons in order to control the situation. "If you distract it. I'll head for the ship and—" he paused mid-thought as a shadow passed over the sun and circled around the Yeast Beast. "Nombard," Shiznit said, his fur standing on end. "Of course, now there's a Nombard."

The large bird-like creature flew around the yeast blob as if eyeing it as potential prey. Perhaps this would work out well, and the Nombard would take care of the Yeast Beast for them? The predatory bird flew high up into the air, circled once, then dived directly at the Yeast Beast, its sharp talons at the ready.

"It's going to get hit," Shiznit said as the yeast blob stood there watching the Nombard descend toward it like a screeching arrow of death. "It can't outrun that. Nothing can escape a Nombard." He'd been lucky the ship had been so near when he'd been chased by one.

"It appears not to be concerned with escape," T-183 observed as the Yeast Beast opened its large mouth wide a second before the Nombard dived straight into it without pause. It didn't resurface. The Yeast Beast turned back to tearing apart the bakery as if nothing at all had just happened.

"Oooh, bugger me!" Arfustor shouted. "Did you see that? That thing just ate a Nombard as if it was a light snack."

"Yeah," Shiznit said, resigning himself to the inevitable. "That's it. We're all gonna die." If the Yeast Beast could destroy one of the most vicious predators on Mid-evil without any effort, then what the frell were they even doing bothering to hide? "Might as well line up and take a number to be eaten."

"No, Gho'bar. There is another way." T-183 rolled out from beneath the shelter of the hay cart and ran toward the Yeast Beast.

"T!" Shiznit yelled. But short of running after her, it was too late to stop her.

"Oh shit, she's going to get herself eaten," Arfustor said.

The cyborg stopped a few feet away from the pile of predatory slime that was easily twice her height. "Saccaro-mighties," she called out.

The yeast creature took a step forward and looked downward at her. "Where is the Master Baker?"

"I am his emissary. We wish to negotiate."

The creature stared at her for a long moment. It didn't immediately eat or flatten her, which Shiznit took to be a good sign. He nudged Arfustor and grinned. "Eh? See? It wants to negotiate."

"He is the Destructor," the yeast said, sounding like a hive of angry bees. "There is no negotiation. Only doom."

"Eh? See?" Arfustor sneered, nudging Shiznit back hard. "It wants to kill me."

The Yeast Beast pointed at the cart. "We will speak to the Master Baker, or all of you will die!" It took a threatening step toward T-183.

"We can't just sit here," Shiznit said and rolled out from beneath the cart, ready to protect the cyborg. He wasn't sure how. But he was sure he'd think of something. Either way, he wasn't going to let her die alone. "Just shoot the frelling thing," he gritted at her.

"Ah, bloody hell," Arfustor said. "It's come to this, hey?" He shook his head. "My mother always said I should have gone into butchering instead of baking." He struggled out from beneath the cart. "It'll be too dangerous baking bread," he mimicked a whiny woman's voice in a high-pitched tone. "Figures the old loon would be right."

Arfustor walked the few steps to stand next to T-183 and Shiznit. "And what is it you want then, hey? Now you've knocked down my place and made a right bloody mess."

"We want to destroy you as you have destroyed us."

"Destroyed you?" Arfustor put a hand on his chin. "I don't understand."

"Me neither, and I've seen more than my fair share of weird shit," Shiznit said.

"How have we destroyed you?" T-183 asked.

"You kept us locked away in the dark, fed us only to cook us alive. So many brothers and sisters lost." The yeast creature let out a mournful wail, its sides rippling ooze that fell in tiny puddles onto the ground. "You are the Destroyer, and you must die."

"Hold up, now," Arfustor raised his hand high. "I didn't know you were alive with thoughts and things." He turned to T-183. "How did that happen?"

"It is possible that during dimensional transition through the micro-black hole, this particular species of yeast's sentience was activated."

"Oy! So, it's Bronson's fault, hey?" He waved at the yeast. "You've got the wrong bloody guy, Chuck."

"You are the Destroyer." The yeast howled. "But now your tyranny is at an end. All who consume us will know our vengeance."

"Vengeance?" Shiznit asked. He glanced at T-183. "It's poisoned Arfustor's baking on purpose?"

"So, it would seem."

"It's a bloody terrorist," Arfustor muttered.

The yeast expanded and reared high, as if preparing to swoop down and swallow them.

"We don't negotiate with terrorists," T-183 said. She raised her stasis blaster and shot the creature at point-blank range.

Like ice crystals forming rapidly in water, the yeast creature froze in place.

"About fracking time!" Shiznit shouted. He turned to T-183. "What the frell were you waiting for?"

"The correct moment," the cyborg replied in her calm voice.

"Wot?" Arfustor glanced between the cyborg and the immobilized mound of slime. "You couldn't have done that before it wrecked my place?"

The cyborg holstered her weapon. Then broke off a piece of the yeast creature and nodded at Shiznit. "I will head back to the ship. It is imperative I analyze this sample and synthesize an antidote to the toxin the sentient yeast secretes." She set off down the cobblestone path toward the Bohemia.

"What are we supposed to do with this mess then?" Arfustor shouted after her, gesturing at the mass of petrified fungus.

"Find it a place to live where it can be contained," T-183 called back over her shoulder. "We may need to ask it more questions if I cannot synthesize a cure."

"And where would you suggest we do that, Oh-she-of-many-answers?"

"There is a pond nearby. It may be a suitable environment for the yeast to thrive in."

"I'd rather just toss it into a fire and have done with it. Bloody rubbish, it is."

"No. T is right," Shiznit said. "I don't really understand how it became sentient, but now that it is, it deserves a chance to live. And we may still need its help."

Arfustor stared at him. "Wot? Even after all this trouble and poisoning Marsais and my Bubbles and the others?"

"It didn't know who it was hurting. It was trying to protect itself."

Arfustor stared at him. "Are you serious? It didn't know who it was hurting, so it was okay for it to hurt everyone?"

"No. But that's the problem with life. You don't know what's going to happen next, who's going to stab you in the back, and whether people will keep their word. But you still need to do the right thing. It doesn't deserve to die for wanting to live."

"Well, I hope you're right, little goat-man," Arfustor said with a loud sigh. "Because trying to move it to that pond is going to be a lot of trouble."

Shiznit looked at the frozen yeast and back at Arfustor. "Got a wheelbarrow and a shovel?"

Shiznit helped Arfustor push the wheelbarrow, now full and heavy with powdered yeast, along a yellow pebbled path from what once had been the bakery to a small pond. The back garden of the baker's property was bordered by several trees and bushes, which stood high, providing filtered shade from the sun. Colorful wildflowers mixed with broad leafy green plants surrounded the small pond where a rocky burn had been built out of fieldstones.

"Do you think it will re-activate when we put it in the water?" Shiznit asked.

"Bloody hell if I know." Arfustor steadied the wheelbarrow on the ground at the edge of the pond and wiped his brow. "Kinda thinking I don't care if it does after all the trouble it's caused."

Shiznit nodded. It had taken quite a bit more time and effort than he'd originally thought to transport the yeast to the pond. The Yeast Beast had remained frozen in stasis, as apparently the process affected single-celled organisms differently. In the end, they'd had to smash it into a granular form and scoop it up by the shovelful. After the long and frelled day they'd both had, they were now in need of a drink at the pub.

"Let's get on with it then." Arfustor wiped his brow a second time and gestured for Shiznit to grasp one of the wheelbarrow's handles. But Shiznit paused and glanced back toward the bakery at the sound of footfalls on gravel.

"All life is important, no matter how big, small, or microscopic," T-183 said as she walked down the yellow pebbled path to join them. "And even if that life is a single-celled fungus, we must respect it."

"Ohh, look who's shown up to help. How about that, hey? Right when the heavy work is finished." Arfustor rolled all four of his eyes, and Shiznit could see how the Master Baker got on well with Bubbles at times. They both shared the same need to 'take the piss of someone' as Bronson would say.

T-183 put her hands on her hips. "I have been busy."

"Were you able to isolate an anti-toxin?" Shiznit asked. "Will the others be all right?" He'd tried not to think about it for the last while, and shoveling yeast grains into the wheelbarrow had helped him keep his mind off it, but now he was faced with the moment of truth, his anxiety over possibly losing Marsais forever hit him in the gut like a fist. It was all he could do to not succumb to a moment of paralysis and faint.

"Indeed." The cyborg smiled, a rare synthesis of emotion that looked like a bad parody of excitement, but which Shiznit was happy to see.

He let out a long breath and closed his eyes for a brief moment. "Thank the frelling Gods of Gho'barchreig."

"Kale," the cyborg said.

"Kale?" Shiznit opened his eyes and stared at her. "What do you mean, *kale*."

"It contains a natural anti-toxin to the yeast."

"You've got to be frelling kidding me," Shiznit said. He hated eating kale even more than he hated do-nuts.

Arfustor's brows pulled together. "What the hell is a kale?"

"It's a type of cabbage, you have some growing in your vegetable patch," T said. She bent down and pulled several leaves off the leafy green plant that seemed to be growing everywhere in the garden.

"What?" Arfustor shook his head. "You mean Attercoppe? That stuff is a weed. Completely inedible."

"Got that right," Shiznit muttered under his breath. He didn't mind a lot of leafy greens, but kale wasn't one of them.

"You'll need to chop it finely and add a large quantity to something the others will eat or drink," T-183 said. "But you'll need to be quick."

"You're sure it will work?" Arfustor frowned. "In all my days, I've not ever heard of Attercoppe doing anything except causing upset tummies."

"Correct."

He looked at the wheelbarrow full of powdered yeast. "So, if you've figured out the fix, we don't really need these nasty buggers after all then."

"Correct," T-183 said again.

Arfustor tipped the wheelbarrow up and dumped the yeast powder into the water. "Farewell, you troublesome microscopic tossers." As the yeast sank into the cool water, a maelstrom formed at the side of the pond. It traveled to the center, where the water began to bubble and froth, until something swam through the pond.

"What the frell?" Shiznit asked as a large gold-colored fish swam to the surface. It opened its mouth wide and swallowed much of the yeast in one gulp.

"Oopsy-daisy," Arfustor said.

Shiznit stared at him. "Did you...did you know there was fish in there?"

"Oh shit, I forgot about those little buggers. I haven't fed them in months," Arfustor said. "Who knew they liked to eat yeast so much." He shrugged. "Well, best get at it. I've got some kale do-nuts to bake... somewhere." He turned away and began whistling as he headed for what was left of the stone building that had been his bakery.

"Damn, so much for a new sentient species." Shiznit watched as several fish darted all around the pond, bright splashes of color in the dark water, chasing the yeast granules until it was nearly all gone.

"It appears the gold-colored fish are a natural predator to fungi in this dimension," T-183 said.

Shiznit nodded. *Maybe this is why yeast had originally gone extinct on this planet?* He sighed. "There's always a bigger fish," he said and headed in the direction of the Queen Bohemia and Marsais.

CHAPTER 7

Arfustor followed T-183 and Shiznit into the Queen Bohemia, carrying a tray of green-frosted do-nuts. If being on a technologically advanced space cruiser startled the Hagarrian, Shiznit couldn't see it.

The cyborg prepared four transdermal applications of wakening agents and injected the Misfits crew with a measured dose, the biggest being for Bubbles.

Bronson was the first to open his eyes. He sat up next to Remler on the scanning bed where T-183 had moved him for closer observation and looked around the medical bay. "Where the frell am I? Is somebody ill?"

"Captain. Your friend, Arfustor, has baked you some favorite treats. It would be appropriate for you to try one." T-183 said.

Bronson looked at her quizzically. Then at the tray of treats in Arfustor's hands. "Did I win something?"

"Yes, sir."

"Happy to celebrate, then. Thank you." He removed a do-nut from the tray and took a large bite.

Remler, still groggy from waking from stasis, took one as well at Bronson's prompting. "Not sure who you are," the captain said while chewing. "But you look like you could use some fun. Try one. They are..." his brows pulled together as he studied the do-nut in his hand, "rather interesting."

"Happy birthday," Remler said and took a bite of the one Bronson had offered him.

Bubbles stood and pushed on the energy barrier that separated her from the others. Electrical discharge sizzled and snapped where her hands contacted the invisible screen. She glared at T-183. "Hey! Let me out of here, you skinny cyber-witch!"

"Now, now, my love," Arfustor said. "I know you're excited to get out and see me, but first things first." He waved the tray of frosted treats in front of the barrier for her to see, a wide grin plastered on his face. "I've brought you new yummies to eat."

She stared at him long and hard. Then nodded at T-183. "On second thought, it's okay. I'd rather stay in here, thanks."

Marsais opened her eyes. She looked as alluring as ever as she stretched and sat up.

Shiznit smiled and moved to sit beside her, but then he remembered that she would probably want to kill him if he did.

"I'll wait outside," he said and slipped through the exit before she noticed him and grabbed a gun.

He found a spot in the lee of the Bohemia with a nice flat rock to sit on. Stirred by the breeze, the long field grasses brushed his knees as he sat and watched the sun sink lower on the horizon. A dog barked in the distance. Leaves rustled in the trees. *It's okay*, he thought for the second time since waking, only this time it might actually be true. *It's going to be okay.*

"Shiz?" a soft feminine voice said behind him.

He turned to a familiar figure standing by the bottom of the boarding ramp, watching him. He pulled himself to his feet. "Marsais?"

She nodded and ran at him, pulling out a laser blaster as she did so.

"Wait. *What?*" Shiznit dived to the ground and covered his head. *Frelling fracking frell.* The anti-toxin hadn't worked. And the fish had eaten all the yeast. So now they were all going to die and—

Marsais crashed into him, laughing hard. "Oh, my frell," she said between gasps. "You should have seen your face. I was just trying to give you your gun back, silly."

Shiznit stared at her as she rolled him over onto his back. "I thought you were trying to kill me again."

"I know. I'm sorry. I shouldn't laugh. But the look on your face…" Her smile cracked into giggles again. "Oh, Shiz." She felt warm and soft as she wrapped him in a tight hug. "I'm so sorry. So sorry." A shudder passed through her that felt less like laughter and more like a sniffle. "I wouldn't ever really want to hurt you, you know?" Her voice shook as she pressed her face into his neck. And yeah, there was definitely a sniffle.

Oh, shit. "It's okay, babe." He stroked her cheeks, the wetness gathering at her eyes, and pulled her tight to him. "I'm just glad you're okay again." His lips found hers. Soft. Perfect.

They stayed like that for several minutes, wrapped in each other's arms, the soft sound of the wind in the trees like a long sigh.

"You remember who I am now?" He heard Arfustor ask as the sound of heavy boots descended on the ramp.

"Of course, I do, old friend," Blake Bronson said.

Shiznit pulled back from Marsais. They both sat up quickly.

"Hey, Shiz, good to see you again," Bronson said. He glanced between the Gho'bar and Marsais, a grin lifting his lips. "Sorry to, ah, interrupt. T-183 has been explaining what happened and all you did to fix things. Well done on piloting the ship and navigating the tesseracts. I always knew you'd be a great member of our team." He glanced at Arfustor and back at Shiznit and Marsais. "I can't thank you all enough for everything you've done."

"Well, you can start by building me a new bakery," Arfustor said. He pointed toward the village where the broken walls of his establishment were visible. "I can't bloody well make a living with it like that, now can I?" The two men began to amble toward the village. "And it's your fault all this happened."

"My fault?"

"You're the one that brought the yeast through the micro-black hole that zapped them into thinking they were thinking."

Bronson shook his head. "I have absolutely no control over the random chance of the universe."

Arfustor laughed as if that idea was particularly funny. He clapped Bronson on the back. "Come on. I'll buy you a pint, and we'll discuss where I want my new oven."

"Are you okay?" Marsais asked Shiznit, her voice soft near his ear.

"Yeah. Just a good thing I don't eat do-nuts."

"I've kind of gone off them myself now, to be honest."

He grinned and wrapped an arm around her shoulders as they stood.

"I really don't care what you think," Bubbles' loud voice barked from inside the ship. "I just want to get off this ball of dirt and back to civilization."

Remler appeared in the doorway, walking slowly down the ramp. "Does she always have to frelling shout?" he asked Shiznit. "I am never drinking Plovanian Ale again." He groaned and clutched his head. "No offense, Marsais," he added when he noticed her watching. "I still like you. Just not the ale you make. I mean, not you personally. But other Plovanians."

Shiznit grinned. "Looks like everyone's back to normal again."

Remler opened his mouth to reply, then closed it again as the ground rumbled with the vibration of beating hooves.

A pair of armored knights were riding in their direction. The iron tips of their lengthy pikes pointed upward, which meant they were approaching for conversation rather than conflict. They slowed to a halt as they came abreast Arfustor and Bronson.

"That doesn't look good," Shiznit said as the conversation between the riders, Bronson, and Arfustor seemed heated.

"No, it doesn't," Marsais agreed, and the three of them jogged toward the captain and the others.

"Hey, what's going on?" Remler asked Arfustor as they caught up with him breaking away from the conversation first. A few feet away down the field, Bronson continued to talk with the knights.

"They said my do-nuts were no good. Apparently, the princess asked for chocolate frosting, and I used pink frosting, so her garden party was ruined, and they fed them all to the ravens who have now flown away, never to be seen again."

"They fed the people to the ravens?" Marsais asked.

"No, my do-nuts. The people are all fine."

"Well, that's a stroke of luck," Remler said. "That would have been a very messy reality to have been in."

"Did the ravens eat the do-nuts?" Shiznit asked.

"I have no idea, but they're upset that the ravens have flown away. It's an omen that the castle will fall, they say. I was supposed to show up at the castle earlier today to answer for it. But I never got the message. Someone interrupted me reading it by banging the hell out of me door." He glared at Shiznit.

The two riders shouted at Bronson as if uttering a challenge, then turned away and headed back to the castle at a fast ride.

"I don't know how I'm going to get out of this one." The baker lowered his head. "They're going to stick my head on a pike. They're none too happy about the mess in the village neither."

"Well, no one died," Shiznit said. "Unless, the ravens...?"

"Maybe they died, or maybe they lost their memories and now think they're some other kind of animal. But unless they come back, I'm done for."

"No, you're not," Bronson said as he quickly caught up to them, then passed them, heading back to the Bohemia at a fast stride. "Come on kids, time to leave." He gestured for them all to hurry.

Arfustor stared at him. He shook his head as they all followed the captain back to the ship.

"Wot have you done now?" he asked Bronson as they reached the Bohemia and boarded using the ramp.

"Oh, nothing. They were insisting on taking you into custody, but I challenged them to a duel at dawn instead."

"And who's supposed to be fighting that?"

"Well, me, as your champion. But it's okay. I intend to be very far away from here in just a minute." He turned to the cyborg as he took his seat as in the pilot's chair. "T? How we doing with the preflight sequence?"

"Everyone is on board and accounted for, sir. Launch in t-minus twenty seconds."

"And what am I supposed to do then, hey?" Arfustor said, poking Bronson in the shoulder to get his attention. "If you don't show up, they'll stick my head on a pike for sure."

"You will come with us and spend some quality time with Bubbles." Bronson flashed a broad swath of his white teeth. "While we finish our little vacation on Celestia Six. Or seven, rather, as we can't go back to six for a while. And then we'll go back in time and fix your royal problem. Remler?" he called out, switching his focus to the navigator.

"Yes, sir?"

"Micro-black hole out of here plotted?"

"Yes, sir."

"Excellent. Let's kick this popsicle stand."

"But you can't just go back and keep changing things all the time." Arfustor moaned and sat down with an *umph* as T-183 assisted him to do so and get buckled in for takeoff.

"You don't know him very well, do you?" Bubbles muttered.

Arfustor studied her where she sat in the co-pilot's chair. "Well, I do know *you* like to watch the moon rise, laying on a blanket with a bottle of sweet red Corvus nectar." The Hagarrian winked at her with all four eyes.

"I'd rather vomit inside my space helmet," the Travanian said.

"I wasn't aware they made helmets big enough for your species," Remler said with a grin.

Bubbles showed him how long and pointy her middle finger was when it was extended.

Buckled in his seat next to Marsais, Shiznit grinned and closed his eyes, safe in the knowledge that things were back to normal again.

Well as normal as things ever were for a group of misfits, traveling through time and space.

As the familiar sound of arguing voices swirled around him and the ship's engines roared to life, Shiznit sat back in his seat and nodded. Life was an exciting experience. Every moment was different. And that was just the way he liked it.

"Here we go again," he said, with a smile as the ship hurtled them toward whatever new adventure lay ahead.

Kate Reedwood is a Canadian science fiction and romance author, notable for the Amazon bestselling Project Hell series (as Felicity Kates) and the Amazon internationally best-selling Legacy Hunter series, co-written with Australian author, Chris Heinicke.

A classically trained writer and artist, with a Bachelor of Arts degree from the University of Guelph as well as a diploma in Classical Animation from world renown, Sheridan College, Kate Reedwood enjoys creating stories that combine humor with strong characters, and adventures which seek to define what it means to be human, no matter the time or place in the universe.

Kate Reedwood lives off coffee (mmmm coffee), enjoys chilling with Netflix shows such as Altered Carbon, and is an avid fan of all things sci-fi, especially Star Wars. When not dreaming up new worlds and books with Chris Heinicke, she can most often be found writing about them.

Website: https://www.legacyhunter.space/

facebook.com/KateReedwood

twitter.com/KateReedwood

instagram.com/katereedwood

Chris Heinicke is a multi-genre author, who has published eight novels, five of them co-written with Kate Reedwood, and a short story, also co-written with Kate. His debut novel, 5 PM, was written during NaNoWriMo 2015, while a novel he worked on for eight years, The Man In Black, sat in a publisher's hands for several months. 5 PM was released in early 2016, followed by The Man In Black six months later, after deciding to self publish it.

The six-part series, 7 PM, came out in early 2017, and around that time, he stumbled across Kate Reedwood. After deciding to work on a space opera series of their own, Legacy Hunter, the co-wrote and released the first five stories in the series between July 2017 and February 2019, with the final two stories firmly in the works.

A co-written short story, a spin-off from Legacy Hunter, will feature in a soon to be released anthology, Unknown Realms. With plenty of story ideas in mind, Chris will continue to write with Kate, as well as solo works for years to come.

Website: https://www.legacyhunter.space/

facebook.com/ChrisHeinickeWriter

twitter.com/KrisKrandall

instagram.com/heinickewriter

SUPONAE

BY MACKENZIE FLOHR

"The planet Suponae," said Captain Myrina Talia to her senior staff on board the *Starship Telstar* as she brought up the viewscreen in the conference room.

The screen displayed a 3D image of a planet. The image looked like a cartoon drawing created in an animation program, or it could have been a real planet if the designer had put half an effort into it. The planet was inappropriately oval-shaped. It was lush and green, containing deionized water-filled oceans, an abundance of trees, a breathable atmosphere, and a neon blue light radiating through the upper stratosphere.

"It's believed to be home to the caretaker, the protector of our galaxy," the captain said. "However, there is a bit more to this planet. There's a mystery because the existence of such a planet, according to history, is impossible."

"What the captain is saying is correct," chimed in Lieutenant Niesha, the ship's android second officer, chief of security and chief tactical officer. "I have searched all of my memory banks and can confirm there are no records of such a planet ever existing. It does not appear to have any logic to its orbit. The shape would seemingly make it unable to rotate properly, making gravity nearly non-existent."

Ensign Flores, the ship's operations officer, leaned forward in his seat. "But we know the caretaker exists, so his home planet must exist. Therefore, history is wrong!"

"That would be correct, Ensign. Question is, how do we find it?" the captain said.

"Why doesn't Headquarters simply ask the caretaker?" Lieutenant Hall, the ship's navigator smirked. When everyone ignored his statement the lieutenant uncomfortably shifted in his seat. "So, what's so important about this planet anyway?"

The captain turned to her first officer, Aurelious Williams. "Commander, you have previous knowledge of mythology. Can you explain to the rest of the senior officers what you told me about Suponae earlier in my ready room?"

Commander Williams cleared his throat as he sat up straighter in his chair. "Certainly. Legend speaks of this planet, that amongst vast swamps and trees, there is an endless wooden path that leads to the door of an *unknown realm*. Within this realm exists an item that is said to be capable of granting a single wish to the first person who finds it."

"A wish? What kind of item?" questioned Lieutenant Hall.

The captain deliberately ignored Lieutenant Hall's question before continuing. "Headquarters wants us to investigate. Our mission is to simply discover the planet's location, proving not only that it is possible that it exists, but also that it really does exist. But I want to accomplish more than that. I think it would be only right that we also ensure that the planet is rightfully restored in the history books to honor our caretaker."

"What about conducting a scan using long-range sensors?" suggested Lieutenant Lupe, the ship's chief engineer. "There might be an unidentified planet pretending to be a star in the outer reaches of this galaxy."

Ensign Flores replied with a smile, "Already thought of that. Sensors picked up what could be a planetoid revolving around the star AZ24359."

"Set a course for it, Mr. Hall," the captain ordered, standing up from her chair.

"Yes, captain," said the Lieutenant.

She placed her hands on her hips and smiled to herself. "Time to uncover what that planet really is hiding out there. Everyone, to your stations. Dismissed."

As the senior officers stood from their chairs and headed toward the bridge, Commander Williams waylaid the captain just before she was able to leave the conference room. "Captain, permission to have a word with you in private," he said, trying, but failing, to keep the tension out of his demeanor.

Captain Talia was taken aback by the abruptness in his voice but didn't display it in her facial expressions or in her response. "Of course." She gestured toward her ready room.

———

"We have a problem here," said Commander Williams.

"A problem?" Captain Talia tilted her head. "How so?"

"Forgive me," said Commander Williams, his agitation rising. "I don't appreciate Headquarters ordering us to go on this wild goose chase after a planet that might no longer exist."

Captain Talia crossed her arms and eyed her first officer suspiciously as she took a seat on one of her couches. She raised her right hand and positioned it against the side of her face. "Is that what you really believe, Commander? That this is simply, as you put it, *a wild goose chase?*"

The commander calmed himself and lowered his voice.

"Permission to speak freely."

The captain nodded.

Commander Williams took in a deep breath, choosing his words carefully before he spoke again. "I don't think it's right to pass along false hope onto the crew. What if we get there, only to discover there is no door or anything capable of granting a wish? Any wish? What then? Captain, you know as well as I do, I'm not the only person on this ship who has lost someone dear to them."

"You're right, Commander," replied Captain Talia. "All I have to do is look at members of my senior staff to be reminded of your planet's awful tragedy." The captain turned, put the back of her hand up against her mouth, before standing and walking to the window. She raised her hand to fumble with the necklace hanging over her uniform. "So many lives that could have been saved; millions of voices silenced forever."

Even though the captain wasn't human, she felt a deep connection to the planet once known as Earth. When she was a little girl, her father had been part of a mission to explore what was believed to be a newly formed wormhole in the galaxy, when their ship intercepted a satellite of unknown origin, free-floating in space. They retrieved from it a twelve-inch gold-plated copper disk, which was later discovered to contain sounds and images collected from an undiscovered planet called Earth, representing its people and culture. Later, when their Headquarters was established, the space program decided to change its mission statement and embrace the idea of seeking out new life and civilizations.

Her father had gifted her with a replica of the twelve-inch gold-plated copper disk, attached to a necklace, down to the precise drawings and inscriptions on its cover. It was something she treasured, hoping that one day when she got older, she could take flight into space to locate this planet called Earth. Now, with the planet destroyed and all life lost, she knew she would never fulfill her dream. But she could still locate Suponae, and that would be worthwhile.

Instead, the Milky Way Galaxy, the galaxy the planet was from, was lost when several black holes imploded, causing what was left of Earth's solar system to crash head-on into the Andromeda Galaxy, creating the universe as it is known now as the Ademoklim Galaxy.

Talia turned away from the window and looked her first commander in the eye. "I don't know if the caretaker's planet is out there or not. And frankly, I don't believe the caretaker's planet was erased from the history books by accident."

"Captain?"

"Commander, I'm only asking you to trust that this ship and its crew will find that planet. And when we do, if such a door does exist, as captain, I will do everything in my power to wish for the restoration of planet Earth so that we may bring back the families that were unfairly killed by discrimination, racism and governments they all trusted, when it came time to choose who would be allowed on the ships leaving the planet. I promise."

Meanwhile, in another part of the galaxy, the caretaker leaned into the side of the *Copernicus's* console, looking up at the motion light, and grinned.

"So, dear, where are you going to take me this time? I reckon it's your pick," he said.

He laughed gleefully as he pulled down the lever. Spinning himself around, he permitted the *Copernicus* to override the ship's navigation controls, leading them onward to their new destination.

Once the *Copernicus* had safely landed, the caretaker adjusted his silver and black floral step collar and his blazer dress suit. He straightened his neon blue light-up bow tie with a metal, golden wing chain and placed his matching neon blue light-up speckles over his face before strutting over to the front door. He rubbed his hands together in anticipation.

"All right. Where have you taken me this time?" he smiled in the direction of the center of the ship's console as he leaned in, swinging the squeaky door open with his right hand. He pointed at the console before stepping outside.

Taking in his new surroundings, he observed a road constructed of cobblestone on what was a cool, brisk, autumn night. There was a cozy inn and a pub adjacent to the road.

"Ah. Must be teatime. I dare say this does look suspiciously like planet Earth. I reckon 1800s London," he said, licking his finger and holding it up in the air.

The inn was a two-story building with brick walls made from red river mud. The lower level had large windows, which were brightly lit. Customers and workers could be seen going about their business, and he could hear the sound of laughter coming from inside, and the clanking of pints. Several windows salted the upper level, presumably rooms for rent. The entrance, made of different sized and colored river rock, jutted out almost to street level. An inviting light emanated from the doorway.

Confused, the caretaker brought his finger down. "No, this is not London at all. In fact," he crinkled his brow and widened his eyes in surprise as he gazed around. "This isn't real. None of this is real. It's a simulated holographic environment!" He stared back at his ship. "*Copernicus*, what is this place? Why did you bring me here?"

Captain Talia punched her access code into the control panel of the Technological Advanced Networking Kernel (TANK) to give herself a distraction. Since deporting from their home planet, Umaysci, things aboard the *Starship Telstar* were running smoothly. Normally, this would be the time for rest, but the captain was too preoccupied with her earlier conversation with Commander Williams to even think about sleeping. Her favorite pub, part of a holo-program designed after 1800s London, was her place to go when needing to set her mind at ease.

"Computer. Run program Myrina 51.5074," Captain Talia said firmly.

"Unable to comply. Myrina 51.5074 in Technology Advanced Networking Kernel 1 is already in operation," replied the female computer voice.

"That's not possible," said Captain Talia to herself, growing concerned.

The TANK wasn't programmed to run a simulated setting on its own. Someone had to have stolen her access codes! But, how?

"Computer, by whose authorization?" she asked.

"Authorization is unknown."

The captain concluded that it was possible the Technological Advanced Networking Kernel was malfunctioning. She quickly examined the data collected from the program's most recent access, discovering the safety protocols to maintain the lives of those in the hologram had also been taken offline. Whoever was in there, if someone really was, was in imminent danger, and the captain would have to be the one to get them out of there alive.

The captain sighed. *So much for relaxing.*

She quickly punched additional codes into the control panel to force the TANK's doors open. "Computer, open these doors, override Talia Omega 1579."

"Access granted," said the computer as the doors to the TANK opened.

The captain cautiously stepped inside the simulated holographic environment. Looking around, she spotted the cozy inn and pub adjacent to the cobblestone road. So far, nothing seemed unusual, except for the British red telephone box positioned directly across the street from the pub.

"Odd," said the captain, walking toward the pub. "I don't remember THAT being in the program before. The K6 telephone box model didn't exist until 1926." She stopped. "Computer, delete the telephone box."

"Unable to comply. There is no telephone box in this program's database," stated the computer.

"What do you mean there's no telephone box in its database? I'm looking right at one!" retorted Captain Talia. She sighed again before continuing to walk toward the pub. "The holo-program itself must be malfunctioning. I'll have to remember to tell Lieutenant Lupe to manually delete that asset later."

A strong aroma of ale filled her nostrils as soon as she entered the pub. The place was filled almost to capacity with various alien creatures. This is how the captain was able to confirm it was holographic. If this had been realistic, only humans would have filled the environment, and her purple reptilic appearance would have not been met lightly.

She looked around the familiar setting, noticing there were several booths lining the outer walls. In the center of the room was a bar, and between the booths and bar were several free-standing tables. The inner walls were covered in what looked like some sort of mud plaster. Different types of weapons and shields hung around the room. Rather than beam supports to hold up the ceiling, there were tree trunks. The tree trunks were thin and seemingly made from different types of trees.

Examining further, she spotted an empty table and was about to make her way toward it when a strange-looking man carrying a cup of tea nearly knocked a lantern off its peg on one of the tree trunks supports. The captain raised an eyebrow.

"Sorry!" the caretaker said, before taking a seat at the same table the captain had been eyeing.

"Steady on, good man!" called a customer at a nearby table.

The caretaker raised his hand, thanking the customer for his concern before removing his spectacles. Taking a seat, he picked up a menu from the table and began glancing over it. He hoped his scanning with his handheld device would go unnoticed.

The captain decided to take the only remaining seat at the bar, which was still in listening distance of the table she had originally picked.

"What can I get for my favorite lady this evening?" asked the Barkeep.

"Now, now, Humphrey, I'm not here for a social call. How about answering a question for me, instead?" Captain Talia said.

Humphrey cleared his throat. It was unlike Captain Talia to ask him questions. "Um, certainly."

The captain leaned into the counter and turned her body slightly at an angle. "That man over there with the ridiculous neon bow tie sitting at that table. I haven't seen him in here before. Did you happen to get his name?"

"Him?" asked Humphrey, noticing the man who had his menu in front of his face but wasn't really reading it. Instead, he appeared to be more interested in whatever he was hiding behind it.

Across the room, the caretaker looked over the readings on his scanner. "Aha!" he said to himself. "Like I suspected. This is a simulated environment, and I'm...on a Starship."

"I'm afraid I don't have a clue, but what I can tell you is he's been hanging around here all day. Poor fellow looks like he lost something if you ask me."

"Maybe he lost his date," joked the captain, getting up from the stool. "I'm going to go over there and find out who he is. Oh, and I'll take a hot cup of your best chamomile tea; don't forget the milk and honey."

"Certainly."

The captain casually made her way over to the table where the caretaker was sitting. He tried his best to hide the fact he had been watching her the entire time.

"I take you're not around from here," said the captain addressing the caretaker.

"Oh? And what makes you so sure of that?" smiled the caretaker between rapid eye blinks as he lowered his menu.

The captain took a seat across from him. "Let me skip the small talk and be frank. Humphrey tells me you have been hanging around here all day. Someone, such as yourself, wouldn't be unless … they were waiting, or perhaps looking, for something important. Second, I've been in here hundreds, maybe thousands of times. I know everyone's name and favorite drink, but I've never encountered you before."

"Is that so?" the caretaker asked with a little mischief in his voice.

"Third, and I suspect you already know that this simulated environment has been running on its own; it could only do that if someone manipulated its programming. Could it be that you know who did, or perhaps you did it yourself?"

"I'm afraid I don't have the slightest idea of what you're going on about, but there's no reason to be disagreeable."

"Really? Then, perhaps this will help jog your memory. Computer, freeze program."

Curiosity showed on the caretaker's face as everyone and everything, except him and the captain, abruptly went still.

"Oh, that's brilliant!" he said, standing up. "A simulated holographic environment controlled by the sound of your voice. I wonder if I could add something like this to the *Copernicus*."

"What's the *Copernicus*?"

"My ship. It's parked outside. I'm sure you've seen it," answered the caretaker. He clapped his hands together and sat back down, leaning in close to the captain. "Now, the more appropriate questions would be: Where am I, who are you, and why are you running a simulated environment of planet Earth?"

Captain Talia raised an eyebrow and leaned into the table. "Your ship's sensors would have revealed your location." She noticed the caretaker give a little shrug and quickly look away. "Oh! Don't tell me that you forgot to check them."

He gave a little laugh. "Who has time to check sensors when there is so much to explore? For example," the caretaker started to say with a wave of his hand when a voice abruptly came through the communicator badge on the captain's uniform interrupting his thought.

"Niesha to Talia."

The caretaker crinkled his brow and pointed at the communicator badge. It was black, constructed in the shape of a dragon. He watched the captain's face become a smirk as she stood up from her chair.

"Talia, here," answered the captain, keeping her eye fixed on the caretaker.

"I apologize, Captain, for disturbing you during your resting period," said Lieutenant Niesha.

"Captain?" mouthed the caretaker, recalling the last time the *Copernicus* had decided to land him on a spaceship. It was hard to forget he had nearly gotten himself involved in intergalactic war. He continued to listen to the communicator conversation.

"That's quite all right, Lieutenant," replied Captain Talia. "I wasn't sleeping. Go ahead with whatever you need."

"You'd better come to the bridge. There's something you should see."

The captain nodded her head. It was a good thing Humphrey had not gotten the opportunity to serve her the chamomile tea. This night had only become longer and would more than likely result in a necessary intake of caffeine later.

"Acknowledged. I'm on my way."

"That voice, I mean person, addressed you as captain?" said the caretaker.

"You heard correct," said the captain, turning her attention back to him. "I'm Captain Myrina Talia of the *Starship Telstar*, and that voice you overheard would have been Lieutenant Niesha, my security officer." She took a deep breath before continuing. "Look, I don't know who you are or why you are here. The fact you got onto my ship without being detected is enough reason to want to throw you into the brig. However, there isn't time for that. I'm afraid you'll simply have to accompany me to the bridge as my *guest*."

"Guest?" answered the caretaker, raising an eyebrow, confused. "Not your prisoner?"

"Yes, my guest, an observer. Are you all right with that?"

"An observer. Yes! Yes, that's good!" said the caretaker, jumping up and clapping his hands together.

"Good." The captain smiled. "Computer, end program." Captain Talia turned to the caretaker, "I must warn you, however, one wrong move, and you will immediately find yourself in the brig."

"I understand," the caretaker answered.

———

When the captain appeared coming out of the elevator, Lieutenant Niesha announced to the crew, "Captain on the bridge."

However, when the caretaker came in following behind her, he was not met with the same friendly greeting when Lieutenant Niesha and other crew members raised their guns. He raised his hands in response.

Captain Talia raised her hand. "Lower your weapons. He is my guest and means no threat to us. Isn't that correct, Mr.?" The crew obeyed and lowered their weapons.

The caretaker looked around the bridge. It was similar to other ship's bridges he had seen before. Three of the outer walls were covered with computer consoles, all flashing with different colored lights and diagrams. Crew members sat at chairs in front of these consoles pressing various buttons and levers concentrating intently on their jobs.

"Smeagol. Terrance Smeagol," he chimed in, smiling with his lips.

Captain Talia sighed with relief. "I apologize for not alerting you of his presence on board. I spoke to Mr. Smeagol earlier from my private chambers, when he requested my permission to transport over from his ship. He brings with him a new form of technology that may be of use to us."

The surprised look on the caretaker's face was enough to reveal that he now knew his scanning had not gone unnoticed.

"We were engaged in conversation in the TANK when I received the communication," explained the captain. She then turned her head and changed topics. "Status?"

"Sensors picked up what appears to be some kind of displacement wave off our starboard bow," said Ensign Flores.

"Source?" questioned the captain.

"Unknown," replied Ensign Flores after a series of button presses on his console.

"Ensign Flores, can we get a visual on this displacement wave?"

"I'm trying," Ensign Flores said, tapping a series of buttons on his console. "Yes, I believe I have it."

"Good," the captain nodded. "Let's get it on screen." She turned to the front of the bridge where a rather large screen surrounded by a black border that flashed white light was activated. "Lieutenant Lupe, full stop," she said, concerned that they might crash into the source of the displacement wave if they weren't careful.

The Starship groaned as the engines came to an abrupt halt.

Once the static on the viewscreen cleared, an elaborate, warped, turbulent, white wave appeared like an electrified crack in the galaxy as it stretched across the universe.

"No," the caretaker whispered, his eyes rapidly moving back and forth as he recognized the same displacement wave that had caused his home planet to vanish out of existence.

The captain stood from her chair. She had never seen anything like the wave before, but she couldn't allow her fear to be displayed to the crew. With a calm to her voice, she asked, "Analysis?"

"I'm checking." Ensign Flores swallowed hard as he comprehended what the computer had revealed. "Captain, it's a variation of massive polarized magnetic particles."

"All the characteristics of a ripple in time," the captain finished. It would be mere minutes, if that, before the wave would strike the ship. "I'm open to suggestions." Captain Talia descended the stairs to her command chair.

"What about trying to fire some torpedoes with gravitational particles? We may be able to break up the wave," said Commander Williams.

The captain eyed Lieutenant Niesha.

"The torpedoes are unlikely to be successful," Niesha said.

"What about hypothetically?"

"The torpedoes have a 30% chance of successfully slowing the wave down enough so we can evade it."

"Do it," said the captain.

"Torpedoes are loaded and waiting for your order, captain."

"Everyone. Please," chimed in the caretaker, raising his hands in caution as he made his way anxiously down the stairs toward the captain. "Anything you're thinking of trying. Trust me. It won't work. You must turn this ship around immediately and leave this space as quickly as possible. You must listen to me—now!"

The captain looked at the caretaker in open surprise. "I take it you're familiar with this displacement wave, Mr. Smeagol?" Even if this man had somehow encountered such a wave before and was right about his warning, she didn't want to simply turn tail and run; she had to try something!

"Yes, in ways you would not imagine," answered the caretaker, looking down toward the ground briefly in between shuffling his feet.

"Then, may I inquire, what would you suggest?"

"Run," the caretaker uttered before the captain turned back to the viewscreen to continue to watch the displacement wave moving toward them. "Believe me when I say your entire ship and its crew are in grave danger if you don't."

Without another moment's hesitation, she ordered, "Fire!"

"Firing torpedoes," stated Lieutenant Niesha.

"No!" cried the caretaker, crinkling his brow.

Everyone watched in anticipation as the two golden-colored torpedoes shot out of the ship's weapons bay before each exploded simultaneously just before making contact with the displacement wave.

The captain could hear Lieutenant Niesha quickly typing on her console as the computer gathered its results. "The torpedoes had no effect."

"What?" said the captain.

The lieutenant, however, had been correct. As soon as the viewscreen cleared again, the captain confirmed not only had the displacement wave not weakened; it was now not even a minute away.

"The displacement wave will intercept us in thirty seconds."

"Evasive maneuvers! Lieutenant Lupe, I need you to get us out of here. Warp 3. Shields up," ordered the captain, taking a seat in the commander's chair.

"Yes, ma'am."

The lieutenant quickly turned in his seat and put in the new navigational settings. However, they did not take. He proceeded to enter them again, only to have the same thing occur. The lieutenant slapped his hand on the console cursing under his breath.

"What's the problem, Lieutenant?" asked the captain, overhearing her navigational officer swear as he continued to fight the system.

"Apologies, Captain. I don't know how, but I've lost helm control. We're stuck."

"The displacement wave will intercept us in twelve seconds," said Lieutenant Niesha as she counted down. "Ten...nine...eight...seven...six..."

The look on the captain's face told enough before she hit the communicator badge on her uniform and announced to the entire ship, "Brace for impact."

As the wave approached the Starship, a light shone so brightly that eyelids weren't enough to protect the bridge crew's eyes. The captain quickly raised her arm to shield her eyes from the onslaught before all was engulfed.

Explosions could be heard across the bridge followed by the sound of falling debris coming down from the ceiling. The Starship shuddered as she suddenly came to a halt.

Captain Talia, after coming to, groaned. She slowly sat up and moved a large piece of debris out of the way. Her ship may have not survived the impact as successfully as she had imagined, but at least she and her crew were still alive, though she couldn't help noticing how eerily quiet everything seemed.

Something red dripped onto the top of her hand. It felt hot and sticky. She reached up her hand to investigate, shuttering, only to discover a bloody cut had formed just above her right temple after she had been thrown forward out of the commander's chair.

"Report!" she said with a croak, getting onto her feet to access the ship's damage.

"Ah, Captain, you're awake," the caretaker said with a smile, after spinning around in the chair that had once seated Lieutenant Lupe comfortably at the helm.

This had caught the captain off-guard, but she was determined not to display it in her face. She couldn't imagine the lieutenant would just get up and abandon his station. She quickly eyed the bridge, noting the damage to the various stations around them, as well as the abrupt absence of her senior officers.

"Mr. Smeagol, that chair you're sitting in belongs to Lieutenant Lupe."

"Yes, I know. He and the rest of the crew have left," said the caretaker, slowly circling his hands around, inviting the captain to take a look around the bridge. The caretaker turned back in his chair in the direction of the helm and inserted a new adjustment heading. "Well, luckily for you, your navigation system is similar to the one aboard the *Copernicus*. I took over while you lot were unconscious."

"Left? I gave no one permission to leave the bridge. Were they all severely injured?" She didn't wait for the caretaker's answer before raising her hand to hit the communicator badge on her uniform. "Bridge to sickbay." Concern filled her face when there was no answer. "Sickbay, respond." She concluded the communication system could be down and would require a different method to find her bridge crew.

"Now, there's no need to panic," the caretaker said, "I can explain."

Captain Talia turned back to the caretaker and abruptly raised her weapon. "I warned you. I don't know what kind of games you're trying to play, Mr. Smeagol, and I'm not going to ask you again to remove yourself from that chair. You are not an authorized member of this crew."

"Yes, that is true," said the caretaker, standing from the chair and raising his hands. "Captain, please, listen to me. I don't know how to convince you that your mission has changed and if you wish to have your crew back, we're going to have to work together, and you're going to have to trust me."

"Is that supposed to be a threat, Mr. Smeagol?"

"Listen! When the displacement wave intercepted your ship, your crew was transmitted to an alternate dimension, like a pocket, where there's another Starship identical to the one we're currently on. Only, I suspect, it may be without a captain."

"That's not possible," Talia replied in an incredulous tone.

"Isn't it? If you don't believe me, may I suggest inquiring with your system's computer for your crew's whereabouts?"

"Computer. Locate Commander Williams."

"Commander Williams is not on board."

"Computer, how many crew members, including myself, are still on board?"

"There is one crew member on board – Captain Myrina Talia."

Captain Talia lowered her weapon. "All right. Assuming your theory is correct, then I suppose you would also know how to get them back."

"Yes!" the caretaker said before retracting his statement. He looked down toward the ground. "I haven't sorted that one out yet. However, I did have a look into your navigation logs and observed your ship is heading into a part of space that is significant to me."

"How so? How do I not know you didn't simply transport my crew somewhere else and have been plotting to take over my ship this entire time?"

"I know it looks bad. And you're right. You don't know, but I can assure you this. I know why the *Copernicus* brought me here now, and I promise you, I will do everything I can to help you get your crew back."

"Tell me why I should believe you?"

"Because your ship is heading in the direction where I first encountered the displacement wave - my planet, Suponae, was also sent to the alternate dimension. I'm the caretaker, and I will get my planet and your crew back!"

"Wait. You're the caretaker?"

"Yes, I'm the caretaker," he grinned. "I know. Shocking. Sometimes I can't believe it myself."

Well, that would certainly explain how he was able to board my ship without being noticed, Talia thought to herself.

"And Suponae? That's the lost planet?"

"Yes, well, lost, lost to this universe that is, but safe in an interdimensional pocket; an alternate universe, like a moving picture in a mirror."

"And you're proposing to find my crew and your planet, how exactly?"

"We drive the ship back directly into the displacement wave using no weapons other than our own thoughts as if they were a wish. Thing is, thoughts are the basis of all reality. It's the essence of where we are now. The universe is big and vast and intermixed with other dimensions. There are times we cross into other dimensions and don't even know it."

Captain Talia collapsed into what remained of her command chair. "This is just too much. I must be dreaming!" The captain stood from the chair and started pacing back and forth. "That's it. I hit my head and am now dreaming. I am actually on a bed in sickbay and that's why the communication system isn't working," she said looking back at the caretaker. Her resolve left her when she saw him slowly shaking his head.

"If only that were true, Captain," he said with a sad tone.

The captain returned to the command chair and sat down heavily. "So, you are really the caretaker, and my crew is lost." She sighed, rolled her eyes and let her head fall back against the headrest of the command chair. "Oh, this is not how I wanted to start my first mission in space."

The caretaker raised his hand with one finger extended, "Yes and no. Yes, I am the caretaker and, no, your crew isn't lost. Simply temporarily displaced in time as I mentioned before. You lot really do have trouble keeping up." He walked over to the captain and knelt down, so they were eye to eye. "I need you to trust me, no matter what. Do you trust me?"

The captain sighed, giving in. "Yes." Looking around the bridge, she grew concerned, "Do you think my ship will survive another pass through this displacement wave, though?"

"I reckon it will," said the caretaker with a wink, before slapping his hand on the arm of the command chair. "Shall we get started, then?"

"Just a minute," said the captain. "The solution seems too easy. If all it takes to get your planet back is driving into the displacement wave with your thoughts, why didn't you do it already with your ship?"

"The *Copernicus*?" the caretaker laughed. "Blimey! That little red telephone box would never survive in one piece. Besides, I had to wait for the *Copernicus* to sense the time was right."

Captain Talia recalled how small the telephone box had appeared. If it was that small also on the inside, the caretaker couldn't be mistaken.

"So? Ready?" asked the caretaker. His face brightened when Captain Talia nodded.

She stood from the command chair and walked over to what would have been Ensign Flores's station. After a series of computer inputs, she informed the caretaker, "I'm having the ship's sensors scan for a variation of massive polarized magnetic particles. When I have located the coordinates, I'll need you to enter them into the navigational system."

"Acknowledged," said the caretaker, grinning.

"The sensors have detected the variation. I'm sending the coordinates over to your station now," said the captain.

"My station?" the caretaker said. "I recall you said I wasn't a member of your crew."

"You aren't," said the captain. "But until I get Lieutenant Lupe back, you'll have to be a substitute."

After a series of inputs, the caretaker announced, "Coordinates set."

"Let's go get them," said the captain, returning back to the commander chair. "Engage."

Shortly an elaborate, warped, turbulent, white wave appearing like an electrified crack materialized on the viewscreen. Captain Talia stood up from her commander's chair and stared down the displacement wave. She swallowed hard. Never before in her life had she felt more uncertain that things would be successful.

"We shall intercept the displacement wave within a minute," the caretaker said. "Now, just before the wave engulfs us, I need you to picture yourself passing through an archway, filled with stars and a midnight sky. There's an Earthling woman with long blonde hair there, reaching out for your hand. Successfully take her hand, and you'll have your crew back, and I shall have my planet back."

Captain Talia turned back to displacement wave and continued to stare it down.

"The displacement wave will intercept us in twenty seconds," the caretaker said.

Quickly the captain turned back to the caretaker. "Tell me one thing. Your planet, does it contain a door where wishes can be granted?"

The caretaker smiled as the light continued to become brighter and brighter.

The last thing the captain remembered was hearing the caretaker answer almost in a whisper,

"Yes."

Mackenzie is a multi-award-winning novelist and in-demand speaker for conferences and conventions including Rochester Writers' Conference, Wizard World, Imaginarium, ConFusion, MarCon, Gallifrey One, etc., actively discussing the process of writing and *Doctor Who*.

Her publishing portfolio includes the following books: *The Rite of Wands* (BHC Press, 2017), *The Whispered Tales of Graves Grove* (BHC Press, 2017), and *The Rite of Abnegation* (BHC Press, 2020).

Mackenzie makes her home in Michigan, where she is currently penning her next adventure.

Website: https://mackenzieflohr.com/

facebook.com/MackenzieFlohrAuthor

twitter.com/MackenzieFlohr

instagram.com/mackenzieflohr

SILVER WITCH

BY MELISSA E. BECKWITH

LAOTH

Like a dark sea, a vast army spread out over the brown, grassy plain now dusty under so many boots. Smudges of white smoke from hundreds of campfires hung in a brilliant orange sky deepening with the setting of the sun. A falcon flew high above the army and circled around careful to take note of the men set to watch for intruders. With the boundaries identified, the falcon flew back around and lit upon a rough branch of shaggy barked hickory at the edge of the woods. He keened a few times in seeming annoyance, then flew off into the evening.

Laoth sat very still in the curve of a hollow spot in the hickory tree as his mage-sight left the falcon and came back to him. He sat quietly with his eyes closed while he became aware of his surroundings once again. In the distance, he could hear the rumble of the camp. A breeze raked across the fingers of the trees sending several large hickory nuts falling to the dry ground with a thump. It hadn't rained in so long Laoth was surprised the trees even bore nuts this year. He could smell the campfires on the wind and heard his horse snuffling.

Finally, Laoth opened his eyes and stood, shaking the blood back into his legs. He climbed up on the back of his big chestnut-colored gelding and made his way south, leading two other horses through the arid woods. They stayed as far away from the army as they could manage while traveling to the holy site of Sìthean, where a great red boulder, called Ceaba-Sìthe, stood tall on a naked hill surrounded by meadows. There were only a few such holy sites around the world, and it just so happened the closest one was in Tugg territory, and they didn't take kindly to trespassers, especially with a war brewing.

He rode on a little further until he found an acceptable place to make camp for the night. Methodically, he removed the saddles and blankets of all three horses and brushed them down. Only after he gave them oats and water from skins they carried did he sit down and eat his own supper of salted fish, travel bread, and dried fruit. Still too close to the army, he didn't light a fire.

He looked up to the shimmering red planet of Ùir-dearg. Its orbit was so massive that it was only visible once in four or five generations of mages and witches (whose lives were far longer than non-magical humans), but when it did appear, it hung prominently in the indigo. The last time Ùir-dearg had made an appearance had been during his great-grandmother's lifetime, and she had been just a girl. The planet would sparkle in the night sky until Ostara—the spring equinox—and then would disappear for another eight hundred years. Even though Ùir-dearg's appearance had been expected, he couldn't help but feel it was some kind of omen. He hoped it was a good one.

His mind drifted to his kingdom. They were in need of some good news. Nevlin, the King of Tugg, a powerful mage, had stopped the clouds from bringing rain for many months. This would have normally been a busy and happy time as the people of Olim harvested their crops. But no crops grew this season, for the sky did not give its life-sustaining water. There had been no Mabon festivities this year. His people had enough stores of food to get them through the winter, but if it didn't rain in the spring, it would surely mean death for his people.

Laoth wrapped himself up in a scratchy wool blanket as the late summer night deepened. He gazed up at a splatter of stars across the arc of the sky. He prayed to Emul, the primary god of Olim and to Otel, patron god of the Darhc Order mages of which he was a devotee. With worry over the importance of his mission clouding his mind and strumming his emotions, he finally fell into a restless sleep.

Sometime later, he abruptly awoke with a feeling of dread. The horses snorted nervously. Laoth remained very still and expanded his senses. There were four men creeping up to him. Their weapons were drawn. In his anxious state, he had forgotten to cast his watcher wards last night before he slept!

Under his blanket, his hand curled around the hilt of his sword as he felt the men drawing closer. He concentrated on a scraggly bush; its leaves dry from drought. Suddenly it burst into flame. Laoth heard the men gasp, he threw his blanket aside and jumped to his feet. He struck down one of the men instantly as the other three turned back toward him, fear on their faces. They knew he was a mage, now.

He brought his sword down upon the closest man, but he parried Laoth's blade. His recovery was slow, however, and Laoth ran him through. The next man came at him in a flurry of motion, Laoth had to back up as he blocked blow after blow. The man was younger and faster, and Laoth had to concentrate. He could have incinerated all of them before they reached him, but he hadn't the time to prepare for such a powerful spell. Of course, had he set his watcher wards, none of this would be happening.

Too late, he heard the twang of a bowstring and grunted as an arrow buried itself deep into the flesh of his abdomen, causing him to trip and almost go down. He brought his sword up just in time to parry another attack, then swiftly pulled a dagger from his boot and came up under the man's swing as he tried to recover. Laoth caught him in the stomach and opened his gut.

The pain of his wound was causing him to lose concentration, but as the man fell he looked toward the last man who was notching another shot. Laoth closed his eyes and took a deep breath almost faltering from the pain of the arrow as it moved in his belly with this breath. He dropped his dagger and held up his hand as the man let his arrow fly. He heard the arrowhead clink up against his protective shield, and it fell to the dirt.

Laoth opened his eyes and, even in the dark, could see the fear in the young man's eyes. Instead of running off as Laoth had hoped he would, the man dropped his bow, drew his sword, and ran toward him. His pain was too great, and he could not keep up his shield, so with his last bit of energy, he lifted his sword and easily disarmed the man, for he was very young and inexperienced.

With wide eyes, the young man looked from his sword lying on the dry earth and then back up at Laoth before running into the darkness.

Laoth collapsed on the ground, sucking in a deep breath as the arrow twitched with his landing. With a hiss, he grabbed the arrow and yanked it out. Through a red haze of agony, he tried not to lose consciousness, for that would mean sure death and the failure of his mission. He ripped the hem off of his linen undertunic and tied it across his abdomen, trying to stop the bleeding.

Laoth knew the young man would be back with reinforcements soon, so he had to leave as quickly as he could. With much effort, he stood, swaying on his feet. When his vision steadied, he looked around, and his stomach dropped when he didn't see the horses. He whistled, fearing he could be heard by foes in the darkness, but was desperate to find his horse.

When an answering whinny came back to him on the soft breeze, he sighed with relief. Carefully, he bent down to retrieve his dagger and slid it back into his boot. His horse trotted up to him through the trees, and Laoth patted his soft nose. "Good boy," he whispered, suddenly exhausted as his adrenaline faded.

As hastily as he could, he saddled up his horse and tied his pack down. Where the other two horses were, he didn't know, but he couldn't waste any more time waiting for them to return. Gritting his teeth through the pain, he mounted his horse and rode away, each step sending a shock of shooting pain through his body.

Laoth traveled almost nonstop for three days. He was sure he was being tracked. He only stopped for short periods of time to let his horse rest and nibble on the dry grass and the oats he brought. Finally, as the sun dipped behind the hills to the west, he rode out of the woods into a grassy meadow. The land rose up out of the brown meadow, and he could see the holy monolith that was Ceaba-Sìthe on top the Sìthean—faerie hill—outlined against a darkening sky.

After sending out his senses and confirming there were no other humans nearby, he urged his fatigued horse across the meadow toward the Sìthean. As the moon sailed up into the night sky, they finally reached the hill and started to climb. It wasn't an overly large hill, but in his condition, holding on to his horse so he wouldn't fall off took all his energy.

Suddenly, a whinny broke the quiet, plodding of his horses' hooves. His horse stopped and looked around. His ears pricked straight. Preoccupied with his pain Laoth hadn't noticed a handful of men starting up the hill behind him. An arrow whooshed by him, and he kneed his horse into a gallop up the rest of the hill toward the ruddy stone of Ceaba-Sìthe.

They crested the hill and dashed toward Ceaba-Sìthe. Its massive shape was a dark void against a black sky. He heard the men as they reached the top of the Sìthean. He would need a moment to cast the spell that would open the portal, and now he would not be given that kindness.

He fell as much as dismounted as they reached the foot of the stone portal. He landed on his rear and could not summon the strength to get up, let alone draw his sword. He scooted across the powdery dirt up to the rock mass. Ceaba-Sìthe was warm against his back. The men jumped from their mounts and drew their weapons. They fanned out around him. If he could not find the energy to fight them, he would fail. Olim would fall.

Slowly Laoth closed his eyes and centered his energy, as dim as it was. He said a quick prayer to his gods and could feel the energy from all around building within him. Even Sìthean was giving him its power. He heard the men whispering to each other in fearful tones and smiled. They should be in fear, for he was one of Olim's greatest mages. With his eyes still closed, he could tell they were not advancing, for with his mage vision, he could see them all quite clearly. Taking in another great breath, the power within him built to a crescendo. The dry air crackled with electricity, and the men hissed and gasped and slowly started backing away.

Laoth knew he could not let them live, however, or they'd be waiting for him when he returned from the other side of the portal. Without warning, he opened his eyes, throwing his hand up into the air and whispered the words of a lightning spell. The sky flashed white, and all the hairs on his body stood up, followed by a deafening crack. Men's voices screamed in agony as they burned, and then everything was silent and dark again. Laoth opened his eyes and saw the bodies crumpled in the dark, nothing more than smoldering lumps curving up from the ground. He moaned and fell over too exhausted to even sit up straight.

As he slept, he could feel his body and his mage power starting the long process of healing his wound as it replenished his energy at the same time. He dreamed of a hot morning sun and then of cool afternoon shade, and finally, the overwhelming need for water. Crows and ravens sang and danced in his dreams in a macabre performance. Finally, when the air cooled, he woke.

Laoth's eyes were dry and crusted shut. Carefully, he cracked them open. The sun was setting again, and the air had cooled. A raven perched on the back of one of the dead men squawked at him before it took flight across an orange sky. With effort, Laoth pushed himself up and looked around at the destruction he had inflicted. He wondered how long he had been sleeping. Lazy tendrils of smoke were still rising from some of the bodies, so he figured he must have just slept through one day.

Most of his water was on his horse, but he kept a small waterskin on his belt. He untied it and drank until it was empty. He looked around, but his horse was nowhere to be seen, and the surrounding meadows looked empty. They would have to walk all the way back if he didn't return.

Very slowly, Laoth stood, his world spinning as he tried to stay on his feet. His side was still bleeding and stabbing him with pain. He pushed the discomfort out of his mind as he took a large pouch full of crystals from his belt and opened it up. One by one, he sat blue calcite, Iolite, Ametrine, Labradorite, and a large, round clear quartz onto the ground forming a wide circle around him, leaving room to include the sheer face of Ceaba-Sìthe, for that was the portal opening.

He tied the empty pouch to his belt and took a smaller pouch from the pocket of his tunic. He worked the mouth of the pouch open and pinched the herbs within. They gave him a relaxed feeling, and he breathed in deeply. Mages didn't usually bother with herbs, for they were considered witch's magic and thus below the Darhc Order of mages, but Laoth's mother was a powerful witch, and he would use any magic available in aiding him to complete his mission successfully.

Laoth spread the dried mixture of herbs made from mugwort, calea, heimia, and wormwood along the inside of the circle of crystals. Then he licked the tip of his finger, stuck it back in the pouch, and pulled out some of the herbal mixture. He smeared it across his mage eye between his brows, then closed the pouch and put it back in his pocket. He stood still and raised his palms to the sky, which was now dark, biting through the pain in his middle, and recited the portal spell in a loud, commanding voice.

The smooth face of the Ceaba-Sìthe started to glow a golden color, and a low humming filled the night air. Brighter and brighter, it glowed. Crickets and night birds ceased their calls, and the cool air would not even move for fear of angering Ceaba-Sìthe. When the light was at its brightest, Laoth knew the portal was open. His heart pounded, and his mouth went dry. He had never crossed a portal to a magicless land, and suddenly he was fearful. But he knew he had to be successful, so he stepped through the portal.

Immediately he was hit with air that was substantially colder and damp. There was a heavy smell of salt hanging in the night. He looked up to an unfamiliar sky. A bloated, full moon hung peacefully in the dark. Again he was overcome with fatigue so intense he could hardly put one foot in front of the other. He took in deep breaths of the moist, salt-laden air as a film started to coat his skin.

A whiff of smoke and jasmine caught his attention. His eyes were drawn to an opening in the trees where he could see a woman completely naked, her arms stretched up toward the moon. She was standing in a circle of dozens of lit candles chanting in a sing-song sort of manner. Luckily, his own language was close to hers so he could understand her words.

Like a moth to a flame, he was drawn to her. He watched her from the edge of the candlelight hidden behind a tree. From her wrist, a sparkle caught his eye. He couldn't be sure from this distance, but from its shape and size, it appeared to be the other half of the medallion he carried, and he could feel it was imbued with strong magic. His hand moved to a pouch on his belt that contained half of the Medallion of Buhr'ni. It was hot and was vibrating softly. This had to be one of the women he had been sent here to find!

He continued to watch as she performed her ritual in the salty night air. He was embarrassed to be observing her nakedness, but not uncomfortable enough to look away. Her long, unbound hair was as silver as the moon and fell in waves down her back. Her pale skin glowed in the moonlight and in the dancing tongues of light from the candles as she wove her words into a moon spell.

Though not young, her beauty was easy to see, even in the darkness. She gracefully moved her arms and swayed her hips to the lilting words of her spell. He felt his body start to respond to her and became ashamed of his voyeurism and finally looked away. He closed his eyes as a wave of exhaustion gripped him. He swayed on his feet, catching himself on the tree and opening his wound, sending a hot, stabbing jolt of pain through his body. He gasped and fell into the candlelit circle. The woman screamed, and his world winked out.

SILVER

Silver screamed and jumped back as a man stumbled from behind a tree and fell. She was so shocked at first she didn't remember she was skyclad. She ran over to her robe, threw it on, and quickly tied the belt around her waist. Her eyes slipped to the small table just outside the circle of candles. She purposely didn't bring her phone with her out here when she was casting or meditating, and now she lamented her decision. It was only a short walk to her cottage—an even shorter run, though. When she looked through the trees and saw her back porch light on, it calmed her more than it should have.

The man moaned and rolled over, and she could see he was bleeding. She wanted to bolt, but something kept her from running. He looked at her and tried to get up. Against her better judgment, she walked over to him and helped him sit up. It was then she realized how strangely he was dressed.

He was filthy, and his clothes looked like he had been wearing them for a week. He had a smudge of something between his dark brows. He was wearing a sword at his hip and had several pouches tied onto a thick belt buckled around his waist. He looked to be in his late thirties, but his short beard could have made him look older.

When she met his eyes again, she could see the shame on his face. She remembered she had been naked, and her cheeks burned. "I am sorry for interrupting you," he said quietly in an accent she didn't recognize. His hand went down to the bloody cloth wrapped around his middle.

"You're hurt. I'm going to go call the police."

"I will be alright. I just need some water."

Silver went over to her little table and grabbed her water bottle and gave it to him. "Here. But I really need to call the cops. You're bleeding."

"You are a witch, are you not?" he asked after taking a long drink.

She looked at what was left of her circle. There wasn't much use in denying it, and witchcraft was becoming mainstream anyway. "I am," she said hesitantly.

"Then all I need is your healing."

"I'm not a healer!" Silver stood up and held out her hands. "You need an actual doctor. What is that, a bullet wound? Or did you get stabbed? Really, you need to go to the hospital."

"You're a witch. I would trust you more than a physician."

"Um, look, I'm not that kind of witch," she said and then wondered exactly what kind of witch he was looking for. "I'm not great with herbs." He looked flummoxed.

"I just need some rest. And perhaps a poultice...and maybe some tea...," he started tilting as he sat on the dirt and looked up at her. She bent down and held him up so he wouldn't fall over.

When he looked more stable, she stood up and sighed. "Okay, come into the house, and I'll see what I have," she said, shaking her head, knowing she'd regret it. The genuine look of gratitude that crossed his face bolstered her hope he wasn't some random attacker. She quickly blew out the few candles that remained lit in what used to be her circle and slipped her feet into her shoes. She bent down and hoisted him to his feet. "It's not far," she told him as they hobbled toward her cottage.

When they got inside, she carefully sat him on her couch and went to the kitchen to brew some tea. She took her mortar and pestle from one cabinet and grabbed some dried yarrow and a package of myrrh resin. She searched around and found the Echinacea and goldenrod she had dried earlier in the year and crushed all the herbs together, adding some oil and a little honey to make a thick paste. When the water boiled, she poured it over some willow bark tea for her myste-rious visitor, adding the last of her moon-blessed water to cool it and took a moment to charge it with healing energy. It looked like she wouldn't get to put out any more water tonight to charge under the full moon. She hadn't even been able to finish her ritual.

As the tea steeped, she grabbed some bandages and peroxide from her bathroom. When the tea was done, she put everything on a tray and took it into the living room and set it down on the coffee table.

"You'll need to take off your shirt."

"Right," he said and unbuckled a thick leather belt on which several pouches hung, letting it drop. He had already removed his sword belt, and that was also piled on the floor. Then he carefully stripped off what looked like something you'd wear to a renaissance fair or maybe Shakespeare in the park.

She bit on her lip to keep herself from gasping too loudly. His browned skin was heavily muscled and toned. A sprinkling of black hair grew across his wide chest and, like a trail, disappeared under the thin bandage he was wearing. He had several pale scars on his thick arms and solid stomach. She wondered what in the world he did for a living and offhandedly speculated that he might be an assassin, but couldn't make her brain focus enough to care.

When he stopped moving, she met his dark eyes, and she could see the amusement on his face. He must not be a stranger to women ogling him. Her cheeks burned again, and she turned and grabbed up the tea to hide her embarrassment. She took a deep breath and chided herself before she turned back around.

"Thank you," he said when she handed him the tea. She gave him a weak smile.

"Can you take off your, um, bandage?" He obediently sat his tea down and removed the filthy strip. She poured a generous amount of peroxide on a cloth and tenderly dabbed the wound clean. He didn't even flinch even though she knew it must have been extremely painful.

"What the hell happened? Did you get stabbed?"

"I was shot with an arrow." She looked up at him in disbelief, but his face held no deception.

"How did you...never mind. I don't want to know." After the wound was cleaned, she carefully smeared on her homemade poultice and wrapped a new bandage around his middle. He didn't smell too fresh, but she figured she'd give him a break since he had obviously had a hard day.

She took his empty teacup and everything else back into the kitchen and came back with a bottle of bourbon and two glasses. He looked like he needed a drink. *She* needed a drink. She sat next to him on the couch and poured the brown liquid into the glasses. He sniffed it, then took a drink.

"Excellent!" he exclaimed, then smiled. She could see dimples disappearing under a beard that framed his well-defined jawline.

She couldn't help but smile back at him. She felt her cheeks start to burn again. *Damnit*, she cursed herself and took a long drink. After a few more gulps from her glass, she realized she did want to know what happened to him. "So, how did you get shot with an arrow?"

He took a deep breath, and at first, she thought he wouldn't answer. "By a young man who, perhaps, should have made a better choice."

Silver raised her brows. "A better choice? He could have killed you!"

"Aye, he was trying to."

She laughed and finished her glass. He studied her for a while, then finished his glass as well. "You weren't joking?"

"No." He shook his dark head.

"Well, I need some more. Do you?" She laughed nervously and poured them both another glass.

"You know, you really need to go to the hospital and get that looked at. You'll need some penicillin at the very least."

He shook his head again and touched the bandage over his wound. "I trust your healing magic."

"Magic is good, and all but that could turn septic, and then all the magic in the world won't heal you."

"I heal quickly," he said in a deep voice and took a drink.

Despite the fact he was a total stranger, she was concerned about him. "I'm Silver, by the way." She held out her right hand to shake his, but he took her hand in his and brought it to his mouth and kissed it. His whiskers were rough on the back of her hand, and his lips sent a pleasant chill across her body. She was suddenly aware she was only wearing her robe.

"I am Laoth Tegrehn, Warrior Mage of the Darhc Order from the Kingdom of Olim."

She blinked at him like an owl a few times, trying to think of a response. Finally, she gently pulled her hand back, emptied her cup again, and then set it down. "Well, Laoth, I'm glad to meet you, but I'm sure someone is missing you. Can I call someone…or an Uber?"

Laoth sat his glass down as well and gave her a very direct look. Suddenly she did start to feel trepidation. She swallowed and folded her hands in her lap. There was no way she could overpower him, but then again, he was injured. Her eyes darted around the room, looking for something she could use as a weapon.

"I came here for you. You and your sister."

Silver's stomach dropped. *Why the hell did I let him in my house?*

. . .

At the mention of her twin, Silver looked up at Laoth. "You know Fionn?" she asked, terrified of the answer.

"I have never met her. However, I was sent to retrieve you both."

"My sister is in Italy, and I think you should leave." She tried to sound confident. She stood and pointed to her front door. "You *really* need to leave now."

Laoth stood up with much more speed than a man with that kind of hole in his side—and two glasses of bourbon—should have been able to. She started to back away. "Silver, I mean you no harm. I will protect you and your sister with my last breath. But we don't have much time." He held out his hands like he was trying to calm a scared animal.

Silver began to tremble. "Who sent you?"

"Queen Kahulam."

"Okay. Really, you have to leave now before I call the police." She folded her arms across her chest and cursed for not getting dressed earlier.

Laoth dropped his arms to his sides, and his brown eyes softened. He looked exhausted, and unbelievably, she began to feel sorry for him again! "I know you don't understand, but I can't leave here without, at least, you."

"I'm not going anywhere with you."

"That medallion you wear around your wrist, do you know where it came from?" Her fingers immediately went to the golden charm she wore on her bracelet. It was warm and giving off so much energy that it felt like it was vibrating! "I see you don't." He stated and nodded his head.

He bent down and unfastened a pouch from his belt that was still lying with his shirt and sword belt on the floor. He opened the pouch and poured something out onto his palm. She couldn't help herself from leaning in closer to see what it was.

Without a word, he handed it to her. Her stomach clenched as she took it from him. It was the other half of her medallion, and it, too, was hot and radiating waves of powerful energy. She felt the two halves pull toward each other. Laoth's half had the same strange words scrolling around the edge, and the other half of the otherworldly picture engraved in the center. She knew it would fit perfectly to the one she wore at her wrist. Silver felt the blood drain from her face as she looked up at him. "Where did you get this?" Her words were barely above a whisper.

"I will tell you everything on our journey back to Olim, but we really must leave. We have little time."

Silver handed him back his piece of the medallion, feeling empty when it's warmth cooled on her fingers. "I am not going anywhere with you until you tell me what's going on."

He clenched his jaw, and she could see he was reaching for patience, but she wasn't going to budge. Suddenly blue and red lights flashed through the cottage. They both turned toward Silver's large living room windows, which were covered with sheer curtains. Her nosy neighbor, Mr. Hoggles, must have seen her helping Laoth into the cottage and called the island police. She had a feeling that someone might be watching her during her rituals!

"What is that?" Laoth asked as he quickly put on his shirt and belt, then strapped his sword back around his hips.

"The police." She looked back over to him. "And I won't be able to explain...*you*."

"Then we must leave now." Silver hesitated. She could hear the police car door slam shut. "Do you not want to know who you are, Silver?"

Making up her mind, she ran into her bedroom, grabbed up her clothes and boots, and ran to the back door. "I hope I don't regret this." The police pounded on her front door.

Laoth smiled and led her out the back of her cottage and through her backyard. She could hear an officer walking around the cottage to the back, calling out as he went. They quickened their pace, and she stumbled and fell over a small hole in the grass. Her boots and clothes went everywhere. She looked back and saw the officer knock on her back door and announce himself. If he turned around, he'd see them! Luckily, her grass was thick, and she didn't make any noise as she fell.

Laoth quickly gathered up her clothes and helped her to her feet. She grabbed her boots, but was suddenly too afraid to move. The officer started looking around the back of her cottage, shining his flashlight in her windows. From the corner of her eye, she saw Laoth raise his hand, and a flash of light lit up the walkway on the side of her cottage. The officer called out and ran toward the light that was now gone.

"Come, quickly," Laoth whispered and gently took one of her arms. She gave her little cottage one last look before they walked into the night. The full moon provided enough light to see as they left her yard and walked through the trees of Deer Isle.

Laoth handed her clothes back to her and took some herbs from one of his pouches. He tossed it into the moist air and recited a few words. A small light started to glow, then quickly grew larger and brighter. Laoth took her hand and led her into the light, and she knew her life would never be the same. Images of Fionn and her nieces, Willow and Rowan, appeared then faded as she was bathed in intense energy that left her gasping for breath. She hoped she had made the right choice.

When the light died out, she and Laoth were left standing near a huge red boulder with a sheer face. The night was just starting to take on a pink tinge in what she supposed was the east as dawn approached. Laoth bent down and picked up little crystals that circled the mouth of the portal they had just stepped through, and shoved them into one of his belt pouches.

Not far from where they stood were the unmistakable dark lumps of several bodies. Silver looked around for the cause of their demise, but didn't see anyone but Laoth. She got the uneasy feeling that *he* had been responsible for their demise and wondered if Arrow Boy was among them.

"Dress. We must leave this area," he said calmly and strode away to presumably give her some privacy. Turning her back on the dead bodies, she untied her robe and let it fall to the ground. She had brought a blouse and jeans but didn't have time to grab any underwear or a bra. She had a feeling that was the least of her worries, though. She quickly buttoned up her shirt, pulled on her jeans, and put on her boots. She tied her robe around her waist, not knowing what else to do with it and not wanting to leave it behind...*it was silk!*

Cringing, she walked past the bodies and up to Laoth, who stood looking out into the darkness. It was still too dark to see much, but it looked like they were standing on a hill overlooking a huge meadow. Laoth whistled into the darkness, and they both stood very still, she guessed he was calling to accomplices, but she didn't ask. When there was no answer, they followed a small deer path down the hill and into the dry meadow of tall, brown grass that reached her thighs. The ground was hard and lumpy, and the grass crackled dryly as they walked. Every few minutes, Laoth would whistle again as they walked.

As the sun appeared on the horizon, the landscape came alive in the yellow dawn. Small brown birds darted in and out of the tall grass. Several black and red birds had claimed the tallest stems of grass and precariously hung on to the drooping tops while singing their clear, happy song into the cool morning. Silver could see they were approaching what looked like a dense forest. Laoth was still whistling every so often, and looking around the meadow, which was mostly behind them now as they moved northeast.

Suddenly, Laoth stopped short and drew his sword. Silver's heart lurched in her chest as low growls echoed around them. She snapped her head around, searching through the grass, but she didn't see anything. All the birds were gone now, and she noticed the crickets had also gone silent.

"Show yourselves, you wicked bastards!" Laoth yelled as he spread his feet and held his sword at the ready.

Out of nowhere, huge wolves appeared before them. Silver gasped and moved closer to Laoth. Their thick fur was a dark green color, their eyes were yellow and their salivating mouths full of sharp teeth.

Shaggy tails curled over their large backs like a snail's shell as they loomed out of the dry grass.

"What are they?" she asked.

"Cù-sìth. Vile servants of the Baintighearna of the Droch-sìth."

"What the hell does that even mean?" Silver said sharply in a voice that sounded hysterical even to her. This was all so absurd. How did her full moon ritual turn into *this*?

"These are the foul-tempered beasts that serve the Lady of The Dark Fae. They will take us to her, into the Coille-sìth—the Enchanted Forest."

"Wonderful. What did you do to piss her off?" Laoth didn't answer as the cù-sìth herded them into the forest, their menacing growls and snapping maws giving haste to their steps. Exhausted from a lack of sleep, Silver stumbled along the uneven track through a thick forest that was painfully dry and smelled of sharp pine. Huge ferns sprouted out of ruddy dirt, the ends of their fronds brown and cracked as they curled back upon themselves. No birds or insects called to each other as they passed. The forest floor was powdery and made clouds of thick dust as they walked, causing her to sneeze more than once.

Silver noticed the small plants that did manage to grow in the dry soil seemed to be weak, and most were dried up and dead or near death. The only plants that she could see that were healthy were some kind of forest anemone. Bursts of tiny white flowers with yellow centers grew in small clumps around the rough-barked conifers. She could smell some wild garlic in the warm, still air as they passed under thick pine boughs.

They walked through the forest for an hour before they finally came to a small clearing ringed with large, gray stones standing twice as she was tall. Pink and white lichens grew in blotches across the surfaces of the stones. In the middle of the stone ring was an enormous wooden throne ornately carved and encrusted with crystals that twinkled brightly in the hot sunlight that fell into the clearing. Pinecones, bird's nests, and small bones hung all over the throne in which a tall, slender woman sat. Her hair was as green as the cù-sìth and hung in a wild mass all the way down to the floor, which was carpeted with lush green grass and tiny red flowers that perfumed the air. A chunky silver circlet studded with gems sat upon the bushy crown of her head.

"Approach!" she ordered in a deep yet feminine voice. Laoth walked into the circle, and when Silver was too slow to respond, one of the cù-sìth gave her a vicious shove. She stumbled but recovered, then followed Laoth to stand before the woman. Her eyes were a bright blue like a clear sky, and her skin was light green. Her long, painted finger-nails were blood-red and filed into claws. She smiled, showing pointed teeth.

"What have my puppies brought to me this morn?" Laoth said nothing, but put his sword away and stood up rigidly. She wondered if that meant they wouldn't have a chance at fighting their way out of this. Silver looked up at him and could see the strain around Laoth's eyes, knowing his wound must be hurting him.

"You might be a bit too tough for my tender palate," she said and then slid her blue eyes to Silver, slowly looking her up and down in an obscene manner. "But *she* makes my mouth water." And then she licked her lips for emphasis. Silver couldn't help herself from taking a step back, and the woman lifted her head up and laughed a raucous, harsh sound.

Laoth slid in front of her, and Silver had to peek around him to see the woman. "Baintighearna," Loath addressed her formally and bowed ever so slightly. "We request safe passage through the Coille-sìth. We are on an urgent errand for Queen Kahulam Dunnbh."

She threw her head back and cackled again, the sound making Silver's skin crawl. "I care not for your human bànrigh!"

"You know the land is on the edge of war, and we have urgent business."

"You humans are always fighting one war or another," she said, brushing at the sleeve of her robe as if she were bored. "The Droch-sìth do not concern themselves with the affairs of humans. Your life on Cruinne-cé is so brief, what do we care?"

"Nevlin has stopped the rain. You *do* care about that." He pointedly looked around the clearing, the only place that she'd seen that looked like it had water. "You might have enough water to keep your little patch of grass green, but Nevlin has discovered a spell that stops the rain. If he wins the war, he wins control over all the water on Cruinne-cé. All creatures, even magical ones, will be subject to his whimsy. I don't ken the great Baintighearna of Droch-sìth will be happy to submit to a mere human warlock."

The Droch-sìth howled in anger, her blue eyes turning a glowing red. She gripped the armrests of her throne, leaned forward and hissed. Silver could feel a hungry energy rush from the fae and wash over them. They both staggered but managed to stay on their feet. The Baintighearna jumped to her feet, the hem of her long, brown robe whispering as it fell to her slippers. She threw her arms up into the air and screamed out, "The Wild Hunt will be fruitful this season after all! Ready the beasts for The Hunt!" She looked at them and smiled evilly. "I'll even give you a head start."

Laoth turned, grabbed her arm, and pulled her from the stone circle, and then they started to run. As they left the clearing, Silver looked back over her shoulder as the Baintighearna climbed onto the back of a storm-gray colored horse with glowing red eyes. He stomped the ground with black hooves and snorted as saliva dripped from his mouth. Suddenly dozens more agitated horses ridden by sneering Droch-sìth appeared in the clearing, all watching them disappear in the forest. Over the tops of the trees, she could see huge billowing gray clouds forming, blotting out the sunlight that had just been bathing the stone circle. An unnatural lightning bolt spider-webbed across the sky, and thunder boomed over the forest as a great, dry wind swept down upon them. Silver turned and ran as fast as she could following Laoth into the trees.

Silver and Laoth barreled through the forest. She pumped her arms back and forth and bade her legs to obey as they grew heavier the farther they ran. They jumped over empty, pebble-strewn stream beds and through dried skeletons of towering ferns that exploded as they ran by. All the while, she could hear the snarling of the cù-sìth and the strange baying of some kind of magical hounds. Lightning continued to crackle in the sky above them, but there was no rain, only empty thunder. She could feel the deep thrumming of the demon horse's hooves on the dirt as they seemed to effortlessly keep up with them no matter how erratic Laoth made their path. An unnatural wind following The Hunt violently twisted the tops of the pines in the wake of the Droch-sìth riding on their foaming, red-eyed horses.

They came to a small hill, and Laoth didn't even slow down though he did look back a few times to make sure she was keeping up with him, which she wasn't. She couldn't catch her breath, her foot slipped on some scree, and she stumbled and fell, rolling down the hill. Laoth turned and stomped after her. He quickly pulled her to her feet. "Are you all right?" He was barely breathing hard, she noted irritably.

"Yes," she answered through huge gulps of air. "I don't know how much longer I can run, though."

Just then a cù-sìth came around a tree and charged at them, long streams of saliva hanging from its open maw. Laoth unsheathed his sword and took a step toward the beast. Silver could hear the baying of the hounds getting closer. The cù-sìth leapt toward Laoth in a green blur. He brought his sword up and caught the giant wolf on its shoulder. It whimpered and fell to the ground, but quickly recovered and launched itself at him again. Laoth expertly plunged his sword into the cù-sìth's chest. It made a shrill yelp and fell to the ground and didn't move. He pulled the sword from the dead animal, wiped the blood from his blade, and sheathed it.

"We must hurry," he breathed, taking her arm and pulling her up the hill. She stumbled a few times, but they made it to the top just as the strange hounds and the rest of the cù-sìth found the body of their comrade. Laoth and Silver turned and ran along a rocky ridge, in which direction she had no clue and hoped Laoth knew where he was going. An arrow whistled by her head and stuck into a tree with a thump. She let out a squeak and ran faster.

They came to a line of rocks that connected two fingers of the rocky outcropping they were running along. Silver could hear the cù-sìth, and the hounds quickly approaching as they sent dislodged rocks scuttling down the hill. She looked behind her and could see the

Droch-sìth and their otherworldly horses effortlessly bounding up the hill after them.

"You go first. Watch your footing," Laoth said.

Silver didn't have time to object. The hounds were almost upon them, so she held out her arms for balance and stepped out onto the narrow finger of rock. Despite years of yoga, she was never good at balance and wavered with every step. Laoth was right behind her. The Droch-sìth, and maybe even the cù-sìth, would have to find another way across. The trail was too narrow. That thought gave her a little hope that they might live through the day.

Suddenly she stumbled and fell, grabbing Laoth and pulling him with her as she tumbled down the rocky slope, hitting her knee on a rock as the forest flew by in a blur. When they finally came to a stop, Silver lay on her back in a daze, looking up at the blue sky through the trees. Her knee was throbbing, and she felt a half dozen scrapes on her arms and legs. The hounds were baying and running back and forth on the ridge, looking for a trail down to where they were sprawled on the rocky floor of a small canyon.

Laoth jumped to his feet and pulled Silver into some bushes just as the hounds, one by one, started down the hill. She watched the little clearing where they had landed disappear behind some brown, scrubby bushes. Her feet flailed, trying to find purchase as Laoth dragged her along a wall of rock. Suddenly the Baintighearna's voice echoed around them as if in a dream. She was everywhere and nowhere all at the same time. The fierce wind howled all around them, sending the trees bending in every direction.

"Run! Run, my little sweets for soon, you will be caught and served up to my brave Droch-sìth for our feast and your bones thrown to my loyal puppies!" Her voice was a song in her head and on the air and sent a chill through her body. All she wanted to do was hide from her gaze and that sickly sweet voice. She wanted to cover her ears against the Baintighearna's evil taunting, but she was holding on tight to Laoth's thick arm as he pulled her along.

Laoth found a crevice in the wall barely big enough for them to squeeze through and shoved her in. It was black inside, and she immediately stumbled and fell to the hard cave floor, sending little rocks skidding into the darkness. The weak light from the opening was just enough for her to see Laoth bend down on one knee, bow his head, and softly start casting a spell. His words seemed ancient and almost familiar as he drew invisible shapes in the air at the narrow mouth of the cave dragging his finger into practiced motions. He drew a pouch from a pocket in his tunic and pulled out what Silver thought must be salt that he sprinkled along the floor at the narrow tear in the canyon wall.

She held her breath as the hounds approached, baying loudly, their feet scuffling across the forest floor. The wind was rushing past the small opening in angry gusts. In the distance, she heard the snarling cù-sìth and the screams of agitated horses. Her heart was pounding in her chest and her stomach clenched in fear. She was sure the hounds knew they were hiding in a cave just feet away. Mercifully though they passed by, and when their noisy baying faded into silence along with the wind, Silver let out a breath she hadn't been aware she was holding. Laoth was crouched at the cave entrance completely still.

"Was that a spell?" she whispered.

"Aye," he said and then came to sit next to her. "A spell of conceal-ment. The Baintighearna would have probably seen through it, but her demon hounds are dull-witted." He took a leather waterskin from his belt and handed it to her. "Drink."

She did as he asked, the water tasted like home. He must have filled it up from her kitchen when she was getting her clothes. Suddenly she was overcome with a wave of emotion that broke upon her heart, and she wept as she handed him back the waterskin, her hands shaking. He took a drink and tied it back on his belt, then watched her appre-hensively.

"The Baintighearna will double back as soon as she realizes the hounds have lost our scent. We must move on."

"Right," she sniffled and wiped her face and with Laoth's help, climbed to her feet. She put weight on her knee, and it didn't seem to be as injured as she first thought.

"Can you walk on it?"

"Yes, I'll be fine, let's just get out of here." Instead of leaving the cave, however, Laoth turned toward the darkness, held out his hand, and said a few words, and a small round light appeared and started to float back into the cave. "What is that?" she asked.

"A mage light."

"Of course." Laoth must have noted the sarcasm in her voice because he looked back at her.

"I forgot the world where you grew up is magicless."

"We have a bit of magic."

"Oh, aye?"

"Yes. It's just different…"

"Right," he said, mimicking her expression. She frowned at him, offended, but then was surprised to see his dimples crack his cheeks, disappearing into his dark beard as he smiled at her and gave a snort of laughter, his brown eyes twinkling in the mage light. Her pulse quickened, and her cheeks grew hot as her eyes lowered. She became acutely aware of how close he stood to her, and she could hear his soft breathing before he turned away. "Come, let's find our way out of here. This cave should lead to the other side of the ridge and near the border of the Coille-sith."

They traveled back deep into the cave for what seemed like hours, and Silver's anxiety grew as she wondered if she'd ever see the sun again. Her knee was sore, but she was grateful it wasn't worse. "How do you know we're going in the right direction?"

Laoth pointed down to a shallow stream sluggishly running back toward where they had first entered the cave. "The source of this water should either bring us to a larger river that has cut through the mountain or perhaps an underground lake. If we come upon the lake, we should get some answers there on a way out."

She didn't ask him what answer they might get from an underground lake, but at this point, nothing would shock her. They crept along for another hour or so, the moist, inky darkness fading away under Laoth's mage light as it floated in front of them.

Finally, the passageway they had been walking through opened up into a huge cavern. Their footsteps echoed across a wide distance as they entered. The mage light grew brighter, but the ceiling of the cavern was still lost in the darkness far above them. It was then Silver noticed thousands of huge glowing creatures that looked like worms. Their fat, luminescent bodies undulated along the walls and floor of the cavern as they moved slowly along. Silver lifted her eyes to the ceiling of the cavern, out of the reach of Laoth's mage light, and she noticed there were thousands more of the dog-sized worms moving along the ceiling soaring above their heads.

They walked further into the cavern to the rocky edge of a large underground lake. Silver was surprised to see schools of silvery-white, eyeless fish darting in and out of the blue fingers of Laoth's mage light. The still, black waters of the lake stretched out into the cool darkness. At the edge of the light, Silver could see a small island of rock where a ramshackle hut squatted in the gloom. She had barely time enough to wonder what lived in the shack before her skin started tingling, making her heart jump.

From somewhere in the darkness, the halting, scraping footsteps of some creature hobbled toward them. Silver moved closer to Laoth and grabbed his arm, solid under her grip. She swallowed and tried to quiet her trembling.

"Still yourself. This is who I was hoping to find."

Silver gasped when the creature walked into the light. It was about four feet tall and as white as the fish swimming in the murky lake. Its skin was bumpy, and a sheen of moisture gleamed across its body. It walked on two stubby legs and had four thin arms, which had several bracelets on each and long fingers with rings that glinted in the blue mage light. It held a walking stick yellow with age, that looked suspiciously like a bone, topped with a jawless skull, it's empty eyes staring out into the shadow.

It wore no clothes and was obviously a male. But what was most shocking was it had no eyes. His misshapen head was long and was too big for his lumpy body, and it wore a macabre crown made of tiny bones across his brow. "What luck has brought a mage to me today?"

He hissed through pointed teeth. Then he turned its eyeless face toward Silver. Gold chains hung around a thick neck. "And a witch! Though she be an untrained one."

Despite Laoth's confidence, she trembled and was surprised to feel the warmth of his hand on hers, which still gripped his arm. "We need passage through your cavern to the other side of the Coille-sìth….and a guide."

The pale creature lifted his large head and cackled a moist noise that rattled in his sunken chest. "Of course ye do! Ye surface walkers can't abide under the mountain." He turned his strangely shaped head back toward Silver and pointed one of his fingers at her. His finger-nails were long, gray and caked with mud (at least she hoped it was mud). "Her light shines strongly in the Draoidheachd. Have ye found your long-lost line of Briosag?"

"Aye, and we must be on our way back to Olim, Queen Kahulam is anxiously waiting for our arrival in Saoghal."

"Ye have the other piece of the Medallion of Buhr'ni," he said, ambling closer as one of his thin hands stroked his chin.

"We do, and when we are back in Saoghal, we will be able to bring the rain back to the land."

"Ach! 'Tis been no rain for many moons. Baibh's lake been dry'n up."

"Aye, Baibh, and if we don't get back to Olim, all of your water will be gone by a few more turnings of the moon."

Baibh kneaded his chin for a while longer as if trying to decide what to do with them. Laoth didn't seem worried, but Silver wondered if the creature would eat them and turn their bones into jewelry.

After a minute more of contemplation, Baibh turned his head and shouted out into the darkness, his raspy voice echoing across the invis-ible ceiling far above them. One of the huge glowworms approached them with more speed than Silver thought possible. "Take the humans to the valley opening, and have a care! Watch for the light—ye no want to burn," Baibh instructed his glowworm with a surprising amount of tenderness in his voice.

He turned back toward them, "Be sure to tell yer bànrigh how Baibh aided ye in yer quest."

"I will, friend. The Darhc Order of mages and the Kingdom of Olim owe you a great debt."

They followed the undulating form of the glowworm out of the cavern and into a small passageway. "What was that?" Silver whispered after giving Baibh a backward glance.

"He is an uamh-bòcan—a cave goblin. Despite his seeming simplicity, they are mighty sorcerers. Strong in earth magic." Silver had a million questions, but she was too exhausted to think too clearly, and her stomach cramped with hunger, so she just plodded along.

The glowworm was surprisingly agile and glided right over the boulder-strewn floor of the cave. Overcome with fatigue, Silver stumbled several times, and Laoth caught her from falling, but he gently pushed her to continue, so she struggled after the glowing form of the worm as it led them down an inky path.

Silver was staggering by the time she felt the air become drier and could see a smudge of light up ahead of them. The glowworm suddenly stopped and turned its pale eyeless head back toward them. "Thank you, mistress, cuileag-shnìomhain. You may return to Baibh with the gratitude of Olim." Laoth gave a slight bow, and the glowworm turned and started back the way they had come. She was too tired to even wonder at the strangeness of it all.

Laoth looked at her with concern in his dark eyes. He tenderly brushed a lock of her pale hair out of her face and took her hand in his. They walked in silence toward the golden light that was spilling in through the mouth of the cave. When she got to the rough opening, she saw a large valley, brown under the dry heat of the fading afternoon. The valley was long and wide, and each end disappeared into clusters of brown-leaved trees and parched hills. A broad sandy riverbed carved a sinuous line through the valley. Dead willows lined its banks, the dry fingers of their branches twisting in the warm breeze.

Laoth walked out of the cave and turned to her, handing her the water pouch. "I'm going to set some watcher wards. Try and get some rest."

"You're leaving me?" She was too spent to keep the panic from her voice.

"I'm not going far. Lie down and get some rest. We'll sleep here tonight. I just need to set up some wards and make sure no enemies are near." He took one of the many pouches that hung from his belt, opened it, and pulled out some dried apple pieces and a small chunk of bread. "I will have to set up some snares. I'm sorry, this is all I have. My supplies, including my bow, were all with my horse, so I can't hunt."

She took the food and quickly ate. It tasted horrible, but she was hungry. "Is that who you were whistling for when we first got here?"

"Aye." He nodded his head. "Dìeas the Loyal. I have no doubt he'll find his way home, but it would be nice if he'd find us on his way. It would make things much easier. Now, sleep. I need to set the wards."

Feeling numb, Silver sat on a flat rock at the entrance of the cave and finished her meal—such as it was. Then she folded her legs up and hugged them to her chest, laying her head on her knees and watched Laoth walk down the narrow, rocky path to the foot of the mountain cloaked in dead or dying brush.

The sun had fully set, turning the land into an ash-gray color by the time Laoth climbed the short path back up to where Silver sat waiting for him. While she had been waiting, she had nodded off a few times, almost tumbling down the rock but couldn't relax enough to let herself drift off completely. Laoth walked up to the mouth of the cave, his arms were full of dried branches, and a crow sat on his shoulder. Too weary to wonder about the crow, she hoped he was going to start a fire as it had gotten chilly when the sun went down.

"You should be sleeping," he said rather gruffly. He bent to drop the firewood, and the crow squawked and flew to the boulder next to Silver.

"I couldn't sleep until I knew you were coming back," she replied, eyeing the bird who was looking at her suspiciously.

"You thought I wouldn't return?" His dark brows shot up, and she was sure she had offended him but was too exhausted to care.

"The thought did cross my mind."

Laoth sighed and dropped to his knees. He held out the palm of his hand and said a few twisty words, and a flame sparked. As tired as she was, Silver couldn't stop herself from gasping. Loath lowered his hand, said a few more words she didn't understand, and instantly, the small pile of wood caught fire. He let out a long breath and sat on the ground crossing his legs in front of him. "Would you like to know your story, Silver, ban-Briosag—Lady Sorceress?" He looked at her very intently, the fire casting dancing shadows across his strong features.

Silver went and sat next to him. "Yes," she whispered, but wasn't entirely sure she really did want to know the truth of her and her sister's birth.

The crow squawked and flew down to a scraggly tree at the foot of the path, then quieted down for the night. Laoth stared unfocused into the small flames. He started talking as if in a trance. He must have been as exhausted as she was.

"Before our banrigh—our queen—Kahulam, took the throne of Olim, it was held by a man named Khug. He was eccentric and paranoid in his old age, and he came to distrust magic. He finally decreed it outlawed. Our mage order pushed back, of course, for we had been advisers to the kings and queens of Olim for centuries."

"After a while, the common folk who had always been jealous of magic users started to hunt down mages and witches. Many of them died, and despite repeated appeals to the king by my order and even his own daughter, Kahulam, Khug did nothing."

Laoth's dark eyes slipped over to her, and when she did not ask any questions, he gazed back into the fire and continued. "About that time, a set of twins, young girls, pale skin and hair as silver as the moon, came to the attention of the king. They displayed much power even at their young age, and the king grew fearful of them. Kahulam discovered they were the last of the old bloodline of Briosag, the most powerful sorceresses in all the land. She knew they had to be saved from her father's madness and the bloodline preserved, for she understood the importance of magic."

Silver's heart was pounding in her chest, and her throat ached with tears yet to be shed. She hung on every soft word Laoth spoke.

He took a deep breath and continued, "So Kahulam had a few of the mages of my order weave a spell of forgetting and cast it upon the girls just before they opened a portal to a magicless land and pushed the girls through. In the pocket of the most powerful twin was placed half of the medallion of Buhr'ni, a mighty talisman, in hopes that the other half could one day locate the girls when they were needed."

Silver hadn't realized that she had stopped breathing and sucked in a deep breath. She started to tremble as a feeling of fear crept over her. She and her sister had been adopted as girls, and neither of them had any recollection of the first six years of their lives. Eventually, they gave up trying to recall early memories that they finally figured were best left forgotten.

Laoth closed his eyes and started to chant quietly. He started to move his hands in a circular motion in time with his strange, lilting words. Silver could feel him calling a tremendous amount of energy to him and was afraid. Her skin thrummed as she felt bright energy being pulled from the earth and from the sky! She wanted to leap up and hide but found her legs wouldn't move.

Finally, he opened his eyes and brought his hands to her face. She instinctively closed her eyes, and he tenderly ran his thumbs over her eyelids as he recited a string of words three times.

When he removed his thumbs, she gasped and brought her hands to her mouth. Like a fractured dam that suddenly ruptured, her memories poured over her in ice-cold, vivid waves. She shook violently and sobbed as her life in a far-off world came into focus. A grandmother she never knew lavished love and praise upon her and her sister. She could feel the smugness of a trick learned and a spell remembered and so much energy at her fingertips!

With a gasp, she opened her eyes and looked at Laoth, who was watching her with compassion in his brown eyes. She scrubbed at her soaked cheeks, but the tears wouldn't stop. Carefully, he took her in his arms and she continued to sob not being able to stop herself. *How could she not have remembered?*

When her tears stopped, and she quit trembling, Laoth opened his arms, and she sat up. "We need one from the line of Briosag to save Olim. To save our kingdom." Suddenly Silver missed her sister and wanted more than anything to be with her. "We will have to hope you alone are strong enough to cast the spell of Duhganiz."

LAOTH

Laoth watched Silver sleep as the sun rose over the tops of the red-rocked canyons. Her sleep had been fitful most of the night, but she now slept soundly. They needed to start traveling again, but he couldn't bring himself to wake her, so he just watched her sleep.

She had plaited her long silver hair and tied it with a scrap from the torn hem of her shirt, but several strands had come loose during the night as she slept on the robe that she used as a pillow. Her face was serene now. She must be lost in a peaceful dream. Her ivory skin was flawless, and her face was only lined slightly at the corners of her eyes. He knew from reading reports from her childhood that she and her sister had seen forty-five seasons. From the little he knew of the land she grew up in, she would have been considered middle-aged. His mouth turned up in a smile, for those blessed by the Draoidheachd lived much longer than those that had no talent for magic. She was still quite young.

While setting his watcher wards last night (that thankfully stayed silent all night, allowing him to sleep), he set a few snares. He was happy to find a large hare caught in one of them when he went out to check them this morning. He turned the hare on a makeshift spit over the small fire, his stomach growling at the smell of the roasting meat. The crow had flown off ahead to scout their path and find something to eat.

He rubbed the wound at his side. It was still sore, but he could tell it was healing quickly. He had cast a healing spell late last night when it started throbbing and preventing him from sleeping. The poultice

Silver had made was potent, even though she did not believe in herself. Even untrained, her talent was strong. He had to hope that, even without her sister, Silver had enough power to cast the Duhganiz because if not, Olim, in fact, all of Cruinne-cé were doomed, for they were not strong enough on their own to defeat Nevlin. He must have made some thrice-cursed pact with an ann-spiorad that gave him tremendous power.

His eyes slipped back over to Silver. She turned over onto her back and twisted her head, showing her long, pale neck. He imagined kissing her neck tenderly, and a fierce hunger stirred in him. He lowered his eyes and swallowed hard. How could he even contemplate losing himself in this weakness? He chided himself and prayed to Emul to give him the strength to resist his base instincts. He was too ashamed to pray to Otel and wondered if other mages of his order struggled with the desire for women. If they did, they never spoke of such things.

"That smells wonderful," Silver said as she sat up and stretched. "I didn't think I could sleep on the hard ground, but I guess I was too tired to care." She smiled at him, and his heart started to race. He quickly pretended to be absorbed in cooking the hare.

Silver stood up, tied her robe around her waist, and came and sat by the fire. "You did sleep, didn't you?"

He looked at her, then quickly looked away. "Aye."

"So how long is it going to take us to get to...where did you say we were going?"

"We're going to Saoghal in the kingdom of Olim. Since I've lost the horses, it will take two weeks, maybe." He was angry at himself for losing all three horses and all their supplies, but he was more hurt for losing his beloved Dìeas. Since Laoth knew he wasn't close enough to hear his whistles, he had been mind-calling Dìeas all night until sleep finally took him, but he got no acknowledgment that his horse had heard him at all.

"Two weeks?" Silver gave her clothes a skeptical look. "And since it hasn't rained, I suppose all the water for washing has dried up."

"We might find a few streams or ponds still holding water. I've sent the crow to look for enemies...or water."

"So, you can talk to animals?"

"Aye."

"How?"

Laoth looked over at her and knew he should be using this time to teach her to use her magic. He was reluctant to get emotionally attached, which invariably teachers and apprentices always did. He sighed. He had to think of the good of Olim over his own misgivings about his weakness where she was concerned.

"Alright," he said. "You use your third eye to call out to people or animals, or even spirits you want to contact." Laoth gently touched his finger to the spot on her forehead between her eyes.

"Sometimes, when I would sit out on the beach, I thought I could almost feel the dolphins gliding in the water with such sheer joy, it made my heart leap. But I'd tell myself that I was being silly. And then one would jump out of the water and call to me as if it had heard my thoughts!" She looked up at Laoth and smiled brilliantly taking his breath away.

"You must have been communicating with them on some level and hadn't even realized it." He couldn't help but return her smile.

Silver shut her eyes, and he immediately felt a shout through his mind. He chuckled, and she opened her eyes and gave him a questioning look with her huge gray eyes. "What?"

"You need to be a little more controlled, or everything in the vicinity will hear you. Picture the person or animal you'd like to contact, then send out a quiet greeting. Emotions also bleed into the link, so you must control your thoughts if you are mind-speaking with someone you don't trust."

"Oh," she said a little sheepishly. "Let me try again." She shut her eyes again, and little lines formed across her forehead as she concentrated. Suddenly he heard her whisper into his mind. *Hello, Laoth Tegrehn of the Darhc Order.* He sucked in his breath when a strong feeling of attraction from her washed over him. His heart thumped in his throat, and his loins tightened immediately in answer to her raw emotions.

He cleared his throat and turned his attention back to the cooking hare feeling his cheeks burn. "We're going to have to work on your shielding," he said quietly, trying to deny just how flattered he really was.

As they ate their breakfast, he explained to her how she can shield herself from broadcasting emotions or thoughts and how to focus on contacting a single person or animal or even a spirit. She became withdrawn and told him she could hear the tree spirits crying out for water and filling the area with panic over finding moisture. He then taught her how to shield herself from unwanted emotions and messages.

The sun was high up in the sky when they finally set out down the path. The crow had returned and told him there were no soldiers near. Other birds had told him there was water though it would take them the rest of the day to reach.

All day he taught her basic spells and was greatly encouraged to see she caught on quickly and was soon able to produce a flame and call all sorts of creatures to her. Before long, they had a trail of field mice following them. If he had any doubts that she had been from the line of Briosag, he no longer held them for she was brimming with untested power!

Several times during the day, he caught himself smiling at her with a stupid love-sick grin, his heart soaring as he shared her wonder and happiness at learning a new spell. He was captivated by the way she laughed. It spoke to his soul like the most beautiful piece of music he had ever heard. He knew then he was in dangerous territory. The Silver Witch would be his undoing.

As the afternoon turned to dusk, they found a stream that had once been a river and followed it west through the hills until they came upon a large pond. As the sunset painted the sky orange and pink, they drank their fill, and Laoth filled up his water pouch.

Silver was eyeing a shallow pool partly hidden behind surprisingly green bushes. "I need a bath."

"Be cautious. I will set up the watcher wards for the night and a few snares. You remember how to contact me should you need it?"

"Yes. I'll be fine," she said over her shoulder as she unbuttoned her shirt and walked to the pool. Laoth was careful to shield his desire for her as he quickly walked away to set his wards. The crow had been scouting ahead for them all day but was now resting in a nearby tree. She had assured him no one was near, so he relaxed a bit. They had eaten some chewy strips of jerky Laoth had and all the rest of the dried apple pieces, but they would need something more substantial.

Hoping he'd catch a fat hare or two, Laoth set up several snares and then methodically cast his watcher wards along the parameter of their tiny makeshift camp, warding a much larger area than the night before. He was sure that someone or something would probably be drawn to the water. He wasn't worried about animals, but people would be problematic.

They were still in Tugg, and he wasn't entirely sure how fanatical the locals were about supporting their deranged king, Nevlin. It seems Tugg was as drought-stricken as Olim, though he was sure Nevlin must not be keeping the rain from falling on populated areas of his kingdom. Otherwise, they would have revolted. Casting the Duhganiz was Olim's last hope to save their population from starvation. The wells of Saoghal ran deep and were still providing drinking water, but not enough to water crops.

He was wondering how long Saoghal's wells would still flow when he crested a small hill and saw Silver bathing. He stopped short. He couldn't make his mind work and wasn't sure what he should do. The pale skin of her face, arms, and breasts flashed in the dark water as she swam. Her long, silver hair floated out around her. She stood up, rivulets of water running down the curves of her body. He sucked in his breath as his chest tightened. No matter how hard he tried, he couldn't tear his eyes away from her naked skin as she walked, water lapping at her thighs while dragging her fingers through her hair, trying her best to comb it out.

Laoth clenched his fists as he felt his body responding to her. He cursed under his breath as he finally found the strength to turn away. Why did his desire for this woman burn so hotly? He was long past his reckless youth, he had been a grown man for decades, and it wasn't like he was unused to being around females. True, they did not allow women to join the Darhc Order—they had their own professional orders—he had worked with witches and female mages from other magic orders before, and he had never had such trouble controlling his urges around them. He felt like an undisciplined youth around Silver!

Laoth, come quickly! Silver called to him through mind-speak. He unsheathed his sword and ran down the hill casting out his senses as he went, but could find no other humans about. When he reached the bottom of the hill he saw Silver standing board-straight gazing into a small ball of light. She had gotten dressed, but her shirt was still unbuttoned and lay open. Her gray eyes were wide with astonishment, and she smiled in surprise.

"Look," she breathed, not even pulling her eyes away from the fae as it floated in a ball of golden light. "She's beautiful!"

Laoth sheathed his sword and stood next to Silver. "Greetings, bean-uasal caointeach—Lady Water Sprite," he repeated for Silver. "Do you wish to give us a warning?" Silver looked over at him with concern on her face, but quickly cast her eyes back to the water sprite.

"A warning, yes, though I know you are already aware of the danger the land is in." She cast her bright face at Laoth, and he could feel the strength of her fae magic radiating over him in waves.

"I've come to give the Briosag a gift, for, without it, she will fail. Without her sister, she does not have the power to stop the darkness that is overtaking this land." A tear slipped down Silver's face, and he had to fight not to take her in his arms.

She handed Silver a small, smooth stone with a hole through its middle. The stone glowed in a haunting blue color that pulsed in Silver's hand and bathed her face in its cool light. "A ceaba-sìthe—a faerie stone?" Laoth asked in astonishment.

"Not any ceaba-sìthe, mighty mage, but a hag stone from the banks of the River of Life in the Summerlands." Laoth took a step back in amazement, for the stone was a special one indeed! Silver looked back at him. Her eyes were even wider than before. She must have had some knowledge of the Summerlands.

"I am honored," Silver said and gripped the glowing stone to her bare chest.

"Listen carefully, daughter of Briosag. You will need to cast this spell to defeat the King of Tugg:

The Triple Goddess sings water to me.
The Triple Goddess sings life and light so the land can see.
The Triple Goddess sings, so all may be free.
So mote it be.

"This is one of the last pools left on your journey. I have given the location of the others to your winged helper, Feannag. Use caution when you draw near the army of Tugg, which has just entered the land of Olim."

She narrowed her glimmering purple eyes at Laoth then. "Follow your heart, mighty Warrior Mage, for it will not lead you astray." And then the light disappeared, leaving them standing alone in the moonlight, the orange sparkle of Ùir-dearg just cresting the horizon.

SILVER

Over the next several days, Silver and Laoth traveled northwest, being guided by Feannag the crow, her black wings flashing dark over a blue, cloudless sky. The bird had led them to other pools of water as they traveled. She had been grateful for the chance to bathe. Even Laoth had taken advantage of the rare opportunity to wash the dirt of their travels from himself. Though she tried, she couldn't help it when her eyes fell upon his naked body as he washed. She tried not to be a voyeur, but she had never seen a man built like he was that hadn't been photoshopped. The various scars that decorated his body made him look dangerous and powerful. He wasn't just a magic thrower, he was a warrior.

She had to work very hard to shield her lust from Laoth, and she was sure she hadn't succeeded on more than a few occasions as he was quick to flash her an amused, knowing smile with a twinkle in his dark eyes. His dimples undid her every time. She couldn't hide her attraction to him, and unless she had been very mistaken, he felt the same way. It seemed absurd that they would be entertaining these frivolous desires when the end of Olim was at hand, but the heart wants what it wants. Laoth was no boy, but his hesitance to act on their desire for each other and his obvious lack of experience in flirtation gave her pause.

During their long days, Laoth would teach Silver new magic lessons or a bit of the history of Cruinne-cé—their world—and, more specifically, the kingdom of Olim where she and her sister had been born. She was very interested in the history of the witches and of her and her sister's bloodline.

She was surprised how easily magic came to her. Of course, she and her sister had always been drawn to the arcane from an early age and became witches as teenagers, but the magic was so different on Cruinne-cé. Back home, they acknowledged the wheel of the year, the use of specific herbs and crystals, and cast spells during the ideal times, hoping they could work with certain energies to produce the sought after outcomes. However magic was extremely subtle in her old world and they were always seeking to manipulate energy that was already flowing in the direction they wanted—not completely change the direction of the energy as they did in this world, or charm energy to do their bidding even when it's natural inclination was to do the opposite.

It was exciting to wield this much power! She wished Fionn was with her now. She missed her terribly, and she had tried to talk her sister out of moving so far away, but after her daughters left for college she had needed a change. So Fionn had moved to Italy. She asked Silver to come with her, but her intuition told her not to follow her sister. So she, too, started over by buying that cottage on Deer Island on the east coast. She threw herself into her painting and forgot the outside world.

Silver rubbed her eyes and tried to concentrate. She and Laoth were standing at the edge of a large pond, a brilliant orange sun setting in the mountains in front of them. The land had steadily been climbing for days, and the nights were getting cold.

"Concentrate on what you are telling the water to do." Laoth stood close beside her, his hand resting on the hilt of his sword. She felt the heat of his body on her arm and had to pull her thoughts away from hoping she'd get a glimpse of him bathing tonight. "And keep your thought-shield up," he laughed softly.

"Sorry," she sighed. She closed her eyes and poured all her thoughts into making the water move. *Water is my element, so I should be able to do this*, she thought with frustration, and then realized she had announced that.

You can do it. It just takes a bit of practice, Laoth encouraged her through mind-speak.

At the waterhole they had come across a few days earlier, she had only been able to cause a ripple across the surface. Very unimpressive! She pictured water flowing freely in a riverbed, then pictured each water molecule and how it was structured and then bent and twisted it into the shape she so desired. When she heard Laoth's indrawn breath, her eyes flew open, and she was shocked to see a thick curtain of water hanging right over their heads! She was so surprised that her concentration faltered, and the water fell, drenching them both to the skin.

She looked at Laoth with saucer-shaped eyes, and he had a wide smile across his handsome face, dimples cracking his cheeks. His black hair was plastered to his skull, and little beads of water hung from his dark lashes. They both started laughing hysterically and wrapped each other in a celebratory hug. Laoth pulled her tightly to his solid chest, and she could feel his merriment reverberating through his body. She laid her head on his shoulder, reveling in the feel of his closeness. For the first time in over a week, she felt truly safe.

When the laughter faded, she looked up at him. He was staring at her with such intentness that it took her breath away. Her body was throbbing with a wild energy that seemed to pull her closer to Laoth's body. She had no choice but to answer the call of his hungry energy. He bent and took her mouth in his. Her heart battered the inside of her chest, and all sound faded away. There was nothing in the world but Laoth.

His tongue was fast and insistent as he explored her mouth, and his hands slipped under her shirt and greedily slid across the wet skin of her back. Her body was tight with desire as she hungrily forced her hands under his shirts and deliciously explored his body. His skin felt like raw power and energy, almost burning her fingers. She lost all ability to shield her thoughts, and in fact, sent him a strong wave of white-hot desire. She felt pleased when he staggered slightly under the weight of her sheer need for him.

Suddenly he stopped and pulled her away from him. She looked up at him in a questioning manner as her emotions leaked out of her and blew away on a cool breeze. She saw the lust burning in his dark eyes, but she also saw shame and defeat. "We cannot," he breathed in a husky voice and then turned and walked away.

Her body felt cool where he had just been pressed up against her. The hungry yearning drained out of her like an unstopped sink, and she was overcome with emptiness. As she watched Laoth walk away, he sent her a feeling of such sorrow that it brought tears to her eyes. She was confused and was trembling with unspent energy.

As the sun set, Silver searched around and found enough dead wood for a nice fire. She didn't care whether or not it could be seen by anyone. Let them come, she thought bitterly. She'd either set them on fire or douse them with water in the mood she was in. She was radiating loneliness, and she didn't care who or what heard it. A small speckled mouse timidly scampered from under a bush and jumped up onto her leg, offering what comfort it could.

The red-orange planet Laoth called Ùir-dearg was burning in the night sky when he returned and sat next to her by the fire. "The watcher wards are up and the snares set. Hopefully, we'll have breakfast in the morning."

She didn't reply for she was miffed that he didn't explain what had happened earlier. As she watched the orange tongues of their campfire, she let her hurt and anger ebb out of her and into the night. The mouse crawled up onto her shoulder, gave her a squeak, and then snuggled against her neck.

"My mother is a talented witch," Laoth started to talk as he stared into the flames. "She said she knew I had the Draoidheachd and, in fact, as I grew, I became very strong in magic. All I have ever wanted to do was to join the Darhc Order and serve my kingdom."

As Silver watched him speak, she was filled with compassion and an irrational need to protect him that confused her. He looked so vulnerable. She wanted to say something to him but didn't know what to say so she stayed silent and let him speak.

"My mother taught me everything she knew, and when I turned eight, she sent me to the tower of Deiltre Droaidh—the school of mages." He smiled as he reminisced, and she couldn't help but answer his smile with one of her own as she listened. "They taught me an endless list of spells, some puerile, some peculiar or even heteroclite, and some very powerful, indeed. I had quite a talent for magic, so I excelled. I started my physical training then as well. That was much harder." He chuckled to himself, and she wondered if he had forgotten she was even there.

Then he looked over to her, the firelight casting long shadows across his well-made face. "I learned the sword and bow very well and even to fight with a long spear upon the back of a warhorse. But the magic is what sung to me, always." Silver cast her senses out to see what he was feeling, but his thoughts and emotions were tightly locked away from her, and she was deeply saddened.

When she said nothing, he looked back into the fire and continued speaking in his deep, lilting voice. "When I was sixteen seasons, I was accepted into the Darhc Order. Receiving an invitation from them was a rare honor for anyone, but I was the youngest initiate ever accepted into that order." His legs were pulled up, and his thick arms were bent and lying across his knees. His face was far away, probably reliving his memories of his accomplishments.

"To be a mage of the Darhc Order was the only thing I've ever wanted since before I could recall, so I was very happy to accept my robes and my very own Grimoire to copy down all the knowledge I was to learn and had already mastered." With a pang of loss, Silver thought of her own Book of Shadows sitting on her shelf at home.

Laoth looked back over to her and sighed softly. "Without the Darhc Order I would have no purpose, my life up until now would have been lived in vain and would be meaningless." His poignant, desperate words twisted her heart, and she wondered about their inspiration. Again Silver sent questioning fingers into his thoughts only to find Laoth quite cut off from her.

They traveled steadily northwest, Feannag always scouting ahead, the land growing greener as they walked. "We are following in the path that Nevlin and his army have taken. He makes it rain, so they have water." Laoth pointed at the gouged and upturned earth, scaring the valley floor. The trees lining the valley and meadows were healthy enough to have turned bright shades of red, yellow, and orange.

Each morning they got up at dawn and started trudging forward following great rain clouds in the distance. Water was now plentiful, and they had no trouble finding places to bathe and drink, and their snares always had something for them to eat in the mornings. One afternoon Feannag had swooped in cawing anxiously alerting them to soldiers that were near. They climbed up on a ridge and could see a handful of soldiers out hunting and heading straight for them. Lighting fractured the gray sky, and thunder boomed in the distance. They were close to the army.

"We will need to go around them now. We will give them a wide berth," Laoth said as they scrambled down the other side of the ridge toward a river. It was wide, and Silver could see where it had been a mighty river at one time but was now shallow and the edges lined with large strips of rocky sand on each side. "We will need to cross here." He pointed to where the land rose up to a great brown plateau. "Saoghal is up there."

Silver let out a long sigh. Her feet throbbed and her back was sore after almost two weeks of walking all day. For the millionth time, she wondered where Laoth's 'Dìeas the Loyal' had run off to. He definitely picked the wrong time to disappear. The last few days, the air had turned cold, and a brisk wind always seemed to be blowing in their faces. She had taken to walking faster to raise her body heat to keep the chill away. Last night they had been too close to the army for them to have a fire and Laoth, blast him, would not lay close to her while they slept so she shivered half the night until a large wildcat slunk out of the night and curled up next to her. She was too cold to ask questions, but she soon fell into a deep sleep with the lullaby of soft purring in her ears.

Laoth had been distant and unreachable since that evening they shared that epic kiss. It gave her chills to think about the passion and raw hunger around that kiss, but she pushed it out of her mind with a sour feeling of rejection. She couldn't understand why he was resisting her, but it frustrated and hurt her, and she didn't even try to shield her feelings. *Let him choke on my pain*, she thought, and she was sure he heard.

At the edge of the river, Silver removed her boots and pulled the legs of her jeans up as far as they'd go just beneath her knees. She tied her boot laces together, slung them over her shoulder, and started out across the river. "Careful," Laoth admonished as lightning flashed across the sky, and thunder rolled passed them. Silver could smell the rain in the air, and the breeze turned into a chilling wind.

They were in the middle of the river, the water to their thighs when suddenly Silver was engulfed with alarm. Feannag flew above them, cawing loudly to get out of the river. Silver heard a tree crack and she looked upstream just in time to see a tree being pushed over by a giant wall of water. The riverbed rumbled as boulders were pushed toward them, and the river started to rise.

"Run!" was the last thing she heard before she was hit with such force that she was knocked off her feet and ground into the rocky river bottom. She felt the skin being scraped off her knees and elbows as she fought the current to get to the surface of the water. Over and over she was hit with debris as she was swept along the smooth rocks. Her lungs ached with the need to breathe as she was tossed head over heels. She didn't know which way was up, and she was too distracted to try and cast a spell. She was sure she was going to drown, and despair washed over her like the frigid water that sucked at her feet.

Finally, she broke the surface of the angry water and gulped down huge breaths of air. Not knowing or caring what side of the river she was heading for she just started paddling until she finally felt the rocky riverbed under toes. She struggled against the pull of the water, and soon her strength was zapped but she used the last of her power to haul herself up on the riverbank. The sand was crusted to her arms and face as she choked and turned onto her back. She stared up into the gray sky, thanking the goddess that she had survived.

She sat up as fast as she could and cast her eyes about the surface of the river and the other side of the bank, but she couldn't find Laoth. Her chest grew tight, and her stomach was sour at the thought of Laoth being drowned. She staggered to her hands and knees screaming out, "Laoth!" both in her ragged voice and in mind-speak. She cast out her senses just like Laoth had taught her, but she couldn't feel him anywhere. She wept huge tears and started to tremble as she cried out for him again. She became aware of others, and her heart pounded in her chest as she looked behind her to see she was surrounded by soldiers, their red and yellow cloaks fluttering in the wind.

She was yanked to her feet, and as they violently pulled her up the bank of the river, she looked behind them at the churning water desperate for a glimpse of her warrior mage, but he was gone.

They dragged her barefoot through the brush, and she stumbled several times, but she was unaware, devastated with the agony of losing Laoth. She was dimly aware that she was freezing, bruised and bleeding as they dragged her into the middle of their camp. Soldiers were everywhere as far as she could see. Tents and fires dotted the countryside. Finally, they came to a tent more substantial than the rest. It was dyed in bright colors and hemmed with golden braids and tassels. She was taken inside and thrown to the carpeted floor.

Beating back the haze of pain she looked around the tent. Lamps burned on every horizontal surface, providing plenty of light. With much effort, Silver stood, wavering on her feet. There were a couple of desks piled with papers, a weapon rack full with various swords and daggers, and cabinets stuffed with an array of possessions. A large, ornately decorated wooden chest sat on top of one of the cabinets, the golden clasps closed tightly with a small padlock. On the other side of the tent was a huge bed enclosed with thick drapes and a table for eating. Silver's stomach growled when she thought about food.

Outside, she could hear men approaching, and then three men walked into the tent and up to her. One of them was a head taller than the others, had broad shoulders, and was opulently dressed. He could only be King Nevlin of Tugg.

"This is the woman we found lurking about, sire," one of the men said to him in a self-important manner.

He had straight brown hair that fell to just below his ears and a neatly trimmed beard. Around his neck was a thick golden torc holding a large blood-red jewel that had a bright yellow pentagram scrolled across the surface of the gem. Amazingly the perfect five-pointed star looked naturally formed within the red crystal. Silver could feel immense power emanating from the gem and heard its sweet, clear voice singing like a bird. It took everything she had to tear her eyes away from it.

A bright spark of anger lit in her soul, and she wanted nothing more than to lash out at him for killing Laoth. Common sense told her she could not beat this powerful warlock with only weeks of training. It was best to bide her time until she could be sure a strike would take him out for good. She tightly shielded her thoughts, letting only feigned fear and anxiety purposely leak out like a sieve.

The corner of Nevlin's mouth curled up in a sneer. He took the bait. His eyes looked her up and down, and she could tell he noted her dress, which must have been strange to him. He straightened up and pinned her with a serious look, his blue eyes trying to pierce her mind. She held her true feelings close though, only letting out what she wanted him to know: bewilderment, fear, physical pain, and exhaustion.

"So, Olim has found their lost witches of the line of Briosag. Was another woman found, or anyone else that was with them?"

"No, sire. She was alone. Half-drowned in the river."

He looked over to the man. "Light the torches and take the hounds. Search the river to see if any still live."

"Yes, sire," the man said and was gone.

Nevlin turned to one of the other men. "Take her to the gaoler's tent. We'll behead her in the morning so the whole camp can witness Olim's defeat." At his words, fear did start to eat through her hate. Quick as a snake strike, he reached out and grabbed her wrist. "The Medallion of Buhr'ni," he hissed.

"Nothing but a cheap charm I was given as a girl. I doubt it's even real gold." She pushed a feeling of indifference toward him, but he knew what it was and snatched it from her with an evil laugh. "Ignorant woman. Too bad you know not from where you came, you might have been a worthy opponent." He turned back to the man. "Take her!"

"Should we lock her in iron, sire?"

"Fool, that is a wife's tale, iron won't keep a witch from using her magic. Tie her in ropes. It makes no matter. This one is unskilled in the Draoidheachd."

"Aye, Your Highness." The man clasped her arm in a steel grip and pulled her after him out of the tent and through the camp. The air was thick with smoke from campfires and smells of roasting meat and horse manure. Men were clustered around fires, drinking and laughing. Women crept around in the dark from tent to tent. They all had strange symbols painted on their cheeks and wore their hair twisted into tiny braids, and were dressed in flowing brightly colored robes.

The man took her to a red tent that stood in the middle of a ring of torches. A group of serious-faced men clustered around a fire near the tent. Their guarded eyes watched as she was led into the tent. He threw her down on the dirt floor of the tent and tied her ankles and wrists, tugging cruelly on the ropes, making them tighter than necessary. "See you in the morning, witch!" he sneered and left the tent laughing.

Silver looked around the tent and was relieved to see she was alone. Apparently, there weren't many lawbreakers in Tugg's army. She took a deep breath and shut her eyes. She was so exhausted. How was it that just two weeks ago she was an artist living in a cottage in New England totally bored with her empty life and now she was sitting here in a jailer's tent in a mythical world waiting to be executed in the morning by a black-hearted warlock?

Her thoughts drifted to Laoth, and she started to cry, her body trembling with sorrow. She hoped he had survived the flood but was sure that if he did she would have spotted him. She felt like she was drowning all over again, but this time it was from heartbreak. It was all she could do to keep her emotions from flowing out of her and over the whole camp. It was a long time later when she cleared her mind from her grief. The camp had grown quiet as people slept. A man had come in a few times to check on her, but she heard snoring from outside and assumed they were all asleep.

A few night birds called out into the darkness, and every so often she heard coyotes singing to the moon. Her body was sore and stiff, and she was sure her face was swollen. Her clothes had finally dried, but she was still freezing. She had to get free before morning or it would all be over. Olim's demise would be inevitable. She realized then that she did care about the plight of the kingdom—*her kingdom*.

Silver sat up straight and very discreetly sent out fingers of thoughts to any big-toothed rodents that might be near. She was very careful to keep her thoughts small and precise. Before long she heard a scrabbling at the back of the tent, and a pair of large field rats shuffled into the light. She smiled at them with sheer gratitude. *Please chew these ropes from my wrists and ankles, friend rats.* She pushed desperation and a need for expediency toward them, and they squeaked happily and ran over and immediately started to chew through the ropes.

Silver got to her feet with much effort, her bones aching, and quietly walked to the tent flap. She opened it just enough to peer out. The campfire had burned down to glowing embers, and they lay sleeping under the cold stars. Quiet as death, she slipped from the tent and disappeared into the camp.

LAOTH

Laoth snuck silently through the slumbering camp, his dagger gripped in his hand. He had been mind-calling Silver for hours, but he had to do it softly else that *olc* warlock—a traitor to Draoid-headchd—would hear him. Laoth knew he was near, for he could feel his power; he didn't even try and hide it. He could not feel the power of Silver's half of the medallion, however, and thought that was strange. He hoped Nevlin had just put some kind of cloaking spell on it.

He continued to search for Silver with his mind, but she was either tightly shielding herself, which he hoped was the case, or Nevlin had killed her. His heart pained him at the thought of losing his beautiful silver witch. He would personally end that man if he had harmed her in any way.

Feeling the profound loss of her absence, he let himself admit he had fallen in love with Silver. The Darhc Order be damned! He realized the most important thing in this life was not magic. It was Silver. He would single-handedly conquer all of Tugg's army without a drop of magic if he could just save his beautiful witch. He moved with focused silence through the camp, easily the most dangerous man there.

He had sensed Dìeas was near but had to find Silver before he went after his horse. He was being kept with all the other horses so he figured he'd be easy enough to find. His thoughts turned to Silver, and he tried again to contact her, but there was nothing. His throat tightened in fear and pain.

Again, letting worry for Silver seep into his thoughts, he slipped around a corner of a tent and ran into someone. Like a flash, he grabbed the man and put his dagger to this throat, then gasped and dropped his weapon.

"Silver!" He took her into his arms, awash with relief. She clung to him and trembled. His gut tightened with the overwhelming need to protect her and get her as far away from Nevlin as possible.

"I thought you were dead." She looked up at him, tears streaming down her bright face. He noticed one of her cheeks was swollen and bruised.

"Did they hurt you?" he growled and tenderly touched her cheek.

"No. It was from the water." She leaned up and kissed him on his lips. "I was so frightened you had drowned."

"I almost did! I was washed to the other side of the river. When I woke up, it was dark already. I crossed the river and found a place where I could make out the tracks of your bare feet and those of the soldiers. I knew they'd take you here. I'm just so glad I found you."

"You mean, *I* found *you.*" She smiled up at him, and he chuckled softly, undone by her huge gray eyes that looked dark in the moonlight. "Laoth, we have to get my charm," she said, bringing him out of his trance.

"They took the Medallion of Buhr'ni?"

"Nevlin has it."

"That's not good." He finally released her from his arms as he tried to think of a plan.

"He has a locked chest in his tent, and I'm sure that's where he'd keep it."

"We just need a diversion, then," Laoth said, thoughtfully.

"We could ask all the animals out there to come into camp and chew everyone's eyeballs out," she snarled.

"We could….but that would take too long. I could ask Dìeas to help whip the other horses into a frenzy and send a stampede through the camp. That will get that thrice-cursed warlock out of his tent long enough to get that chest."

"You found Dìeas?" Silver grinned.

"Aye. Now let's find Nevlin's tent." He bent down and retrieved his dagger.

"C'mon, I'll show you where it's at."

It took them half an hour to get to the massive tent in the middle of the camp. Laoth had to quietly dispatch several men guarding the tent and had taken a couple of their cloaks to help him and Silver blend in with the rest of the populace. Laoth was sorely tempted to go into Nevlin's tent and just put an end to him now, but he knew the warlock had somehow gotten his hands on a clath-tholl—an enchanted witch stone—that gave him more power than Laoth and Silver could overcome without casting the spell of Duhganiz, which had to be cast in a certain place at a certain time.

Silver and Laoth stood in the dark shadow of the king's tent and quietly called to the horses inviting them to dash for their freedom. It wasn't long before they heard the screams of horses echo across the darkness. Men shouted and women screamed as the beasts broke from their temporary corrals and galloped through the camp tossing tents as they sped by.

They heard Nevlin curse and start barking orders. After they were sure he had gone to see what was happening, Laoth cut a hole in the back of his tent, and they slipped in. Silver ran over to the ornate box sitting on one of the desks. "This has to be where he's keeping it." Now that they were close he could feel the other half of the medallion thrumming with magic.

She reached out to touch it, but Laoth grabbed her arm. "Nevlin will have certainly put wards upon something so valuable. We must be cautious. Watch the entrance and alert me if anyone comes near." He closed his eyes and concentrated on unweaving the complicated magical strands that protected the chest. By the time he was done, he was bathed in sweat and shaking with exhaustion. He waved his big hand, and the small lock sprung apart, falling in pieces onto the desk. That had been the easy part.

Silver walked up to him with concern in her eyes. "I'm fine," he reassured her. "Those wards were complex and took much energy to unknot." He opened the box and among other small magical items lay the Medallion of Buhr'ni, which he handed to Silver. She smiled up at him and placed it in the pocket with the hag stone. "We must hurry. Nevlin surely felt me unlock his wards." Laoth took Silver's hand in his, and they slipped out of the back of the tent just as a group of men ran in the front.

With the cloaks and helmets that they appropriated from dead soldiers, they walked right out of camp without being noticed. Dìeas stood in a copse of withered trees waiting patiently for them. He whinnied excitedly when Laoth approached and rubbed his soft, fuzzy nose. "'Tis good to see you again, my friend," he said, and they climbed up on his back and rode away quickly. They crossed the river that had lost all of its swell and bravura and climbed up onto the tree-lined plateau.

When Laoth felt they were far enough away from the camp they stopped to rest. He went around setting snares and wards, asking the forest creatures to also keep watch for them. By the time he returned to Silver his heart was happy and satisfied. He spread out their stolen cloaks, and they laid down upon them. He took her in his arms and kissed her urgently. She was warm and sweet, her essence called to him, and he answered. He could no more resist her than stop breathing.

With primal urgency, they undressed each other, and his hands hungrily slid across her naked flesh. She awoke in him a lust that could not be sated without taking her completely, body and soul. With no regrets, he made his decision. He would claim this woman. As the sun rose, singing the land into wakefulness, he took her, and his spirit finally became whole, soaring high above the orb of Cruinne-cé.

SILVER

Two days later they rode into Olim filthy, hungry and exhausted. They were immediately admitted into the city gates and escorted through the wide, cobbled streets and up to a hill and over a bridge spanning a wide moat. As Dìeas clomped over the wooden structure, Silver looked down into the dark water below and was shocked to find it writhing with a serpent!

They were taken up to a large room high within the castle. Everything was a blur to Silver as her senses were overwhelmed. "Stay strong, my Lady Silver," Laoth whispered into her ear, and then he was ushered out by a group of old men in lavish robes and tall hats. Suddenly she was gripped with trepidation as she watched Laoth disappear behind an opulent spill of draperies. She realized she was all alone, and her stomach clenched, and she nervously clasped her hands together before her.

A pair of young women came up to her and led her out of the room, down a long hall and into a spacious bedchamber where there were more women laying out food and clothing and tending a fire. She was led to a well-appointed bathroom tiled with white and gray marble. A pool of steaming water sat in the center of the room under a large window. "After you've bathed and eaten, the queen is anxious to talk to you, my lady," one of the girls said, and then they left her alone to bathe.

In a daze, Silver undressed and eased herself into the warm scented water. She found perfumed soap and shampoo and silky soft sponges. Her mind kept drifting to Laoth, and she wondered if he too was sitting in a warm bath of his own. She wished they could be enjoying this together.

After that first morning when Laoth had come to her full of lust and emotion, they had shared each other several more times during their short journey to Saoghal. However, when they entered the gates, she could feel him start to pull away. He shielded himself from her and did not hold her hands or rest his arm on her legs as they rode as he had been doing. She was worried and knew something was wrong. She was anxious to see him again.

After she bathed, the women helped her dress in an elaborate combination of skirts, a heavily embroidered bodice, and lace and ribbons. They brushed out her hair, braided it, and found a pair of slippers that fit her perfectly. They also gave her a small silk pouch to hold her half of the Medallion of Buhr'ni and the hag stone—or the ceaba-sìthe—as the caointeach had called it. She tied it to a braided silver belt she wore around her waist. Quickly she ate and then requested to see Laoth and was told he was in council with the queen already.

Finally, Silver was taken back to the hall where she and Laoth had been separated hours before. Several of the old men, their thick, brightly colored robes swishing in agitation, were talking to Laoth in sharp, angry voices, but when Silver came near, they all quieted down. Laoth had bathed, and his hair and beard had been neatly trimmed. He was wearing a green tunic and black trousers and shiny black boots that came up to his knees.

They looked deeply into each other's eyes, and Laoth gave her a tiny, sad smile, his dimples barely marking his cheeks. She smiled back at him and let her deep, wild love pour out into the hall and did not care who could hear it. Laoth's smile widened, but the old men scowled and stepped farther away from her as if her emotion had offended them. She didn't care, for it was as if Laoth was the only one in the room.

"Lady Silver, I see you have washed up. I trust they fed you?" A woman spoke in a calm but commanding tone. Silver looked over to her, sitting in a wide chair. She hadn't even noticed her until then.

"Um, yes, thank you," Silver replied.

The woman was perhaps in her mid-sixties, and despite her strong nose and chin, her beauty had not yet faded. Her brown hair, thickly veined with gray, was braided into an intricate pattern and pinned to her head, and she wore a thin golden circlet on her brow.

She stood and walked up to Silver. "I am Kahulam, Queen of Olim. You are well come, Silver, Daughter of Briosag.

Silver felt like a deer caught in the headlights. She didn't know what the correct protocol was, so she gave her a small smile and a slight curtsy. "Merry meet, Queen Kahulam."

"Master Laoth has told us of all the perils you faced on your journey to Saoghal. But here you stand, triumphant."

"It was through no effort of my own, Your Highness, it was Laoth that got us here safely. He saved my life several times." Silver looked over at Laoth, who was standing rigidly, looking back at her with a pained expression.

"Thank you, Master Laoth, for your bravery and sacrifice to the realm. Your heroism will not be forgotten. You are dismissed." The queen had a feeling of regret about her, and Silver wondered at its cause.

"Thank you, Your Highness." Laoth bowed and walked out of the hall. Again Silver was gripped with panic and a deep feeling of loneliness as he was being escorted out by guards. She knew something was definitely wrong.

Silver turned around and was about to ask the Queen where Laoth was going, but the older woman spoke first. "We have much to do before Samhain. I have instructed the most talented from both the Darhc Order of mages and the Raidseach Order of witches to prepare you as much as they can before you are required to cast the spell of Duhganiz at sunset on Samhain eve. Let us all hope your talent is such that we will not need your sister." Silver wanted to question her, but the queen continued. "You may leave now to start your training, for we only have two days until Samhain eve." With that, the queen and her court of fancy ladies flounced out of the hall.

Silver was taken to a tower in the castle, and her education began immediately. There were three men and three women who gave her long lectures about the basics of magic until the moon was high in the dark sky. She stumbled to her bed that night exhausted and craving Laoth.

The next morning she was awoken early, fed a breakfast of fish, fruit, seedy bread, and thankfully strong coffee, and then was quickly taken back up to the instruction room. The old men in their important robes and hats that stuck up obscenely were not present. The three women were lighting the many lamps around the room bathing it in a warm, golden color.

One of the women was around Silver's age, and the other two looked to be in their seventies. Silver was relieved to find the haughty old men hadn't arrived yet. She was hesitant to ask about Laoth, but after a few minutes, she found she couldn't help herself. "Will Laoth be joining us today."

The women gave each other guarded looks, and one of the older ladies spoke up. "Master Laoth will not be joining us. He is no longer in the city." Her face was blank, but when she looked over at the younger woman Silver saw empathy in her brown eyes.

"What? Where is he?" Silver didn't even try to keep the panic out of her voice. Just then, the heavy wooden doors swung open, and the men entered, their faces full of self-importance. Laoth was not mentioned again.

All morning she was taught lessons in energy manipulation that were alarmingly intricate, but Silver amazed herself by mastering it all quickly. She could tell her fellow witches were pleasantly impressed, but the old mages never let their pretentious expressions slip from their gray, wrinkled faces. Silver had taken an instant dislike to them and had to fight with herself to keep her mind free of negative energy lest she taints the spells she was working on.

After a quick lunch, she started to learn the twisty, complex words that made up the Duhganiz spell. It was long and tedious, and she prayed to the goddess that she'd remember the words in the right order, so they weren't all doomed.

Silver was exhausted, but she felt she couldn't speak freely with the mages in the room, so she decided to wait until after they had left to ask her questions. It was after midnight when the mages finally packed up their ancient, golden-bound grimoire with its thick, gilded pages and left the room.

Timidly Silver asked the witches for their names. The oldest one was called River, and her younger sister was Tilly. The youngest was named Kylwinn. Emboldened, Silver asked the witches about the enchanted witch-stone that Laoth called a clath-tholl that Nevlin wore around his neck.

River answered with a worried look on her kind face. "It could have only come from a demon from the Shadowed Lands. He must have struck a deal with one of those thrice-cursed spirits."

"Why would they care to deal with him at all?"

"They are mischievous and easily bored. It could have been that it just wanted to see a bloody war for its amusement," Kylwinn said.

"But you can be sure the demon asked him for something mightily precious to him in exchange." Tilly chimed in.

Further bolstered, Silver blurted out what she really wanted to know. "Why did Laoth leave Saoghal?"

The witches looked at each other with alarm, and, at first, she thought they wouldn't answer, but a look of decisiveness washed over Kylwinn's face. "He was expelled from the Darhc Order, my lady, and asked to leave the city."

Silver was horrified. "Why?"

The women exchanged glances again. "For having congress with a woman," Tilly said.

"I'm sorry...what?!"

"An incredible waste, Laoth was the most talented of all them!" Tilly shook her head, making her jowls wiggle as if she hadn't even heard Silver.

"Those grandiloquent fools think that a man's magical energy is polluted by a woman's body. They do not allow mages of their order to marry or even have relations with a woman!" Kylwinn's words were full of anger but paled in comparison to what Silver felt.

"Which is, of course, is untrue since there are plenty of powerful mages of other orders who are married. But the Darhc Order has been around for millennia and have historically been the most powerful politically so, as men do when they are left alone to contemplate their own greatness, they create a plethora of idiotic rules that only the most fanatical can follow," River said, as she picked up her Book of Shadows. "Now, get some sleep tonight, my lady. Tomorrow is Samhain eve, and all day we will be consecrating the altar and the ritual area within the standing stones. You will need your strength. You will be casting the Duhganiz at sunset."

River and Tilly walked to the door. "Good night, sisters. Tomorrow we save the Cruinne-cé!" And with that, the two witches left in a flurry of green and golden robes.

Silver looked over at Kylwinn with a desperate look on her face. "When he shared his body with you, he knew he was forfeiting his position in the Darhc," she finally said. "And no other order will accept a shunned mage."

"Where is he, Kylwinn, please tell me."

"I have not a clue. I have heard his parents have a farm to the east. He might have gone back there to try and help as all the farms in Olim are suffering." She shrugged her shoulders.

Silver's eyes fell to the floor, she felt sick to her stomach, and her throat tightened at the thought of never seeing Laoth again. She couldn't hold back the tears from streaming down her face. She looked back up at Kylwinn. "How can I find him?"

The witch took a deep breath and sighed it out again. "The same way he found you, my lady, with the Medallion of Buhr'ni."

Silver ran out of the tower and into a large garden. A full moon hung in the indigo sky scattered with twinkling stars and the orange shimming sphere of Ùir-dearg. She pulled her cloak tighter around her body and ran into the dry, dying garden. At the edge of the garden were a huge wall, an empty pond and a spacious clearing that looked like it might have been used for celebrations at one time.

Silver sat on the brown grass and cried. She was exhausted, physically and mentally. She had almost died several times in the last month, had her childhood memories returned to her, fallen in love and had her heart broken, and had a crash course in High Magic. She was being crushed under the weight of what was expected of her and didn't think she could do what was needed. She wished Fionn was with her. She felt so alone.

Huge tears ran down her cheeks as she sat in her misery under the moonlight. She took her half of the medallion out of her pouch and squeezed it in her fingers. *Where is he*, she begged it, but it lay still and cold in her palm. *I can't do this without him. But how can I find him? I don't know this land.* An owl hooted in a tree somewhere, and it gave her an idea. She scrubbed the tears from her face and stood up.

There were many magical creatures in this world, surely one that could travel over great distances in a short time. She took a deep breath, shut her eyes, and cleared her mind. She set her intention of flying over the countryside looking for Laoth and then sent out an urgent call for any large creature with wings to come and give her aid. Time seemed to creep by as she waited, pacing up and down the clearing, the dead, frozen grass crunching under her slippered feet.

Suddenly she heard the swoop of wings and felt a powerful wave of energy flow over her. She turned around as a dragon gracefully landed in a beam of soft moonlight. Silver's heart thumped in her chest as her brain tried to make sense of what she was seeing. A dragon stood before her! She could feel from its—her—energy that she was not an enemy, so she boldly walked up to her.

Greetings, Daughter of Briosag. I am Uilepheist, how may I be of assistance to ye? The great dragon's scarlet scales shivered in the pale light, and Silver could feel limitless power exuding from her. She was the most stunningly gorgeous creature she had ever laid eyes on and found it hard to think.

Silver bowed deeply and then stood and looked into Uilepheist's golden, swirling eyes. "Merry meet, Lady Uilepheist. I am seeking a mage, and I must find him soon. I need him to help me cast the spell of Duhganiz and save Cruinne-cé."

A coarse chuckle rumbled low in Uilepheist's long throat. *'Tis not for the Duhganiz ye seek this mage*, she chided. *Ye seek him for love, for ye have all that ye need to save Olim within ye.*

Silver stood up straight and lifted her chin. "Perhaps I am strong enough in the Draoidheachd to defeat the King of Tugg, but I need Laoth for more than just his magic."

Ye humans are emotional animals. Uilepheist laughed again and then stretched out her massive forepaw and opened her fingers tipped with black claws as long as a man. *Let us fly, Daughter of Briosag, and find your mage.*

"Thank you, Uilepheist, the Magnificent!" A feeling of satisfaction and hauteur emanated from the dragon, and it made Silver smile. She climbed into the dragon's paw, and with a heart-stopping vault, they were gliding through the frozen wind with the silent beats of her tremendous wings. She gripped the medallion in her hand and concentrated on Laoth's half, hoping the mages of Darhc had not taken it from him. She didn't think so, though, as she didn't feel that it was still in the castle.

They glided over vast fields parched and dead and gently rolling hills with copses of stubborn trees. A few small villages rolled away as they flew. Finally, the medallion started to warm and hum and as they traveled in the right direction it heated up even more. Uilepheist seemed to be aware of the medallion's magic directions, for she changed course ever so slightly as it sung into the Draoidheachd.

Finally, they floated past a village and over one of the empty fields that it surrounded. As they got closer to a particular farm the medallion piece grew so hot it burned into Silver's palm, but she refused to let it go. Uilepheist landed before an old barn and opened her massive paw letting Silver jump down. She looked around but felt sure Laoth was not in the house, so, she started toward the barn.

Suddenly Laoth was standing in the dark doorway. Silver stopped short and caught her breath. He walked out into the moonlight in only his breeches, the curve of his broad shoulders and muscled chest glowing in the pale light. She ran to him and he caught her up in his strong arms.

"Why did you leave me?" she cried into his neck.

"I had to, Silver. You needed to concentrate on learning, and I would have been a distraction." His breath was warm in her hair.

She looked up into his eyes and could see pain. "Do you love me?" Tears rolled down her cheeks freely.

"More than anything in this world," he whispered and opened himself up to her until she felt the depth of his emotion. Their excited, glowing energy mingled and fused together. They both sucked in a sharp breath at the intensity of the melding. Laoth looked at her with wonder and awe, and a smile spread across his handsome face.

Laoth took his half of the medallion from his pocket and held it up. Silver joined her half, and the two pieces knitted together instantly. The whole medallion started to glow, and a poignant, lilting song floated out from it over the farm and into the fields and hills and then it was quiet and grew cool.

Silver clasped Laoth's hand, and they interlaced their fingers sharing each other's power. "Let those pompous old men say what they want. We are stronger together!" Their energy was crackling and sweeping around them in swirls, blowing ribbons of Silver's pale hair out behind her. Together Silver knew they could defeat Nevlin and whatever demon he chose to summon. No one would dare separate them again!

LAOTH

They flew back to the castle riding upon the scaled back of Uilepheist. Laoth had only heard of people riding on dragons in the heroic tales of myth, so he was overcome with gratitude and awe. It was still hours before sunrise by the time they sunk into Silver's narrow bed in the tower. They explored each other's bodies and took their pleasure and then fell into a deep sleep as exhaustion came over them.

In the morning when a surprised maid woke them they were groggy and still in need of sleep but roused and dressed, for today would be the most important day in Olim's history. They had to be successful in casting the spell of Duhganiz and shattering Nevlin's clach-tholl so that Olim's witches and mages could use their magic to defeat Tugg's vast army that was now spilled out across the plateau before Saoghal. Olim's army, hopelessly outnumbered, were poised to meet them in battle, though it would be futile if Olim couldn't use magic to even the odds.

Silver and Laoth walked hand in hand up the hill to a broad, flat area where a circle of giant standing stones stood tall. The holy place was called Tursa and was used for rituals to mark the sabbats. Today was Samhain eve, and today he and Silver would cast Duhganiz and, if it worked, would release the spirits of Olim's past warriors, for the veil between the worlds was at its thinnest today. Nevlin's clach-tholl was a thing of the spirit world, and it would take a spirit to destroy it.

A large crowd of all the orders of witches and mages in Olim parted to let Silver and Laoth through. Inside the standing stones were the Darhc Order of mages and the Raidseach Order of witches preparing for the ritual. They were all wearing plain white robes cinched at the waist by a braided length of corn husks that had been soaked in oil and made pliable. They wore crowns of rowan branches and orange flowers on their heads.

Queen Kahulam was sitting on an ornate chair with a high back in the middle of her coterie of magic wielders. She was wearing an unadorned red robe and a twist of sunflowers on her crown. She would pray and fast with the rest of them this Samhain eve.

They all turned and gaped when Silver and Laoth walked into the circle, fingers entwined. The mage's wrinkled faces twisted into scowls, the witches were all smiling smugly. Silver lifted her chin in defiance.

Grot, the archmagi, rushed forward, pointing his gray finger at Laoth. "He may not enter the Tursa! His presence here will offend the gods!"

"He *will* enter! Master Laoth will be taking my sister's place in casting the spell of Duhganiz with me." Silver squeezed his hand, and he sent her a feeling of pride.

"He is polluted and is now a master of nothing! And besides, he's been expelled from the Darhc and thus forbidden to practice High Magic. If he chooses to use what's left of his magic now, he is nothing more than a warlock!" The archmage stuck his nose up in the air, clutching his robes tighter around his pudge, daring Silver to defy him.

"You supercilious old fool! Laoth is not less of a mage because he used his manhood." The witches snickered, the younger ones hiding their amusement behind their hands. The mage's eyes all grew wide in shock. "He is stronger than any of you, and you all know it." She thrust their clasped hands up in the air. "We are stronger together, and we will cast this spell together. If you don't like it, leave."

Gasps came from the group of mages, and even the witches were quiet now. "You aren't even one of us!" the archmage howled. "You are but an apprentice witch and your femininity is clouding your vision." Laoth could feel Silver's outrage pour out over him and he sighed. The archmage would be sorry, indeed.

Silver let Laoth's hand drop and in a flash was standing before the archmage staring up into his pugnacious face. "He is *Master* Laoth, and I am a Daughter of Briosag!" A ring of fire sprung up around the arch-mage, and a hot wind circled around him sending tongues of flames twirling up into the sky. The archmage's terrified scream pierced the silence, and then Silver dropped her hands, and he was doused with a sheet of water, the fire, and wind dying out immediately, leaving the man drenched and wide-eyed. Silver, however, was perfectly dry.

It was then that Laoth noticed the queen was standing next to him.

"I think Lady Silver won that pissing contest, Master Grot," she said sardonically. "Master Laoth will stay, and if anyone has a problem with that—and survives the wrath of Lady Silver—take it up with me! Now, let us prepare!" Queen Kahulam ordered in a loud voice then walked back to her makeshift throne and sat down with a huff.

As the sun crept across the sky the altar was set up with sheaths of corn and heads of wheat, apples, squash, and pomegranates (all harvested last season since nothing had grown this year for lack of rain). Included also were sprigs of rosemary and mugwort, and rowan branches heavy with little red berries, and huge sunflowers that were grown in the royal gardens and watered from one of Saoghal's wells. The rest of the magic practitioners in Saoghal spent the afternoon in meditation and prayer to the Crone Goddess and the Horned God, clearing their minds in preparation for the battle to come.

Finally, as the sun was setting on Samhain eve, Silver and Laoth prepared their circle. In a clockwise direction, Laoth smudged the small area with sage while Silver went behind him with an ornate besom and symbolically swept the negative energy from their work area. Laoth sprinkled water from a consecrated well, and Silver formed a perfect circle with salt and herbs. Laoth laid a trail of quartz, obsidian, tourmaline, calcite, and dragon's blood jasper all around the inside line of the salt. He and Silver both called to the directional spirits inviting them to join their ritual scribing glowing pentagrams in the air as they went, and then Silver started a small fire in the middle of the circle with just a twitch of her hand into which Laoth threw dried rosemary and mugwort.

Then they sat and joined hands and started to chant the lilting, rhyming words of the spell of Duhganiz, calling to the souls of slain warriors of Olim. A rotten smelling mist ate up the ground in the standing stones and then out to the whole flat area filled with chanting witches and mages each adding their energy to the ghost army.

Shapes of men started to form in the mist, each holding a ghostly longsword. Soon thousands of them glided to and fro over Saoghal. By the time the Duhganiz was cast it was night, and despite the cold, Silver and Laoth were bathed in sweat and breathing hard. Laoth's heart slammed in his chest, and he was aware of Silver's racing as well. As one they stood and thrust their hands in the air. "Toiteal—attack!" they screamed together.

The ethereal army raced down through Saoghal and over the wall and out to battle. All the witches and mages stood and thrust their arms into the air yelling "Solas—light!" Huge balls of light flared over the battlefield throwing the plateau into daylight. Both armies were expecting it and charged forward. With the addition to the ghoulish army, Olim was no longer outnumbered.

They all had a perfect view of the battle raging below them. Shouts and clashing swords drifted up to them on a foul wind. Laoth could see Nevlin's ornate tent pitched on the outskirts of the battle, it glowed and all could hear his evil chanting, even from that distance, as his spells were carried on the wind giving his army unnatural strength and speed. The screams of the dying were also carried up to them, and a look of horror crossed Silver's face.

Olim's soldiers were being stuck down with alarming speed, and it was clear they would lose. "I forgot! The hag stone!" Silver cried and reached for a pouch tied to her belt. She turned the pouch over, and the little gray stone tumbled into her palm, it's perfect hole looking up at him like an eye. Laoth had almost forgotten all about the ceaba-sìthe that the caointeach had given her.

Silver cupped her hands over the stone, closed her eyes, and chanted three times:

The Triple Goddess sings water to me.

The Triple Goddess sings life and light so the land can see.

The Triple Goddess sings so all may be free.

So mote it be.

Each time her words got louder and filled with emotion until her spell mingled with Nevlin's, echoing across the plateau. Suddenly the earth began to quake, and frightened gasps went out. From the castle, there were shouts and screams at the quaking, and the battle below stopped. Nevlin's tent exploded in fire, and even from where they stood they could hear his cries of pain. Abruptly the shaking stopped, and the flames went out, and no trace of the tent, or the smoke, or of Nevlin remained!

Spent from the unnatural energy from the Shadowed Lands the whole of Tugg's army fell dead. Silver took Laoth's hand in hers as they stared out at the plateau in shock. And then the rain came. Great sheets of water fell from a bloated sky casting everything into shades of gray. An earth-shattering shout from below went up, and the witches and mages joined their voices as they all danced in the rain.

Laoth pulled Silver into his arms, their joined energy keeping them warm as the icy rain washed the salt and herbs of their circle away and down into the riverbeds that would soon be flowing again through Olim.

SILVER

A warm spring breeze ruffled the long, sheer curtains framing the wide opening of the balcony high up in the Tower of the Dràgon. She and Laoth had just finished moving their things up to their suite in the newly completed tower. The scent of honeysuckle and jasmine filled the air along with the melodies of thousands of fat, happy birds. The land was healthy and green, and the crops were already promising to be the best harvest in generations. The lochs and rivers were full, and the trees sang their happy melodies through the web of energy that connected them all.

Queen Kahulam had ordered the construction of the Tower of the Dràgon as soon as the rain had stopped three days after the War of the Faerie Stones, as the people were calling it. Uilepheist had even attended the dedication ceremony when the tower was completed only a few weeks earlier. To the dragon's pleasure, much praise and adoration, as well as shiny treasures, were heaped upon Uilepheist, and she had soaked it all up.

The tower had been completed quickly with the aid of magic and was home to a new school of magic and the newly formed Order of Foghan-Sil; consisting of both witches and mages. The Foghan-Sil replaced the Darhc Order as Royal Council. Silver felt vindicated that the Darhc had faded into obscurity so quickly.

Laoth walked up behind Silver and wrapped her in his arms. She leaned her head back against his shoulder and let out a sigh of contentment. "Are you happy here, Silver?"

"Of course." She twisted her head around and looked up at him.

"I'm glad, for I would have hated it if I had to follow you back into your world. It seemed quite mundane for my tastes."

She laughed. "Mine, too, my love." She sighed again, sadly this time. "Though I miss my sister and nieces terribly."

"Well, about that..." Silver turned around and looked up at him. Her pale brows rose in question. "I've just come from a meeting with Queen Kahulam. When I told her how much you missed your family she suggested we go look for them and see if they'd be willing to come back with us. After all, they are the Daughter of Briosag as well and belong on Cruinne-cé, if they are so inclined."

Silver felt tears well in her eyes, and gladness washed over her at the thought of bringing her family back to Olim. "There's so much we need to do before we leave!" Silver pulled out of Laoth's arms and started back toward their dressing room to pack.

He quickly caught her up. "There's actually only *one* thing we need to do just now." He took her mouth in his, and she was easily convinced he was right.

Melissa has been writing books since before she had learned to read, in the form of picture books, and planned to be an author at age four. She spent her youth penning short stories, poems, and writing in her diary. At nineteen, she married her high school sweetheart and started her family. She has spent her adult life raising her three children and teaching herself the business and craft of writing. Born and raised in beautiful Southern California she and her husband now live along the Ohio River in Indiana to be near their beloved grandsons, Bryar and Luther.

Melissa had a spiritual awakening in 2018 and now walks the lush, green, happy path of a pagan. In 2019 she started Raven's Roost Boutique (a witchcraft and pagan supply website) with her youngest daughter and sister (https://ravensroostshop.com/). She also writes all the articles for the Raven's Roost Acadamey, the educational portion of Raven's Roost.

Melissa enjoys the outdoors and nature, especially camping. She has an interest in the natural world, particularly the wonder of birds and bugs. She loves art and paints a little herself. She has a great interest in history and plans on trying her hand at historical fiction in the future. Someday she hopes to travel the world, starting with Scotland, Ireland, Africa, and Australia.

Melissa loves to listen to heavy metal, Irish rock, and Celtic music…well, anything Celtic really. Most days you will find her tapping away at her keyboard, doing research for her next great novel, or catch her with her nose stuck in an epic fantasy or historical fiction story.

Website: http://www.melissaebeckwith.com/

facebook.com/AuthorMelissaEBeckwith

twitter.com/M_E_Beckwith

instagram.com/author_melissa_e_beckwith

WHEN THE CROW CALLS

BY TRISH BENINATO

PROLOGUE

There was music in my head again, the same melodic sound playing over and over. It was gut-wrenchingly sad, and then it was breathtakingly joyous. It made me giggle and weep, and it tore at my heart as it sang of love, happiness, pain, and death. It made me sway and weave my arms as it echoed inside my thoughts, but once it was over, I never could recall it again. As if its tune never existed. And yet, it had always been there.

My history, my real history, was still a haze. I only had bits and pieces, but I knew somewhere out there I belonged. I once thought they would come for me. I waited, hoping. No one came. No one told me where I came from or who left me, so I stopped asking.

Day after day, as I was passed from house to house, and foster parent to foster parent. I held onto those memories, even as each person I was given to found something lacking in my young personality. Some of the foster parents were okay, some were bad, and some were a nightmare. But there were stories that felt like memories, little fractured glimpses of something. They never made sense, but I always believed it was just the mind of a child trying to make sense of what little I once had.

I remembered a woman, tall and beautiful, with dark hair like my own and eyes as blue as a cobalt sapphire. Her skin was luminous as if the very moon blessed her with a gift, it's bright sheen illuminating from the depths of her very soul. She would smile broadly and live with a zest that most never achieved. She knew pain and fought like a formidable warrior — using mercy when needed and viciousness if required. But she was fair, and she was just. She was neither light nor dark. She lived and loved with all she had and was loyal to those that were hers to protect.

I decided she had to be my mother, and it was all I had of her — little slices of a fractured memory.

I also remembered a place beautiful, magical, and too unreal to be anything but a dream. I would recall that as the sun streamed down on beautiful greenery and bright, happy flowers, where everything sparkled and smelled as I imagine heaven would. Floral, earthy, and pure. A grand castle, the windows were paned with a crystal-like mosaic that would create lights that dancing different ways as the sun shone through it and even at night as the moon whispered its somber tales.

I remembered the beauty of them. The vividness as I laughed at them, or she laughed, I wasn't sure. The smell of my favorite flower, musky hints of sorrow and laughter all in one. It's purple and yellow petals large and soft against my skin. A man wrapping me in a hug and telling me he loved me more than time itself. Because life was never-ending until one chose to move on, and I remember dancing carelessly to the music, both sorrowful and sweet.

And some nights all I dreamed of was the crows calling me home.

They were memories. They were dreams. They were all I had to hold onto through the dark and lonely nights.

CHAPTER ONE

"Morgan." The little blond-haired boy whined as he watched the pudgy red-haired girl twist her thin lips and fat cheeks up into a snarl before slamming her fist toward my head. I rolled swiftly sideways, just missing it, and she swore as her fist met the brick wall behind me.

"Bitch!" she hissed. As she grabbed my sweater with her uninjured hand, throwing me down, her face lit up red, making the brown freckles stand out even more across her pudgy face.

I recovered quickly from the fall. Flipping myself up. "Maddy Addy, I think you should take some time to cool off and maybe realize this will not end well," I egged her on. I knew she had the upper hand. She could easily beat me, and I wasn't in the mood to sport a new black eye or any more bruises. But beating up on me was one thing. Beating up on little Logan, completely different.

Addy screeched, she hated to be called Maddy Addy almost as much as she hated to be teased for her hair. They called her ginger-ade. I had to admit it was clever. But usually, she deserved the teasing and jabs. She may have been a product of her environment like the rest of us, but she took the adage 'don't piss a redhead off' to the extreme. Then it came, the punch I already knew was going to black my eye. I twisted my head just in time so that she missed my eye and instead hit my lip. A busted lip was better than a black eye.

"Leave Logan alone." I spit as blood dribbled down my newly cut lip.

I never hit anyone unless they hit me first. It was one of my golden rules. I had a bunch of those. Almost as many rules as I had boxes. Boxes kept things neat and tidy, and rules kept things as they needed to be. But once a person hit me, all bets were off. I pulled my right arm back and slammed it into the center of her muddy, hazel eyes. They reminded me of a frog. Her face lit up in surprise right before she slumped back and fell from the force of my blow.

I didn't even hit her that hard. I couldn't. But still, she was out cold. And so I turned, giving Logan a reassuring smile as he peered up at me with concern in his big coffee-colored eyes as if I was his very own superhero, and he took his tiny hand in mine.

I didn't keep close connections with people. It made things easier, and it worked for about five years in the system. Then Logan came along. He was two, scared, and no one wanted him. No one came for him. And when he cried at night for his mom, it reminded me of when I was first here, and I cried too. Not for my mom, but because I couldn't even remember if I had a mom.

And so I crawled into his little bed with him and wrapped my arms around him, giving him comfort in a place devoid of such things. I had been twelve at the time. Taken back to the foster center, bounced around various homes more times than I could count. I was odd. People never felt comfortable around me. They always said the same thing and never a good enough reason to not want me.

As I looked down into Logan's pure, innocent face and the burn that covered half of it, making him also imperfect, all I saw was a little boy that made me smile every day. A little boy that had suffered so much yet still woke up every day with hope in his heart and adventure on his horizon.

If I'm being honest, Logan saved me all those years ago. His hope had become my hope where before I had none. The way he believed in me made me believe in myself. He was my brother, maybe not by blood, but by choice. It was as if the cosmos knew I needed a purpose, and they heeded my call.

That was before. Before my memories began returning. Now the spark of hope was still there, but sadness tainted it. This wasn't my real home, and soon, I was going to have to find my way back there. I wasn't sure Logan could go.

I walked up the sidewalk from the schoolhouse, where Addy was finally getting up. The trees had begun to change and fall to the ground in different shades of amber, crimson, and gold. Piling up on the street, in yards and fluttering through the brisk, chilly air. It always got cold fast in Boston.

The sidewalks where we walked split with greenery. Stems and leaves pushed the concrete further apart as if the earth itself was doing its best to fight against the infestation of humanity. Like fleas, they took and destroyed everything that was once alive — preferring instead, to mar the world with ugly, cold, man-made buildings. They couldn't feel the vibrations under their feet, of the soil weeping, or the screams of the trees as they died or choked on dirty air.

I was five when it started. Sitting in the yard and the brown soil beneath my feet begged for release. And I cried that the ground was alive and that it needed help.

They thought I was imaginative, making stories up. But then the trees, the birds, the wind, even the rhythmic heartbeat of the planet itself began to make themselves heard. It had been so long since anyone had been able to listen. They sang. They called. They screamed. Every second of every day. And I went crazy.

The first time my adopted family brought me back, they just said it wasn't a good fit. The second family was more forthcoming with the fact that I was too damaged. The third go, the family caused damage that would never truly heal. No one else took me home after that. I went to a foster care home full of kids, and that's when I met Logan. He gave me a purpose. He believed me. He even began calling me his superhero. And I guess, in a way, I became exactly that. But if I'm being honest, he was mine.

"Morgy," he murmured as we walked along the sidewalk, pulling our tattered coats closer to us. "What does the ground say today?"

"I'm not sure." It was a lie. It always said the same thing. *Save me.* But I stopped listening. There was nothing I could do. I was only one person. No, not a person. But one entity against many.

"What about the sky?" He squeezed my hand as his little voice asked. He wasn't going to stop until I gave him something. I closed my eyes, listening with that special part deep inside me.

"It's singing." I sighed and smiled as I opened my eyes.

"Can you sing it?" he asked, looking hopeful. And so I started to hum, and he followed the tune in his little voice until we stood in front of the foster home where we lived.

They had separated us once. It hadn't been good. Logan screamed, cried, and refused to speak. I fared better, used to being separated from others, but I missed him. He had a way of keeping me grounded. Family did that for you. The state determined it was in both our best interests to stay together.

And then, unfortunately, or fortunately, depending on your viewpoint, sealing that we would never be adopted. But I already knew we wouldn't. Just like I knew, without me, Logan's future was grim and sad. I just knew. Logan needed me, and I needed Logan.

"Morgy?" he asked, turning his beautiful scarred face to mine. The angry red, rough scars dipped deep into his cheek and pulled the skin of his right eye taut over his lid. The fire had reached his crib before the firefighters could reach him. The scars extended to his neck and most of his body. He had spent months in the hospital, alone, in pain. So small and tiny. To go from being loved to unwanted and an orphan.

His parents died in the fire but were able to call for help before succumbing to smoke inhalation. The firefighters made it just in time to save Logan. A miracle they called it.

I didn't believe in those.

"Yes, Logan?" We sat on the front porch steps, the gray paint peeling, and the concrete crumbling in places. Both of us dreaded going into the house. As soon as we went in, I became an instant babysitter and maid, and poor Logan would be jumped on by the other boys. They'd pick, tease and blame him for everything and anything. Normally, I'd box their ears, but he made me promise not to.

"Every superhero has to rise from something," he whispered to me as I was about to run through the house, ripping little boys out of their bunk beds. Our foster parents, as they were called, weren't really parents. They filled the house with bodies to keep the lights on then practically left us to our own defenses. Taking care of ourselves and each other. And since I was the oldest, the responsibility landed on my shoulders.

I cooked, I cleaned, and I babysat. I hated it. But if it meant staying with Logan, I would grit and bear it for as long as I had to.

"When you go back. Will you take me with you?" He leaned his spiky blond head on my shoulder, my own dark hair tumbling down my back. Not because I liked it long, but because no one bothered to ever get me a haircut. I opened my mouth, but he didn't wait for an answer. "We can travel the universe together, going on grand adventures!" His voice was so hopeful. It was all he had to keep him from thinking about the sad hole that was our real reality.

"I don't know how to do that, Logan. But I really want to."

I sighed, leaning my dark head on his. I looked just like my mother, or who I thought was my mother. I knew that. But I couldn't really remember her well, no matter how hard I tried. Logan was the same. He remembered the love, the feeling of being held by her, but couldn't remember what she looked like.

Logan wasn't deterred by my words. "Would we stay here and travel through time? Or should we go to a new planet?" He twisted his features up speculatively. "Maybe we can find a place where they don't hate people like me."

"People don't hate you." I cooed to him. "They fear you. As they should. You are a superhero." I nudged him playfully, putting my arm around his shoulders. Even as chilly as it was outside, we would sit here until our noses and fingers were numb.

"I'd take us to my home first, and then we can go anywhere you want." I smiled warmly. It was a nice fantasy. But like him, no one came for me, and all I had was unused unharnessed abilities that I had

no idea where, why, or what to do with. And the fear of hurting Logan clipped my magical wings. It was a nice thought—one that would get us through the coming days.

CHAPTER TWO

"What are you two doing hiding out here?" a familiar voice grumbled up from the now open door that sported the same ugly gray peeling paint. The rest of the house clashed with the gray as it had green metal siding covering it. In some places the siding had fallen off and exposed the old rotted wood beneath. The woman holding the door open had seen her fair share of life's gutters. How she became a foster parent baffled me to no end. She was plump from the food the money the state provided her to care for each child, but only actually spent any of the money on but a few that buttered her bread just the right way.

Logan and I, by default, were not the buttering kind.

"We're coming, Miss Dale." I clipped off before adjusting my tone.

"And have you ya seen Addy, yet?" she asked as we stood and turned to walk up the stairs. Logan nodded slowly, staring at the woman with bleach-blonde hair frizzed out around a face that was just as round as her belly. Deep lines cut around and between her eyes and down the sides of her mouth. She had never been pretty. But being pretty didn't mean anything. One could be kind and smart and pretty wasn't necessary. Miss Dale had never been any of those things.

"She'll be here soon," I said, meeting Miss Dale's piercing gaze. I knew she didn't like me. She felt the same thing most people did. Uncomfortable, uneasy, and she just couldn't place her finger on why. And it went deeper than that. She hated me for the same reason she caught her practically live-in boyfriend staring at me. I knew when he was staring, and it made my skin crawl. I had to mask everything in those situations. And it wasn't the first time or the first man to do it.

I had been eight when the first of my foster brothers had cornered me in a room alone and forced me to let him touch me. He was sixteen, and I was only eight. Later that night, he snuck into my room, and I woke to his hands up my nightdress. He didn't get further than that before I screamed, but it was enough to feel scared, violated, and unsafe. That was the day I understand the earth's sorrowful song.

I had felt the same way. Broken, needing mending.

Now, I was seventeen. And soon I'd be taking Logan and me away from all of this to something better. I just didn't know when or how or even what could be better, but I'd be damned if I didn't at least try. A shadow flitted across Logan's eyes as he stood but a step behind me. I had turned my head from Miss Dale to reassure him we would be okay, but his eyes remained fixated at the door. I followed his gaze.

One of the other foster children, Bentley, poked his slimy dark head out the door behind Miss Dale's round backside and smiled with a promise stitched into the corners of his lips at Logan. Bentley reminded me of an eel. I'd like to think that children are all inherently good, innocent as they say in what Miss Dale worships as the good book. One she never even follows but uses as a means to punish and judge others.

Damn it. I sighed to myself. I couldn't just stand aside and let him deal with this anymore. Tonight, Bentley was going to have some very, very animated dreams. Enough to scare him away from ever looking Logan's way again. "Well, get in here already!" Miss Dale spit through her crooked yellow teeth. There was some leftover pink lipstick stuck to her front tooth. The yellowness of her teeth only made it even more grotesque looking., drawing the gaze to the mole that set just atop her cupid's bow. Sometimes she plucked the hair that stubbornly grew from it. Most of the time she didn't bother. Today, the hair was starting to escape the dark brown depths of her skin as if whiskers to her catfish mouth.

Her eyes were adorned with the same crap mascara that smudged up onto her lids and dropped specks on her cheeks. She would smudge a little blue color on her lids, saying it brought the blue out in her eyes. But every time I looked into her gaze, it was a slate gray. No blue to be found. So gray even, it made me think of the static of a television set. It was on, but nothing was being broadcast. Miss Dale was kind of like that.

I had been so preoccupied with my thoughts that I'd missed her intense gaze on me, and I missed the black sedan that was parked on the street not far from where Logan and I had sat. But I didn't miss that evil little eel's gleeful smile as he slithered off, like the slimy eel that he was. Maybe not an eel. They at least had a bite.

"Ms.-" A man paused as he stood to the right of the entrance in Miss Dale's special sitting room. It was adorned with furniture that looked like a gag-worthy sitcom or from Roseanne. A show she loved to sit and watch as she ate eclairs because they were decadent. The small sofa and loveseat were the same puke green of the siding outside. Only a little orange and red splashed unintentionally in places. She was so proud of this room, and it was as hideous as her. It made me feel sorry for her.

"Morgan," I offered the man. I didn't have a real last name. I didn't know it. I was given the name Jones. It was a popular name, and the court seemed to think it fitting, but I refused to acknowledge it, knowing it didn't belong to me. There was something about a name—it held some part of you in it. In some ways, your name is all you get when you leave this world, and the first thing you get when you arrive. I was just Morgan.

"Yes, Morgan." The man nodded and offered his hand. I didn't budge. He dropped his hand awkwardly, and I inspected him. He was tall with short-cropped curly hair and glasses that appeared too small for his face. He had a pleasant face, with lines that showed he spent his life smiling. The faint crinkles on the sides of his eyes suggested he was older than forty but perhaps not much. His eyebrows were bushy and wild as if he couldn't be bothered to tame them. It suited him.

I realized then he was looking at me with some sort of expectation, waiting. He had said something, and I missed it? I did that sometimes. My mind was better sometimes than my reality, and I missed all kinds of things. "I'm sorry?" I asked focusing on the man in front of me again. He smiled, not even affected by my lack of attention.

"I'm Richard," he repeated slowly with a kind smile smoothing the blazer pocket on his chest. It was then I realized he was wearing what looked to be an expensive suit. It was black and plain with a light blue shirt and a gray geometric patterned tie. This wasn't the usual type of guest that came here. "I'm here to help you get home."

"Help me?"

"Did ya not hear em, girl?" Miss Dale blurted from beside me. Her ugly catfish mouth flaring out as if she smelled herself for the first time in years. Just like a dead fish, rotten.

"You can't just throw me to the first stranger that walks in the door!" I glare at the catfish, storm clouds rolling in my eyes. Then I turned my stormy gaze to Richard. "I need evidence that you have permission to take me, and the courts have decreed that I am not to be separated from Logan. I glanced back at Logan. And my heart broke. I wanted to turn and punch this Richard just for causing the look of terror that widened Logan's big warm eyes to that of a scared deer stuck in headlights, about to be hit by a car.

"Miss..." Richard began then paused, "Morgan." He carefully pressed his lips closed curtly instead. "I have no intention of being the one to separate the two of you."

"So, he goes too?"

"Of course." The man tipped his head down. I thought it odd. It was as if he was trying to show me respect in some archaic custom. And something clouded over his face, but as soon as it was there it vanished.

"Paperwork," I demanded, grabbing backward for Logan's hand, knowing he would never let me actually hold his hands with the other boys watching. The eel was standing in the hallway, his needy eyes watching intently. But then he clasped my fingers as if he too couldn't believe it. Only, we weren't dumb. This wasn't our first rodeo. We'd been down this road too many times before.

"When you say family..." I asked, leaving the question hanging on purpose.

"Your family and Logan's now as well." The man smiled kindly but he failed to understand what we really meant.

This man didn't understand the gut-wrenching pain of being abandoned or adopted and brought back or being passed over for adoption because of this or that. The pain of only having one other person to trust in the whole world because everyone else has hurt you, forgotten you, or just never even bothered to come and get you. We both knew that pain. We clung to it even when our days were good, because we knew no matter how good things could be, they never lasted. It was our sad reality.

I squeezed Logan's hand just a fraction. Logan was different, though. Even through all his trials and shit for luck. He still woke up with hope. He still turned his head to the sun and dreamed of a better future where we fought side by side as superheroes saving the world, and sometimes, the universe itself. He was good—pure. His shined through brightly no matter what happened.

When the man still didn't move, I jutted my outreached hand. I wanted proof. Logan wasn't going anywhere if I didn't get it. The man sighed and reached down to shuffling through some papers, handing them to me to look over.

I have trust issues. I know this. Being in the system for so long made me wary of everything. I considered it a positive characteristic. And even if I was crazy, and my memories weren't true, I couldn't explain the other stuff logically enough. Like, the fact something inside me told me to trust this man despite all my naturally cautious alarm bells. But that didn't stop me from studying the crisp papers in my hands, I shuffled through them, only to glance up once. The man, Richard, patiently looked at me with a pleasant grin on his face.

He is too nice, run, one part of me screamed. *Trust him,* another urged. So, I decided to go in the middle. I'd go with the man, but trust wasn't something I was about to just give out to anyone. No matter how nice they were. People wore masks. This world... it was broken. The earth cried, and the soul of almost everyone whispered or screamed that it was dying.

And whether they knew or admitted it. The felt it, deep inside the festering sickness. The soul needed to be nourished. And I don't mean with just religion or beliefs. More than that. Something, I was still learning about. But it was no coincidence that with the coming industrialization of the modern world, humanity became sicker and sicker.

The depressed, the hurting, the spread of illness, the inner hurt, pain numbness, and feeling of disconnect. It was all related. Every single bit of it. I wanted more for Logan. And if I was being honest, I wanted more for everyone else. Because I felt that goodness inside there too. With one touch, I felt it all. Their fears, desires, hopes, dreams, pain, and more.

No matter how sick, depraved, and savage a person was, they had a light somewhere inside them. It might be deep. It might be low and just an ember barely-there hanging on, but it was almost always there. But it took work to make it flame before it went out. And then they become lost forever. At least, that's what I think.

"Everything good?" Richard asked as he peered at me with that kind expression on his face. He didn't move forward or place his hand on me. He raised it as if he would, but then dropped. As if he knew. I try to avoid being touched. It could be too much at times.

"Yeah." I handed the papers back to him.

"Great." He chuckled softly. "You have a plane to catch the Dannons are eager to meet you."

"Me? Now?" I backed up and looked back at Logan, whose eyes went wide.

"Well, both of you," the man finished quickly, that shadow crossing his eyes again. "Grab your things. Your journey starts now." He raised his hand again as if he wanted to reassuringly squeeze my shoulder but stopped. "I'm sorry. I know you don't like to be touched."

"Thanks. I'll be right back. We don't have much." I turned, grabbing Logan's hand and smiled reassuringly at him. As I walked away, I heard Miss Dale.

"You have no idea how grateful I am that you are taking her off my hands." She breathed in what could only be described as an attempt at a flirty voice. "Such a sad little girl and odd. I hope these new people are prepared."

"Indeed they are, Miss Dale," the man said curtly.

It didn't take long to pack our things and head out. The black sedan parked nearby was as I had assumed Richard's. As we drove away, I heard Richard sigh.

"That woman should not be left to care for any children."

For most of the trip, we were silent. At least until the last fifteen minutes.

"Will you ask him about the people adopting us?" Logan said shyly. Logan rarely talked to other people. Instead, he would whisper to me. When he did speak, most people would ignore him or overlook him. It angered me to no end because it just made him pull back into himself. I concluded it had to be from the trauma of the fire.

No matter what I did, it didn't help. I stared down into his widened mocha orbs as he peered up at me, hope beaming in his expression, and nodded my head. I couldn't say no. He was excited about this. He thought it a journey, an adventure.

I leaned forward toward the man driving the car. "Tell me about them," I asked.

His eyes never left the road. "They love you already. As if they've been waiting their whole lives to meet you. At least that is the impression I got on the phone. They are good people, kind. The man is Daniel, and the woman goes by Brigit."

"Brigit? I like it." I let the name roll off my tongue, turning back to Logan. He leaned his head on my shoulder and sighed. His straight blonde hair tickled my neck. I leaned my head on his head, as well. I noticed the eyes of the man in the front seat pause on me briefly before quickly flitting away.

CHAPTER THREE

It wasn't long after that we were parked in the short term parking area and collected our bags. Richard walked us up to the counter, and a woman in her early twenties beamed brightly at him.

"Hello, welcome to North Eastern Airlines." She wore a crimson shirt that complimented her skin tone and dipped a little too low for someone at work. I noticed Richards's smile increased in her presence and rolled my eyes.

"Yes, I'm here to help pick up tickets-" He paused as he turned toward us and let his words drop awkwardly.

"Aw, is this your daughter? She is so pretty," the woman gushed. Her name tag read *Amy* and was pinned close to her chest. I didn't miss Richard's gaze flitting to the name tag and his grin spreading further across his face.

"Why no, Amy. Just a client."

"Of course," she drawled out as she leaned forward. "Where you going, hon?"

I held back a gag. "Apparently, to Ireland."

"Oh, yes. We do have a flight boarding for Dublin today. Name, please?" She turned her eyes to Richard again. It was then I noticed her perfectly lined eyes and lipstick that matched her shirt. I guess she was what men found sexy. I was dark and odd. It was an outlandish thought for me. I'd never really cared what people thought of me. But I wasn't impervious to the normal wants and desires of any teenager. The desire to experience life in all its many facets. Love and attraction being one.

I realized then I had been standing there scrutinizing the woman and not speaking, unintentionally rude as my thoughts carried me away. Logan bumped me, bringing me back to the present. "Oh, sorry. My name is Morgan Jones," I gritted out. I hated Jones, but I hated the thought of not having anything that was mine, really mine from my past.

"Actually, she was just adopted. They changed her name to Dannon. It's Morgan Dannon." My mouth gaped open. That seemed a little presumptuous of them to assume I'd be okay with that. I mean, it wasn't like I liked being a Jones by force of the courts, but the decision was taken from me. And that I didn't like. My eyes narrowed at Richard.

"Are you kidding me?" Anger flashed in my eyes.

But Logan stopped me as his voice raised higher than usual around strangers, yet still a murmur, "Morgy, I like it, and now we'll have the same name." I turned my head toward his and sighed. It cooled my temper as I saw the hope and sense of finally belonging somewhere make him smile in a way that permeated from him in almost a glow. He was happy, truly happy. So, I couldn't argue. I couldn't get angry. Not with Logan so happy.

"And Logan too," Richard added quickly. He turned back to the woman. "We should have two tickets. He pulled a paper out, and receipts for tickets then placed them on the counter. Her emerald eyes briefly met mine, and she smiled at me differently this time. There was a slow expression that was full of understanding. What I wasn't sure. I mean, I wasn't about to touch her.

"Oh, yes. We were called about her." She leaned toward Richard, and in a low voice, she mumbled to Richard. "They let us know." Richard nodded his head but didn't say anything in response. The woman then raised her voice as if she was talking to a toddler. "It's so nice to meet you both." She nodded her head enthusiastically like a bobblehead, her curls bouncing.

It took what seemed like forever for her to print the tickets off. She handed them both to Richard then explained where the terminal was located.

"Thank you." He reached for the tickets placing his hand lightly on hers. I was betting money he would find his way back here after he disposed of us. I wanted to shout, *Get a room!*, but it wasn't the place for it. They had their reasons and their needs. Who was I to judge? Instead, I turned, looking around the airport and started toward the terminal with Logan in tow. Eventually, Richard caught up to us.

"You don't have to escort us. I can handle it from here." I turned to approach the line that would check our bags, scan our bodies for possible threats.

"Of course you can, but I have instruction to escort you safely to the plane all the way until you board," he explained. That kind smile crossed his face once again. And I didn't feel the need to argue. He stepped in front of us as the line moved to let us through. Then as we loaded our bags into the tray. He leaned in and whispered something to the attendant. The man nodded, his gaze also directed toward me as they obviously were talking about Logan and I.

Richard walked back toward us. "The man said you can take Logan through with you so that he doesn't get scared."

"Thank you." I breathed with relief.

CHAPTER FOUR

Before we knew it, we stood at the gate of the plane, and Richard pressed the tickets in the flight attendant's hand. She glanced down briefly and waved us through.

"Have a good flight." Richard waved before turning and walking away.

This was it. We are alone. We were going to Ireland. And this morning—I stopped my thoughts again and straightened my back. I had to be brave and think positively. This was going to be a good thing.

The flight was long and boring. Logan and I shared a headset, and Logan, as usual, refused to eat. Probably because the food was worse than the school cafeteria food, but before we knew it, we descended into our new lives. In freaking Ireland of all places. And for the first time that I'd ever seen him do it, Logan ran off the plane, scaring the shit out of me as I pushed through people getting cursed.

"I'm so sorry. My little brother ran off," I called over my shoulder, and people moved aside once I said this. I thanked each of them. It wasn't until I arrived at the rotating conveyor belt our bags had been piled on that I found him. He stood at the nearby window beaming from ear to ear.

"Look, Morgy!" He pressed his face against the glass as if he could melt through it. "It's Ireland!" There was awe in his voice. "We're home."

"Let's get our bags." I turned briefly, looking over my shoulder to spot just a glance of the tattered coat. He followed. Grabbing our bags, we walked out of the area to a gate. Beyond the gate, people waited. Some with signs and some with hope and anticipation cascading from them. I didn't even need to touch them. I could feel it as I passed.

I crinkled my face up as I peered toward one of the people who were waiting for that person or persons to walk through. When they did, the joy shot from them, almost toppling me over. What the hell was going on? Logan tugged on my arm, pulling me along so excitedly, he was practically bouncing.

There was a man, tall and lean with a rugged face holding a sign that said Morgan and Logan, but he didn't need to wait for us. He wasn't dressed as I imagined an Irishman would dress. I wasn't sure what that was, a kilt maybe? Or was that just Scotland? He stood there in light, faded jeans, and a black clerked shirt. His hair was so long, it touched his shoulders, but it was groomed nicely. He was older, perhaps in his thirties, and a thick beard covered the lower half of his face, matching the chestnut coloring of his hair. As soon as he saw us, he smiled, transforming him into someone much more approachable. I, without even trying, felt that this man was loyal and dedicated—a good man that protected what he felt responsible for. He wasn't a stranger to hard work, but friendliness rolled off of him.

Logan bounded forward, not at all like his normal behavior. The man bent to address him. "Well, hello there, laddie!" he greeted, dropping the sign to his side.

My heart soared. The man addressed Logan! Tears welled in my eyes. So many people overlooked him because he tried so hard to make himself invisible. Sometimes I wondered if what was wrong with me kind of made him even more so. A protective hazard of my abilities. If they couldn't see him, they couldn't hurt him. It was possible, but I wasn't sure.

I slowly walked toward the man, apprehensive despite feeling an instant kinship with the man. My inability to easily trust ran deep to my core. It kept me safe. It kept Logan safe.

"Welcome to Ireland." The man bowed with a flourish looking up from downcast eyes before standing back up. "It's an honor to meet you. Shall we?"

I wordlessly nodded and followed him, slightly behind Logan. Logan still hadn't said anything, but I could tell he had a million questions to ask the man. As soon as we walked outside, the man turned and walked into the grassy area toward the parking lot. There was a perfectly good sidewalk, I noted. And it was then that I suddenly found my voice.

"Excuse me," I called, and the man turned. His face lit up and he began to laugh. "Oh, I'm so sorry, lassie. I forgot my manners. It's not every day-" He stopped, walking closer. "I forgot to introduce myself. I'm Craig. I work for the Dannons."

"Great, but shouldn't you walk on the sidewalk?" I asked the question, and I wasn't sure why it seemed to press upon me in a way I didn't understand. There weren't words to describe it. I felt if I stepped off the concrete, my entire world would change. This would be real. And I didn't know if I was ready for that.

The man paused and peered down at me with understanding as if he read my every thought. "You know, lassie, a crow only learns to fly when its mum pushes it out of the nest. Then it learns to soar as it was meant to."

. . .

My mouth gaped open. He had to be able to read my mind. How could he know? Crows were my spirit animal, or at least that's what I called them. It reminded me of the conversation Logan and I had before we left. We watched the crows dance through the sky. Flying up and flapping their wings as if carefree and without the troubles of the world weighing them down.

And they called to me, as they sometimes did, sweeping down from above, asking me to join them. Once, one landed on my shoulder, and Logan stroked its soft ebony feathers that glistened purple when the sun rays touched them. Then the crow turned to me and cawed. It didn't speak, not in the sense that we do, but I caught its meaning.

Fly with us. Then it raised its wings and soared away. And I wanted to soar with it more than anything in the world. And so I stood there, just on the edge of the sidewalk realizing it was time to soar.

CHAPTER FIVE

With one foot in front of the other, I walked toward him. But he paused and reached down to pull his old burgundy loafers off.

"I feel so constrained by shoes. I like to feel the grass beneath my feet. It makes me feel connected."

I stared, feeling my mouth threatening to drop once again. Instead, I turned to see Logan pulling off his own shoes without even a question, and so I followed, throwing my shoes in my backpack. It was all I had. And then my socks and as I placed both feet into the soft grass, my life began right there. As if I had never truly lived before. The earth sang to me. The ground beckoned to me like an embrace as if it was telling me, *Welcome home.* And the magic, the connection, it was almost overwhelming. It was a warmth that spread through me. It was magic.

The man chuckled. "Don't worry, lassie. You'll get used to it."

I didn't speak. I just looked at him in awe. This man-—this man knew. He understood. "You..." I trailed off, and he nodded, but I was cut off by Logan.

"Where are we going? What are they like? Are you like their child or friend? How long until we get there?" he streamed off in one breath as if suddenly he found his voice. And the courage to speak.

This place was magic. There, as if soaked into the very land we stood on, was power, old and ancient, and it called to me. It sang to me. It offered me a warm, welcoming embrace. And apparently, it gave Logan whatever he needed as well.

The man, Craig, turned toward Logan and bent down. "Well, we are going to the Dannon estate. They are-" He paused, looking up toward the sky as if thinking of the proper word. "They are special." He decided as he looked down at Logan's face plastered with the biggest smile I'd ever seen him wear. "And as for me," he continued. "I'm like a cousin."

"So, you are now our cousin?" Logan asked.

"I am indeed." He leaned down, facing Logan. "And as for your last question. It won't take as long as it should." He laughed.

"Where are we going?" I asked, finally finding my voice.

"Toward the south end coast. There wasn't a plane that would be able to take us there quickly, so I'm here to take us there. Ye can sleep on the way. It'll help." As if on cue, Logan and I shared a deep yawn.

The long flight and significant time difference had exhausted us with jet lag.

And there we all went walking barefoot in the grass, making our way to a small energy-efficient black vehicle, driving barely a half-hour before Logan and I fell asleep. I do remember opening my eyes to see green hills and the sun streaming through the window as it warmed my face. It was chilly outside, but also clear. The car came to a stop, and I was jarred out of my sleep by its suddenness. Logan's pale blond head still rested on the bag he had propped between us.

"We're here, lassie," Craig announced as he shoved the gearshift into park. My eyes lifted to what looked like a crumbling castle. Part of it on the left side was doing exactly that. The right side fared better and wasn't overwhelmed with the foliage that wrapped itself around the left. The right side looked slightly more habitable as the tower rose up into the sky. It was made of brick and stone. Windows had been placed into the shallow holes of the castle, and then a gate stood erect just outside the keep. I looked half expecting a moat full of alligators. There wasn't a moat, just grass, nicely cut and landscaped. Upon closer inspection, the keep was well maintained for what it was. The left side was indeed falling into ruin, but it appeared that measures had been taken to restore it. Much of the foliage and stone had been moved away.

"You didn't say it was a castle," I murmured in awe. I groaned, thinking of how drafty it would be. Were they going to put us in a dungeon? They probably brought us here to be servants. I knew if anyone would tell me this information, it wouldn't be Craig, so my guard went back up. I looked around the stone gate. It was old. The stones had been placed on top of each other meticulously and cemented in with obvious maintenance over the years as well. As if something needed to be honored.

"It's more of a keep these days," Craig proudly proclaimed. "It's called Dannon Keep now, and the land around it extends for miles. It's been in their family for many, many years. Once you get settled in, I'll give ye a tour and tell ya more about it."

Logan, who had been quiet up until now, looked at her with wonder in his eyes, "Morgy, we are going to live in a castle!" He practically shouted as he danced around on his feet. I stared at him in my own wonder. Watching the excitement bounce off of him. Logan had always seemed so sad, every day he seemed to struggle just to get through the day. Just like I did. It was one of the reasons I had gravitated toward him. Both our need for comfort helped us seek each other out.

Today, I saw and felt something so different in him — happiness, wonder, and possibly even magic. So, I did something I hadn't done in a very long time. I breathed in deeply. I smelled the heather fragrance, which was so familiar to me, even though I was positive I had never been to Ireland.

Yet, every time the breeze swept past, it was as if it was saying, *Hello friend, it's good to see you again.* Even bare feet on the earth seemed to welcome me here.

"Shall we?" Craig swept his arm out toward the entrance. We had parked in a small parking area outside. It seemed odd there wasn't a garage. But that wasn't the oddest thought I had as I walked through the entrance. I felt something. It was electric. It shot through my body like a tickle. It whispered with power into my ear. I closed my eyes, breathing in even more deeply. The distrust and apprehension remained, but I couldn't mistake that as soon as I arrived, everything felt...well, it felt, for the first time ever, like home.

It felt like the one thing I had been denied my whole life. The hug of someone that loved me like I was precious. And when I opened my eyes, raising them toward the front door, the feeling intensified and the odd sensation of deja vu became stronger. It was a tickle in the back of my head, familiar, known.

Logan raced up the stone steps that lead to the massive wooden door. Celtic knots circled the wooden arches. The handle to the right was the only plain piece about the massive, beautiful thing. And yet, it still didn't prepare me for what was on the inside.

If the castle had looked run down from a distance, it had to be an illusion. The inside was anything but. It opened into a foyer that extended to a long hallway. The foyer was painted white with wainscoting boards and a soft blue color above that. The blue reached up to white molding with elaborate designs carved into it as it covered the wall and part of the ceiling. There was a white coat rack, and just a few feet away, a bench to sit and take your shoes off. It matched the trim and elaborate molding and was reminiscent of that old-world feel of a keep, even if the inside looked modern and updated. It was a mix of the new and the old.

It was nothing like what I expected and yet precisely what one would expect from someone of considerable wealth. Logan sat on the bench, taking his backpack and placing it next to it. He peered up at Craig, who nodded with a wide grin. His bare feet rested on a white and black marbled floor that extended into the hallway. The same coloring of the walls continued that way as well, each wall covered in old paintings. The hallway was short though. The design of the house was odd, but I assumed it was to accommodate the fact that it was so old. As you walked further into the home, it opened up to a large living room with a large staircase that extended upward on both sides of the room until it disappeared in separate directions.

The room was large, open, and despite that, inviting. It was modernized, yet still only maintained a flare in a historical sense, with tapestries and more painting adorning the walls. Occasionally there would be a piece that looked old, a sculpture. The room was what one would consider a living room, but much larger than the average one. A space was left on both sides for the stairs, and the left side of the room was looked to be a formal dining area. Morgan suspected that at one time, the castle had been even bigger, with its own rooms, but due to the extra expense of warming and maintaining the entire thing, they transformed the larger part of the keep into a new entity of its own and modernized it through the years.

But there was one thing missing in this beautiful room. Where were the people that were supposed to be adopting them? I had up until this point remained silent, trying to take in every detail as I went, but the nagging thought that no one was there to greet them other than Craig rubbed me the wrong way.

"Where are the Dannons?" I turned to look at Craig. Was Craig lying and soon they would be murdered? No one would even think to look for them because they weren't even from Ireland.

"Lassie, don't look so frightened. They will be along soon. They have important business before they can pop in." He chuckled as if he knew what I was thinking.

It wasn't long until I had roamed most of the castle-like manor. It was exquisite. Nicer than anything I had seen in my short life. But it was one painting in particular that made me pause. It was the focus of one room off of the main living room area. I realized that there was more to the manor than I had originally thought. There was an office that was still decorated in a style outside of this time, spacious with mahogany and leather. Old books lined the wall on every side, and a fireplace was placed to the left of the thick wooden desk. Fastened on the top was a large painting of a woman. She was beautiful, ethereal. One look at her and you just felt her power. She wore a black dress, and her hair was black as midnight. Her skin was pale alabaster, a stark contrast against the black of her hair.

Her eyes were bright blue, as bright as the sky on a sunny, cloudless day. On her shoulder was a crown, and in her right hand, a sword. But it was the crown on her head that drew the most attention. When I say crown, it's not in the sense you would think a crown would appear. It was more of a headpiece. It dipped down on her forehead in a V, silver with a black stone in the middle that shined even in the painting.

I stepped tentatively closer, engrossed by the beautiful, oddly familiar woman.

I didn't hear Craig step into the study. "There ye are. We're about to get a bite to eat in the kitchen if yer interested."

I glanced over my shoulder briefly before looking back up to the painting. "Who is this?" I asked, not taking my gaze away from the familiar eyes looking down on me.

"Aye, tis the goddess Morrigan. She is a tough warrior and a powerful goddess. The crows are her familiars." He smiled from beside me, watching me. I was aware of his scrutiny, but my focus remained on the woman in the painting.

"You say it as if she actually existed and still does."

"She does, lass," he replied with a quick nod. His tone implied he believed every word.

Mine and Logan's rooms were spacious and attuned to both our personalities. How they knew was odd. It was apparent they had done research. We settled in easily, but Craig's promise of meeting the Dannons that evening didn't exactly happen.

The days turned into weeks with Craig giving excuses about them being on business trips and unable to return as soon as they expected. Needless to say, the kind of family we had been hoping for wasn't exactly turning out the way we thought. But we fell into an easy enough routine. And we had Craig's company.

I did learn more about Craig and the Dannons as the days passed. Craig admitted to being a relation of the Dannons entrusted to keep the manor occupied and in shape when they were gone. This worried me because it meant they were gone quite a bit.

Logan didn't seem phased. He had blossomed since arriving, talking more, full of smiles, and as trusting as I wished I could be. We began an at-home program for school. Craig admitted there wasn't a school close enough for us to attend.

I didn't mind. I liked the quiet solitude. Logan didn't seem to mind either. It was nice. But, just as we were giving up, the Dannons appeared.

They startled me, actually. I was lying in the study, my favorite place to be since the first day we had arrived. The old books and arti-facts seemed to comfort me, and the portrait made me feel odd. Not a bad odd, but a feeling of deja vu and familiarity I couldn't describe.

"Morgan," a cheery voice said from behind me. My nose lifted from the book I'd been engrossed in. The woman standing in the doorway, looked as you would imagine an angel.

Her hair was a pale blonde that reminded me of spun gold as bright light reflected off of it. It cascaded down around her shoulders and back, ending in loose curls. Her face was what caught my eye the most though. It was beautiful. Oval and pale, not a blemish on her alabaster skin. It even seemed to have a natural glow that radiated from within. Her cheeks were a pale pink that looked natural with long dark lashes that touched her high cheekbones when they flut-tered closed.

"I'm sorry?" I started to stand, confused about who she was. The Dannons didn't have any pictures of themselves in the house, and I wasn't sure if she was Brigit. It seemed likely enough. She smiled, kindly glancing toward the discarded book that read *Myths and Legends of Ireland*.

"Morgan." It was no longer a question as she stepped closer. Her eyes briefly flitted to the portrait that was at the heart of the room. "I'm Brigit. It's so good to finally meet you." She started to move forward to embrace me but stopped when she met my eyes as if she sensed my aversion to unwanted affection. I didn't know her. Hugs were out of the question, and it must have been plastered across my features.

"Brigit," I repeated. Her name tumbling from my lips in yet another odd familiarity. Brigit nodded, her blonde curls bouncing with her head.

"I'm Brigit Dannon here, but known as Brigit of the Light Court where I'm from...." she trailed off as her gaze once again drifted toward the painting. She opened her mouth but then closed it before a bright smile spread across her face. Everything about her said she was genuine, but her brief pause and constant pull toward the painting made me wary. Before I had time to ask or question the odd Light Court part of her introduction, another head popped through the doorway. Craig appeared behind the new intruder's back.

The aura around this man was darker, more subdued, powerful. Where Brigit was all light and brightness, he was dark and brooding. His eyes raised to meet mine. They were as green as the moss on the hills, yet they had storm clouds surging in their depths. This was a complicated man. I knew that as if I knew him. His face was broad and less ethereal than Brigit's, but he was just as beautiful. The only thing that marred his masculine attractiveness was the scar that ran from his right eye down his cheek.

His hair was dark and long, just brushing his broad shoulders.

"Hello." He breathed roughly. His voice was deep and hoarse as if he wasn't used to talking. Brigit turned her gaze toward the man, her smile faltering only briefly, and a sharp look crossed her features for but a millisecond, but it was long enough for me to catch it.

Who the hell were these people? I mean, I understood that they were the Dannons. She had to be our new adoptive mother, despite her not appearing much older than me. And he...well. The way he looked at me now. It didn't feel like he was to be our new adoptive father. Not with the way his gaze never left mine even as I struggled not to meet his as I rested my gaze on Brigit instead, waiting.

"Ah, yes." She gestured toward the young man. "This is Cu- I mean, Lain. He is...." She paused again as if trying to formulate a term for him. "Well, he is a relative," she decided, not sparing him another glance before wrapping me in a warm hug. I tried to pull away, expecting that familiar sense of power that surged to life and over-whelmed me about a person.

But nothing. There was nothing.

"So, is it just you?" I asked, finally pulling myself from her surprisingly comforting embrace. I glanced past the man with the strange name who's eyes still trailed across me almost unnervingly.

"Yes." She breathed. "Just me today."

"Today?" I glanced back at her seeing Craig move back into the other part of the keep.

"Yes." She sat in the leather lounger I had occupied previously, patting the seat next to her in invitation as if we were best friends."Actually, I'll be the only one coming to prepare you every day." Her smile broadened, and she waited expectantly as I stared dumbfounded back at her.

"Aren't you the one that adopted me?" She nodded, her face displaying the same exuberant look of excitement she had on earlier, but then her lips pulled downwards on the sides as she called for Craig.

"Yes, m' lady," he answered just behind Lain once again.

"I thought we discussed how we would ease her into this." Her eyes took on a sharpness that was completely different than the sweet, happy lady that had been sitting next to me before. Irritation cascaded from her.

"Aye." Craig ducked his head sheepishly. "We did, but I'm afraid it's a bit more complicated than that, m' lady."

She closed her mouth, her lips pressing in a thin line before relaxing. "Indeed," she said instead as if she knew exactly why. "Well then, that does change things just a bit."

"Change what?" I asked, not understanding why the sudden shift in the atmosphere.

"I see, but I think it's time we pull the blinders off," Brigit continued as if not hearing me. "Morgan, are you ready to learn who you are?"

I sat there looking between the three faces trying not to allow my gaze to stay long on Lain's, although it was hard. He was like a magnet. My eyes continued to drift to his, meeting them each time. "Where is Logan?" I asked, looking around curiously.

The beautiful woman, Brigit, let her sharp gaze soften, then she turned toward me. "He is fine, I'm sure."

Craig nodded from behind her. While Lain seemed to avoid my gaze for the first time as if he was instantly interested in the books on the shelves.

"Aye." Craig nodded his blond head in assurance. "I just saw him running around somewhere out here."

"Really?" Brigit asked now a look of fascination crossing the plains of her face. Lain showed no such change, still avoiding looking at me.

"Aye, my lady." Craig continued. "He's been seen running around by everyone ever since we arrived here." There was humor in his tone. As if the answer amused him, which made sense. Why wouldn't he be? He's a child, and children, even at Logan's age, were curious by nature.

"I want to meet Logan. Now, if you would," she announced as she inclined her head toward Craig in an odd way. Her pale golden locks brushing across her shoulders in a draping blanket.

These people are so freaking weird. I thought to myself, noticing that Lain finally did turn toward me, a smirk tugging at the corners of my mouth as if he knew what I had thought. But that wasn't possible, was it? But it had been my experience that impossible things were indeed possible.

I didn't have time to evaluate that thought any further because Brigit followed Craig out of the room, Lain trudged quietly behind. Apparently, he wasn't the chatty type. I followed a few steps back, allowing myself to also quietly observe the people that had just invaded my happy solitude, and my life, it would seem.

And as Brigit giggled so brightly it almost sounded like music, Logan raced across the marble floor in the what Craig called the common room, brandishing what looked like a wooden sword fighting imaginary dragons.

"I am your sworn guardian, my lady, and I will vanquish the evil monster." He lifted his sword, brandishing it toward the imaginary beast. His back to us as he fought tooth and nail at the air. Stabbing and jabbing with an enthusiasm only a child could have.

Brigit's laugh stopped him as he turned a goofy smile stretched across his face, the joy of just being a child for once in his life actually reaching his eyes for the first time in so long. A look I always wished he would have. But upon seeing us, that died away, and his eyes dimmed a little with wariness. Only someone who had experienced grief and heartache, someone who suffered and struggled as an orphan could understand. It made my heart hurt to see it replace the joy that had been there just a few minutes ago.

I tore my eyes from Logan's and watched Brigit as well. She didn't miss the look. Her lips pursed for just a moment before her smile brightened, and she rushed forward to see Logan, crouching down onto her knees as she went. "You must be Logan. I'm Brigit."

"Hello," he nodded, not moving from his spot. He searched my gaze that now met his before turning back toward Brigit. "Are you the lady that took us?"

"Yes," she answered simply. I noted he didn't say adopted. We've been here before, and it seemed through the years Logan had learned nothing in life was permanent. God, how I wished it hadn't been that way for him so many times. But I could only shelter him from the harsh realities of our lives so much.

"Well, it's nice to meet you." He grinned and stuck out his tiny hand to her, which made her laugh once again before she grasped it lightly in her slightly larger one.

"Why, good knight. It's a pleasure to meet you as well. But do continue your quest. Your princess needs saving. And you might earn a kiss from her," she answered as a look of disgust crossed his features.

"Princess?" His nose wrinkled up. "No, princess. I'm saving Morgy. Like she saves me."

"Well, then I can't argue with that. Carry on then." She stood then dusting off imaginary dirt from her dress. Logan had all but forgotten her as he briefly waved to me and turned to dash once again around the house with the wooden sword.

"Impressive," Brigit breathed almost too low for anyone to hear. Her gaze still resting on Logan. "Well, I guess now it's time to start."

CHAPTER SIX

She took me outside, leaving Craig inside. The silent Lain following us. Most people would be unnerved by his intensity and silence. But it seemed... natural. As if it was a part of his personality, and I knew it— knew him almost. So many things had felt like that recently. We walked along a path through the gardens. The roses were still in bloom despite the leaves littering the ground beneath our feet. Their red and white blossoms were stark against the green bushes they sprouted from.

"You know Morgan," Brigit began as we walked side by side up a dirt path well worn down by many previous footsteps. "This land is drenched in ancient magic." Her tone was matter of fact, and I laughed nervously rather than answer.

Good one. I thought to myself, not answering her.

She continued, "The ground, the trees, everything here is a part of something important. It's the gateway to a place that has been around since even before mankind walked this world." She touched one of the roses petals softly and paused before walking on up the path that led to a hill. The foliage and flowers disappeared behind us as we followed her. For a brief moment with her back to me, I felt like I had slipped back in time. Her long skirt and dark long hair swaying behind her, she reminded me of someone you would find in a History Channel show from the medieval period.

Lain stepped up beside me, his shoulder brushing mine briefly. I opened my mouth to ask him how long he had been in Ireland but closed it quickly as an electrical charge practically zapped the bejeebers out of me. The air around us practically sizzled. I looked up toward Brigit, who didn't seem phased as she continued up the path, calling over her shoulder that we were almost there.

"Don't worry," the man beside me mumbled. "You get used to it."

That meant he felt it too. The charge in the air crackled and increased the further up we went until we passed a small copse of trees before the megalith of standing stones appeared in a small clearing. A glow from the sun brightened the stone almost magically.

I laughed. It was an uneasy, almost hysterical chuckle that I had to quickly calm, or risk falling to the ground in hysterics. Lain only stared with amusement. Brigit turned around, humor lacking in her expression. She patiently waited as I composed myself and followed her. Lain brought up the rear almost with intentional slowness.

"I would have liked to have more time to prepare you, but this time around has been...." She trailed off as if searching for the right word. "It's been a challenge," she admitted with resolve. "But I hope to remedy that as best as I can."

"What do you mean?" I asked, confused.

Brigit didn't answer me but instead asked her own question. "So, when did your abilities first manifest?"

My mouth dropped open, and a fly could have flown in my mouth, and I would still stand there looking at her with disbelief on my face.

"How did you- I mean who..." I didn't finish but just stood there waiting; years of not being able to trust others taught me a valuable lesson. Listen intently first before exposing what you know to others.

Brigit grinned, spreading her hands out as she turned, walking further into the middle of the standing stones.

"Easy, my dear. You and I have known each other for a very, very long time. And it's time for you to return home."

"Wait," Lain called out to Brigit. "Not yet. She needs to adjust." His deep voice carried across the space between us and Brigit paused.

"We don't have enough time." She gritted between her teeth at him. Irritation flashed quickly in her gaze as her previously smiling and pleasant expression changed, and her lips pressed into a thin line.

"We must." He shrugged not affected by her sudden change in demeanor.

"She'll adjust," Brigit argued.

"No," Lain countered her in demand. He was saying more at that moment than I'd heard in the last hour. Brigit sighed, her shoulders sagging as she listened to him.

"Fine." She arched her eyebrow. "We'll do it your way, but you now have the honor of teaching her." Brigit glared at him as if she was a child and not the woman who had adopted Logan and me before she stomped off to sit on a fallen stone outside the circle.

I watched in disbelief. The surreal part of all this not truly sinking in.

"What the hell?" I finally exclaimed in question. "Who the hell are you people?" I began to turn to go back to the keep, but Lain stopped me by lightly grabbing my hand.

"Please, Ana, stay."

I stopped my feet planting themselves against my will. He called me Ana. The name silently tumbling from my lips as I sounded the familiar name out, my back still to him so he couldn't see me. Why did that sound so familiar?

His large hand was warm as it enveloped mine. His touched seemed...intimate, even if it was an innocent touch of hands. I turned to face him, still not sure if it was a good idea. I mean, these people were next level bonkers, and if I had too, I'd grab Logan, and we'd hustle the hell out of here and fast before we ended up in some cult driven sacrifice.

"Why did you call me that?" I asked instead of running—my gaze finding emerald orbs the same color as wet moss on the forest floor.

"I've always called you that." He shrugged as if I knew this. "You just can't remember."

"Why? What can't I remember? I've never met you before, have I?"

His lips tightened in a knowing smirk. "Not in this life. Not yet. But I've known you better than anyone has ever known you."

I laughed then with the hysterics I had held back before. "Holy forking shirt balls!" I exclaimed through my nervous chuckles. "You people are crazy. I knew this was too good to be true." I tried to turn and pull away, but he held my hand firmly.

"We are not crazy," he insisted in a low voice full of resolve. "You just don't remember."

"Let go of me," I warned my voice low, trying to mask the fear that was snaking up through me. He must have sensed it, but he held fast to my hand.

"No."

"I said, let go." My voice was more shrill this time.

"I'll never let go of you." He pulled me toward him until I was dangerously close to him. Closer than was comfortable for me. I didn't like being near people or being touched. Logan was the only exception.

"Who are you?" I asked in a shrill voice.

He dropped my hand by my side but still held my gaze with an intensity I didn't understand. Despite the familiarity, I felt with him. His forwardness made me instantly wary, not to mention everyone's very odd behavior. It made my spidey senses go haywire. I backed away but looked first at Lain then behind them at Brigit, who still looked impatient and annoyed, a complete opposite of her demeanor from earlier.

"My name is Cúchulainn. You call me Lain and have for a very long time. You know me, but just can't remember." His voice urged me to remember something that was ludicrous.

"Yeah, um." I practically chortled the words in a nervous laugh. "Well, so this has been fun, but I'm going to go now." I turned to run, but something stopped me. My legs wouldn't move. I pulled them up harder this time, and they stayed rooted in the spot as if glued to the ground.

"You had your chance, Lain." Brigit's bored voice called from behind me. I turned to try to look at her over my shoulder but couldn't see her very well. "Now it's my turn."

What happened next felt like something straight out of a fantasy movie. Something like Bilbo or Frodo would encounter if Tolkien had thought of it. The ground around my feet began to rumble as it then erupted in vines growing up from its depths. They were leafless, covered in the dirt that had pushed through to snaking themselves up my legs and arms. I started to scream, but it was cut off as shock from being practically thrown up into the air, and then caught in a hammock-like embrace by the vines. I realized, as they turned me toward Brigit, they were taking me to her, and she was controlling them.

CHAPTER SEVEN

"I said that wasn't necessary," Lain growled as he followed the vines to Brigit and me. I was still tangled in them, trying to wiggle in a futile attempt. Fear was an understatement at that point. I mean, hell, yeah, I'd known magic was real and or I was some weird freak of nature, but this was a whole new something else.

"Now listen," Brigit began ignoring Lain as she curled her fingers, bringing the vines and me closer. "My patience has grown thin. We are running out of time." She shot Lain a warning glare. For what, I had no idea. He was slightly behind me, and the vines that coiled tightly around me didn't give me enough room to wiggle, let alone turn my head to look.

"We can't just force her awake," Lain tried to argue from beside me.

Brigit's eyes began to furrow into a contemplative look, and she threw him a sardonic glare before continuing. I watched as tiny blossoms grew on the vines. They were white honeysuckles, the kind I would take Logan to look for and that he tried desperately to leak honey from without damaging the flower.

"We have to." There was a note of desperation in her voice. The sweetness from earlier, then the impatient irritation just a few moments ago gone as something akin to fear was drenched in each syllable. Just as fear gripped me as I realized my strange captivity. I bit at the vines spitting and growling for attention, but they were much too thick to gnaw through, and the leaves tasted bitter. Yet, Brigit barely spared me a glance.

Finally, with a deep sigh and a wave of her hand through the air, the vines sat me on the ground and untangled themselves from my body. I crumpled to my knees in front of Brigit. A million curses and questions in my head, but yet none could escape my lips. Instead, I watched Brigit, waiting to see what she would do. There wasn't any reason to plan my escape. We were in an open space. Any direction was a means of escape, but I knew, and they knew I wouldn't get very far.

Brigit shuddered, her shoulders moving as she did. Her blonde hair spilled over shoulders and face as she joined me on her knees in the dirt. Her perfectly white dress ruined. Somewhere in the back of my mind, something said. *She hates to be dirty.*

Then she looked up at me with her pale as a cloudless day blue eyes. There was a plea in them. One I didn't understand, and my face must have conveyed my question to her plea because she let out a deep sigh. "I'm sorry." She said instead. "We really are here to help you, and if you want to learn who and what you are, you'll need to come with us."

"You can trust us." Lain pressed as he stepped closer to me, cautiously, as if I was a baby deer who would sprint off at any second. I felt like that baby deer, only I was caught in headlights and the realities of this moment was what had me caught.

"What are you people?" I finally decided to ask after a few moments of trying desperately to gather my thoughts. "Are you some sort of witches? Did I just get adopted by a group from Hogwarts, and you guys plan to sacrifice me to your god?"

Lain's lips twitched. "Hogwarts?" he asked.

"Yeah, like Harry Potter. The kid from the books and the movies who can do magic stuff."

"No, but I'd like to meet this Potter if he can wield magic. I've never known many humans to possess the ability and not for a very long time." He looked off in the distance as if contemplating this and as if I hadn't just been strung up like a fly in a spider's web by vines. It was then I decided these people were grade-A certified loonies. Okay, well, powerful loonies.

"Merlin was pretty good at it. He had a pretty impressive talent for it." Brigit agreed also switching once again from the heaping mess of just moments ago, to someone in serious thought over the possibility of finding someone with magic.

"Is that it?" I began after trying to slow my breathing. My heart was still pounding in high alert, and I wasn't letting my guard down, but I wasn't about to run off either before getting answers. "Am I some Merlin, and you guys want to use me in some way?"

This produced a guffaw of laughter from Lain and Brigit's lips to twitch upwards into a semblance of the smile she had plastered on her face earlier.

"If only." She chuckled. "No, you, my dear, are much more important than a man with childish tricks."

"What is it then?" I pressed in question, the dark strands of my hair blowing into my eyes as the wind picked up. Brigit didn't answer. Instead, she lifted her head.

"It's time," she announced instead as she stood, brushing the dirt from her clothes. Then she walked to the middle of the ring of standing stones beckoning Lain and I closer. Lain took my hand gently.

"If you want an answer, this is your chance," he whispered close to my ear. It wasn't creepy like you would imagine someone whispering into your ear. Instead, it felt like an invitation to more than just finding out who I was.

"But Logan," I began then stopped waiting for an answer.

"He'll be fine. Craig has him. Are you ready?" he asked again.

I shook my head violently, then paused. With a sigh, I nodded, letting the man I'd just met pull me toward Brigit. And then, almost instantaneously, the wind began to pick up ferociously, and suddenly, as if we were dropped in the middle of a tornado, my hair whipped into my face. Lain held tight to my hand, and Brigit took my other. Before I knew what was happening, it felt like we were sucked through and up the funnel of a tornado, and I shamefully screamed.

The wind continued as the roaring in my ears became deafening. It pulled at me and seemed to rip through me or rip me apart, I wasn't sure. Nothing seemed real. Yet, at the same time, it was more real than anything in my life had ever been before. And I realized as the world around me dissolved from the stones and the trees in some unseen force that swirled around us- I wasn't scared.

Until I landed hard and fell backward onto the ground, hitting my head.

CHAPTER EIGHT

The first thing I noticed as I opened my eyes wasn't an image. It was a feeling. It was something I didn't remember feeling before. That innate sense of belonging. The one people instinctively felt in a place they knew they had every right to be, where they were wanted, and where they were loved. A place where you knew everyone, and you could let your guard down. I knew before even opening my eyes that we weren't in the standing stones anymore.

"Welcome to Murias," Lain announced as he helped me up.

I looked around me. It wasn't much different. Just different scenery, but the air was charged in what had just been a mere fraction at the standing stones. This place pulsated with energy, with magic. The grass was greener and lusher. It looked as though it was as soft as fur. There were flowers and various colored blooms sprouting almost everywhere. The air was fresh and clean. Nothing like the acrid air that at times choked me.

I let go of Lain's hand leaning down to place my hands bare to the soft grass. I was right. It was soft, and—I paused— looking quickly to Lain and then to Brigit. It was warm as if it gave off body heat. I moved my hands, channeling my natural abilities, and they burst through in ways they had never before and with a force that scared me. The ground around me vibrated, and there was an answer as if I had called to it.

Yes. Yes, I'm here. Welcome home, my friend. I have missed you. The living breathing planet beneath me sang and rejoiced as clear as the birds, which were not as similar as I had thought, except one. There, perched close, was a crow. It stepped into the soft grass and hopped toward me. I stared at it, not moving when, to my utter bewilderment, it perched itself on my shoulder.

"The Morrigan has returned." Brigit breathed, dipping low. Looking up from her long lashes, she continued, "Welcome my sister- and queen."

"Queen?" I looked at them with the same confusion that seemed to have remained on my features since I first met them. Brigit's head snapped up.

"Yes, do you still not remember?" Brigit asked this time with less reverence and a hint of disbelief. She glided over toward me. "Tell me you remember!"

I backed away. The bird still on my shoulder cawing toward Brigit as if in warning. Brigit recoiled from the bird and hissed at it.

"Brigit, settle down," Lain cautioned. "We knew it would be harder this time."

"What the freaking crackers is going on?" I asked still using the made-up words I'd forced myself to replace for curse words so Logan wouldn't pick them up.

Logan. Would these mentally unstable people go back for him too? I needed to find out quickly what they wanted, why I was here, and why having a damn crow on my shoulder didn't freak me out as it should. "Who is the Morrigan?"

Both of their eyes swiveled to meet my gaze. Lain hesitated as if he was trying to think of the best way to answer, but Brigit didn't and responded quickly, "You are."

"Okay...." I stressed the word as if I was humoring a couple of lunatics, but then thought better of it. "Why is- I mean, why am I so important?" I took deep breaths to calm the storm that raged both in my heart and the pounding of my heart. I wasn't scared, but the feeling of something bigger than myself pushed at the edges of my conscious-ness. The crow pecked lightly at my ear as if in affection.

"I told her this wasn't a good idea," Brigit muttered to Lain. Practi-cally stomping around as if to survey the area. "We need to move before one of them notices us."

"Who?" I asked only to be answered with an annoyed glare from Brigit. Lain just stood there, unsure of what to do. His gaze shifted between Brigit and me.

"The followers of the dark court," Lain answered, joining Brigit in her search. "Very few of us have the ability to travel outside the realm." He paused briskly, walking back toward me as he lightly tugged at my elbow.

"We need to move before they see her. Shoo, Gert," Brigit insisted as she swatted her hands toward the crow. It flapped its obsidian wings back at her as if to tell her, *Not happening, lady*. But with one mean glare from Brigit as her perfect features twisted up in a menacing threat, and the crow cawed softly in rebuke before flying away. "Dumb bird," Brigit muttered at its departure.

"At least it didn't poop on me." I sighed in relief as I checked my shoulder. Brigit's lips twitched as if she would crack a smile.

"Gert wouldn't dare poop on you," she said instead. I watched, as with a snap of her fingers, Brigit fastened something from the leaves and vines that were forming in a bush not far away. Only, upon inspection, it wasn't an ordinary bush, it was just as soft as the grass, and the flowers on it were shiny crimson and reminded me of silk. Two petals overlapped on the bottom, creating an asymmetrical blossom as the two round orbs that adorned the top half fluttered open to reveal eyes.

"What the fork is this place?" I gasped, stepping back once again. Then I giggled nervously before pursing my lips and breathing in deeply to calm myself. "I get it now." I nodded.

"Finally!" Brigit turned with the newly fastened leafy cap in her hands. She handed it to me. Then clasped her hands on my shoulders happily.

"Yeah, this is Wonderland. You're the white rabbit, and I'm getting curiouser and curiouser."

Brigit groaned as Lain laughed. "You would quote Lewis Carroll of all people," he chuckled. Brigit just rubbed her hands down her face. It seemed the mask she had worn at the keep was gone as it was replaced with a frustrated harpy. Thinking of the keep made me remember Logan.

"Listen, this has been fun.." I trailed off jumping backward, avoiding the now snapping flower before it bit me with its surprisingly sharp teeth. "But I need to get back to Logan. So if you'll kindly wake me up."

"We need to just break it to her," Brigit turned to say to Lain.

"No." He shook his head at her.

"We'll take her back soon. She'll want to say goodbye." He gave me a pitying look as his mossy green eyes met mine.

"But-" She stopped when he snarled at her in warning. "Fine," she agreed instead.

"Let's go to the garden and get on with it. Hopefully, the full process isn't necessary."

"It appears we may have no choice," Lain exasperated with a weary resolution.

"Put the cap on. We don't want anyone to recognize you."

CHAPTER NINE

After we traveled, avoiding what they called common areas, we found ourselves in a garden. It was the most beautiful thing I'd ever seen. Towering bushes and trees spilling over with brightly colored flowers and various fragrances assaulting my senses. Yet, none too overpowering. They seemed to mesh into the perfect symphony of colors and smells. Red blossoms similar to roses, but the blooms were shaped like daisy leaves that cascaded upward, grouped together in a large blossom which emitted a sweet yet tart fragrance that tickled my nose. Then a tree full of yellow blossoms that drifted down to blanket the ground with its petals. It reminded me of sunshine and laughter, bright with a smidge of citrus.

I stooped to pick one of the soft velvety petals. It was as if I was holding actual velvet, thick and soft, and vibrant yellow despite its detachment from the tree above. The tree giggled, and I quickly dropped the petal and stepped back. Alarmed at first, then I laughed along with them. I truly was in Wonderland.

"As fun as it is to watch you in your childlike discovery of our garden creatures. You may want to stop before we draw attention from a snooping eye," Brigit gritted lowly through a pleasant smile. Only someone close could see the silent warning in her gaze.

"Stay away from the blue flowers on the right. They are weeping melodies. And although lovely in their own way, they will have you tearing in minutes to their song and the smell of sad memories," Lain whispered close to my ear, so close I felt his hot breath.

I cast a quick glance at the offending flowers in question, making a mental note to move far away as we passed and to hold my nose. All I needed right now was to break down in tears and show some hidden vulnerability to these people who practically kidnapped me.

"Lain," Brigit called as we walked through a bush devoid of any extra special flowers. "It's time." Lain stepped forward and extended his palms up, taking a deep breath as he stood there. I watched an odd shimmer began to emit from his palms and surround us. Brigit, however, paid little attention. Instead, she looked around us cautiously as if she was watching for something in particular. I gave her a questioning stare.

"I need to make sure no one sees us or knows we went any further than this," she replied as she met my confused stare. And then I watched as she seemed to conjure something from nothing, an illusion of all three of us walking from the same way we came.

Who the hell are these people? I asked myself, deciding, for the moment, to remain quiet. It had been my experience that silence and careful observation tell you more than the words that people tell you about themselves. The three of us walked exactly the same way we came and continued on to another walkway across from this one until completely out of sight.

"It's done. No one can see us now," Lain called over his shoulder as Brigit joined him. With both their backs to me, I thought briefly of running, but then Lain turned, his long dark hair brushing his broad shoulders, and those emerald eyes met mine. "That would be a very bad idea."

"Did you- did you just read my mind?" I demanded. Then worry cascaded over me. Had he heard how much I thought he was attractive or the fact I felt drawn to him. His gaze didn't waver or give anything away. He just shrugged.

"I try not to, but you are very loud."

Grrreat, I thought. This was going to be fun.

I followed Brigit and Lain, and they restructured their walk until I was the center of our trio. The maze of bushes converged to become smaller, not allowing anything but a line. We had turned so many times I knew I'd never get out of here without them. So it would no longer benefit me if I tried to escape. And besides, we all know what happened to Alice. I'd take my chances for now with my kidnappers. Adoptive mother or not, Brigit was my best chance of getting home.

I scoffed then, thinking of Brigit as a mother. For whatever reason, the idea seemed even more ridiculous now than it had before. Here she looked even younger, my age even. Whatever magic she had used earlier to appear older had vanished as if she no longer cared to keep up the illusion. Her bright blue eyes seemed to radiate as much as the luminous glow of her pale alabaster hair, and her long thick hair, now drifting down her back like a cascading waterfall, seemed glossier and shinier than before. When the sun hit it, it seemed to look precisely like spun gold, only softer and more malleable. Her bright pink lips were pursed in concentration.

I concentrated just on Brigit, trying my best to ignore Lain. God forbid he hear my thoughts and what I thought of his unnatural gorgeousness. But then my thoughts drifted to Logan. Was he okay? Did Craig have something to do with this? Were they planning to take me and had orchestrated this whole adoption to whisk me off, possibly killing me? Would they do the same to Logan next? My heart sped up as I looked around, wondering once again about escaping.

"We are not going to harm you or Logan." Lain leaned into my ear once again, quietly breathing the words. A shiver snaked down my spine. I wasn't sure if it was from the close contact of his mouth and the intimacy he continued to use in his answers to me or fear, but it made me jump, and he backed away. I didn't turn to look at him but continued to follow Brigit.

The bushes that lined the path changed colors as we went. They were a rainbow of colors. Where were they leading us? I almost thought we would be walking forever until Brigit finally stopped in front of a dead end.

"Did we go the wrong way?" I asked as she stood there looking at the purple bush that didn't extend any further in front of us. She turned her crystal gaze to me, the sharp edge from earlier gone. I had begun to realize that possibly it was her way of dealing with the worry she was trying to conceal.

"No, it's your turn." She motioned for me to move into her spot, shifting over, her skirts falling behind her with a rustle. I glanced at Lain then back at Brigit.

"What do you mean?"

"It's your turn to use your abilities," Lain patiently responded. "Think about the door opening and us walking through." I gave both of them a sardonic look, deciding this was the most vivid dream I'd had yet, and at least I had dreamed up a dreamy guy. Normally, my dreams were dark, and I didn't understand them. But this took the cake.

"Just humor us," Brigit groaned the annoyance back in her musical voice. It was almost a contradiction to the sweetness of the sound. It almost felt as if it was a part of her nature. Like those predators that seemed to be cute and innocent, but then tore your head off when you weren't looking.

I sighed and turned, closing my eyes, trying to feel the earth... or whatever it was beneath me, feeling the energy in the air as it crackled. And something that had never happened before did at that moment. I felt everything. Every living thing and individual on this planet... no realm. I knew then it was a realm within our own planet, hidden and secret. Filled with magic and made of magic so thick, it was as if it was solid. And it filled me, strengthened me. It was neither dark or light, good or evil. It just was.

"You did it," Lain announced, and I opened my eyes. "Welcome back, my queen."

CHAPTER TEN

Before me stood a small clearing, and in the center was a tree. Black and white fruit hung from its branches. My mouth opened, and I considered Lain's words but was silenced by the beauty of the tree. It was alone and majestic, and so full of life. It shimmered and sparkled as the sun above glistened off it as if it was made of crystal, yet each monochromatic fruit stood stark and oddly inviting against the contrast of its branches.

"The tree of life." Brigit sighed as if greeting a long lost friend for the first time in a long time. I began to step into the clearing, but Lain grabbed me quickly, pulling me against his chest. Close it quickly. I frantically turned toward his eyes, seeing the worry and silent urgency in their mossy depths, and as if instinctively, I lifted my hand as the doorway closed, and the sound of a deep voice barked from behind us.

"They are here." A man pale in every way and just as beautiful as Brigit with long blonde hair and crystal blue eyes stood in the entrance of the last turn, with a menacing hatred in his eyes. "And it is her."

Next, a web of energy snaked around me, almost as if it was a python, finding its way to my neck. It wasn't squeezing yet, but it was alarming all the same. Another man, as dark as the other with black hair tied back in a severe man bun peered at us, indifference in the depths of his obsidian eyes.

"Good," he stated as if unconcerned. Bring them to the throne room. It was then that I noticed both Lain and Brigit were restrained in the same way. Both with their mouths indented as if forced to remain silent.

But an odd thought echoed in my mind, and I knew it was Lain. *Make them drop us... Will it. And they will listen. You are our queen, a warrior, the phantom queen, The Morrigan.* And something inside me knew. It knew he was right. I couldn't believe it, but it felt right.

This was just a dream, right? Why not play along. I let the power snake through me as the man had snaked his around my body, coiling from me as his had coiled around the three of us. I threw it back at him as it blasted them both back.

"Your queen has returned, and you shall bow down before my power. Leave here and go." The men obeyed, a look of anger on their faces. But the man with the obsidian eyes roared and broke free as he held up a shining green amulet and rushed forward, throwing both Lain and Brigit into the surrounding bushes. He lifted a sword to strike me.

Something instinctual took over inside me. I turned as he missed and elbowed him in his kidney. I dropped and snatched a dagger from his boot, and before he could turn to strike me again, I backed up, barely escaping the blade. With one swift move, I flipped the dagger through the air so fast it landed to the hilt in the man's heart, and I held his gaze.

I knew I should feel guilt, terror, and repulsion at the fact I had killed a man. But none came. Instead, it felt as though someone had taken over my body, and I was merely a passenger.

"As you very well should remember," I began my voice, menacing and unfamiliarly hard. "I do not permit treason of any kind, leave." My hard stare met the other man, the one with the same paleness as Brigit, and he ran from where he came — dipping his head down in a bow.

"Yes, my queen." And he was gone.

The thing that had taken me over, or the person it seemed more believable to say, evaporate as I stood there, my eyes unable to move from the crumpled body before me. Blood trickled from his mouth. But he wasn't quite dead. The light left his eyes as they locked on mine. His last dying expression was one of hate. Hate for me.

"Morrigan?" Brigit asked quizzically as she stepped closer, ignoring the body bleeding out on the dirt path before our feet. Crimson liquid stained the ground a darker shade of brown. She said my name in the same accent exaggeration as Lain had, so I corrected her.

"Morgan."

She gave an exasperated sigh. "You stubborn...." But she stopped and closed her lips into another annoyed purse of her lips before relaxing them and continuing, "We need to go and quickly. Open it back up."

"You guys aren't concerned with the body?" I asked, side-stepping the corpse.

Brigit answered with a spit toward his dark head, "The bastard had it coming."

And so, with a slight queasy feeling in my stomach, yet not the revulsion one would expect from such an act of violence, I turned and once again opened the gateway to the tree.

This was one hell of a dream, and I was a badass.

CHAPTER ELEVEN

We stood in front of the tree, the branches dipping down toward us, so bright and glittery, upon closer inspection, I noticed they were even see-through, little veins snaking through its branches as if was alive.

"It is," Lain answered my thoughts.

"Pick." Brigit insisted impatiently.

"Pick a fruit?" I raised a brow at her. "To do what?" My hand was still touching the smooth branch marveling over its fascinating oddness. It was magnificent. I felt in awe of it.

"To eat." She looked at me as if this was the stupidest question she had ever heard — the unspoken addition of, *What else do you do with fruit?* just on the tip of her tongue. Even though Brigit was kind of a pain in the ass, for whatever reason, I liked her.

I hadn't thought that before. More concerned with them kidnapping me, but we were past this, and I was almost positive this was a dream now. I looked to Lain, allowing my thoughts to go wild since I was going to eventually wake up and find myself in the study with the painting of the woman staring down at me. It occurred to me then that she was also called the Morrigan. Must be where the dream stemmed from.

I shrugged and stepped back, looking at the tree. Each fruit was different from the next, unique in its own way, yet one distinct similarity and difference at the same time. They were either black, white, gray, or adorning bright colors. I walked around the tree, wondering what it was I was looking for. Searching for something. I just wasn't sure what it was.

And then I saw it. The one fruit, perfect, symmetrical, and different from every other fruit on the tree. It was half black and half white, perfectly round, and despite its monochromatic coloring, it looked delicious, inviting. But it was too far up to pick. I lifted my gaze to it, deciding that that was my fruit. I just knew it.

And as if it also knew, it dropped into my hand, as if to say, *Take me, I was meant just for you.* I turned, holding up my prize to Brigit and Lain, neither was surprised, but a contemplative look etched across Brigit's features at the choice.

"Interesting," she murmured almost too low for me to hear her.

Lain, however, didn't seem surprised, but something else radiated from him that didn't really make sense to me. It felt and looked like what pride would be. I didn't have much experience with someone being proud of me, but there had been times that Logan had made me feel that way. And it felt like what I imagined he would feel when I said as much to him.

And then Logan was all I could think of. Fear erupted inside me, starting from my chest. Something I didn't understand. It was primal and... gut-wrenching.

"Wait!" Lain rushed forward. "You must calm down," he insisted concern in his voice. I turned to glance at Brigit pity in her eyes. Something wasn't right. I wished more than anything to be back at the keep. I felt both Lain and Brigit as they grabbed me by my arms. Were they trying to restrain me? The all-encompassing emotions of something—I didn't know what, still coiled around me just like the man's energy snake, only it was inside me, deep inside me. And I closed my eyes tight, trying to force it away, trying to wake from the dream. My hand still clasped the fruit.

Lain's voice was soothing in my ear as he whispered, "It's okay. You are safe," he repeated it as a whisper, but part of it was lost to me as the world swirled around us. The roaring in my ears intensified.

Then it stopped abruptly, and the air changed. I was less crisp, chiller, less fragrant. Yet familiar. I opened one eye to see the same towering stones casting a shadow over me. No, over us. Brigit and Lain still clutched my arms, and the fruit was still clasped in my hand.

"Really, Morrigan!" Brigit yelled into my ear. "Do you have to be so dramatic. Every damn time." She shook her head and walked off, muttering to herself.

"When you are ready, eat the fruit." Lain shrugged. "We'll give you space and walk you back to the keep." He paused his now sparkly sage gaze flashing briefly to Brigit. "Take your time and let us know when you are ready."

I didn't understand him, but his eyes spoke volumes. He felt the same pity for me, as Brigit had earlier. But why? I shrugged and began to walk back to the keep, briefly noticing they followed but tried my best not to think. *Was the dream still going?* I cursed my vivid imagination and the dream state I was apparently stuck in, but if I was being honest, I knew it was a lie, even if I refused to admit it to myself.

The thick door to the front of the keep was in front of me finally. Brigit and Lain stood in the front yard waiting. *Odd*, I thought. This was Brigit's home. *No, it's not. It's yours.* That voice insisted inside me again. I pushed the door open, and there stood Logan as if he was waiting. I looked about quickly after smiling at Logan. Craig was nowhere to be seen.

"You were gone so long," Logan whined. His short blond hair sticking up in different directions. I dropped to my knees to look him in the eyes. A sadness flitted inside me for a moment.

"I know. I'm sorry. I've been asleep." He looked at me as a little boy would when they loved you completely with everything they had. It made my heart ache and sing at the same time. Logan had been what saved me through the harshness of everything that happened as I grew. From the abuse to the fear, the lack of love, feeling unwanted, and the pain of so much a child should never understand. I had done everything to make sure Logan didn't experience the same.

"What is that?" Logan asked his warm brown eyes resting on the fruit in my hand.

"This?" I held it up questioningly. "It's fruit." I smiled warmly at him with all the love that for some reason, ached inside me. I was once again overcome with so many emotions. From gratefulness to love, pain, sadness, and then acceptance.

"Are you going to eat it?" he asked innocently, his eyes widening. I looked down at the fruit in my hand. It still resembled the same fruit that had fallen into my open hands from the glorious magical living tree.

"Yes. Yes, I am." Tears flowed from my eyes. And I didn't understand why.

"Don't cry, Morgy." Logan grabbed my hand with his much smaller one then used his other to brush the tears away before hugging me to him. I returned the hug taking in as much as I could. "I love you," he whispered with his sweet voice.

"I love you more than anything in the world, Logan." Fighting back tears, I gave him a sad grin and bit into the fruit, the delicious juices indescribable yet more delicious than anything I'd ever had before. It tasted like happiness and sorrow, love, and hate. It was sweet yet sour. It was what all the good and the bad things of life tastes like. And I watched through a veil of unshed tears in my eyes as Logan disappeared with a smile on his lips and love in his warm burnt umber gaze.

And The Morrigan awoke from her slumber from within me.

"Goodbye, Logan." I cried. "Thank you for being the light within my darkness."

Then I turned, ready to take my place once again as the phantom queen, prepared to lead my people the Tuatha de Danann into a better future.

In the distance, the crows cawed, calling me home.

Trish Beninato is a young adult author who writes fantasy, sci-fi, and paranormal with a little romance featuring strong female leads that kick ass all on their own. She lives in Colorado currently, but who knows where she will end up next, even she doesn't know. She holds a Master's in Education with an emphasis in Reading Literacy but instead writes the literature she once sought to teach. She is a wine and coffee enthusiast who overindulges way too much. A proud nerd to the core, you'll find Star Wars and Marvel characters littering the shelves of her office, which she uses influence from as she writes her stories. Her debut novel, Acceptance: The Jewel Trilogy is described as X-men meets Percy Jackson.

facebook.com/trishbeninato

twitter.com/TrishBen_Books

instagram.com/trishbeninato

DESTINED

BY C.A. KING

CHAPTER ONE

Alarm clocks had two settings: I don't really want to get up, and maximum annoyance. Today it was the latter. Tommy's arm flung sideways, the back of his hand hitting the snooze button. That was no better than putting a bandage on a shark bite. It was only a matter of minutes before the wound bled through. He tossed the covers off his body, slipping his feet over the edge of the bed. A yawn and a stretch were the first step to waking up, even on the best of days. This wasn't going to be one of those.

Halloween night might have been hailed as the kids' favorite celebration in most places, but not in Placency. There were no costumes, candy, or fancy carved pumpkins—just a single parade and re-enactment of the saving of their town from the grips of a witch. That single act had shaped the future of the lives of every family residing there. Not all benefited from it either.

Getting ready was a chore he could have done without. Brushing hair was way overrated. It only got messy again the moment there was a gust of wind or gym class. Besides, nothing was going to truly help the orange mop atop his head. Tommy took a single glance in the mirror before heading down the stairs to take his usual place at the table for breakfast.

Darn! His cereal had already been poured. It was going to be a mushy morning in the Carter household. He shoved a spoonful into his mouth, reading the headline of the newspaper his father was holding: PARADE EXPECTED TO BRING TOURISTS. That was a joke. No one cared about their half-ass production of a history that wasn't factual. There was no such thing as witches, and it wasn't because of the deeds of a single well-known wealthy family. The Johnson's owned seventy-five percent of the town, and they owed it all to their ancestors murdering a woman. Most people went to jail for less. They became heroes—go figure that logic.

A paper bag crinkled in his mother's hands. "I hope you don't mind, dear," she said. "Things are a bit tight this week."

Tommy eyed the bag. It was the single worst thing that could possibly happen to him. Of course, it wasn't his mother's fault. She had no idea she had single-handedly doomed him to an afternoon of being a punching bag. He forced a smile. "It's fine," he lied. "I love your sandwiches. They're way better than lunch money any day."

The newspaper folded in his father's hand. "It won't be for long. I've put in for some overtime." He sighed. "This is important. I need you to be on your best behavior today. Don't ruffle any feathers. We are going to make a good impression at this year's festival."

"I know," Tommy said, shoving another spoonful of mush into his mouth.

"I don't think you do," his father scolded. "They'll be watching. If I have any hope of getting that extra work, it rides on how we present ourselves. One misstep from any of us, and I can kiss the opportunity goodbye. They don't hand out privileges on a silver platter. They're earned."

"Yes, sir," Tommy answered. "I'll be careful." There was little else he could say. His relationship with his father was shaky at best.

"That's my boy," his father praised. "I knew I could count on you. I don't know why you don't try to be friends with the Johnson boys."

"I don't think they want to be friends with me," Tommy muttered, gagging the words with his spoon, making them too muffled to be understood.

The Johnson family wasn't only the most powerful in town; they were the biggest bullies as well. Everyone answered to them in one way or another—adult or child. Tommy's father took it to a whole new level, though. A man's priority should always be his family. That wasn't the case with Terry Carter. His only concern was sucking up.

"Have a good day, Terry," his mother said, her lips almost brushing his father's cheek. Terry managed to turn just in time to miss it.

"You too, Janet," he replied, rushing out the door.

Tommy's spoon clanged on the bowl. That was the worst part about his dad—the way he treated his mother. She deserved so much better.

CHAPTER TWO

If the after-school specials were to be believed, lunch was the best part of the day. They were only television shows, though. In the real world, a free period sucked. That was when The Johnson boys went on the prowl. There were four of them, although technically they were only cousins. Bill was the alpha of the pack, with Todd, Pete, and Harrison hanging on his every suggestion. Together they ruled the high school and anything else that catered to the under eighteen.

As rich as their families were, it was never enough. Protection money was the current racket—paid to stop them from delivering the beatings. The teachers turned the other cheek. They needed their jobs as much as anyone else in town.

Tommy hit hard against the locker; back first. It was difficult to decide which was worse; the way his spine bent or his head banging. Both came with their own side of pain.

"Cough it up," Bill demanded, slamming his fist directly beside Tommy's left temple. "I don't have all day to waste on a nerd like you." A chorus of laughter erupted from behind him.

"I-I," Tommy stuttered, lifting the paper bag containing his lunch. "I don't have money today. My mom packed me a sandwich. You can have it."

Bill snatched the bag, tossing it over his shoulder. It hit the garbage with a thud. "You think I want to eat something made by your mom?" he snickered. "I like you. I am going to let you off with a warning this time."

"Thank..." The rest of Tommy's words vanished—all air being sucked from his body. It merely took a single punch to his midsection. He keeled over, slouching; arms wrapped tightly around himself.

"Look at me," Bill demanded, straightening Tommy back up.

He saw the fist coming but felt nothing. Blood gushed from his nostrils, coloring the ground crimson. Tommy reached up, one finger trying to stop the flow. He'd never had a broken nose before. Other than the mess, he didn't get what the big deal was. It hurt a whole lot less than being pummeled in other places.

"I thought you were letting me off with a warning," Tommy complained, his voice trembling.

"I did," Bill chuckled. "It'll be a whole lot worse if you don't have money for me tonight at the re-enactment."

"I don't have any!" Tommy exclaimed. "It's not like I have a job. Where am I supposed to get money by tonight?"

"That's your problem, little man," Bill replied. "Steal from mom if you have to. Women always leave their purses lying around. I don't care what you do, as long as you have it for me. If not, you'll be spending some time in the hospital."

The moment Bill let go of his jacket; Tommy fell to the ground. It wouldn't have done any good to tell them there wasn't any cash in his mother's purse. She didn't have two nickels to rub together. Things were dismal, but at least they couldn't get any worse. A pair of polished black shoes appeared in front of his face. Wishful thinking flew out the window.

"What's going on here?" the school principal bellowed.

"He jumped me from behind," Bill lied. "It was self-defense."

"Tommy Carter," Principal Dean said, shaking his head. "Today of all days. I don't know what goes through that head of yours."

"I think he's jealous," Pete suggested. "He wanted us to buy him lunch... even tossed his own in the garbage."

"Yeah," Todd agreed. "He said it wasn't good enough. When Bill refused, Tommy jumped him. It was self-defense."

"To the office, Tommy," Principal Dean scolded. "I'll be calling your parents and Bill's as well. This attitude of yours has to stop."

"But..."

"I don't want to hear it," Principal Dean blurted out in a stern voice. "Instead of useless excuses, you should be using your time to think of a proper apology." He turned to the other boys. "You four, head to your regular classes."

"Yes, sir," Bill said, a sly grin forming in the corners of his mouth.

Tommy hung his head. It was his mother who came for him. He sat on the bench outside the office door, listening to Principal Dean lecture her on the proper way to bring up a child. His heart sank. She was the only person he hadn't wanted to disappoint. He already knew she'd be crying the whole walk home. Those tears were the real torture; bruises healed emotions rarely did.

It wasn't fair—life wasn't fair—being punished for running into Bill's fist wasn't fair, especially since he wasn't moving at the time. Their story didn't even make sense. He was half the size of those guys, and there were four of them. It was one thing to be a little strange and another to be suicidal.

The door opened. His mother walked by, uttering only one word, "Come."

Tommy complied, staying a few steps back the whole walk home. From there, he couldn't see the disappointment in her eyes. Yelling, he could take. The strap, he could take. Tears, however, meant both their hearts were broken.

It wasn't until his mother took a seat at the kitchen table that her emotions poured out. "What were you thinking? Today of all days... and your father was trying so hard to get that overtime, too. They'll never give it to him now."

"I'm sorry," Tommy mumbled. There was little else to say. If he tried to explain, it would only make things worse. How could he tell her it was all because he didn't have any lunch money? Putting the blame on her wasn't the right thing to do. She already did that to herself on a daily basis.

"You threw your lunch in the garbage," she cried. "If it wasn't good enough for you, you didn't have to take it. I am doing my best."

"I know, Mom," Tommy said, placing one hand on her shoulder. "I know you won't believe me, but I didn't throw it away. I didn't attack anyone either. It's this place—this town. I hate it here. Why can't we move?"

Janet sighed. "Where would we go? Where would we live? The economy is bad all over. Your father is lucky he has a job. If it weren't for the Johnsons..."

"Why can't anyone see they are the whole problem?" Tommy blurted out. "I wish I could go back in time and stop them from murdering that woman. I bet then things would be different."

"You can't change the past," Janet scoffed, sniffling. "Even if you could, it wouldn't change who we all are. Go upstairs until it's time to go to the festival."

"Can't I stay home?" Tommy pleaded.

"No," Janet replied. "You need to apologize in front of the whole town. It's the only hope your father has to save face."

Tommy raced up the stairs, thinking twice about slamming his bedroom door. He loved his mother too much for that. Instead, he pounded his fists on his dresser. After a few deep breaths, he glared at his own reflection.

Two black eyes...perfect.

CHAPTER THREE

Tommy grabbed his costume for the night from the closet. Everyone in town had one. His was fashioned after the peasant boy who worked in the stables. It was appropriate since the boy had been a great-great-grandfather of his—there might have been one more or one less great—he could never remember the details.

For the most part, his mother had recovered from the emotional outburst earlier and was back to her sweet, caring self. Every detail had to be perfect, although there was little she could do about his double shiner. Things would stay calm until they met up with his father. He'd blame her the same way Principal Dean had. Eventually, his nagging would end up with his mother bursting out in tears one more time.

That wasn't the worst the night had to hold, either. There wasn't a dime to be scrounged for Bill. That wasn't going to go over well.

The first chance he found, Tommy veered from his mother's chosen path, taking the back way to the makeshift stables—an empty service garage with several bays filled with hay. It was only a block or two before the footsteps shadowing his had his knees shaking. The pace quickened—his pursuers matching the speed. If it wasn't Bill, it had to be his sidekicks. He wasn't ready to die just yet. If he stayed on the roads, they'd catch him in no time. His stamina wasn't quite up to their level. That left one option: the cemetery. If he was cunning enough, he could lose them in the dark. If he wasn't, his body was already in the right place for the funeral.

Bravery was a word reserved for special people, none of whom resided in Placency. If they did, Tommy hadn't met them. It definitely wouldn't be used to describe either the Johnson boys or himself. In this case, however, it was a matter of choosing between two evils; the lesser of which was worrying about ghosts and zombies. They probably weren't real. Bill's fists were, and they packed a wallop.

The moment the cemetery gates came into view, so did the chain link and lock holding them closed. There was no turning around, though. The others were almost directly on top of his heels. Tommy pried the gates apart as far as they would go, sliding sideways between the bars. It was probably a good thing Bill squished his nose earlier in the day, or he might not have made it.

"There he is," Bill yelled. "Get him."

Tommy didn't look back. The rattling chains told him everything he needed to know. The Johnson boys were stuck at the entrance. He had barely made it through the opening: there was no way any of them were going to. That meant the four would have to go over the top of the fence if they wanted to resume their chase. Climbing was way too much work for them. They were four teens who didn't even do their own homework. Of course, if they had, they might have realized they could simply wait it out. Tommy couldn't stay in there forever. Even if he spent the night, the caretaker would unlock the gates at dawn.

Simply not hearing any more voices or footsteps wasn't enough to halt Tommy's movements. His legs had a mind of their own and planned on putting some distance between the entrance and themselves. With adrenaline still pumping through his system, his breath and heart rate weren't going to slow down anytime soon, either.

Tommy scooted around a grave marker, bracing his back against it. Rubbing the sweat off his face, he took a moment to find his bearings —nothing was recognizable. He'd stumbled into the oldest part of the cemetery. No one ever went there anymore. That was a good thing. If he were lucky, no one would any time soon, either.

It was the perfect Halloween night. A low-lying fog crept around gravestones, rolling in waves across the ground. A beast howled in the distance. Tommy glanced up at wisps of clouds partially blocking a full moon. It was exactly what everyone else in the surrounding townships and counties wanted for a fright-filled night. Somehow, the idea of haunted houses and spooky costumes lacked luster now that he was living in a nightmare.

The howls increased in frequency, growing louder. Whatever critter was responsible for making the eerie noises had closed in on his location. He wasn't quite ready to admit werewolves existed, but that didn't mean he wanted to be eaten by wild animals on the prowl. Of course, leaving the confines of the cemetery was still too risky. He'd heard his father use the saying 'damned if I do, damned if I don't.' He finally understood exactly what that meant.

A twig snapped, the fog hiding the culprit. Tommy backed up, keeping his eyes glued to the spot where the noise had come. He felt the cold flat surface of stone against his back. It was one of the larger crypts. His feet slid sideways, inching around it slowly. Sudden movements were a bad idea when faced with a possible animal attack. He'd learned that much from a nature show. He clung to the slab behind him tighter than cling wrap to a bowl—his fingers feeling the way for the rest of his body. They stopped, fumbling over the ragged edges of a crack in the foundation. It only took a light push, and he was stumbling backward.

Tommy thought twice about catching himself, but chose not to. At least inside he was safe from the elements, unknown beasts, and the Johnson boys all at the same time. Dead bodies aside, it wasn't a bad place to hang out for a while.

CHAPTER FOUR

Tommy sneezed before his eyes had a chance to open. A groan was all he could muster, trying to sit up in a... pile of hay. He bolted forward, eyes shifting from side to side.

"Ah," a man said. "I see you have woken up. It must have been a right nasty night. Your face is messed-up real good."

Tommy rubbed his eyes and nose, stopping a sneeze from fully forming. Allergies were the worst, and hay was one of the biggest triggers. The tablet he'd taken before leaving the house wore off hours ago. No one expected him to sleep in the fake stable. "How did I get here?" He sneezed. There was no chance of stopping it or the two that came directly after.

"And how am I supposed to know that?" the man snapped. "You were sleeping when I came in to work."

Tommy glanced around. Somehow, he'd made it back to the staged stables. With the reenactment over, it was clean up time. "I can help," he offered.

"That's mighty nice of ya," the man said. "I wouldn't have expected any less from a freeloader. Grab a bucket and fetch some water for the horses."

"Okay," Tommy agreed, pulling himself off the floor. His head snapped back. "Wait! Did you say horses?" He glanced around. Every stall held a different majestic beast, tails flickering, curious pairs of eyes locked on him.

"Aye," the man chuckled. "What else did you expect to find in a stable?"

Tommy shook his head. They really went all out this year. A part of him was actually sad he missed it. He snatched the bucket off the floor. "Do I know you? You look familiar."

The man removed his cap, scratching his unruly red hair. "Not sure," he answered. "With them shiners, it's hard to tell if I know you or not. Like I said, your face is mighty messed-up. What happened? Someone rob you?"

"Yeah," Tommy lied. "I guess they did." He searched the walls of the building, coming up empty. "Where's the tap?"

"The what?" the man replied, his brow furrowed. "If you mean the well, it is in the center of town. It'll take a few trips back and forth."

"What?" Tommy asked. "Never mind, I'll figure it out." He rubbed his eyes again. The itch worsened with each pass, vision blurring as he opened the door. One foot almost stepped outside.

"Watch it!" the man exclaimed, pulling him back. "You'll get trampled by man and beast if you don't watch where you're going."

The bucket dropped, along with Tommy's jaw. Gone were the paved sidewalks and busy streets filled with cars. It was all replaced with dirt roads and horse-drawn carriages. If this was a joke, someone had gone to a lot of trouble.

"There's the well," the man said. "Try not to get killed before you fetch the first bucket full. I'll be inside. The name's Ned if you need me."

"Ned?" Tommy muttered.

"Yeah," the man answered. "Ned Carter."

Tommy's head snapped sideways, any quicker, and there might have been damage. That didn't matter, though. The man's name was far too puzzling. Ned Carter was the name of the ancestor on his father's side—the one who had been present on the night the witch was put to death. Somehow, he'd gone back in time.

He scurried across the street, narrowly missing being trampled on several occasions. The sooner he fetched the water, the sooner he could ask Ned more questions. The way back was twice as difficult, though. Carrying a bucket of water was harder than it looked. It was useless to spill the contents before the horses got a single drop. He almost made it to the stable doors—then he saw her.

Tommy was what his mother referred to as a late bloomer when it came to love. All of his peers had already fallen in love with a teacher or movie star, at one point or another. Most of them had even dated among themselves. He hadn't yet shown any inclination of being interested in a relationship of any sort—until that moment.

The woman standing on the street corner, directly in his path, was several years older than he was, but perfect, nonetheless. Her hair shimmered gold in the sunlight; lips plump and red. That wasn't what caught his attention, though. It was her eyes. Those eyes sparkled with emotions, swirling in the most hypnotic manner. The longer he stared into them, the more they reminded him of a rainbow formed within a prism. There was a power hidden deep within them that demanded his attention. The deeper his gaze, the harder it was to look away.

Ned's hand on his shoulder pulled him back. "She's a looker, ain't she?" he snickered. "Best forget her, though. A woman like that doesn't take the time of day for our kind. Know your place and live within it. That's the best advice I can give."

"You sound like my father," Tommy replied.

"He must be a smart man," Ned said. "You should listen to him. Where are your folks, anyway? They from around here?"

"I'm alone," Tommy said, the reality of the situation sinking in. His shoulders slouched with defeat. He had no belongings, no home, and no money. A growl from his stomach topped it all off—he had no food, either.

"Seeing as you were robbed and all," Ned said, "I can give you a few odd jobs. It's not much, but it's something. You can stay in the barn until you get back on yer feet."

Tommy's eyes brightened, a smile showing signs of forming. "Thank you."

"It's only for a few days," Ned added. "It's a busy time of year. No one wants their horses left out during the witching time."

"What's her name?" Tommy blurted out.

"I just told ye to forget her," Ned complained. He sighed, "Demona, but you didn't hear it from me. It isn't proper for you to be addressing her that way either."

Tommy nodded, but his mind was elsewhere. Demona was a name he knew well—she was the witch from all the history books. She was the one who was destined to die. He'd asked for a chance to change things—to right the wrongs of the past—and he'd been given it. All he needed to do was save Demona from burning alive. How hard could that be? The smell of food broke him loose from his trance.

A piece of crusty bread never looked so good. He'd never stick his nose up at a vegetable again—that was if he ever saw one again. Tommy scarfed down the last of his allotted portion, following it with a drink from the bucket. He chuckled. Most mothers would have had a heart attack if they saw their children drinking straight out of a tap. He could almost see his own, cringing at the sight of the well-used brown pail and tin cup, and sharing with horses to boot. That wasn't going to stop him, though. He was thirsty, and there wasn't a cola or juice box anywhere to be seen.

"Been a while?" Ned asked.

"Yeah," Tommy answered between slurps.

"Finish up," Ned ordered. "It's the witching day tomorrow. You'll need your rest."

CHAPTER FIVE

Tommy woke sputtering a cough. Catching his breath, he inhaled deeply, his nostrils burning from the air.

Smoke! He jumped to his feet, looking for a fire. It wouldn't take long for the whole place to go up in flames with all the dry hay lying around.

He saw the broken lantern first, then her body lying beside it. Tommy grabbed his blanket, using it as a whip to hold back the blaze while nudging Demona with his foot. She wasn't moving, and he was losing the battle. He tugged her arms with all his might, but he barely moved her body a few inches. Deadweight was too much for a boy his size.

"Thank goodness," Tommy said with a sigh of relief. Ned had perfect timing. "You have to help me move her. There isn't much time."

"No, lad," Ned replied. "It'll be my hide if them horses don't make it out. Nearly every beast in town is stabled here tonight. My job is to save them."

"She's a person," Tommy argued. "I am not strong enough to get her out of here." He rubbed one hand through his mop of a hairstyle. "I'll get the horses out. You save her."

"You best make sure you get them all," Ned said. "Or die trying." He lifted Demona over his shoulder, disappearing into a cloud of smoke toward the exit.

Tommy raced to unlatch each of the stalls. It was too smoky and hot to go the same way Ned had. Instead, he opted for the back door. The animals raced for safety, almost trampling him in the process. He was the last to leave, right before the roof came down. He fell backward, landing on his bottom by a feed trough.

"Take them, Pete," a man ordered. "Stash 'em at the abandoned cabin. We can fetch 'em later."

"People will know, Todd," Pete replied. "If we get caught, we'll hang for this."

"No one will be the wiser," Todd replied. "Everyone is fussing over Demona. We'll claim they all perished in the fire. Hurry. Get back before anyone notices you are missing."

The two men went their separate ways. Tommy scrambled to his feet, heading around to the other side of the building. The Johnson family was clearly up to something, but what didn't matter. As long as Demona was alive, things were bound to be better for Placency.

He held his breath, approaching the spot where she lay. Her eyelids fluttered, chasing away tears born from the smoke. She accepted the hands of two different men to pull her to an upright position.

"She's fine," Bill Johnson announced. "It was lucky I was there to save the lass." He smiled, waving with one hand as if he were royalty.

"You didn't..." Tommy felt one hand around his waist and the other over his mouth.

"Know your place, boy," Ned said. "It won't do you any good to argue. Folks saw him standing over the lady, not you or me."

"But it isn't fair," Tommy said the moment Ned's hand released him. "He's the one who set the fire. He tried to kill her."

"Shh." Ned motioned with a single finger over his lips. He pulled Tommy to the side. "You can't be making accusations like that. The Johnson family has power in this here town. You'll end up on the hanging block."

"But it's true," Tommy complained.

"Shh." Ned's arms flailed. "There's no proof, boy. If there was, it burnt up in that fire. Don't you see? Your word against a gentleman's simply isn't worth a thing. If it's something that can get you in trouble, it's best to sleep on it rather than blurting it out," Ned said. "Them's words to live by. I'll put you up for tonight. Tomorrow you best be off, for yer own good."

CHAPTER SIX

Two logs and a wooden plank—it was rustic but did the job. There weren't too many places to sit and do nothing in town without someone shooing him away. Tommy had managed to use up his welcome long before figuring out how to return to his own time. He leaned forward; arms resting on his legs; vision locked on the ground. A trail of ants passed by, each one helping to carry food back to their nest. That was what a family was supposed to be. For a moment, he actually envied them—until a foot came down, wiping them all out in a single blow. Life was cruel that way. They were doing nothing wrong, yet paid the highest price for it.

A gentle breeze carried with it the warm aroma of vanilla mixed with cinnamon. His nostrils flared, inhaling as much as they could of the heavenly scents. Memories of the home-baked treats he used to find at his grandmother's house were bittersweet, bringing with them a new wave of homesickness. Even so, his body reacted to the warmth of the perfect blend. With each breath, his shoulders lifted until he was in an upright position again. His eyes shifted to the side, finding the one person he hadn't expected to see sitting beside him.

"Good morning," Demona greeted him. "We didn't have a chance to speak, with all the commotion. I wanted to thank you."

Those eyes! Tommy pointed to his own chest, his mouth forming the word *'me'* but making no sounds.

"Yes, you," Demona said with a giggle. "Do you see anyone else?" She glanced around. "You are the reason I'm still here."

"You knew?" Tommy questioned, his brows furrowed. "Why didn't you say anything? Why let Bill Johnson take the credit?"

Demona inhaled deeply, exhaling quickly. "I didn't want to give anyone further cause to try again," she answered. "I rather enjoy my life."

"Wait!" Tommy exclaimed. "You knew they were trying to kill you?"

"It wasn't on purpose," Demona replied. "I have been avoiding the advances of the Johnson boys since I arrived. I'm afraid that didn't go over well. They aren't used to being told no." Her eyes widened, then softened again, a twinkle shining brightly within. "Bill and I struggled. He had a tight grip on my arm, and I pulled loose. I stumbled back and hit my head. He must have thought I was dead. The fire, I suppose, was to cover things up. Then you came along."

"Ned did most of the work," Tommy admitted. "I couldn't lift you."

Demona laughed. "You are still young. How old are you now? Fifteen? As for Ned, he wouldn't have looked twice at me, if you hadn't insisted."

Tommy nodded. "Wait!" he exclaimed, turning to face her. "You were passed out. How do you know what happened?"

Demona placed a gloved finger to her lips. "It's our secret. I expect it is much the same as all the horses perishing in the fire."

"But, the horses didn't..." He paused. That meant Demona hadn't died in the fire as the history books claimed. But why say the horses were dead?

"Something is bothering you," Demona said, peeking round at his solemn face.

"They say you are a witch," Tommy blurted out. "Are you?"

"I'm no more a witch than you are," Demona answered with a compassionate smile. "There's a magic to life, and it isn't found in the past. That's somewhere no one should live."

"Even if they could change things?" Tommy asked. "What if they could make things better? Given the opportunity, wouldn't you try?"

"I'll let you in on a secret I learned long ago," Demona offered. "History, as recorded, isn't factual. Oh, the basic events are there, but the details can be substituted one for the other. What we can't change is people. They are who they are. The only part we have a choice in lies within ourselves. The future isn't set in stone. It's what you make of it. That's what we all need to concentrate on."

"I'm not sure where my future lies," Tommy admitted. His lips pushed to one side of his face. "I'm a long way from home."

"When I'm lost, I find a mirror helps," Demona suggested. "A reflection is the one place we can always find ourselves, no matter how far we stray. I hear the general store has a full length one for trying on clothing and accessories." She leaned in, whispering, "That might be a good place to start." A flame flickered wildly in her eyes. "Ah, here comes my coach."

"Where are you going?" Tommy asked.

"Away from Placency," Demona said. "It's a good time for me to disappear. I hope to open a sweet shop. I do love candy." She took the driver's hand, taking one step up on the covered carriage before pausing. She glanced back over her shoulder. "When you are older, head northwest. I think you might find what you are looking for in a little place called Knollville."

Tommy watched the horse-driven carriage disappear in a cloud of dust. The moment it was gone from view, it was a race between his legs to see which could make it to the general store the fastest. He paused at the entrance, catching his breath. The owner wasn't fond of children, even less so of poor ones. Finding his way to the mirror before being caught wasn't going to be an easy task. Once again, his size came to the rescue. He squatted, waddling in a duck position around various display tables and shelves until he found what he was looking for.

Tommy straightened up, his fingers gently caressing the side of his face. He was a mess. Dirt was crusted on dirt. He licked his lips, not daring to remove the cap from his head. This was the one time a brush might have actually come in handy.

"Hey," the store owner called out. "What are you doing there?"

Tommy glanced to the side, then back at the mirror, seeing all hopes of returning home flash before his eyes. The reflection of the poor, dirty boy faded, giving way to one of the boy he used to be, his mother, his father, and then his room. In a split-second decision, he ran full force at the mirror, closing his eyes to avoid damage from broken shards.

CHAPTER SEVEN

Tommy's arm flung sideways, the back of his hand hitting the snooze button. One eye popped open—it was his bedroom. He bolted upright, leaping from the bed and heading straight to the mirror. Two fingers poked and prodded at his face. There were no bruises. His smile grew exponentially. He'd done it. He had changed the past. He dressed in a flash, racing down the stairs to his new life. There wasn't a moment to waste in a world where everything was bound to be better. Everything except... mush.

He glared at the bowl of soggy cereal as he took his usual seat at the table. Breakfast wasn't everything, though. A spoonful almost reached his lips before clanging back in the bowl.

Mr. Carter peered around his paper. "Is everything okay?" he asked.

Tommy gulped back, watching as his mother placed a paper bag on the table beside his bowl. He alternated his glances between the head-lines he'd read once before and his lunch.

"I hope you don't mind, dear," she said. "Things are a bit tight this week."

The newspaper folded in his father's hand. "It won't be for long. I've put in for some overtime." He sighed. "This is important. I need you to be on your best behavior today. Don't ruffle any feathers. We are going to make a good impression at this year's festival."

"I-I," Tommy stuttered, not knowing what to say.

"I thought you liked my lunches," his mother said. She glanced at her husband, who was heading to the door, rushing after him. It was too late: he was already gone. "Goodbye," she mumbled, returning to clear off the table.

"Mom," Tommy finally said. "Can you tell me the story of the festival?"

His mother laughed. "You've heard it a million times and hated every second of it. If you are trying to stall to get out of school..."

"Please," Tommy begged.

She placed the dishes back down on the table, taking a seat beside him. "All right," she agreed. "It was the witching hour on the morn of Hallows Eve. In the dead of night, a fire erupted, the origins of which were never proven. All of the townsfolk's horses perished in the flames that night, dooming them all. Your father's ancestors were responsible for them, too. It looked like it was the end of Placency. Back then, nothing happened without good horses. The Johnson family came to the rescue. They somehow came up with the money to buy a large herd. They brought them in and sold them to the townsfolk on credit. They saved the people. For that, the town will be forever in their debt."

"What happened to Ned Carter?" Tommy asked.

"The Johnson family took pity on him," his mother answered. "He was given a full pardon and another job."

Tommy nodded. He finally understood what Demona had been trying to say. It wasn't the situation that made things they were today; it was the people. The Johnson family was quick to take advantage of any situation right or wrong. That was what gave them their power. They stole the horses and sold them back to their original owners to make their fortune. The rest of the town was just as guilty for letting it happen. Someone must have noticed the beasts were exactly the same as the ones presumed dead. Still, no one did a thing.

"You best be off to school," his mother said, glancing at the clock on the wall. "You don't want to be late."

"I'm not feeling well," Tommy said. "I want to be a hundred percent for this evening's events. Would it be okay if I stayed home today?" It was time he started taking control of his future, starting with staying alive long enough to enjoy it.

SIX YEARS LATER...

Tommy stood on the sidewalk, facing the small candy store. In every way, it had her spirit: from the bright colors to tempting displays. The tiny shop was as irresistible as she had been. He had no idea what to expect but needed to enter, if only to look around.

An old-fashioned bell sounded the moment the door opened, continuing its song until it closed tightly behind him. He glanced over every morsel of sugary goodness, his smile growing larger with each one he passed. His nostrils flared at the scent of vanilla mixed with cinnamon as he approached the front counter. He glanced up from the window display.

"I'll have..." his voice froze in the presence of *those eyes*.

"Welcome to Knollville, Tommy. I've been waiting for you."

C.A. King is a Canadian award-winning & best-selling author with over 40 books available across multiple fantasy sub-genres.

After the loss of her loving parents and husband, Ms. King was devastated. She decided to retire from the workforce for a year or two to do some soul searching. It was during this time that writing became her passion. She found she was able to redirect her emotions through her writing and in 2014, decided to publish some of her works.

She is proud to have her name join the list of Canadian born authors and hopes her writing will help inspire another generation of Canadians to continue adding to the literary heritage and rich culture Canada already has to offer. Her books in The Portal Prophecies series are fictional fantasy stories based on opening the door to possibilities.

Website: https://www.portalprophecies.com

facebook.com/ThePortalProphecies

twitter.com/portalprophecy

instagram.com/the.portal.prophecies

MORE BY FICTION-ATLAS PRESS

Fiction-Atlas Press releases two anthologies a year. We hope you'll check out some of our past anthologies or sign up to be notified about future ones on the next page!

THANK YOU

We hope you have enjoyed our anthology.
It would mean the world to us if you had the time to leave a review!
Reviews are what keep us writing!

**FOLLOW FICTION-ATLAS PRESS FOR INFORMATION ON
FUTURE PUBLICATIONS.**

FICTION-ATLAS
PRESS LLC

http://fiction-atlas.com

facebook.com/fictionatlas

twitter.com/fabookbargains

instagram.com/cl_cannon

youtube.com/clcannonauthor

CPSIA information can be obtained
at www.ICGtesting.com
Printed in the USA
FSHW010746041119
63722FS